T0372378

A Dark and Snowy Night

Books by Sally Goldenbaum

The Seaside Knitters mysteries:
Murder Wears Mittens
How to Knit a Murder
A Murderous Tangle
A Crime of a Different Stripe
A Dark and Snowy Night

The Queen Bees Quilt Shop mysteries:
A Patchwork of Clues
A Thread of Darkness
A Bias for Murder

A Dark and Snowy Night

Sally Goldenbaum

Kensington Publishing Corp.
www.kensingtonbooks.com

This book is a work of fiction. Names, characters, businesses, organizations, places, events, and incidents either are the product of the author's imagination or are used fictitiously. Any resemblance to actual persons, living or dead, events, or locales is entirely coincidental.

To the extent that the image or images on the cover of this book depict a person or persons, such person or persons are merely models, and are not intended to portray any character or characters featured in the book.

KENSINGTON BOOKS are published by

Kensington Publishing Corp.
900 Third Avenue
New York, New York 10022

Copyright © 2022 by Sally Goldenbaum

All rights reserved. No part of this book may be reproduced in any form or by any means without the prior written consent of the Publisher, excepting brief quotes used in reviews.

All Kensington titles, imprints, and distributed lines are available at special quantity discounts for bulk purchases for sales promotion, premiums, fund-raising, educational, or institutional use.

Special book excerpts or customized printings can also be created to fit specific needs. For details, write or phone the office of the Kensington Special Sales Manager: Attn. Special Sales Department. Kensington Publishing Corp, 119 West 40th Street, New York, NY 10018. Phone: 1-800-221-2647.

The K with Teapot logo is a trademark of Kensington Publishing Corp.

First Kensington Hardcover Edition: October 2022

ISBN-13: 978-1-4967-2941-5
First Kensington Trade Edition: September 2024

ISBN-13: 978-1-4967-2942-2 (ebook)

10 9 8 7 6 5 4 3 2 1

Printed in the United States of America

For my shining hopes for the future—
Luke, Ruby, and Dax McElhenny
Atticus, Julian, and Sebastian Goldenbaum

Cast for *A Dark and Snowy Night*

Birdie Favazza (Bernadette): Sea Harbor's wealthy and wise octogenarian, widow of Sonny Favazza

Cass Halloran Brandley (Catherine Mary Theresa): Co-owner of the Halloran Lobster Company; married to Danny Brandley; baby son, Joey

Izzy Perry (Isabel Chambers Perry): Former attorney, owner of the Sea Harbor Yarn Studio, married to Sam, award-winning photographer; toddler daughter, Abigail (Abby)

Nell Endicott: Retired nonprofit director; Izzy Chambers Perry's aunt; married to Ben Endicott, retired lawyer and family business owner

Friends and Townsfolk

Archie and Harriet Brandley: Owners of the Sea Harbor Bookstore; Danny Brandley's parents

Beatrice Scaglia: Mayor of Sea Harbor

Darci Lou Fox: Member of the catering team

Dirk Evans: Member of the catering team

Don and Rachel Wooten: Owner of the Ocean's Edge Restaurant (Don) and city attorney (Rachel)

Ella and Harold Sampson: Birdie's housekeeper and groundskeeper

Elliott Danvers: Owner of a Sea Harbor investment bank

Gus McGlucken: Owner of McGlucken's Hardware Store

Harry and Margaret Garozzo: Owners of Garozzo's deli

Jake Risso: Owner of the Gull Tavern

Jerry Thompson: Police chief

Lidia Carson: Celebrity chef and entrepreneur; married to Oliver Bishop

Liz Santos: Manager of the Sea Harbor Yacht Club

Luna Risso: Cass's next-door neighbor

Mae Anderson: Izzy's Sea Harbor Yarn Studio manager
Mary Halloran: Cass and Pete's mother
Mary Pisano: Newspaper columnist; owner of Ravenswood-by-the-Sea B and B
Molly Flanigan: Cass and Danny Brandley's nanny
Oliver Bishop: Nell's college friend
Pete Halloran: Cass's brother; co-owner of the Halloran Lobster Company
Shannon Platt: Waitress and childhood friend of Molly Flanigan's
Tommy Porter: Police detective

Chapter 1

Nell Endicott and Oliver Bishop's college romance had lasted approximately seventy-two hours, two sessions of Lit 201, and one dinner at a noisy college bar. It ended by mutual consent and relief, and was happily replaced by a friendship that deepened through college courses, graduations, marriages, careers, and life changes.

And one devastating death.

When they met at the front door of the Ocean's Edge Restaurant that night, Nell's first thought as she looked into Ollie's eyes was of Maddie. Oliver's late wife. Nell's forever best friend.

Neither Nell nor her husband, Ben, had seen Ollie since Maddie's funeral a dozen years ago, and this reunion made her happy and sad at once. They'd invited Ollie and Maddie to come visit many times, and for one reason or another, it had never worked out for both couples at the same time. And now here Ollie was, finally.

But without Maddie.

"You look wonderful, Nell," Ollie said. They hugged, arms wrapped around their puffy winter coats.

Nell finally pulled away and looked into Ollie's face. "I'm so glad to see you, old friend," she said.

Ollie reached out and held her shoulders, tilting his head and looking at her as if he were afraid she would disappear if he stopped.

Finally he said, with meaning that spoke of years of friendship, "The years slid right by us, Nellie. Gone in a heartbeat. How did that happen? How did we lose touch?"

"We haven't lost touch, not completely. Or if we did, we found it. And I'm happy for that, even though surprised. This event is a little beneath the world you live in, Ollie. Are you helping your wife? Doing any of the cooking, I hope?"

"No cooking. Or helping for that matter. That's Lidia's department, and what she's a master at—being the chef extraordinaire. I came to see you and Ben."

"You won't even be sous chef?"

"Would you trust me with a knife?" He held up his right hand so she could see the scar running across the width of his palm.

Nell winced, then put a smile in place and took his arm. "Come, my dear friend. I asked them to save us chairs by the fireplace."

"Sounds perfect, and warm. The little lady running our B and B says we're in for a lot of snow. I hope it doesn't spoil the event, which I still don't quite understand. It's a Christmas party?"

"Kind of, yes. It's an annual holiday party for the town, but it's slightly different this year. In addition to other changes, the mayor is using it to show off her new house."

Ollie laughed, more heartily than her pleasantry deserved, but still a welcome sound that eased Nell's discomfort a bit. Although they'd been close those years ago, it had been a long time since they'd seen each other. What changes had the decades brought in both of them?

She put the thought aside and steered him into the restaurant's lounge to a granite fireplace, flanked by two leather armchairs. A reserved sign sat on a small table.

Ollie looked at the sign. "So I'm guessing they know you here, you and Ben."

"It's our favorite place to bring our favorite people."

The waitress appeared almost immediately and set a plate of garlic oysters on the table, a basket of cheese straws, and took their drink orders. "Compliments of the owner," she explained with a smile.

"Friends in high places," Ollie said.

"The owner is a good friend of ours. You'll like Don Wooten, Ollie. I'll introduce you."

Nell took the glass of wine Ollie handed her. Then he picked up the tumbler of Scotch the waitress had poured for him, leaving the bottle on their small table.

Nell took a sip of wine and sat back, thinking of Ollie's musing. How had all those years slipped by them?

But she knew. *It's life,* she thought, then almost immediately corrected her thought. *It was Maddie's death. That's how it happened.*

She looked back at Ollie, his face still handsome, though lined now with the years that life had etched there. His prominent cheekbones were flushed from the fire crackling beside them, or maybe the Scotch, Nell thought, and his chin was more chiseled, more set in place than she had remembered.

"I like this place," Ollie said, taking in the comfortable sitting areas and the bank of windows looking out to the sea. "I'm an expert critic for these sorts of places, you know."

Nell laughed. "Yes, you are, and yes it is. A Sea Harbor gem."

In daylight, the Ocean's Edge lived up to its reputation with the most coveted panorama—and consequently the most coveted real estate—in all of Sea Harbor, and possibly of the entire northeastern seaboard. Nell was sorry not to get to show it off

for Ollie, for him to see it through her eyes. For now, at cock-
tail hour, winter nighttime erased the Atlantic Ocean. It turned
the view from the large windows black, with only the occasional flash of a faraway ship, harbor lights catching the white
curl of a wave, and the regular, reassuring beams of the light-
house.

Where did they begin, attempting to fill in the years between
them? Or did that matter, and should they just let them lie?

As she loosened the hand-knit scarf around her neck, Nell
thought about her niece Izzy's yarn shop and considered telling
Ollie about that part of her life, the part that lived here in Sea
Harbor since she and Ben had retired and moved to his family's
vacation home. About Izzy, who left her Boston law firm and
opened the local yarn store, and the two other women who had
become her dearest friends, women she grieved with and
laughed with and celebrated life's mysteries with.

She might tell him how the four of them had originally come
together at Izzy's store one Thursday night, each for her own
reason: Nell to bring a meal to her niece, who was working late;
Birdie to pick up a pair of needles she'd ordered; and dear Cass,
knitting impaired back then, who came in because she had
smelled the amazing aromas of Nell's seafood casserole.

And all of them had stayed.

They'd bonded quickly in the way women sometimes do,
and kept coming back every Thursday night, week after week,
year after year, forming a circle of friendship that would last
forever. And then some.

But she decided not to, at least not now.

Ollie was smiling at her now, seemingly pleased with the
moment, comfortable with the silence.

Across the room, a long-haired guitar player was singing
mellow cover songs, as if the singer somehow knew that some
of the customers that night were reliving the past. Ollie
watched him for a minute, then tilted his head back and drained

the glass, setting it down on the small table with a thud, and focusing again on Nell. "Being with you like this, it all comes back. Lots of years."

The noise level rose at the bar where a younger group was gathering to watch the final plays of a Celtics game.

Nell leaned in toward Ollie to be heard. "We've known each other nearly half our lives, Ollie. That doesn't go away easily."

Nell watched the lines in her friend's face deepen. She could see him touching on certain memories, lingering there too long.

"I miss her, too, Ollie," Nell finally said. "She was the closest friend I ever had. Maddie's death hollowed out a part of me—but it also left something that will be there always."

"I know that. Sometimes I was jealous of whatever it was you two had. It was so . . . I don't know, intimate, like the two of you wrapped yourself in a bubble and no one else could get in."

"But I introduced you and Maddie, don't forget that. I found you the most amazing wife. So our bubble wasn't ironclad. Ben found a way in there, too."

Ollie settled back and stretched out his legs, a long swatch of graying hair falling over his forehead. He lifted his glass toward her. "We had some good times, the four of us."

They did have good times. And Ollie was right, too, about her friendship with Maddie. They were soul sisters, almost from the first moment they met that gray September day. Nell sat back in the chair, took a drink of her wine, and slipped back into time, remembering that day, climbing up the steps in the old dorm building, the musty smell in the old wood floors.

She remembered walking down the narrow hallway until she found a closed door with a brass number nailed to it. She was *here*. Eighteen years old and excited and nervous in such huge waves she thought she might be sick. *Harvard.* This Kansas girl's dream. She took a deep breath, released it slowly, and opened the door to her assigned room.

There, tan legs folded into a pretzel, a girl in a torn sweat-shirt and shorts sat on a narrow bed. Her hands were dotted with neon-green paint and hair pulled back into a ponytail. She looked up, her entire face opening in a smile. On her lap and bed were scattered the makings of a collage, a sort of WELCOME sign. Somewhere in the mess Nell spotted the letters of her name.

A voice lifted from the bed.

"You're finally here. I'm Maddie. Welcome to our suite."

Nell stared as words tumbled out of the woman's perfect mouth, her face spirited and happy and blotting out every bit of gray from the thick September sky.

Madeline Solomon. Her first roommate. And her last.

It took fifteen minutes, or maybe less, for the two young women to know they were destined to be together in one way or another through the arduous, thrilling, enormously life-changing roller-coaster ride of college. And life thereafter, no matter where they were.

Nell shook herself free of the memories and brought her thoughts back to the man in front of her. The sadness in Ollie's eyes, the grief etched into the lines of his face, were still fresh and new these years after Maddie's death. Some things seemed to defy the passage of time.

"Enough about the past," Nell said lightly, trying to shift the mood. "Tell me about your New York restaurants. And your wife. Ben and I are looking forward to meeting her."

Ollie's body seemed to relax as he shifted back into the present. "Lidia. Well, how much time do you have?" He laughed softly. "She's talented. A fine chef. Not as good as I once was, but almost."

"No one will ever be as good as you. You were the sole reason for our 'freshman fifteen.' Amazing meals cooked up in that dingy Somerville place you lived in."

"I remember well. Anyway, Lidia would have come tonight, but had an interview or something in Boston. You'll like her,

Nell. Everyone likes her. Unless they don't." He took a long drink.

Nell frowned, trying hard to read her friend's face. "I read somewhere that she gives you credit for giving her a start."

"I suppose you could say that. Although Lidia isn't the kind of person people actually give things to. She decides what she wants, and then she takes it. People think they're offering her things, but that's because Lidia makes them feel that way."

Ollie's face and tone of voice gave Nell few clues as to whether that was a good thing or a bad thing.

"She came into the restaurant kitchen on a particularly bad day. Maddie was in hospice, I was distracted, the restaurant was suffering. And there she was at the alley door. She stepped inside, looking around, almost as if she'd cased the place first. I watched her from the glass window in my office, slightly wary, although I couldn't tell you why. She walked around, waving steam from soup pots toward her face, checking out the combination of spices. I even saw her stick a finger in a pot of thick sauce and was about to charge out of the office and send her back out the door.

"But then she spotted my office, headed over, and walked in, as if I had been waiting for her. She checked out the mess of papers on my desk, a couple of crates on the floor, a dirty coffee cup. The expression on her face as she looked around was pure disdain. But when she looked at me, it disappeared. It was business-like, I remember, not flirtatious. She announced that she was there to work. She could start right away.

"I thought she was on something, but she went on, telling me she knew kitchens, and mine clearly needed her. It was a mess, she said, but she'd straighten it out. Prep chef, fry chef, expediter, on and on, naming a half-dozen positions. Then she added that it didn't really matter. She'd do whatever needed to be done, and from what she could see, that was nearly everything."

Ollie shrugged, then half smiled at the memory.

"That didn't unhinge you?" Nell asked. "You never liked people telling you what to do, especially when it had anything to do with cooking. You were one scary cook if anyone got in your way."

Ollie laughed. "Yeah. Maybe. But you'll get what I mean when you meet her. Besides, she was dead right. The restaurant was failing financially, although the news of that hadn't quite leaked out. I wasn't handling things well back then—"

Nell glanced at his large hand again, its veins prominent, strong fingers that once whisked butter and wine and fresh herbs into award-winning sauces. But it was the angry scar across it that stood out. An angry scar caused by anger. A meat slice in the wrong place.

A reputation Ollie Bishop had finessed. Nell hadn't seen his anger often, but she'd heard stories of him yelling at sous chefs and cursing at fallen soufflés. Maddie had laughed off the anecdotes, saying, "He's just under a lot of pressure. I don't ever see that side of Ollie."

"So, did she? Did she straighten things out?"

"She did. I was mostly absent, being with Maddie, trying to make her live."

Nell looked at her old friend, then fell into the sad, shared silence. In the distance, the old Al Green song "Let's Stay Together" filled the bar, as if the guitarist on the tall stool knew it fit into their memories.

"Things calmed down at the restaurant without me," Ollie went on. "Lidia fired and hired people right and left. Paid off old debts, unpaid bills. She just did it, going way beyond any authority she had—which was basically none. But I couldn't have cared less. In the end, her decisions were smart, effective, calculated. Visionary, almost. When I think back, it was eerie that she dropped into my life that way. And that she stayed. Things got better . . ."

"But . . . ?"

"*But?* No buts. It's all okay." Ollie stretched out his legs and looked into the flames. "She teaches a class here and there, is on the board of some of the elite culinary schools in the city. Lidia gets around."

Nell listened quietly, trying to imagine that world. She had gone to New York to sit with Maddie shortly before she died. Ollie had mostly stayed away that day, giving the two of them space. Maddie talked little. Nell had held her hand, their love passing wordlessly through the gentle clasp. Nell knew when she left that day that she wouldn't see Maddie again. Not on this planet. But neither woman said good-bye. Their embrace was enough to cement that they would carry one another with them, wherever they were.

And then a few years later she and Ben received a wedding invitation. And Lidia replaced her dearest friend in Oliver's life.

"It sounds like Lidia's good for you," Nell said aloud. "Maybe Maddie had a role in this? So you wouldn't completely screw up the magnificent restaurant she'd help you build, the one you both put your hearts and souls into."

Ollie shrugged. "Who knows? Things aren't always smooth, but it works out. Mostly. Or will—"

The marriage or the business? Nell wondered.

"Lidia has a head for business. Half the time she forgets to tell me about the newest grand plan until I see proposals, whatever. She's got some new plan going on now. It was the incentive to come up here."

"Catering the Sea Harbor mayor's annual holiday party?" Nell chuckled. "That's 'big' for Sea Harbor, maybe. Our mayor, Beatrice Scaglia, is sure she won the lottery, having a famous chef cater her event. But *big* for Oliver Bishop? For his famous wife?"

Now it was Ollie's turn to laugh. "No, not the mayor, although she's a character. She came to New York to charm us. Dressed to the nines and flirting with me shamelessly, not realizing that it was Lidia she should have been impressing. But the catering was calculated, something my wife is good at. She's always looking ahead to—"

Nell lifted a hand, interrupting his sentence. She half stood, looking beyond Ollie to a tall man coming in from the dining area. She waved to get his attention, then glanced at Ollie and pointed across the room. "I'm sorry to interrupt you, but I just spotted the friend I want you to meet. You have lots in common."

Don Wooten spotted Nell at the same time. The owner of the restaurant and lounge smiled and waved back, raising one finger that he'd be over in a minute, then continued toward the bar, where a bartender was gesturing for the boss's attention.

"Who?" Ollie said, his forehead wrinkling, straining to see where Nell was pointing.

"Don Wooten," Nell said. "The owner."

Nell settled back in the chair. "It looks like he's busy right now."

But Ollie had stopped listening, his attention focused on the large television set above the bar.

"You asked about meeting my wife—" He lifted his drink in the air, pointing toward the screen. "Nell, meet Lidia Carson."

Nell looked up and saw an attractive woman with pitch-black hair pulled back into a knot. The television camera highlighted a narrow face, high cheekbones, a polished smile. Ollie's wife was sitting across from the evening newscaster, a popular Boston interviewer, who was guiding viewers' attention to clips of Lidia appearing as a guest on the Bobby Flay cooking show. Next was a large image featuring an architect's rendering of a nearly all-glass restaurant. Nell couldn't hear what the interviewer asked or what Lidia answered, but she could see ocean beyond the modish glass walls. "What a beautiful structure," she said aloud. "Exotic." She looked over at Ollie and just managed to get out the words "Your wife is beautiful, Ollie" before the screen flickered, then went black.

Next, a shocking crash interrupted everything.

For a startled second, the bar noise was muted, too.

And then, another sound. Behind the bar, Don Wooten slammed the remote control device down on the bar surface, shattering it to pieces. Batteries skittered across the polished teak. Next to him, the young bartender squeezed a towel in his hand as if for protection, his eyes wide. Several bar regulars sitting close to the usual easygoing restaurant owner teased him for his bum choice of a television. Others pitied the bartender who may have caused the commotion.

But all were happy the television hadn't failed them earlier during the game. And happy that their team had won.

Laughter and voices picked up almost immediately and drinks were slid across the bar surface. The guitarist packed up for the night, and loud, recorded hits filled the Ocean's Edge Restaurant lounge, bringing the area back to its after-dinner spirit.

But what Nell felt wasn't the crowd's spirit, and what she saw wasn't a room of happy revelers.

What Nell saw was her good friend Don Wooten, his face darker than the wintry night, moving around the end of the bar with great urgency, then disappearing through a service door and onto the icy cold, wave-soaked deck.

Chapter 2

Nell stepped into the welcoming warmth of home, shutting the door to the garage behind her. She could hear male voices coming from the den and smiled at the bass and tenor melody of them.

At the sound of steps, Ben came into the family room and wrapped her in a hug that helped her bones start to thaw out.

"Ah, Nellie, I'm glad you're home," Ben said. Then he took a step back and helped her out of her coat.

"Me too." Nell looked toward the den. "Who's our late-night company?"

"Tommy Porter."

"Tommy? Why? Has there been a crime I should know about?"

"Internet mess. Something has made away with our connection. Tommy was at his parents' house, fixing theirs, and saw our light, so came over to straighten ours out, too."

"So we now have the town's most amazing police detective fixing our computers?"

Her comment traveled into the den and to the young man she glimpsed hunched over Ben's desk.

Without turning around, Tommy sent her a muffled "hi," along with a request to keep Ben out of his way.

"I'll distract him," Nell laughed. She stepped back into Ben's arms to give him an improved embrace. "You're nice and warm, I think I'll just stay here."

"Sounds good to me. So give me the scoop," Ben said. "How's he doing?"

"Hmm. Well, it was wonderful to see Ollie, but honestly, Ben, I don't think I can tell you how he is. At first, he seemed a little depressed and dispirited—"

"Oliver?"

"I know. But then he livened up and seemed like Ollie again. I think he's still adjusting to changes in his life."

"The marriage, you mean? But they've been married a few years now—"

"That's true. And he praises Lidia. It sounds as if he's stepped back from both cooking and running his restaurants, leaving most of the responsibilities to her."

"That's a lot for Ollie to get used to. Ollie was always a bit controlling of his business, I thought."

Ben nodded toward the large stone fireplace at one end of the room, flames leaping in the grate. "Looks like I've been banned from the den, so let's make use of my fire before it dies on me. A better place to talk." He headed to the kitchen island at the other end of the room and returned in minutes with a steaming hot toddy for Nell and a glass of Scotch for himself.

Nell curled up in a corner of the couch near the fire, taking the warm mug in her hands. "It's a perfect fire."

From the den, Yo-Yo Ma's soothing strings and Abigail Washburn's amazing voice filled the warm air with languages foreign and familiar, singing about "Going Home."

Nell cradled her mug in her hands, welcoming the warmth to her fingers and Ben's long comforting body beside her. "A hot toddy and Yo-Yo Ma," she said. "What more could I ask for?

But something tells me you need it, too. How did your committee meeting go?"

Ben looped his free arm over the back of the couch and began a one-handed massage of her neck and shoulders. "The usual. Some easy town issues. Some disruptive. The holidays seem to bring out the argumentative side in some folks."

"Our friend Ms. Risso was there, I presume."

Ben laughed. "Right. Luna Risso never misses open meetings."

"She told me the other day that those meetings are more entertaining than *Judge Judy*. What was she objecting to tonight?"

"She's upset about the holiday party being held at 'Beady's' mansion, as she calls our mayor. There's something about Beatrice's new house that irritates her. And she's also upset that the annual town event is by invitation this year."

"Good for her. Luna charges in where others fear to tread. And she's right about that event suddenly becoming exclusive. Plenty of people are upset about it."

Ben nodded his agreement. "She ended her objections by saying she just might run for mayor and put Beatrice in her place if she didn't behave."

Nell laughed. "Well, she brings chocolate chip cookies to all your meetings. That might earn her some support." She sipped her hot drink slowly, its warmth easing her body. "What else was on the agenda tonight?"

Ben kicked off his loafers and stretched his legs onto the coffee table. "Some commercial real estate ventures from out of towners—always a hot topic. We get reamed out by people who don't want Sea Harbor to change, especially if it involves new fancy restaurants along the harbor. And then there are the ones who think we'll die if we *don't* change." He leaned forward and set his glass on the table. "But you already know all that. I'd rather hear more about your evening with Ollie. How's the old guy doing?"

"The old guy, who's one year younger than you?"

Ben laughed and raised his glass to her.

"If it's any comfort, you look a lot younger than he does. But the woman he's married to now seems to have helped bring him back to life. She's younger, attractive, at least from what I saw on the TV screen." Nell paused, rethinking the evening's conversations. "I don't think she's anything like Maddie—"

"That might be good. He could never find another Maddie. But how's she different?"

"I guess we'll find out at the mayor's party."

A shadow in the den doorway pulled their attention to their young policeman/computer wizard. He held his jacket in his hand.

"All done, folks. You'll be relieved to know you're back on social media, Ben."

Ben laughed, the term being nearly foreign to him, as Tommy knew.

"You're the best, Tommy," Nell said, pulling herself off the sofa and walking his way. "A man of many talents."

"Yeah, that's what ma says." He pulled on his jacket and tugged a ski hat over his ears, looking more like the teenager who used to take care of Nell and Ben's yard than a respected member of the Sea Harbor Police Department.

"Are you ready for the holidays?" Nell asked, getting up.

"Almost. Things even slow down at work, letting me sink into my Santa skills. I love this time of year."

"So crime takes a vacation, too. That's a good thing." She gave Tommy a hug.

A siren in the distance broke their hug, followed by a strange ringtone on Tommy's cell phone. With an apologetic grin, he pulled it out. "I'm off duty, but you know how it is. Gotta keep tabs on the new guys." He looked down at the screen.

"What is it? A cat in a tree?" Ben guessed.

"In this weather?" Nell said. "Cats are too smart for that. Besides, I thought people called the fire department for cats in trees."

Tommy looked up. "Yeah, they usually do. Sometimes we

vie with them for that job. You'd be surprised how many cookies appear after a cat rescue. But this one"—he tapped his cell—
"this isn't anything to fight the fire brigade over."

"Anything serious?" Ben asked.

"Probably not. The homeowner reported a peeper, but considering the source, ah, sorry, I shouldn't say that."

They looked at him expectantly.

"Ms. Risso. It's a call to check out her house. We get a lot of
calls from Luna. She patrols the heck out of that neighborhood.
Town too. It's probably nothing, but I may drive over and see
what's up."

"I hope she's okay," Ben said.

Tommy turned to go, then stopped and looked at Nell.
"Hey, Cass and Danny live up on Coastal Road now, right?"

"Yes, why?" Nell's brows lifted, along with her voice.

"No worries. I just remembered that they live near Ms.
Risso."

"Yes, next door," Nell said, suddenly concerned.

"Luna was at the council committee meeting tonight," Ben
said. "She riled a few people up. I hope this doesn't have anything to do with that."

"I doubt it does," Tommy said. "Not unless she really
hacked off someone and now they're spying on her. It seems
she saw a trespasser. Or, in Luna's words, 'a Peeping Tom or
Jane'—she wasn't sure which."

"That would be frightening."

"Agreed. But it also could have been just a shadow or the
wind. A stray animal. If it was a prowler, we'll get him."

With a final hug for Nell and a handshake for Ben, Tommy
went off into the night.

Chapter 3

Nell crawled into bed a short while later, curling up against the warmth of Ben's body. Ben murmured his approval, then turned off his reading light.

"You're still thinking about having seen Ollie tonight," he said.

Nell nodded in the dark. Decades of marriage had given them that power to read one another's thoughts. Whether intended or not.

"Or is it the unknown, the wife, that's on your mind?"

"Maybe."

"We'll meet her soon enough. Unless chefs at the mayor's party stay in the kitchen."

"I don't think that happens when they're famous chefs. Beatrice will want to show her off." Nell thought back to Ollie and Lidia's wedding in Italy. She couldn't remember now why she and Ben hadn't gone. And then, without Maddie to cement the friendship, they'd drifted apart.

"I'm surprised that Ollie doesn't resent the fact that she's a famous chef. Ollie never liked to be one-upped."

Ben had a point. It was a trait of Ollie's that Nell never gave much mind to. She and Ollie had become fast friends the day they debated the "Nature of Being" in a freshmen philosophy class. His "self-assured and healthy opinion of himself," as Maddie described it, was something those who liked him ignored or thought funny or joked about until they got Ollie laughing at himself. But even Maddie admitted it was there, that often-competitive edge. Along with a slice of anger when challenged.

Nell, Ollie, and Maddie were already friends when Ben, a year ahead of them, met Nell and they fell in love during a ten-minute walk through Harvard Square. Ben got along fine with Nell's close friends, although it was the two women who provided the glue among the four of them. But no matter, it had worked, and the four had traveled together, partied together, and celebrated each other's highs, consoling each one's lows. One of the highs was Ollie's surprise inheritance from his wealthy grandfather, one that helped him along the path to being a multiaward-winning restaurateur and chef.

"You're right about that competitive streak," Nell said. "I guess age can change a person. We'll see. But seeing him tonight brought back a flood of memories. Maddie was very much with us—it felt good to have the old threesome together again."

"Hmmm," Ben said, his breathing slowing, and his body relaxing beneath Nell's touch.

Nell smiled into the dark, then leaned over and whispered to his sleeping form, "Good night, my love,"

Hours later, Nell turned on her side and looked out into the black night. Sleep was coming raggedly, her thoughts tangled up with images—an uncomfortable mix of memories, moving around in her head like ghosts. As she reached for one, it disappeared, just out of her grasp. And then another and another. And another.

Familiar figures floating about in a fog. An old friend grieving. And another, her soul mate, Maddie, fading away on the edge of the dream, never completely there. She reached out, trying to pull Maddie back.

And then another figure, this one out of place with the others. An angry Don Wooten, disappearing and returning and disappearing again, until he finally faded completely into a blustery night.

Chapter 4

Danny Brandley slipped his cell phone into his pocket, grabbed a jacket, and headed for the kitchen door.

Cass looked up from the table and the week's mail. "Hey, where're you going?"

"No place. Just next door. Luna called. She said it was urgent."

He grinned at Cass, acknowledging what they both knew: coming from Luna Risso, "urgent" could mean anything from "help, somebody's trying to murder me" to "help, I can't find my comb."

But Danny always went.

He flicked on the porch light, lighting a view of their driveway and garage. It was weak, barely lighting the short path from the one-car detached garage, where their nanny lived in an apartment on its second floor. Danny reminded himself to change the bulb to better light her way from the garage to the house.

Cass had inherited the small house from Finnegan, an old and lonely fisherman with whom she'd become good friends.

She loved the cottage-like house, and when she married Danny, he'd fallen in love with it, too, with all its charm and history, its leaks and creaks.

The floor in Joey's bedroom creaked the loudest; they could hear Molly's steps from rocking chair to crib and back again, a noise that pleased Cass every time she heard it.

But the house was only half of why Cass loved living here: Coastal Road was aptly named: a dead-end street of small, old-but-ordinary homes with million-dollar views of the sea hidden from the street. A modest windbreak of evergreens in their small backyard didn't entirely protect them from nor'easters, but it allowed a view that made it worth their while to wear sweaters in the house, lay extra blankets on the beds, and latch the shutters if the winds grew fierce. In the summer, with the bedroom windows open, they went to sleep listening to the soothing rhythm of the waves upon the shore.

A north wind was blowing this night, curling around the houses, setting wind chimes clanging and porch swings swaying, the windows tightly closed.

"What about your brownies?" Cass called after him, just as Danny slammed the door quickly to keep the cold air out.

She glanced at the stove and frowned. Molly Flanigan was expanding Danny's love for baking, but it was too closely related to "cooking," something Cass dutifully steered clear of.

She hoped Danny could check them on his return from saving Luna from a mousetrap going off or whatever.

The sound of sirens interrupted thoughts of mice and brownies. Cass got up and headed for the kitchen window that overlooked part of Luna Risso's yard and house.

Maybe, just maybe, there was a real emergency this time.

A floor above, Molly looked down on a sleeping Joey Brandley and felt her heart expand. The young nanny couldn't remember being quite this happy. It was what she'd felt as a child. *Cherished and loved and secure.*

And then, when she grew up, it fell apart.

But already, after these weeks in Sea Harbor, those old feelings were finally settling down inside her again. The water and sky and light lifted her spirit, the sunsets so brilliant that even on gray days you had to shield your eyes from the blinding beauty. She loved the ocean, the crashing waves, the hard winter sand for running.

But mostly it was Cass and Danny Brandley and their amazing baby who had wrapped her up so tightly. These unlikely people—a woman who ran a lobster company and her mystery-writer husband—had made her feel the way her parents had: loved and secure and valued.

This life had come out of the blue. But not really. Shannon had come to her rescue, something they had done for each other their whole lives.

Shannon Platt—her friend from preschool, her backpacking friend, her secrets-sharing, spirit-soothing friend. Shannon had settled in Sea Harbor, waiting tables at restaurants and bars all over town, taking any job she could find, on any day for any shift, to pay for night classes at North Shore Community College. Molly knew that Shannon, a belated college student, would excel no matter what she did. And she'd fight anything or anyone who got in her way. Courageous Shannon. And loyal. Definitely proven when she found Molly this job.

It happened during one of Shannon's waitressing shifts in Harry Garozzo's deli. She'd overheard Cass, Izzy, Nell and Birdie—her most favorite customers—talking about one of them needing a nanny. And not only a nanny job, but Cass had said she'd toss in a "a potentially terrific room" over the garage if they could find the right person.

Shannon had known from the rumor mill that Cass's reputation regarding nannies wasn't stellar. A revolving door of nannies. But it didn't deter her. Her friend Molly was special and could do anything. And after what she'd been through, she definitely needed a dose of Sea Harbor.

"I know somebody," she had said to the four women. And then she'd made promises to them that nearly scared Molly off when she heard. "I told them you're perfect, smart, an amazing cook, and babies love you."

"Geesh, Shannon," she'd said on the late-night call.

"I miss you. You need to move on, Mol. Together we can recapture those old dreams," Shannon had said.

Dreams that had crashed before Molly even got them going.

Molly leaned over and kissed the top of Joey's curly head, then slipped out of the room and down the back stairway to the Brandleys' kitchen.

"Cass, what's burning?" she yelled, racing into the room.

Cass was at the window, staring out. She spun around. "What?"

Molly opened the oven door and looked in at the brownies. In quick order, she turned off the heat, grabbed two hot pads, and pulled out the pan.

"Serves Danny right," Cass said, coming over to examine the extra-crispy brownies. "He knows better than to leave me alone with a turned-on stove."

"They'll still be good in the middle," Molly laughed. She looked across the room toward the window. "But what's going on out there?"

They went to the kitchen window as circling red lights flashed outside.

"I'm not sure. Lots of lights, but I can't see much. Luna called Danny a few minutes ago—he seems to be on her speed dial—and ordered him to come over. Maybe someone is camping out in the stable she put up for Christmas." She turned and grabbed a parka off a hook near the back door. "I'll go find out. You'll stay with Joey?"

"Sure. He went right back to sleep. Well, after a little songfest. I think he's a Beatles baby, Cass. His favorite is their 'Good Night' lullaby. Right now, he's dreaming baby dreams, making that little whispery sound."

"I love that sound."

"He looks like he's dreaming of flying on an angel cloud with his stash of cuddly polar bears beside him."

Cass smiled at the image. "Thanks, Mol. You have the magic touch. Don't ever leave us. Please stay until Joey graduates from high school."

They both laughed as Cass disappeared out the back door and across the drive to the neighbor's house.

Chapter 5

Cass shivered as she stepped into an onslaught of windy, cold air.

She spotted two empty squad cars parked at the curb, their circling lights playing off Luna's extravagant holiday decorations. The wind was buffeting around the big plastic Santa Claus and a reindeer, setting them bopping to a winter beat. Rudolph's red nose blinked along with the police cars.

Cass had heard that years before, neighbors had to prevail upon Luna to turn off the lights by ten p.m., so they could get some sleep. It had taken stronger persuasion by the police to convince her to shut down her loudspeakers blasting "Silent Night" and "Winter Wonderland" until midnight.

Cass had also heard that just when most of the neighbors had decided Luna was a pest and a menace, they had awakened on Christmas morning to discover that she had left lovely, beribboned boxes of her delicious homemade Christmas cookies on their doorsteps. For the two Jewish families on the block, she'd added menorah-shaped cookies and a dreidel or two. That was Luna in a nutshell, Cass thought: you might want to strangle her on a Tuesday, but you'd be thanking her by Friday for some outrageously generous thing she had done for you.

Cass_looked across her driveway and spotted policemen standing beneath a window, flashlights drawn like lethal weapons, slowly panning across the house and a haphazard pile of logs scattered among the frost-covered bushes. When Rudolph's nose flashed again, she recognized one of them as Tommy Porter and waved.

Danny and Luna stood nearby, Luna hugging her wind-blown_purple_robe around a flowered nightgown. Puffy ear-muffs sought for space among a gray head of curlers. Every now and then, she turned toward the front of the house and gave a queen's wave to the neighbors who were gathering on the front lawn.

Cass walked over to Danny. "What happened?"

"It was an ogler," Luna said, authority in her voice.

"Og—what?"

"It looks like someone may have been trying to look through Luna's bedroom window," Danny said.

Luna patted his arm and looked up into his face. "It was an *ogler*," she said, emphasizing the word. "I was terrified, of course. And it was more than just a 'try,' Daniel Brandley. I saw a face, a head with a ridiculous ugly cap stuck on it. Atrocious colors. He was right there." She jabbed the air, pointing to a window on the side of her house.

"All looks okay around your house, Miz Risso," a policeman said as he came around the side of the house from the backyard. "But we'll search the whole neighborhood wicked good. No need to worry."

"The bedroom window is high. So you think someone climbed on those logs to see better?" Cass asked, pointing to the scattered logs. "They look like he got off in a hurry."

"They look that way because that's what happened. He jumped off when I screamed," Luna retorted.

Cass stared at the window and shivered. "That must have been terrifying, Luna. Did you recognize him?"

"Couldn't see his face. Just an ugly orange ski hat with some crazy horseshoes on it. Pulled down so low I couldn't see much else. I assume it was a *he*. A girl wouldn't have been seen in such attire."

"There's nothing you can do out here, Cass," Danny said. "Why don't you go back inside before you freeze? I'll stick around with Luna for a while, and watch the police do their thing."

"Good idea," Cass said, shivering. "You'd better get Luna inside, too."

"I'm staying right here," Luna said, grabbing Danny's arm and hooking elbows with him.

"Okay, but you're not dressed for—"

"For *ogling*? I'm glad I wasn't *un*dressed for ogling."

Cass bit the inside of her cheek to keep from smiling. She had a feeling that Luna didn't always know when she was funny, but suspected this wasn't a tactful time to test her theory.

She turned and started back across the driveway, then stopped short.

A young woman was standing on the edge of the neighborhood crowd. She didn't remember seeing her in the neighborhood before, but maybe she had moved in recently. Or was she a relative? The woman's black hair escaped from beneath a blue wool cap pulled down over her ears. The cap matched a blue cloth coat, more stylish than useful in a Sea Harbor December. Boots up to her knees completed the look. They looked uncomfortable to Cass, but she guessed it was the "in" style that had escaped her, as most "in" styles did.

The young person had her arms clasped around herself, as if freezing, and Cass wondered if she should help her out somehow. Invite her in? She seemed to be alone, standing apart from the other neighbors. And then Cass noticed something odd.

The woman wasn't joining in with the neighbors, or even watching Luna or the police to figure out what was causing the commotion. She wasn't even looking at the extravagant holiday decorations that had taken over Luna's front yard.

The stranger was focused on Cass's house. On her own front door.

Cass followed the woman's stare.

All she saw was Molly, standing on the front stoop of their home, looking over at Luna's front-yard activity.

Under the porch light, Molly's curly blond hair looked silvery as moonlight. Poised there in suspended movement, dressed in a wooly sweater and snug jeans, she looked like a model on the cover of a magazine.

Cass looked back at the frowning dark-haired girl standing at the curb. She was attractive. And seemed upset. Afraid, maybe? Maybe she was worried about the police presence? But it looked to Cass like something other than worry. Upset? Whatever it was, it made Cass uncomfortable and she was tempted to walk over and ask her . . . ask her what? She wasn't sure.

Her thoughts were interrupted by a scolding voice at her elbow.

"If you left that precious child with your nanny," Luna said in a sharp tone, "you'd better get back there right now, because she's not doing her job." She pointed toward the front step. And then, in what seemed a total non-sequitur, she added, "And now she's teaching your husband to cook, he tells me. What's the world coming to?"

Cass looked at Luna and laughed. "You're jealous, Luna. And you have no right to be. Joey loves you. And he loves the many incredible sweaters you knit for him. He's a fashion icon, the envy of every twelve-month-old in his Kindermusik class."

When Cass looked back, the young woman who'd been standing at the curb, was gone.

And then Luna was gone, too, disappearing inside her house, then reappearing almost instantly with a platter of chocolate chip cookies for the remaining neighbors.

Cass waved off an invitation to join them, then scurried through the back door to the light and warmth of her own home.

Chapter 6

Cass hurried in the side door, closing it against the wind.

Molly had moved back to the kitchen, watching the activity as best she could from the window.

Cass quickly relayed what the police were saying, which wasn't much. "But apparently Luna really did see a face in her window. Someone with an ugly orange ski hat with horseshoes on it. But she's tough. She'll be fine."

"Horseshoes?"

"I know. Weird that that's all she noticed."

Molly nodded, shivering slightly. "It must have been a really scary thing for her."

"You're right, Mol. It must have been." She paused, then added, "And for you, too, being so close and all. Your bedroom overlooks the crime scene. Will you be okay?"

"Oh, sure. I'm fine. Scared for Luna, I guess."

"How about we have a glass of wine after I look in on Joey? Something to erase the creepy thought of someone seeing Luna in her nighty?"

Molly was silent for a second, focusing on lights beyond the window. Finally she looked back to Cass and thanked her for the invitation. "It sounds great, Cass, but I'm bushed tonight."

"Joey can be a handful."

"Joey is a love. He could never be a handful." Her expression softened at the thought of the sleeping baby upstairs.

"Well, I hope you can get to sleep, Molly. They're still making some racket out there, but not much. If they're too noisy, let me know and I'll send Old Dog after them."

From his bed near the coatrack, the Brandleys' stray mutt flopped his tail and raised his head, then slowly lowered it. Slightly deaf and with signs of cataracts, the dog, who had shown up on the Brandleys' steps the day of Joey's birth, couldn't scare away a fly. But Old Dog, as he was affectionately called, loved the family—Molly too—with a loyalty that made all those other things pale by comparison.

Molly laughed and patted Old Dog's head, then headed back out the door, pausing briefly as she saw flashlights bouncing off the side of Luna's house, a policeman appearing, then disappearing again.

She pulled herself away, trying to dislodge the images from her head, and climbed the staircase to her small apartment above the Brandleys' garage.

She flicked on the lights and walked through the small sitting area to the bedroom, an alcove area big enough for a bed, armoire, and dresser, not much else. She stood at the side of the bed and looked at the window on the other side, realizing that she'd rarely opened its blinds, nor noticed how close it was to Luna's yard. She walked around and slipped two fingers through the blinds, looking out at the remaining group of neighbors still milling about in Luna's yard.

Luna Risso loved the holidays almost as much as babies and picketing City Hall, and her small house was transformed in December with blinking, multicolored lights, the windows and door looped with swags of greenery, and the front-yard trees transformed into steeples of light. Beneath them, wooden reindeer lifted their proud heads, looking, it seemed, into the stable and manger. It was like a giant glittery ornament, Molly thought.

And there was Luna in the middle of it all, passing out chocolate chip cookies.

Molly watched as the neighbors began wandering off to their own warm houses, their warm beds. She watched the police come back from canvassing the neighborhood, then disappear inside Luna's house. Shortly afterward, they emerged again, carrying paper plates of what Molly suspected were more cookies.

The sound of the kitchen door opening and closing between the garage and the house told her Danny was home, too.

Luna's door lights blinked off and soon the bedroom shades were pulled tight, the lights off, plunging the house into darkness.

The neighbor's window was scarily close to her own, with only the stretch of grass, dark and muddy now from many footsteps, between them. Her apartment was higher. But still, so close she could have called out to whoever wanted to spook Luna. To have scared him off. Would she have done that? she wondered. She squinted, trying to see the ground below Luna's window, the scattered logs Cass had described, a brown twiggy bush.

Then she looked back into her own bedroom.

And then her eyes went back and forth from Luna's window to her own place, growing larger as she replayed the scene. Her thoughts ran off in new directions, collecting fear as she envisioned what Luna must have felt and seen through her window. She pressed one hand against her heart, calming it, and another to her temple to slow a headache's advance—to block out the feeling snaking uncomfortably through her.

A sudden movement on the side of Luna's house startled her. She leaned closer to the window and stared at the shadowed logs, the dark grass. A scuffling sound.

A cry.

Molly's breathing stopped, her body painfully stiff.

Suddenly a white cat leapt out from behind one of the logs.

A cat. It's only a cat. The painful release of Molly's breath clouded the window. She repeated the thought, calming the beating in her chest.

Finally she turned away from the window, her scattered thoughts taking shape inside her head. She walked into the soft light of the cozy seating area. It was home.

Her friend Shannon had insisted on her having something red and had brought over the hugest poinsettia plant Molly had ever seen. It covered most of the small kitchen table, right beside a photo of Joey, which Cass had framed for her.

But she wasn't seeing or feeling the coziness or safety this space usually brought to her. She was seeing a shadowy face in a window, frightening her older neighbor. A face that may have been peering in the wrong window. The wrong house.

She walked to the door, grabbed a flashlight and her jacket, and climbed down the stairs into the dark night, memories of the last time she had felt this frightened chilling her bones.

Chapter 7

The small notice in the Sea Harbor Gazette went unnoticed by most people.

But not by Birdie Favazza, who read the paper religiously every day. She read it *all*, from the front-page charity and city council events and fishing restrictions and expected storms, to the inside reports on the Patriots game, the obits, and on to her two favorites columns: the police blotter and her dear friend Mary Pisano's "About Town" column.

"Therein one finds the faces of Sea Harbor," Birdie would say with a smile to those who questioned her reading habits. Mary's folksy "About Town" column highlighted things in Sea Harbor that the Ravenswood B and B owner deemed interesting or inspiring or important for people to know—like a gentlewoman shoveling her elderly neighbor's sidewalk. But it was the police blotter Birdie read with glee, visualizing a policeman being called to rescue an immature gull caught in a lobster trap, or a report of dog walkers getting too close to the newly hatched piping plover chicks on the beach.

It wasn't just the small-town updates that intrigued Birdie; it was the fanciful way they were written. Peppered with words like *sternutation, recalcitrant, bunkum*. Birdie was quite sure the current writer was a young, would-be fiction writer who had been assigned the blotter, and then turned the assignment into a chance to practice her prose on the reported crimes of Sea Harbor. At the least, Birdie thought the enthusiastic writer's efforts deserved readership, and she often sent in complimentary notes praising the posts.

The item that caught her eye Thursday morning wasn't the entertaining prose, but rather the street name: Coastal Road, a narrow town lane that wound along a quiet area of old homes above the Canary Cove Art Colony. It was her dear friends Cass and Danny's street.

With the paper smoothed out in front of her on the kitchen table, Birdie pushed her blueberry muffin plate aside, straightened her reading glasses, and read on. Seconds later, she looked up.

"Ella, you must come read this."

Birdie's housekeeper wiped her hands on a dish towel and walked across the kitchen to Birdie's side. Straightening her own reading glasses, she leaned over and peered down at the newspaper.

She read aloud, as Ella was prone to do.

" 'Wednesday night, 9:03 p.m.: With efficient haste, police responded to a call from 2 Coastal Road, where they found a verklempt, quaking woman in a voluminous nightgown.'

"Good Lord above," Ella said to the top of Birdie's white head. "Who in their right mind writes like that?" She straightened her glasses and continued.

" 'The woman reported seeing a shadowy figure peeking into her bedroom window. A possible scopophiliac was invading the quiet neighborhood. Police inspected the holiday-bedecked property, peering inside the stable and behind the wooden reindeer and plastic cows, the mute Nativity figures, all unable to provide further details. After diligently patrolling the well-kept area, the police assured the solicitous gathering of neighbors that they were all safe from any minacious prowler. Eventually, after time spent calming the homeowner over steaming mugs of hot chocolate and homemade cookies, they bid the now-pacified woman 'bonsoir' and departed into the wintry silent night.'"

Ella shook her head, laughing. "Well, now you have it. Crime in the big city. And the homeowner, as sure as I'm standing here in this kitchen, is Luna Risso."

"Of course it is," Birdie said, relieved it wasn't Cass's home. She chuckled at the fanciful description of the event and hoped Cass and Danny's baby had slept through the commotion.

The outside door off the kitchen hallway opened and closed with a bang, bringing in a gust of cold air. Harold stood in the doorway, rubbing life back into his hands.

"Did you catch this one on your police radio?" Ella asked her husband, waving the newspaper. "Luna has had a snooper come a-calling."

Harold Sampson, as tall and thin as the *American Gothic* farmer, laughed heartily and nodded. "Lucky for whoever it was that Luna didn't catch him. But I got other news for you two ladies. There's a car just pulled in your drive, Birdie. It's parking in the circle near the front door. Too early for anyone I know to be here."

Nearly as old as Birdie herself, and having lived and worked on the Favazza estate for decades, Harold knew nearly everyone in town. And as Birdie's trusted driver of her decades-old Lincoln Town Car, he especially prided himself on identifying the town's automobiles—make, model, and owner. "It's a Volvo XC90. Got a rental plate," Harold said. "Didn't know they rented Volvos."

"Is there a person driving the car, Harold?" Birdie asked nicely.

"Looked to be a lady. I was about to go check her out, but wanted to know if you were expecting company first. If it's a sales pest, I'll run 'em off."

Birdie was already standing, brushing muffin crumbs into her palm.

"No need. I'll go, Harold."

"Who rents a Volvo around here? Nobody, that's who." Harold spoke to Birdie's back as she walked out of the kitchen and headed toward the front foyer.

She opened the front door to find an attractive woman, dressed in slacks and a long coat, a gold Tiffany knot necklace bright against a black turtleneck sweater, standing on the flagstone steps. The woman's smile was professional, polite.

Birdie frowned, trying to figure out if she'd met this woman before. She looked vaguely familiar.

But before she could assemble her thoughts, the woman spoke up, in the way someone used to being in charge might do.

"Hello," the woman said. "You are Mrs. Bernadette Favazza?"

Birdie nodded, trying again to find the woman's face somewhere in her memory. An attorney? One of her bankers?

"I've come to talk with you about a restaurant," the woman continued.

Birdie opened the door wider, the giant wreath on the door brushing her short crop of gray hair. A myriad of tiny laugh lines fanning from the corners of her eyes deepened. She wondered if she had somehow misheard the woman. A hearing aid checkup was in order, perhaps. Or was the stranger inviting her to lunch? Or perhaps she herself had missed one on her calendar.

"A restaurant," Birdie repeated, trying to put the visitor's words into some understandable context. She moved aside, allowing the woman to step out of the cold and into the pine-scented foyer, its winding stairway roped with freshly cut garlands.

The woman removed her boots and set them beside the door.

Then, while Birdie stood quietly, waiting, the woman turned and faced her, straight as a bamboo knitting needle, Birdie thought.

Waiting was a trait that came naturally to Birdie, honed over many years of living—waiting thoughtfully for the other to speak. Letting the silence settle between them until she knew what to expect from the other.

The woman waited, too, seemingly undeterred by the silence.

When she spoke, her voice was pleasant, business-like: "A restaurant, yes, that's correct," the stranger said. "I'm going to buy a restaurant here in Sea Harbor. And you, Mrs. Favazza, are someone who can help me make that happen."

Birdie smiled, bemused and intrigued, and wondering if this seemingly intelligent woman knew that she didn't have a single restaurant to sell. Or buy. But she was always open to dining at one and did so often.

"You may call me Birdie," she said, and, curious now, she led the stranger through the wide foyer and into the rarely used front living room. Perhaps her quiet morning would be more interesting than she had anticipated. At the least, it would provide some tidbits for knitting night that evening at Izzy's shop.

Molly Flanigan woke up early that same morning. But she didn't need to read the paper. She had experienced Luna's adventure firsthand, and she had taken it to bed with her, letting it punctuate her dreams. A Peeping Tom with an ugly hat. How many men could wear a hat that ugly and not feel silly? Or be made fun of? Only one, she thought. A man with looks and ego that would overshadow unsightly clothes, even making an ugly hat look awesome. A man who could turn another's life as ugly as his hat.

But it didn't make sense and she knew she was letting

dreams, a neighbor's scare, and memories play into her psyche, making an awful, fearful mess of it. And she would not let that happen. She loved this job, this life, and this town. No. She would not let that happen.

Shannon, was always telling her that she should see a therapist. Talk to someone about bad dreams. About horrible experiences. Get help in letting go of them.

Maybe she would.

But not today. Today she and Joey were going to his Kindermusik class again. Joey had perfect pitch; of that, Molly was fairly certain.

Chapter 8

Thursday night knitting usually began in a staggered fashion, with Nell the first to arrive, carrying an Instant Pot or casserole dish with hunger-inducing aromas leaking out as she set it up in the cozy back room of the yarn shop. Izzy would be somewhere in the yarn shop, finishing up the business day with Mae, her shop manager. Birdie was usually next to arrive, a chilled bottle of Pinot Grigio in one hand, her knitting bag in the other. Cass Halloran Brandley would straggle in last, after a long day of managing the Halloran Lobster Company and squeezing in sufficient cuddle time with baby Joey.

But this Thursday evening gave rise to a confluence of friends at the yarn shop's blue door, piling in together as Mae Anderson, bundled up in a puffy coat, opened the door to go home.

"Well, will you look at this," the shop manager said, miming a group hug. "Such eager faces. Must be a lot of gossip or news or mysterious whatnots waiting to come out of those knitting needles tonight."

Nell smiled at Mae's comment, but inside, her heart

squeezed a bit, as if her meddlesome dreams of the night before—images she had described to Ben over breakfast that
morning—were a strange kind of portent. The kind of dream
that pulled the past into the present, with the passage of time
clouding events and adding a touch of sinister to it all.

That morning, Ben had stirred his coffee and listened in that
silent way he had, his expression attentive, providing Nell
space to talk her own way out of the hazy dream, scattering it,
or putting it aside for the moment to make room for the day.

And she had done exactly that, although Mae's words brought
back a vague discomfort, something that the evening at Ocean's
Edge with Ollie had left her with.

Birdie, as she often did, caught Nell's look. She closed the
door after the shop manager left and walked over to her side.

"Perhaps our Mae is prescient," she said. "I feel a certain unrest myself. Maybe it's the weather. It seems to hold a threat
today."

Before Nell could reply, the music from the back of Izzy's
yarn shop picked up. Like a wave at high tide, Lady Gaga's
powerful voice rolled up from the cozy knitting room a few
steps below.

" 'When the sun goes down,' " Cass began to sing along with
the music and the artist, relieving Nell of a package of rolls,
then leading the way down the steps to the fire-warmed room.

Izzy looked up from the corner where she was kneeling
down, poking logs in the fireplace grate to life.

"Home at last," Birdie greeted her, shrugging out of her coat
and hurrying over to give Izzy a hug. She then sank into an old
leather chair, which Ben Endicott had donated to the yarn shop
when his and Nell's niece had opened it those years ago. It was
the closest chair to the fire, Birdie's favorite. She leaned in toward the crackling flames, rubbing the blood back into her
small hands.

"That's how I feel about this room, you know," she said to

anyone who might be listening. "Our home away from home. It's like that wonderfully soft alpaca blanket you knit me for my birthday, Izzy. The room wraps us all up in comforting folds."

Izzy uncurled her long body from the hearth and stood up, her cheekbones rosy from the fire. She smiled and brushed a kiss over the top of Birdie's white head, whispering, "I love you, too, Birdie."

Cass had already uncorked the wine Birdie had brought and was filling four glasses on the low coffee table. "Hey, did any of you hear about the wild time in my peaceful little neighborhood last night? We even made it onto your police blotter, Birdie."

"Which, of course, I have read, word for colorful word. I fretted for a bit when I saw it was on your street," Birdie said. "So much better it was at Luna's. It will please her to repeat this story for years to come."

Nell looked up from the old library table and stopped stirring the pot of chowder. "Tommy Porter was over, and he said something about a call concerning an intruder. So it *was* Luna's house."

"Right." Cass quickly filled them in, dramatizing it, along with Luna's attire.

"That's crazy," Izzy said.

"Yep. Luna saw an ogler, as she called him. *Ogler.* Have any of you ever used that word in your life?"

"Did she know the person?" Izzy asked.

"She told Danny she saw him through a glass darkly. I think she meant her windows were dirty. Basically, she saw an ugly orange ski-type hat in ugly colors with blurry horseshoe symbols or something on it. Could have been anybody. Maybe a neighborhood kid. Who knows?"

"The poor woman must have been distraught. Seeing someone looking in her window at night like that? How frightening that would be," Birdie said.

"Most of the neighbors were lighthearted about it, I guess because of Luna coming out looking the way she did. But a few were scared. And I think Molly was, too, though she didn't say much."

"Our Molly?" Birdie said. "She's so strong and practical and in charge of things. It surprises me."

"She's protective of Joey. Maybe the thought of a prowler in the vicinity worried her," Nell said.

"Maybe," Cass said. "I don't know. But it was weird."

"Why weird? I'd be scared, too," Izzy said. "Just the thought of some guy peering in the window scares me."

"Yeah, I guess. But later, when we were getting ready for bed, Danny went in to check on Joey. I guess the idea of a prowler had stuck with him, because he checked to make sure all the windows were locked. When he looked out Joey's window, he could see a light reflecting off the side of Luna's house. Then it moved and headed toward our garage. It freaked him out at first, but he soon realized it was Molly—holding a flashlight like her life depended on it."

For a minute, they were all quiet, surprised at what could have been dangerous. And not very wise.

Finally Izzy said, "You know, it kind of fits. I can see Molly not being able to sleep until she was sure the three of you were safe."

"Did you ask her about it this morning?" Nell asked.

"Danny did. He wondered if she'd heard another noise. She brushed it off, kind of embarrassed that Danny had seen her. She thought she'd seen something on the ground, she said, and had gone over to find it."

"Well, I suppose that makes sense," Nell said.

"Well, anyway, the police didn't find anything, nor did Danny, Mister Super Sleuth. I think he has a scene in his new book about a neighborhood in peril or something."

"Luna would be a great protagonist," Birdie said.

"She's a character for sure," Izzy said. "She came in the shop yesterday when it was packed, then proceeded to let Mae and me have it, scolding us in front of the Wednesday morning knitting group for not having enough help."

"She may be bossy, but she's a beautiful knitter," Birdie said.

"Joey is testimony to that," Cass said. "His sweater wardrobe is bigger than mine. But anyway, last night was a bit exciting for the quietest neighborhood in Sea Harbor. Danny's take was that Luna's peeper wasn't very smart or he'd have found a more interesting neighborhood to prowl around in."

Their laughter and thoughts of the peeper's surprise when he spotted Luna in her nightgown and curlers turned to sharpened appetites as Nell set down a tray of steaming bowls of chicken corn chowder on the coffee table. Thoughts of Peeping Toms were put on hold and the conversation turned easily to the creamy chowder, the thick Aran jumper that Birdie was knitting for her groundsman, and the weekend holiday extravaganza Mayor Beatrice Scaglia was hosting in her home.

"Beatrice is psyched about this party," Izzy said. She passed a basket of warm rolls around the table.

"It will give her a chance to show off the house," Cass said. "What bank do you think she robbed to afford that place?"

"Inheritance," Izzy said. "Or so the morning knitters' circle said."

"I hear it's quite beautiful, in a gilded sort of way," Birdie said.

"Well, I'm going for the food, not gold-plated faucets," Cass said.

Izzy refilled glasses, then sat back and looked at Nell, her brows lifted. "Speaking of food, how is your friend, Aunt Nell? The celebrity chef's husband? You had drinks together?"

Nell held back a smile. Izzy didn't hide the fact that she found her relationship with this man from her past intriguing. Mysterious, Izzy had told someone. Oliver Bishop provided a sneak peek into her aunt's youth, which Izzy hadn't been around to see for herself.

"Yes, we met at the Ocean's Edge. Ben was invited, but had a meeting come up. It was nice to see Ollie again."

Cass scraped the bottom of her bowl, wiped a dollop of cream from her face, and began collecting empty bowls and plates. "So, what's the guy like? Were you guys—how did they say it back then—an item?"

Nell laughed. "Sorry, no scoop there, unless a very short-lived relationship qualifies. I realized quickly he was better suited for my roommate. They were a good match and we all stayed friends. It was good to catch up. He's been through some rough times, but seems to have landed on his feet." Nell got up while she talked and wiped off the table, readying it for soft piles of yarn.

"He'll be at the mayor's party, right?" Izzy asked.

Nell nodded. She settled back in her chair, put aside Ben's sweater for a while, and pulled a half-finished cowl from her knitting bag. "You'll like him. But it's his wife who's the head-liner these days. He's mere backstage help, he says."

Izzy reached over and ran her finger along the broken rib pattern. "This is a beautiful cowl, Aunt Nell. It's rocky, like our coastline."

"It's for your mom, Izzy. Maybe it'll remind my sister of our coast here, and lure her back for more visits. Growing up in Kansas, we didn't have many coastlines, rocky or otherwise, as you well know."

Izzy laughed and pulled out her own project, her annual gift for her husband: argyle socks. And like her uncle Ben, he always expressed utter surprise. She began moving her needles, a movement as natural as breathing, miraculously turning the orange, green, and blue merino strands into diamonds. Nell reached over and touched the fine yarn, smiled, then went back to manipulating the chunky needles creating her sister's cowl.

"I got a glimpse of the chef being interviewed on the news last night," Cass said. "I missed most of it, though. Joey woke up. And we took him into our bed."

"We saw that, too," Nell said. "Or a snippet of it, anyway. Ollie was giving me a virtual introduction to his wife when she appeared on the lounge TV, but it went black before I had a good look." She paused, as if rethinking what she was saying. Or the mysterious, unpleasant incident that followed it. But then she continued, setting discomfort aside. "Ollie says she's an amazing chef, but also a shrewd businesswoman. She's made guest appearances on some of the cooking shows and has been approached to do one of her own. She's an entrepreneur, he said. Ollie wasn't that good at thinking up new ventures, investments, that sort of thing. His love was cooking, not ledgers."

Cass and Izzy chimed in with questions. There was something intriguing about the well-known chef who was married to an old boyfriend of Nell's, however briefly that might have been.

Birdie sat quietly in her chair, fingering the ball of pure Irish wool in her lap. And listening, her thoughts soon shifting to her early-morning visitor.

The woman had provided business details, economic advantages, statistics. And utter confidence.

There was little chitchat in the visit to Birdie's home; the woman was all business.

And it took little time for Birdie to realize that the shrewd businesswoman was suggesting that Birdie partner with her in an enterprise.

One that would betray a close friend of hers, although the visitor probably didn't know that. Although, would it have made any difference? Of that, Birdie wasn't sure.

Thursday nights were never just about Nell's cooking, the cozy back room, and the comfort of knitting. They were about friendship and sharing. About secrets and sorrows, thoughts and emotions and life. The four women trusted one another to make sense, and to make peace, with all that life brought to each of them. And to all of them.

But for reasons Birdie couldn't articulate, she held back sharing her unexpected meeting with the shrewd businesswoman.

The meeting had been presented as a confidential one. And the woman was clearly an extremely capable woman, an award winner. But deep down, Birdie felt the woman was other things, too.

And when they finally closed up Izzy's shop and walked out the door that evening, her unexpected conversation with Nell's college friend's wife went with her.

Chapter 9

Molly Flanigan woke before dawn Friday morning, feeling more like herself than she had in a couple days. It was Joey, his sweet laughs and thrill at pounding on a drum at music class the day before that convinced her she might not need a therapist. She simply needed to enjoy each day of her life and move forward. That's what a twelve-month-old did for her. Made her see what was real. That's what it was all about in the long run. Learning from an infant-cum-toddler was a gift, and she was going to make the most of it.

She turned toward the window as she pulled herself out of bed, as if the house next door would look somehow different, the recent event that happened there simply a dark spot in all their imaginations.

The house was still there, still lit with Christmas lights competing with the dawn for center stage. And that was good, she told herself. Life was normal.

She turned away and headed for the galley kitchen and the coffeepot.

The strong coffee brought her to full alert, and she thought about her day, about her job, about her life with these people she loved dearly.

She looked around the room that Cass, with help from her friends, had made as cozy as possible, and Molly loved it. Izzy had donated knit throws, Nell a cushy slipcovered couch and chair, and Danny had refinished a table he'd found in the attic. It was at that small table she sat every morning to drink her coffee. She loved her coffee time, but loved even more what came next. Sweet baby Joey, and a day filled with warmth and purpose and helping this family that had become part of her life in such a short time. A good family.

She rinsed the coffee mug and hung it on a hook, then headed for the shower, ready to move into her day.

It was late morning when Molly finally had time to take Joey for a walk. And she even had a mission.

Shannon had suggested she come by the mayor's new home, where they were getting things set up for a big party she was working at the next night. "I was called in last minute by the mayor, who said they needed one more server." Shannon admitted she didn't know anything about the party, but the house sounded great and the job paid well. That was enough for her.

"Bring Joey by to say hello," Shannon had said. "It would brighten my day."

"Shannon will be hungry," she explained to Joey, who was settling into his plush stroller, his lids heavy and ready for a nap, and his tiny hands clutching a stuffed polar bear to his chest. "We'll bring lunch."

The mayor's home wasn't far from downtown, Shannon had told her, then sent the address to Shannon's phone.

After stopping at Harry's deli to pick up a two provolone and ham sandwiches for Shannon and herself, she and sleeping Joey found the lovely old home easily. Shannon was waiting in the drive.

"It's awesome, Shannon," Molly said, looking up at the gracious home, the festive decorations, the lovely lawn, and the long drive.

"And, like I said, pays well," Shannon said with a grin, hugging Molly, then spotting the bag from Garozzo's deli tucked in the back of the stroller.

"One for each of us," Molly said. "Joey insisted."

Shannon pulled it out and gave it a whiff, exclaiming that it was her favorite of all of Harry's specials. "This will keep me alive for an hour or two," she said, immediately unwrapping the sandwich as she walked with Molly to a low granite wall near the driveway. They pulled their puffy jackets close and sat on the cold surface.

"So what's going on here?" Molly asked as she talked around bites of ham and melted cheese, looking up at the house.

"I know nothing," Shannon laughed. "Haven't even met the rest of the crew yet. They should be arriving soon for us all to get the lay of the land."

Molly looked around the wide yard, the old grand house made new again. "This is really lovely."

"Someday you and I will each have a place like this," Shannon joked.

They talked for a while longer, finishing up their sandwiches just as two young women walked up the long drive and waved.

"Those must be my kitchen crewmates," Shannon said, wiping crumbs off her lap and standing. "Sorry this was so short, but guess I better follow them in. Don't want to make a bad first impression."

She grinned and leaned down, sending an air kiss to a sleeping Joey. "Wish me luck," she said, giving Molly a quick hug before following the others up the drive to the back of the house.

Molly smiled at Shannon's back, looked once more at the beautifully decorated home, and stood and began to push the stroller down the sidewalk and toward home.

She'd barely made it to the next stately home on the street when a loud grinding *vroom* caused her to lean down, checking on Joey as if she could protect him from the awful sound. She looked up to somehow chastise the monster vehicle that had almost awakened Joey. But what she saw was a black motorcycle turning into the drive of the mayor's house. The cyclist's eyes were on the house. His helmet was missing, an unfortunate-looking ski hat in its place, and his face clearly visible.

Molly's heart squeezed so tightly she could barely breathe, but she managed two long calming breaths, then turned away from the mayor's house, explaining to a sleeping Joey that he shouldn't worry. She'd get him home safely.

And she did.

And shortly after, she put in a call to Luna Risso.

Chapter 10

Cass Halloran was ready for the weekend. It had been a long week, filled with company decisions, calming fishermen, and wondering if she needed more office help in the thriving Halloran Lobster Company, a company built by her father, Patrick, and carried on through good times and bad by Cass and her brother, Pete. The company that had provided a decent life for the Halloran family. And a company Cass and Pete were determined to keep going and growing and making Pat Halloran damn proud, as he always said of his kids.

She pulled on a down parka and shouted to her assistant in the next room, "I'm outta here, Ruthie. Don't burn down the place."

Ruthie's answer was muffled by the sound of wind filling the office as Cass pushed open the door of the Halloran Lobster Company office and stepped outside.

"Geesh." She watched her breath rise up in front of her, a hazy gray plume against the black night sky, then hurried across the parking lot and climbed into her SUV, starting the engine.

As she waited for the car to warm up, she breathed in the frosty air and let go of the week, her thoughts turning to home.

Home—the very thought of what that meant dismissed all concerns of missing buoys and replacing old lobster traps, of computer glitches and the million other things that had crowded the last hours of her day. *Home.*

It was just a few years ago that home for Cass was a small rented apartment above a fishing supply store, then a cottage rental from her good friend Izzy. Family then was her brother, Pete, and their remarkable mother, Mary, who worked at Father Northcutt's church and prayed for her son and daughter a lot. And her knitting forever friends—Izzy, Birdie, and Nell. And now here she was, with a home of her own near the water, a husband that loved her no matter her multitude of failings, and an incredible baby. *Going home* took on a whole new meaning. How rich could one sinner get, she often said to her mom, who would laugh and light another candle for her. Just in case.

Home to baby Joey. To Danny. To a cozy house and a home-cooked meal Molly would have managed to put together in between folding laundry or playing on the floor with Joey or singing him sweet songs as she danced him around the house.

Cass turned onto the narrow road that wound through the Canary Cove Art Colony. Decorations were up, gallery windows filled with artsy gifts, with notices of holiday shows and events at the tiny galleries crowding the road. At the end of Canary Cove Road, she made a turn onto Coastal Road, a narrow hilly street that climbed up to a dead-end, a street filled with small homes but with exceptional views of the sea.

She clapped one hand over her jacket at the familiar tightening and winced. Baby Joey was hungry. Just the thought of the robust baby boy waiting for her warmed her insides and caused her breasts to tingle. Some counseled her that it was time to stop all that nursing. Wise Izzy had silenced everyone else's comments and said, "You go for whatever's right for you and Joey."

Izzy, as always, won out. And so had Joey.

Soon, sweet baby boy.

And thanks to Marvelous Molly, dinner for her and Danny would be taken care of, too. Spectacular, unusual dinners. She didn't talk often about her unusual ability to create meals out of nothing. But Danny and Cass both agreed that Molly could easily be a chef at some fancy restaurant. But they didn't say it too loudly. They were extremely happy with the present arrangement. In addition to creating culinary masterpieces, the twenty-three-year-old woman had singlehandedly brought harmony and order back into their chaotic home in a million ways. As her mother, Mary Halloran, often said, "It was a miracle."

Neither Danny nor Cass had anticipated the changes a baby would make in their forty-something lives. Danny's writing success brought publishing expectations and demands for serious writing time, and Cass had a lobster company to run, but they were older. Mature. A baby in their lives would be a breeze.

It had taken nearly a year, but finally, after months of sleepless nights, brains that seemed to be on hiatus, a household turned on its head, and a revolving door of nannies, the Brandleys' very own Mary Poppins had dropped into their lives. This magical one appeared in jeans, with tousled blond hair tucked beneath a baseball hat, and boasted a smile that cast a spell over all of them.

Thanks to Molly, Cass and Danny began sleeping again, and so did baby Joseph Archibald Brandley.

Cass pulled into the driveway and smiled for no reason other than she was home with a weekend of family ahead of her. Maybe they'd take Joey to a tree farm to cut down a tree. Build a fire in the firepit and count the stars. And watch in amazement as Joey tried to pull his plump body up on the edge of a chair and grin magic into their days.

The only time away from the baby over the weekend would

be Saturday night—an obligatory showing at the mayor's holiday party. But she and Danny had become experts at sneaking out of events early and hurrying home to be with Joey, even though he'd be fast asleep when they arrived.

Flashing lights, brighter than a theater marquee, drew attention to Luna's house and her heart missed a beat. Another prowler? Geesh. But no, the yard was empty of people, the street devoid of spinning police lights, like they'd had a few days earlier. The flashing lights were all Luna's, lighting up the yard. As festive as a Macy's Christmas window.

Cass glanced over at the stable, knowing it was just a matter of time before blown-up elves and angels joined the circle of reindeer and cows. Joey loved it all, giving her and Danny reluctant appreciation for Luna's holiday extravaganza.

She grabbed her laptop case and slid out of the car, hurrying into the kitchen through the back door. Standing at the coat hooks for a minute, she closed her eyes and breathed in the enticing aroma of garlic and sweet onions and curry. Fresh parsley. Nell Endicott had better watch out. Molly Flanigan was definitely competition.

The kitchen was spotless, the table set. The sound of a rocking chair in the distance added to the Norman Rockwell moment. They'd be in the den together—Molly and Joey, as thick as hand-knit fishermen hats. Old Dog would be in there, too. With Molly's arrival, the dog had given up meeting Cass at the back door, preferring his spot at the feet of the baby boy he protected and the young blond woman he adored.

"My sweet Joey," the lobsterwoman whispered, a surge of joy filling her so completely that her heart thumped loudly in her chest. She dropped her parka on a hook and headed through the short hallway to the den. The rocking chair faced the window, and Cass paused at the door, taking in the slow rock of the same chair she herself had been lulled to sleep in. Evening shadows fell across the rag rug and idyllic scene.

Cass frowned, then focused more carefully on the rocker. The head that barely reached the top of it was devoid of streaked blond locks cushioning the headrest. Instead, thin wisps of long, graying hair flew about at the edge of the rocker.

Cass's spirits fell. *Good grief. Why is she here? I hope Molly didn't invite her for dinner.* She tried to swallow her disappointment, her image of an evening in front of the fire with her family beginning to fray at the edges.

Luna Risso turned slightly, just far enough to glance back at Cass. Thick rimless glasses slipped to the end of a short, wide nose. The woman pressed a finger to her lips, shushing Cass before she could speak.

Cass walked into the room, leaving her irritation at the door and looking around the room. "Hi, Luna. Where's Molly? Grocery store?"

Luna wagged a finger at her not to wake the baby, her squinting face turning into a dried apple doll.

Cass nodded, hoping to hear Molly bounding in the back door soon.

"I sang him to sleep," Luna whispered.

Cass smiled. Danny was right, the woman had a good heart. And there were the chocolate chip cookies, too. "So, where's Molly?" she repeated, walking to the chair.

Luna focused on the sleeping baby, a smile softening her face. Before she could explain, Joey opened his huge brown eyes, saw his mother, and stretched his arms to her, a dimpled smile filling his face.

Cass leaned down and scooped him up, holding him close, nuzzling his soft brown locks. Luna and the rest of the world nearly disappeared as she cuddled her baby.

"He's a very good boy," Luna said softly. She watched from the chair, her eyes focusing on the child.

Cass nodded, breathing in the sweet smell of her baby. Finally she pulled her attention back to her neighbor. "So, how

are you, Luna? I hope you're over that nasty prowler scare."
She kissed the top of Joey's head as she waited for Luna to explain why she was there and where her nanny was. She rubbed Joey's plump cheek with the back of her finger. *Probably picking up some exotic spice we need for dinner . . . or a diaper run. Or someone . . . someone what?*

She glanced out the window into the dark night, a small smidgen of anxiety inching into her heart from some unknown place.

And then somehow, in that instant, Cass knew, even before Luna pulled herself out of the old rocker to a standing position and faced her, her round face looking up into Cass's worry.

"You should have listened to me, missy," she said. "The girl is gone, of course."

Before Cass could breathe, Luna headed for the den door, wrapping a heavy shawl around her shoulders as she moved. She paused at the hallway, looking back just once, her small eyes accusing Cass, as if the unfolding mess of her life was all her own doing.

"And you might as well know it now, that sweet old pup of yours is gone, too."

Chapter 11

Izzy was rattled. The text from her practical friend didn't make an ounce of sense. And it had arrived way too early on a Saturday morning.

Iz—Help! I need you. Now!

Sam was up, too, already pulling out the makings of Abby's chocolate chip pancakes. He turned from his mixing bowl and nudged Izzy with his elbow. "Go, Izzy. Cass isn't an alarmist. If she needs you, I say . . . go. And bundle up. There's snow in the air."

"Bossy pants," she said as he kissed her smile.

So Izzy went, jogging away from the house and down Harbor Road. In minutes she had reached the coffee shop where Cass said she'd be.

The place held its usual bustling Saturday crowd. Izzy stood at the door for a minute, adjusting to the noise, then headed toward the back of the coffee shop.

She heard Cass's words before she actually saw her.

"She's gone, Izzy. Vamoose. My life has ended."

Cass's voice was plaintive, sad, angry—all in a frightening

mixture that was turning heads in the steamy room. Izzy followed the mournful sound to its source, a distraught figure huddled near the fireplace in an old, overstuffed chair that Cass had long ago claimed as her own.

Some customers actually thought it *was* her own. That Cass had absconded with the chair from somebody's curb and planted it in a prime spot in Coffee's, a place she frequented so loyally that the owner had granted her the privilege of shooing others out of "her" chair.

"Who's gone?" Izzy caught her breath and pulled up a chair from a nearby table. She leaned toward Cass, her eyes searching her friend's face. "Your message was crazy, Cass. Is Joey okay? Danny?"

"Molly. Molly's gone."

"Molly? Why? When? Gone where?"

"*Gone*, Izzy. Like she's moved out."

"Oh, good grief. She's not gone. To the store maybe? Getting her hair cut?"

Anger was now winning the battle on Cass's face. "I don't know where she is. But listen to my words. Watch my mouth. She is G-O-N-E. I came home from work last night, and she was gone."

"Last night?" Izzy's thoughts went immediately to Joey, but Cass quickly continued. "Joey's safe. He's fine. But I'm not. And Danny isn't, either."

The anger on her face now dissolved into sadness. And then worry.

"Okay, slow down and tell me."

"I came home from work last night, expecting to find Molly there, right? Like always. And I stepped in and dinner was cooking as usual, but it was Luna who was babysitting, not Molly. Luna said Molly asked her to stay with Joey for a while—"

"Why?"

"She didn't say why. Even Luna thought it was weird—that she'd just up and leave without telling where she was going. Luna told me that before Molly left, she walked over and picked up Joey from his crib, and hugged him so tightly he woke up. And then, with Luna yelling at her for waking him, she left. Just left. Got in her car and went I don't know where. She left Joey, left dinner in the oven. Left. Who does that, Izzy? Who leaves like that?"

Izzy flagged the barista for a cup of coffee, then turned her full attention back to Cass. "This doesn't make sense, Cass. We all know Molly. She wouldn't just leave you and your family. Not any of you. Sure, you might get on her nerves now and then, but Joey and Danny were always there to make up for it." She forced a smile.

"You're wrong. She left us. And she took Old Dog with her."

Old Dog . . . Izzy sucked in her breath. Then she let it out and made herself calm down. It wouldn't be helpful to get as frantic as Cass—her usually steady, levelheaded friend. "Okay, wait. Molly didn't come back last night?"

"Nope, I told you. Not this morning, either."

Izzy leaned back. "That makes no sense. None of it. All of it. What does Danny say?"

"That she must have had a family emergency and that we'd hear from her soon. She'll be back, he said."

Izzy nodded. Of course. That was it. "Well, Danny's right. Molly would never leave like that—without a very good reason. You'll hear from her soon."

"No note. No phone call," Cass said, her lower lip starting to tremble.

That, alone, scared Izzy. Cass was no crier. Although, lately, Izzy had been touched to see her friend's eyes get moist whenever someone asked her about her baby boy. They'd found themselves the perfect nanny, and Joey loved Molly, and now she was . . . gone?

"And you've tried texting her, calling her, emailing her—"

"Over and over again."

A barista shadowed their space carrying two espressos. "You both look like you need this," she said. "I'd add a dash of whiskey, except my boss'd fire me. Everything okay?"

Izzy and Cass looked up at the same time, as if the young woman had given them a winning lottery ticket. "Shannon," they said in unison.

Shannon Platt, a sometimes barista or waitress, sometimes a gardener at Birdie's home—and Molly's best friend from childhood—smiled down at the two women. She was a redhead, with her long, thick hair pulled back into a swinging ponytail that suited her cheerful personality. Shannon laughed. "I don't usually get that kind of welcome. I know the coffee's good, but I don't even make it."

"It's about Molly," Cass said quickly.

Shannon's brows shot up. "What about Molly?"

"Do you know where she is?"

"Oh, *where* she is." Shannon looked relieved as she carefully set their cups in front of them and took away Cass's empty one. "I thought she was hurt or something. She's probably taking Joey out to look at the lobster boats, Cass. She likes early-morning strolls."

"Shannon," Cass said, "Molly left our house late yesterday afternoon without telling us where she was going or when she'd be back, and we haven't seen or heard from her since. Are you sure you haven't talked to her?"

"What? That's impossible. And no, I haven't talked to her today, but I saw her and Joey yesterday. She was fine. Great." Shannon stopped for a breath. Then spoke more slowly. "Okay, now you're scaring me. Don't you live close to Luna Risso, Cass? I heard she had a prowler. Have they caught him?" Her eyes widened and she looked terrified for a moment. "You don't think that has anything to do with—"

"No, no," Cass said. "We're next door, but he wasn't at our house. He was very definitely at Luna's. And anyway, that was two nights ago. That guy is long gone."

"What if he saw Molly, though, the prowler?"

Suddenly the image of Molly standing under the porch light came to Cass and her stomach turned over. She didn't tell Izzy and Shannon, not wanting to make them feel as queasy as she did at the moment.

"I know she'd have left you a note somewhere," Shannon said, her hands waving in the air. "Did you look for one?"

"Maybe not carefully enough," Cass admitted, sounding as if she would cling to the idea as a ray of hope. "I think I'll go get Danny and we'll give the house a going-over until we find it."

"Molly is great, the closest friend I've ever had," Shannon said with an earnest expression they'd never seen on her face before. She looked very young to Izzy and Cass at that moment. "With my jobs and working on my belated degree, I don't have much time for socializing, but I can always count on Mol. We're soul sisters."

Hearing her name shouted out from the counter, Shannon looked over, then back.

"I gotta go," she said, "but please let me know if you find a note? I'll see if I can get hold of Molly, and if she shows up here, I'll have her text you, Cass. Oh, and I'll see you guys tonight at the gala. And by then, Molly will be home cuddling Joey."

"*Gala?*" Cass said, as if it were a word she'd never come across before.

"The mayor's party? I got myself a job helping in the kitchen. It has some downsides, but I need the money."

"The mayor?"

"Yeah, she called me herself at the last minute. Said there weren't enough helpers. Though maybe she just didn't like the ones the chef brought. I don't, either, but I like Mayor B. She may be fussy about things, but she's generous, not matter what people say. She makes taking the job bearable."

With that, she was off, weaving her way across the room.

"Geesh," Cass said, already gathering her belongings. "I forgot all about that event tonight. Of all the things I don't want to do—"

"Hey, we'll make it fun—and short. And by then, you'll have solved the Molly mystery. Knowing her, and the way you don't cook, the freezer probably has three days of dinners socked away."

"It doesn't, Izzy."

"Well, she'll be back before the cupboard's bare."

"I hope so." Cass stopped only long enough to give Izzy a quick hug, some dollar bills, and a hurried 'thanks'. Then Cass, too, was off, leaving her second cup of espresso to cool off, untouched.

Motherhood had turned her dear friend into a worrier of the first order, Izzy thought as she took a final sip from her own cup. Welcome to the club, she thought with affection, sympathy, and, she couldn't deny it, a touch of worry.

She knew she had to leave too, or Mae would have her head.

Izzy hurried toward the door, waving to several friends along the way.

Maybe Molly just needs a few days to herself. Personal business. Everyone has some.

She paused on the sidewalk outside of Coffee's, glancing up as a few snowflakes settled on her cheeks.

Although, why would she take the family dog with her?

Izzy forced the unnerving thought away and hurried toward her yarn shop.

Cass or Danny will find a note. Or Molly will contact them, full of apologies for not telling them sooner that she had to leave. She'll explain everything, and it'll all make perfect sense.

Izzy pulled up the collar on her jacket and hurried across Harbor Road.

As she neared the curb, a black motorcycle came too fast out of nowhere. The rider had to curve around Izzy to miss hitting her, throwing her slightly off balance.

Izzy's breath caught in her chest as she stepped up on the curb. She looked back, staring at the man straightening his bike, then speeding on, cutting a curving track around cars in front of him.

A young, helmetless woman riding behind him turned her head toward Izzy, glaring at Izzy as if she had caused the crazy driver to swerve through traffic like a madman.

Izzy took a deep breath and turned away, carrying into the shop the image of a dark blue winter cap with long, dark hair flowing out from under it, and an angry face glaring at her.

Chapter 12

"Mae, be about your business. I'm not leaving. This place is a mess."

The brassy voice traveled across the crowded main room in the yarn shop and stopped Izzy just inside the door. She knew the voice even before she spotted its source.

Luna Risso, hands on hips, stood like a stalwart warrior in front of Mae Anderson's tall, skinny frame at the checkout counter.

But Izzy's shop manager never cowered to anyone.

Mae stared down at Luna. "It's not a mess. We're just incredibly busy. Look around you, Luna. This place is gorgeous. See all the smiles? All Izzy's hard work. Some of mine, too, I dare say. So stop criticizing for once and appreciate success when it happens." Mae brought a smile back to her face as she turned to the next customer, handing her a festive bag filled with yarn and a complimentary word about the woman's knitting. She turned back to Luna.

"Here comes Izzy, Luna. Be nice or go home."

Yikes, Izzy thought. Luna might be a pest sometimes, but

she was also a loyal and frequent customer. And truthfully, the room *was* kind of a mess, albeit a happy and colorful one.

The store was packed with holiday customers shopping the bins and cubbies and display tables, or admiring the knitted samples hanging from festive wreaths and swags of greenery. Others were heading down to the knitting room for a morning beginner's class. But what drew Izzy's delighted attention was the growing line of women waiting for knitting help or to check out their purchases.

In that moment, the shock of the motorcycle near miss and the worry about Molly Flanigan gave way to the happy feeling that her store, packed with knitters, gave her on days like this.

She loved the bustle, and not just because it portended good Christmas sales, but also because she loved filling the world with knitters. Young, middle-aged, and old knitters. Men and boys. Women and girls. Black knitters, white knitters, knitters of all colors and shapes and sizes and political views and religions and life histories.

Feeling like a hostess at her own festive party, she made her way through a group of shoppers to the counter.

"What's up, ladies?" she asked, smiling at Luna and Mae as she hurried by, pretending not to have heard their spat.

Then she felt a small hand grab hold of her left shoulder.

"This place is a disaster, Izzy Perry," Luna said without a preamble. "Unpacked boxes are taking up space, blocking people's way, customers are needing help. What are you thinking?" Her short arms shot up in the air, but not in surrender.

That it's the beginning of a busy season. And that's a good thing. And we're working our tails off. But she also knew Luna was right.

Before Izzy could come up with an answer, Luna shrugged out of her bulky coat, talking loudly as she managed to loop it onto a nearby hook.

"Okay, okay, I'll stay. But it will cost you. I'll work my own schedule. And one thing's for sure, I'll bring some order to this mess if it kills me."

Izzy glanced back to the counter and the long, deep, threatening frown taking over Mae's face. But just as the manager was about to move Izzy's way with her strong objections to Luna's comments, several more customers crowded into the checkout line, blocking her from weighing in.

Izzy breathed a grateful sigh. She wasn't up for a boxing match today. And a showdown in front of customers wasn't good. Mae could handle Luna. Mae could handle anyone, as could Luna.

If the two women were boxers, there'd be even odds on them.

She started to speak to Luna, but the woman was already heading across the room toward a distraught customer. The young woman was holding up a half-finished sock with noticeable holes and a very tiny heel. Her eyes were moist.

Luna pointed the customer to a small love seat beside a table display, and squeezed in beside her. Izzy watched as Luna's demeanor turned almost soft, and soon a trace of a smile appeared on the sad knitter's face.

Luna's short fingers began untangling yarn and promising, in a gruff voice, that the woman's sock would hold a foot someday *if* she listened carefully and followed Luna's instructions to the letter.

Izzy watched for another minute, then glanced over at Mae and saw that she was watching, too, a trace of a smile lifting her lips.

Ah, 'tis the season, Izzy thought, then hurried into the supply room, aka her office, for a new shipment of a cashmere-silk blend she'd been waiting for.

Luna had patience with children and beginners that she lacked with "people who ought to know better," as she liked to say. If Luna meant what she said about helping out during the

Christmas rush, Izzy was sure she and Mae could somehow make it work.

It was midafternoon before the crowd thinned out enough for decent conversation. Izzy looked around for Luna and found her down in the back room, the hub of knitting projects, collecting stray needles and helping out a few women sitting around the long table.

Luna looked up and announced, "Well, Izzy, I'm out of here for now. I have plans for the evening."

Mae looked up from her spot near the fireplace, where she was unpacking a shipment of winter wool yarn, her brow furrowed.

Izzy spotted the look on Mae's face and knew Luna's work ethic was about to be questioned. Before that could happen, Izzy stepped in, thanking Luna for her help. "I saw you helping Jessica. Thank you. She's a new knitter and that will help her stick with it."

"All thumbs, that one," Luna said, but her pink cheeks betrayed her pleasure at Izzy's praise.

"Got a big date tonight, Luna?" one of the women knitting at the table joked.

"Who knows," Luna answered, a mysterious inflection in her voice.

"Oh?" Izzy asked.

"What are you up to now, Luna?" another women asked as a good-humored eye roll traveled around the table.

"Just a place I need to be. I'll see you there, missy," she said to Izzy. "Apparently, it's the 'place to be' tonight."

All eyes were now shifted to Izzy, as if she were on the other side of a tennis net.

"You're talking about the mayor's event?" Izzy asked. But she knew it was, of course.

"Mayor Scaglia is pulling out all the stops," a young woman knitting a baby blanket said. "It will be lovely."

The comments made Luna pause for a minute, her face unreadable. Finally she said, "Well, now, we'll see, won't we? That house wasn't intended to keep people out of it. Our mayor might not have the Midas touch tonight. We'll see." She pointed one finger at Izzy, as if expecting a note of protest, and then headed for the steps leading up to the main room. She turned around at the top archway and looked over at Izzy again.

"We'll hope for the best, right? But who knows what that is?"

And then she waved an attempted festive good-bye, some of her exuberance lost in the exchange, and left the store.

Chapter 13

When Cass reached home, she realized right away why Danny hadn't answered the text she'd sent, telling him she was headed home and needed his help.

Her husband was ensconced in the den in his favorite chair, with stocking feet on a stool, a mug of coffee next to his right arm, and a baby monitor close by. On his lap was his well-used laptop, typing in new lines, checking old ones, poring over every word, every sentence, every comma, of his most recent manuscript.

Cass stood at the door, watching, reluctant to disturb the image of this man she loved, blocking out the world, unable to hear anything short of an air raid siren except for his son's heartbeat, or his sweet *da-da* words when he awoke.

Cass had been amazed those few years ago when Danny had moved into her house and she had so proudly brought him into the den she'd arranged for him, filling it with plants and bookcases and her fisherman dad's old rolltop desk and well-worn high-backed chair. "Ta-da, your very own writing sanctuary," she'd announced.

Danny had loved it all, and especially its decorator, he said—but only if he could move the furniture, his back to the view. He claimed that when he was writing hard, four of his senses vanished—smell, taste, hearing, touch—and all he knew was the sight of words rolling out of his imagination and then onto a page on a screen. He'd know he was done for the day when he heard a jingle, and realized it was Old Dog clinking the tags on his collar. Or, on a day like this, a snowplow. Or, now, Joey starting to stir.

Cass loved to see him like this, his glasses on his nose, his brow slightly furrowed, his mouth expressing something of the mood of whatever he was reading or writing: a slight smile when it was lighthearted, a grim look when his characters were in desperate straits.

Being something of a loner herself—Cass felt lucky to love a man who needed periods of quiet and solitude as much as she did when she took her boat out for a solo run.

She had not gotten over a feeling of wonder that Danny loved her back.

Normally, Cass would not have interrupted him for anything short of fire—or maybe if Joey had the hiccups. He'd been patient as she absorbed his writer habits and peccadilloes. In return, she had patiently taught him that yes, *cruise ships* were *ships*, not *boats*, but her *lobster boats* were *boats*, not *ships*. And when she came home from a day of managing the company bills, broken traps and snagged lines, he had never said, "Here, take the baby." He gave her however much time she needed to take a shower and change clothes so she could scoop up Joey without perfuming him in eau de shellfish.

"Danny?" she said now, in a loud-enough voice to make him look up.

When he did, looking dazed, as if he were still in his imagined world where murders were solved and justice was served, she asked, "Have you heard anything from Molly?"

He shook his head.

She chewed her bottom lip, then said she'd talked to Molly's friend Shannon. "She made me wonder if we'd looked hard enough for a note Molly may have left. I need you to help me look. I'm starting to get really worried about her, Danny. So is Izzy. So is Shannon. Let's go check her room."

Danny was silent. He took off his glasses and absently rubbed the glass. "I don't know, Cass. That's kind of an invasion of her private space. I promised Molly when she moved in here that the apartment was hers, and that we didn't believe in landlords who checked up on renters."

"What if she needs help and left a note that said that?"

Baby sounds emerged from the monitor on the table.

They looked at each other.

Molly would have fetched Joey if she'd been there.

Old Dog would have followed her up the stairs.

"I'll get Joey," he said, looking fully present now.

Cass expected to find Molly's room neat and clean. It was clean, but definitely not neat. Danny walked in with Joey in his arms. "Looks like she was in a hurry."

The closet door was open, with obvious gaps in the line of clothes.

Two drawers of the dresser were partly open, too, and several pieces of clothing littered the bed.

"It looks like she left plenty behind," Danny observed. "So that means she's coming back, right?"

Cass felt too anxious to speak.

In lieu of blurting out her fears, she kissed Joey all around his hairline, making him giggle.

"Do you think we offended her?" Danny asked.

Cass sat down with Joey in the small chair in front of the desk, using the open drawer as an excuse to stare at its contents.

"I don't think so. I don't know." She leaned over Joey to look at the photos tucked into the edge of the mirror behind a small desk. "No, Molly isn't that kind of person. She'd tell us if there was a problem."

Joey patted his mother's chin.

"What do we know about Molly, Cass?"

"Not a lot, I guess. I checked basic references, and then we met her. And she seemed perfect." She thought about it, then added, "She *is* perfect."

Danny walked around the room, checking the bookcase.

Cass watched him, knowing he didn't want to touch anything. This wasn't Danny's thing. People in his books snooped, but he didn't.

He turned toward her.

"This looks to me just like what it would look like if things happened the way we thought, that some kind of emergency came up, and she had to get there in a hurry."

Cass nodded. But her worry persisted. "Maybe she scribbled a note and it fell down or got covered up?"

Danny went back to halfheartedly moving the toaster and checking around the couple of chairs in the room.

Cass forgot any qualms she had about Molly's privacy, and started pushing around stray papers and pencils in the desk drawer.

"Nothing," Danny said at last. "What's that?"

Cass touched a corner of a brochure that Joey was trying to nibble on. "Take a look at this. I think Molly listened when we talked about her becoming a chef. Not, of course, 'til Joey is twenty-five, but after that? Maybe she's considering it. This is from that culinary school in New York." She read the front cover: "'Institute of Culinary Education.'"

She eased it away from her son and handed the brochure to his father.

"Interesting," Danny said, pushing his glasses up on his nose. He opened the brochure. "Some heavy hitters on the school's board, too."

"What would you know about famous chefs?" Cass teased.

"I know everything," Danny said. "That's what writers are. World Books on legs. That chef who's catering for the mayor's party? Lidia Carson? Her name's on this thing." He walked over and showed it to Cass.

Cass looked at it, squinting at the small print, then looked up, thinking out loud. "This woman—the chef—is married to Nell's old college friend. So . . . let's say that Molly wants to go to this famous culinary school? And she gets this brochure, and realizes that she has a good chance to actually meet one of its teachers. So, what does she do? She throws some clothes in a bag and leaves town? That makes no sense."

Danny managed a laugh. "Hey, you're storytelling here. Molly isn't much interested in Sea Harbor parties. I doubt if she even knows there's a chef coming. And we don't know if she's interested in becoming a chef."

"Danny, this is . . ."

"Fiction. What I do for a living."

"Could you . . . Should we say something to the police, just in case . . ."

"Molly is an adult. She can come and go as she pleases, even if it doesn't make us happy."

"But what if . . ."

Danny lifted Joey out of Cass's arms and made a funny face at him that made the little boy laugh again. Then he set him down on the floor. "Maybe Joey can find a clue."

They watched him toddle across to an overstuffed chair.

"Besides," Danny said, "if we reported Molly as missing, Tommy Porter will tell us she'll have to be gone three days before they'll do anything."

"It will be three days tomorrow, Danny."

"Two. And if she's not back by then, and we still haven't heard anything—"

"We'll lay it all out." He watched Joey lose interest in the chair and head for a giant ficus tree in a large earthenware pot, filled with tempting-looking soil. "And I'm taking this little guy back to the house."

Cass half stood and tried to jiggle the old drawer closed. Several loose photos slid to the front and Cass immediately picked the top one up. It was of Joey and Molly playing at the beach last summer. "Aww," Cass said, holding it up for Danny to see.

Cass shuffled through the rest. There were a few more of Joey, then some of Molly and Shannon Platt, looking sunburned and happy with worn backpacks slung across their backs. Then more of them with European monuments behind them. Then the two girls closer to home, sitting in Central Park, drinking coffee. She put them back in the drawer, then noticed one more stuck to a roll of tape. It wasn't an actual photo, but an image used in some kind of advertising.

The group image featured young adults wearing aprons, standing behind a long butcher-block island, with bowls and cooking utensils in front of them, like students in a cooking class. One woman stood apart, distinguished-looking, wearing a chef's uniform, complete with toque.

The image had suffered from life in a cluttered drawer, slightly torn and faded, but the group looked ready and eager to learn.

Cass's finger pointed to one figure. The face was indistinct, but the woman had curly hair and was smiling.

Danny looked at it. "It looks a little like Molly," he said. "But it's so small it could also be Izzy or anyone else with good looks and blond hair." He started out of the room.

Cass glanced at the photo again, focusing on the figure next to the attractive blonde. It was a good-looking young man, with one hand on the woman's shoulder. The two centered the photo, two attractive students decked out in white aprons, grinning happily for the camera. Cass shoved the photo into the pocket of her jeans and followed her husband and baby back to the house.

Chapter 14

By Saturday afternoon, the wind off the ocean had picked up, turning the morning flakes into perfect sledding hills. But by early evening, the sledding hills gave way to snow-covered cars and roads, and the sound of snowplows rumbled through the streets of Sea Harbor.

"I'm not sure about this, Ben." Nell looked from the window, back to her dresser mirror, and fastened a chain of large, flat turquoise beads around her neck. She turned to her husband and straightened his tie. "What if we get stranded there? The forecast isn't great."

Ben chuckled. "Stranded at Beatrice Scaglia's home with half the town. Imagine the plots Danny would get out of it? *Bel Canto* revisited."

Nell laughed. But it was a shallow sound. She usually loved snowy days. Especially during this more leisurely time in her life when events and appointments were seldom urgent. Days when a fresh blanket of snow brought quiet and comfort, an excuse to slow down the day and savor an evening in front of the fire with Ben.

Tonight the snow fell in artful drifts, blanketing the earth in silent beauty.

But all Nell felt was a growing, unwelcome discomfort.

Birdie was ready when Danny and Cass rounded her circular drive. Thanks to Harold's thoughtful efficiency, the drive was cleared of snow and already sprinkled with salt.

Danny got out and walked Birdie back to the car carefully, although there were days when the sprightly gray-haired woman outbalanced them all.

They all looked over and waved at Harold, who was watching them from a distance, not sure at all that they should be going out in a winter flurry. He was leaning against the door of the carriage house, where he and Ella lived. A few feet away stood the riding snow blower, ready for another round. It would be a long night for the aging groundskeeper.

Dear Harold, Birdie thought. She knew he worried about her. And was thinking he was a far better driver in the snow than the lot of them. But she also knew they'd all be fine and safely home very soon. Now that Cass and Danny had a baby, they left parties on a schedule Birdie liked.

She settled into the backseat of the Brandleys' SUV, close to Joey's car seat. Tonight it was littered with cracker crumbs and a ragged stuffed polar bear. Birdie picked up the bear, squeezed it gently, and smiled. "Who's with our sweet little guy tonight?" she asked Cass, who was sitting in the passenger seat in front of her. Her voice lifted, hopeful that the answer would be "Molly, of course."

But the look on Cass's face when she turned her head matched the text messages that had circulated among Izzy, Cass, Nell, and herself that day. **Molly is gone!**

Danny confirmed it. "No word from Molly yet. Soon, though. But hey, we're off to a grandiose affair tonight. And even though Cass promised her mom—the greatest babysitter in the world—that we'd be back in forty-five minutes, I say let's celebrate the season and have a good time."

Cass was silent.

Birdie held her silence, too, her eyes focused on the mounting snowbanks beyond the window, and her thoughts on a party that would hold little pleasure for her, not after meeting the woman catering it.

Cass's cell phone chimed into her thoughts and startled all of them.

Cass took a deep breath, digging frantically in her bag for her phone.

"Joey's fine, Cass," Danny said, used to Cass's worry when a babysitter called. "My bet is it's your mom, wondering if she can keep Joey up playing blocks for another couple hours."

"My mom never asks my permission for anything," Cass mumbled, finally pulling out her phone.

Danny was partially right about Joey being fine. Finer than he had been when Cass and Danny left, Cass's mother said. "Guess who showed up to snuggle with my sweet grandson and me?" Her voice was loud enough that everyone in the car could hear.

Cass held her breath, her heart lifting.

But Mary's message was mixed. Good and bad in one single confusing package:

Old Dog was home! Clean and fed, and happily allowing Joey's small body to be pressed tightly against his own. He had simply lost his way, not unusual as one aged, Mary Halloran explained. And he had found his way back, a good fortune, and one she would wish on herself in a like situation. The pup's return was worth a celebration.

But Molly Flanigan was nowhere in sight.

Across town, Izzy and Sam settled their sleepy Abby into bed, gave final instructions to the babysitter, and headed out into the black-and-white night. Izzy skidded on the front step, just in time for Sam to collect her in his arms.

"Hey, you're good," Izzy said. She straightened up, then looked up into the wintry sky, one hand now tucked tightly under Sam's arm. "They say every snowflake is unique," she said. "How do they know that?"

Sam leaned over and kissed a snowflake off the tip of her nose. "The snowflake gurus know that because they do. Believe them."

Izzy stood still, as if pondering the thought.

Finally Sam nudged her to get into the car, which he had already preheated for the ride. He strapped himself in behind the wheel and looked over at his wife, slowly getting into the car. Izzy was still concentrating on something, her eyes now focused beyond the windshield.

"That look's way too pensive for snowflakes, Iz," Sam said. "What's going on?"

Izzy shrugged and settled back into the seat. "I don't know. I guess it might be the weather. The possible storm—and here we are, heading away from our daughter. Maybe . . ."

But there was no "maybe" and they both knew that the weather didn't merit concern. She and Sam would get home to Abby if they had to snowshoe back. Or more certainly, leave when sensible Sam said it was time. The frustrating part was that Izzy knew she was a bit off, not making total sense. But she didn't know why.

"Maybe Cass's nanny going AWOL is bothering you," Sam offered. He pulled away from the curb and drove slowly down the snow-quiet street.

"Maybe. It's sure bothering Cass. But Molly'll be back. It's strange, though, that she didn't give Cass a call. But somehow that fits into the week. Everything has seemed a little off kilter—even the energy in the store. I mean, having Luna Risso storm in and take over the way she did? That was strange. And Mae lost some orders. She never does that. Then there's the customers' incessant gossipy chatter about this event tonight. Some are ready to throw the mayor under the bus for sending out invites rather than having an open house. She could lose the next election because of her awful decision, someone said. Even our Thursday knitting night wasn't quite normal this week. And don't ask me why, because I can't tell you. Birdie was too quiet, as if she wanted to tell us something, but didn't. Nell, too, was distracted. And then . . ."

Izzy stopped talking and looked over at a quiet, listening Sam. "Okay, Sam. I'll stop. I'm crazy, right?" She forced a smile.

"Nah, not my Iz. Maybe things are a little off-center. It's a busy season for you, Izzy. You've been working nonstop. And then there's me, doing an easy, fun photo assignment capturing a day of ice fishing for *National Geographic*. I'd fail miserably holding that shop together and dealing with all those customers of yours." He turned the windshield wipers on and focused on the drifts of snow blowing across the road.

"You're right. Crazy busy. My head is too full. So let's go party. Meet Aunt Nell's old boyfriend. Eat the incredible food made by the old boyfriend's acclaimed wife, and . . . and then, as soon as politically correct, sneak out the back door and come home to warm up in our cozy bed."

She tried to send a coy smile, but just then, Sam turned onto a narrow, unplowed street and the car skidded wildly on an icy patch of snow. The SUV careened toward a tree. But just as quickly, Sam gently maneuvered the wheel, correcting the slide, and pulled the car back into alignment.

Beside him, Izzy's gloved hands were pressed against the edge of the dashboard, her eyes on the road ahead.

"Hey, it's fine, Izzy," Sam said. "You know I'm a pro on ice and snow." He reached over and laid a gloved hand on her leg. "Everything's going to be okay—"

Izzy was silent, her thoughts tangled. She trusted Sam more than anyone in the world. But she wasn't at all sure everything was going to be okay. Something wasn't right in the world.

She could feel it.

Chapter 15

A group of Dickensian carolers, the women in elegant velvet capes and white muffs, the men in top hats and tails, were gathered on the wide steps leading up to the mayor's home. Their gloved hands held librettos, while their perfectly pitched voices floated into the winter night air, inviting the well-heeled guests to "come a-wassailing."

"It's a Currier and Ives portrait come to life," Birdie said. "Absolutely enchanting." She smiled at the singers as she walked up the walkway between Cass and Danny. She squeezed Cass's arm tightly. "And now we have something to feel festive about. Old Dog is home."

"And Molly Flanigan can't be far behind," Danny said. "I feel sure of it."

Cass managed a smile.

They all looked up at several enormous evergreen trees, wrapped in tiny gold lights and forming a canopy over the guests.

The house itself was old, with some signs of its previous life still visible: an outbuilding to one side, a low granite wall in

need of masonry work. But most of the house had been renovated, its granite block construction repaired, a new roof, a
long landscaped yard with gaslights lining the drive.

It now fit in with other houses on the tree-lined street, some
with brass plates on the door, indicating historic registry status.

"It's a golden evening," said a familiar voice behind the trio.
Mary Pisano sidled up beside the group, her black coat wrap-
ping up all five feet of her. "Who would have thought Beatrice
Scaglia could pull off something like this?"

"I suspect our dear mayor had plenty of help," Birdie said.

"I can see your column headline for tomorrow, Mary,"
Danny said. "Something about a Gilded Age reborn, although
you will be far more creative."

Mary laughed. The Pisano family owned dozens of news organizations in the area, and although Mary had little interest in
them, she loved her chatty "About Town" column in the *Sea
Harbor Gazette*. "It's certainly an event, and I'm happy to ex-
pound about it, but it's not what folks are used to. Beatrice may
have made a bad move here."

Mary didn't need to expand. The mayor's decision to send
out invitations for a holiday event that had always been a community open house—a "town tradition" officially marking the
holiday season—didn't sit well with many of them.

Birdie brushed the snow off her sleeve and moved ahead, her
cheeks tingling from the cold. She looked ahead at the well-
dressed guests being met at the door, their warm coats being
taken away. But none of them were Aaron, her mailman, or the
bus driver or sundry other Sea Harbor folks who would miss
the annual holiday event this year. She shook her head, her faux
fur Cossack hat moving along with her small head. She'd gently
told the mayor a month ago that it would be unwise to forgo
the festive open house tradition. Apparently, being "gentle"
hadn't worked with Beatrice this time, and Birdie wondered if
the mayor would regret it.

Cass leaned over, whispering into the fluff of Birdie's hat. "Let's get this over with. The sooner we go in, the sooner we can come out."

Birdie chuckled, and taking Cass's arm, they followed Danny into the warm foyer. In seconds, a young helper was there to whisk away their coats and hats, to help with boots and wraps. They spotted Mayor Scaglia, beaming beside a gigantic blue spruce. Her stilettoes lifted her up and her long, sequined dress sparkled like an elaborate ornament. She hugged a guest, then stepped aside to give directives to a young man coming in with a tray of champagne glasses.

"We should say our festive hellos to Beatrice before it gets too—" Cass began, her words cut off by a brisk pat on her back. She turned around to a smiling, familiar face.

"Looks like we represent the hoi polloi, neighbor," Luna Risso said in a stage whisper. She grinned and turned to Birdie, giving her a hug. "Well, not you, Madame Bernadette Favazza, but Cass, Danny, and I are from the other side of town." She chuckled, and this time a few heads turned, then turned away.

But one head did not.

In the next minute, Beatrice was at their side, a glare of deadly daggers aimed at Luna. She ushered all four of them into a small room off the foyer, then turned to Luna.

"What do you think you're doing here?" she hissed.

The others stared at the hostess, except for Luna, who was looking around the small room as if it held a secret on one of its shelves.

"Beatrice," Birdie began, but a wave of the mayor's hand and controlled smile stopped her short.

"Of course I don't mean you, Birdie. Nor Cass and Danny. You are all invited guests." She turned away from them then, as if there were no one else in the room now but Luna and her.

"Remember this room, Bea—" Luna began, but she was cut off immediately.

"Stop it. You will do anything in your power to embarrass me, to ruin this. What are you planning, Luna? To poison the food, trip a guest, set the house on fire? We're not kids any-more. That was a long time ago. You're acting like a fool, a lu-natic. Leave now."

Then she touched a stray hair back in place, turned, and walked through the doorway and into the foyer, a polished smile already in place, and a gracious greeting ready for the next guests walking into her festive home.

"Well, that's that. I guess we've said our hellos," Cass said.

Beside her, Birdie was looking at Luna, a frown in place. "Luna?"

Luna shrugged, a giant knit shawl shifting on her shoulders. "Don't worry about it, Birdie. Old feelings die hard some-times." She glanced out into the foyer. "Beatrice has been a thorn in my ample side my whole long life. But I'm definitely not leaving the party. I have as much right to be here as she does." She patted a velvet-upholstered Queen Anne chair in the corner, as if greeting an old friend, and said, "The evening is young."

With that, Luna smiled, tiny lines spreading out from the corners of her eyes, the small Christmas bells hanging from her ears jingling, and walked into the foyer.

They watched as she greeted people along the way, smiling broadly, as if completely at home in the mayor's home.

Birdie's frown was still in place. "I do wonder what that was all about."

"It's just Luna," Danny said. "More importantly, Sam texted that they're sitting in the library, which is somewhere toward the back of this great old house. Beatrice has done a nice job of bringing it back to its long-ago glory. I'm feeling fascinating skeletons in every closet."

"And you've already written chapter one in your head," Birdie said. She smiled, pushing Luna and the mayor from her mind, and followed Cass and Danny through the wide-planked halls.

Enticing aromas from the dining room paused the group at a wide doorway.

Danny took a step in, straightening his glasses. He looked hungrily at an antique wooden table laden with platters of rare beef slivers on tiny rounds of toast, spears of shrimp and lobster, hunks of crab meat surrounded by small colorful bowls of sauces. In the center, tiered vintage serving stands were heaped with finger-sized delicacies that filled the room with amazing aromas. From a corner speaker, Andrea Bocelli's rich, sweet voice wished them a white Christmas.

"Danny, you're drooling." Cass elbowed her husband as he stepped closer to the table.

Birdie followed them in, waving to several friends who were delightedly filling small plates. She waved to Don and Rachel Wooten, standing on the other side of the table, and walked over to say hello.

She gave Rachel a hug, then turned to Don and smiled. "Are you getting appetizer ideas for the Ocean's Edge, Don?"

Don offered a small smile, but the look faded almost immediately. He looked around the table, toward the kitchen door, then back. The pleasantness on his face had all but disappeared and his voice had an edge to it when he spoke. "I don't steal from other chefs, Birdie."

Birdie's white brows lifted in surprise. "Well, of course you don't, Don. You know I was teasing you."

Don looked down, then back at his friend. "It's this whole mess, Birdie. If she knows what's good for her, she'll keep her hands off what's mine."

His wife put a hand on her husband's jacket sleeve. "Don, please calm down. This is Birdie we're talking to."

Birdie frowned. Don might have been speaking in code, but it was a code she understood.

"Don," she began slowly, her voice quiet and calm, "your restaurant is wonderful and so are you. The Ocean's Edge is important to our town, and we protect things important to us."

Rachel looked at Birdie, clearly grateful for her words. "I didn't want to come," she said. "Don insisted."

"It wouldn't have looked good not to be here," Don said. "But thanks for your words, Birdie. I figured Ms. Carson might have talked to you, and it sounds like she did. I don't know what to think. She's . . . a vicious person. I'm not sure what will stop her. I'd like to—"

"Don," Rachel cautioned.

It was Birdie's time to put a hand on the restaurant owner's arm, her small, slightly bent fingers pressing gently into the cloth. "You are a good man, Don Wooten. With a fine restaurant, a wonderful wife, and a good life. Things will work out."

Don nodded, his face showing little. He gave Birdie a brief hug.

Rachel gave Birdie a grateful look, then suggested to Don that they put in the appropriate "mingle time," offer their gracious thanks, and go home.

But Birdie knew that wouldn't happen. Between the two of them—a restaurant owner and the city attorney—they knew everyone in Sea Harbor. And though they both looked like they'd like nothing better than to go home, other guests wouldn't let them.

Birdie walked back around the table, concerned for her friend, but things would be fine, hopefully. She hadn't yet talked to the others who had, along with her, invested in Don's restaurant, although she'd noticed on the guest list that they were invited to the party. She wondered if Lidia Carson had requested that. But no matter, she hoped they would be like-minded. The Ocean's Edge was a treasure—and one didn't give away treasures, no matter the cost.

As she looked over the table, she admired again the incredible, artistic presentation the chef had created. Chocolate desserts that looked like majestic flamingoes, delicately fanned salmon, and ice sculptures holding tiny shrimp in graceful swirls. It was difficult to imagine the hardened businesswoman who had shown up at her door as the artist behind this gorgeous display. She looked around again, hoping to catch a glimpse of her in this environment. Wondering if she'd see a completely different person.

A parade of young people, dressed in starched white aprons with LIDIA CARSON, MASTER CHEF scrolled across the bibs, carried trays in and out through a butler's pantry. But there was no sign of Lidia herself.

One of the servers came up beside her. Shannon Platt set down an icy tray of oysters on the table. "Some shindig, Birdie, right? Can you believe it?"

Birdie laughed. "You show up everywhere, Shannon. A woman of many talents. I imagine this is helping fill the coffers for your degree."

Shannon laughed. "It's the only reason I'm here."

Birdie paused for a moment, then asked, "Have you heard from your friend Molly yet?"

Shannon's brows shot up. Then her face went blank, as if at first she hadn't understood Birdie's question. "Molly? Oh, you mean . . ."

Birdie squeezed Shannon's hands sympathetically—they were cold from carrying the icy tray. She didn't mean to cause Shannon stress, if that was what she was reading in her face. Although it seemed more that she was keeping something from Birdie. Whatever the reason, there was no place for that tonight. She changed the conversation quickly. "So tell me, what is it like to be working for a famous chef?"

Shannon paused before answering, then said, "Well, she runs a tight ship, which is good. She's all business. And the money's great, which is the reason I stayed after meeting some of the crew. I could definitely do without a couple of them. I hope the instant the gig is over, they leave town."

"They probably don't work as hard as you," Birdie said. "Nobody does."

Shannon glanced toward the kitchen, then looked back, as if collecting her thoughts. When she spoke, her voice was hard. "There's a pretty horrible guy. *Despicable* is putting it nicely." Her face was as dark as her voice, as if conjuring up thoughts she'd rather not have.

"Are you all right?" Birdie said, surprised at the sudden change in the friendly woman. "Is it someone you know?"

Shannon stopped for a minute, then tried to lighten her voice. "Know? No. Well, he's one of those guys who think their looks make them special. And one of the women helpers cares only about getting as close to the irritating guy as possible. We're small-town peons to them."

"You will never be a 'peon,' Shannon, no matter how small a town."

Shannon smiled. "Thanks, Birdie. Sorry for dumping on you like that. You're just too darn easy to talk to. But anyway, I'm glad to have the work. And in spite of working with horrible slugs, the food's beyond awesome."

She leaned in and cupped her hand close to Birdie's ear, whispering, "The blini napoleons are to die for, but they're going fast—grab some for Danny over there before they're gone."

Birdie chuckled as the waitress hurried back to the kitchen. She scanned the room once more for the chef, remembering Ella's old adage that "the chef is always in the kitchen."

But Birdie wasn't at all sure that the woman she had met earlier that week was the kind to hide herself behind pots and pans or aprons with her name on them.

Chapter 16

A rope of mistletoe marked the library doorway at the far end of the home. A proper mayor's den, Birdie thought, looking around at plaques and framed photos hanging on the walnut-paneled walls. In each photo, the mayor stood or sat alongside someone notable. In true Beatrice fashion, the library, like the rest of the house that Birdie had seen, had been put together by an interior designer with fine taste.

In the far corner, the Perrys and Endicotts had taken over a comfortable group of leather chairs, not far from a double set of French doors opening to a snowy patio. And in the middle, sitting between Izzy and Nell, was a distinguished-looking man, who smiled and stood as they approached, setting an empty glass down on a small table.

Oliver Bishop looked as Birdie had visualized him—a strong man, good-looking, but his face showed the wounds of losing a loved one far too early. Just as Birdie herself had experienced when her Sonny had died early in their marriage.

But before Birdie could give Nell's longtime friend a suitable welcome, Ollie turned toward someone calling his name. Heads turned as a woman walked quickly toward them.

Oliver swept one arm out in a welcoming gesture, wobbling a little, then recovered quickly and wrapped an arm around the woman's shoulder.

"Here she is, my friends. Your chef for the evening."

Introductions were made around the group, with Lidia Carson resting one hand on Ollie's arm, and shaking hands with the other. She greeted Birdie with extra charm, but didn't refer to having met her before.

Birdie held back her surprise. She wouldn't have recognized this person as the woman who had appeared at her door. Tonight Lidia Carson presented herself as an image directly off the pages of *Gastronomica*. Her chef's whites were crisp and perfect. The toque blanche sat snug on her sleek black hair, the white double-breasted jacket fit perfectly, and pants in a black-and-white houndstooth pattern were tailored to perfection. She was every inch a chef.

Lidia greeted each of them with a reserved kind of warmth, seemingly pleased to meet Ollie's friends, even though they'd probably never be close friends of hers. But it was the semblance of warmth that Birdie hadn't noticed at their previous meeting. Lidia had been strictly business when she was trying to sell Birdie a bill of goods—a bill that wasn't good at all.

Hmm, Birdie thought. *Am I a bad judge of people's motives?* She straightened up and smiled at the woman.

"It's such a pleasure to meet Oliver's friends," Lidia was saying. "I hope you enjoy the food. Oliver had a part in planning many of the appetizers." She smiled up at her husband and patted Ollie's arm.

Birdie wondered if she was the only one to whom the credit looked and sounded patronizing, more like a chef encouraging a kitchen novice than one famous chef giving credit to an even better-known, and longer-known, one. Birdie instantly pushed away the feelings, trying to concentrate on Lidia in the here and now, and not allowing her first meeting to color her impressions.

Oliver brushed off his wife's words, moving the conversation on to more neutral topics, like Mary Pisano's B and B, where he and Lidia were sleeping on the most comfortable beds he'd ever slept on. And then he expounded on his impressions of Sea Harbor.

"I always knew you two would find a perfect place to settle in," he said to Nell and Ben. "It fits you both."

"It's a beautiful area," Lidia added. "My family vacationed for a few summers in Annisquam and we came over to Sea Harbor sometimes."

"You'll have to come back to see old Saint Nick come in on one of our lobster boats," Cass said proudly.

"Santa on a lobster boat. What a clever idea," Lidia said. "I'll remember that . . ."

Before Lidia could expand on her thoughts, the mayor, standing in the doorway, spotted her and began waving. A guest and a local photographer stood with her.

Lidia looked slightly annoyed, then seemed to recognize the guest and waved back, excused herself, and walked back across the room.

Birdie recognized the guest, too, and frowned. The man was a prominent business owner, an acquaintance of hers, and one of her coinvestors in Don Wooten's restaurant.

"Ollie, you should go, too," Nell said. "You're a part of this."

But Lidia was already gone from the room—and Ollie was already headed to the bar in the corner of the den to refresh his drink.

Ben and Nell exchanged looks, then followed Ollie across the room.

✳   ✳   ✳

As more guests arrived and rooms became crowded, Cass and Izzy escaped, stepping out onto the wide, covered portico that ran along the back of the house. They stood beneath an outdoor heater, each of them with a glass of wine in hand and the lemony dill taste of Lidia's mini caviar parfaits lingering on their tongues.

Several arches framed the enormous snowdrifts covering bushes and benches and towering trees in the home's backyard. As in so many Cape Ann yards, the landscape was filled with granite boulders, big and small and thousands of years old. Tonight their craggy shapes were turned into works of art.

Low gaslights lit the winter wonderland scene as the snow continued to fall.

"It looks like a field of creatures from a strange planet," Cass said. She shivered, stepping closer to the heater.

"It's eerily beautiful." Izzy wrapped her knit shawl closer and looked down the porch. Light from glass doorways and windows across the back of the home spilled out into the night. At the far end, the kitchen windows were cracked open and sounds of food preparation were heard, muted voices, water running.

Izzy watched the shadows of servers moving around the inside. Tantalizing aromas of spicy dishes floated out to the portico each time a kitchen worker walked out carrying bags or boxes to the catering van or refuse area or garage.

Izzy pointed to a familiar figure coming out alone, her arms full of boxes. "It's Shannon," she said. "Let's give her a hand."

Before Izzy could call out, a tall man came out the door behind the server, catching up and stopping her with a hand on her shoulder.

"Looks like a Sir Galahad beat us to it," Izzy said, and she and Cass turned to go inside.

But a low, distinctly unfriendly, male voice stopped them. At first, the man's back was to Izzy and Cass and his words were inaudible. But the look on Shannon's face was clear and enough to hold the two women still.

Shannon's eyes were wide, her body stiff. She turned to walk away, but the man stopped her again, catching her arm. Standing sideways now, his voice was more distinct, his profile silhouetted from behind.

"I saw you both the other night," the man said, his voice hard as his words carried down the back of the house. "You stupid woman. You're all alike. Useless. Tell me where, or I swear I'll . . ."

Shannon turned around then, holding the boxes between them like a coat of armor. In the pale light, the shock they had seen earlier on her face was still there, but coated now with anger. And strength. "Or you'll what? You'll do nothing, that's what you'll do. You've already done enough harm to last a lifetime."

The man tried to speak, but Shannon seemed to forbid it, her own voice louder, angrier. "You get out of my face right now, you despicable, horrible person. If anyone knew the things you've done, you'd be in jail." Her voice was steady and cold. She seemed oblivious of the wind that blew snow onto the covered portico, dampening her hair.

Izzy and Cass could see the waitress's expression even more clearly as she shifted her stance and the garage security light fell across her face. Confident, cold, and angry. The man had stepped back slightly. He was taller than Shannon, with wide shoulders now covered with a dusting of snow. A barrage of words lost in the speed of delivery were thrown at the woman standing in front of him. Harsh, profane, insulting.

Shannon planted her feet firmly on the snowy surface, glaring at him. "You're mean, misogynistic, hateful, and a dozen other words I don't choose to use. Don't you ever, ever touch me again or come near us, or I will report you—or worse."

With that, she shoved the boxes into his chest, spun around, and walked back into the kitchen.

After the door slammed behind her, the man opened his arms wide and let the boxes fall onto the floor of the portico. A couple of half-empty wine bottles spilled out of their box, a river of red staining the light covering of snow.

A minute later, the kitchen door opened again. Izzy and Cass stepped closer into the shadows, watching and listening. They half expected an angry Shannon to come back out and smack the guy.

Instead, it was another white-aproned server, her black hair tied back. She walked around the boxes, reaching out toward the man.

Another confrontation? Izzy and Cass stood in silence, waiting for act two.

The woman, however, spread her arms wide and took the man into them, holding him close. Her head rested on his shoulder.

The man's head was raised, his eyes focused on the kitchen window. He shrugged the hug off, glanced back at the mess on the ground, gave a short laugh, and walked back inside, the woman following close behind.

"What a disgusting jerk," Cass said. "He dropped those boxes on purpose. And what was that sweet hug all about?"

"Kitchen drama. But let's clean that up so Shannon doesn't get blamed for it."

Together they went over and put the intact bottles back, their hands raw from the cold, then stacked the boxes neatly against the side of the portico.

A sound nearby caused Izzy to look up, then turn to her left, where a back door led to a hallway off the kitchen. She'd seen it earlier while wandering around the house. A perfect mudroom, she'd thought, and wished she had one. And then she wondered what Beatrice would do with a mudroom.

She stood and saw that the winter storm door was open a crack, a shadow beyond the glass.

Someone else had been listening to the drama on the porch.

As Izzy took a few steps toward the door, it was pulled shut. She took a step closer and looked through the glass at a determined figure moving away, down the darkened hallway. The figure paused, then stood still at a kitchen door farther down the hallway. A light from the kitchen fell into the hallway, casting a shadowy light on the figure. But instead of revealing an aproned kitchen worker or a guest, what Izzy glimpsed was a white double-breasted jacket and a perfect chef's toque.

"Weird," she said, then walked back to help Cass finish the job. Maybe she was seeing things.

Izzy straightened one of the boxes and thought about the scene they'd witnessed a few minutes before with Shannon. "I can hardly believe that was the same Shannon we know."

"*Really.* Part of me thinks, 'Good for her,' and another part of me thinks, 'Don't ever get in an argument with Shannon.'"

"She was impressive. Do you think we should go in and check on her?"

"I think she took care of it, whatever *it* is," Cass said in a wry tone. "Did you recognize the guy?"

"No," Izzy said, "but something about him looked familiar."

"I didn't see much of his face. There was something, though. The shoulders? Can shoulders look familiar?" Izzy stood up and brushed the snow off her long red dress.

"I don't know," Cass said. "But mine are freezing. Let's go in."

As they started back toward the French doors, Izzy glanced

back once more at the hallway door. She poked Cass lightly in the back. "Hey, Cass, one more minute. Follow me."

"What?" Cass said. "I'm freezing." But she turned and followed.

Izzy retraced their steps along the edge of the portico, just beyond the low lights. They walked stealthily past the tall windows and the well-lit kitchen, filled with workers scurrying around.

"Izzy, what are we doi—"

Izzy turned her head and whispered "shh," just as she reached the end of the kitchen.

"Who do you think you are? The Pink Panther?" Cass whispered back.

Izzy stopped just at the edge of the storm door. The dim lights inside highlighted jackets hanging on wall hooks, cubbies for boots and hats. And farther down, beneath a brighter light, two figures: the chef she'd spotted before and a man in a white apron, glaring at the woman as her arms flew in different directions. Her face was a contorted angry mask as she seemed to be spewing words at a face and body stoically standing in front of her.

"Geesh," Cass whispered. "What's going on? Glad I don't work here."

They couldn't make out the words, but they didn't need to. The woman's actions mimed all they needed to know.

Someone was in serious trouble with the boss.

Cass tugged on Izzy's arm. "I am totally turning into Frosty the Snowman, Iz. Let's get out of here."

Izzy gave the thick window in the door a serious stare. Then she looked one last time, getting so close to the window her breath formed clouds on the glass. The man's shoulders did look familiar.

Finally she gave in to Cass, allowing her to pull her along the portico, both of them trying to avoid ice patches in their path. "Did you see that?" she whispered.

"Yes, I saw it. A chef chewing out that dude in a major way."

"No. Well, yes, that. But the other thing. Someone was watching them."

"That was us, Izzy."

"No, at the opposite end. There was a mirror or glass or something in that back hall. And it was right across from the kitchen pantry. At least I think it was the pantry. I wandered in there earlier. The glass reflected a shadow in it. Someone was hiding there, listening."

They'd reached the French doors that led into the warm den, and before Izzy could explain further, Cass ushered her inside and over to the fireplace, where they rubbed their freezing fingers back to life and accepted cups of hot spiced cider from a passing waiter.

And soon, giving in to the comfort of the fire defrosting their arms and legs and fingers, Izzy's shadow in the mirror was forgotten.

"We three are heading out," Danny announced later in the evening, handing Cass her coat and glancing at the grandfather clock in the foyer.

Izzy and Sam agreed. It was time for them to leave, too.

Birdie was already waiting at the door in her puffy coat, her furry hat twice as large as her head.

"Where are Nell and Ben?" Cass asked, looking over at a group of people putting on coats and pulling on boots.

"They're looking for Oliver," Birdie said. "He's been wandering around tonight, slightly inebriated. I found him coming into the den a short bit ago, covered with snow. Escaping the crowds, he told me."

Cass laughed.

"He's a character after having a few Scotches. I think Ben wants to give him a ride back to the B and B. He said we should regroup tomorrow for a postmortem. He has some juicy tidbits," Birdie said.

They laughed at the thought of Ben Endicott gossiping, something the man had never been able to pull off.

With a wave and a thank-you to Mayor Scaglia, they pulled their collars up and walked out into the dark and snowy night.

Chapter 17

"I found him," Ben said, walking into the library a short while later with Ollie at his side.

"I wasn't lost," Ollie said, appearing slightly chagrined. He leaned against the doorframe, looking at Nell, who was waiting patiently with their coats in her arms. "I was looking for a cup of coffee and ended up stepping outside. Fewer people out there. And it's beautiful. All this snow." His voice was uneven as he attempted to sing a line of "Winter Wonderland."

"It looks like you brought it in with you," Nell said, brushing white flakes off his shoulders and handing him his coat.

"I love the snow. Thought about building a snowman out in the back, but it was too dark."

"Maybe tomorrow," Nell said.

"We're heading home, Ollie," Ben said. "I thought we'd give you a ride back to the bed and breakfast."

"Unless you need to wait for Lidia," Nell added, looking into Ollie's bleary eyes. The possibility of Ollie driving anywhere wouldn't be prudent. Or legal.

"Lidia?" Ollie said.

"Your wife," Ben laughed.

"Oh, that Lidia." Ollie attempted a chuckle, then tried to sober up. "A ride back to my bed sounds good." He looked at Nell, then to Ben, nodding, his eyelids heavy. "Good friends taking care of old friends . . . I like that."

"I'll let Lidia know we're leaving and meet you at the front door," Nell said to Ben, handing him his own coat, and heading across the hall.

Nell walked into a nearly empty dining room and through the butler's pantry into a chef's kitchen. It made her smile, knowing how Beatrice was a match for Cass in the cooking area, opening cans being a primary skill.

"Is the chef around?" she asked to a noisy, bustling kitchen crew, now packing up supplies and loading the two dish-washers.

A handsome man, whom Nell had noticed earlier in the evening, shrugged. Beneath his striking features lurked an un-pleasant expression.

"Out in the catering van probably," the man said. "Making sure nobody filches a bottle of the fancy wine. Or maybe more interesting things. Who knows? Those vans have seen lots of things, if you know what I mean." He looked at a dark-haired girl standing close to him, and she laughed, loud enough that others in the room grimaced.

Nell ignored the reply. "I need someone to give Chef Carson a message," she said, looking around at the others in the room. But there was no interest in adding another task to the night among the dishwashers and those packing boxes. Nell walked back toward the butler's pantry, discovering it was no longer empty.

Shannon Platt was there, talking on her cell phone.

At the sight of Nell, Shannon immediately slipped the phone into her apron pocket. A guilty look crossed her face. She re-placed it with a smile. "Hi, Nell. What's up?"

"I need someone to give a message to Lidia Carson for me."

"Sure. What's up?"

"I just want her to know we're giving her husband a ride back to the Ravenswood, where they're staying."

Shannon looked over her shoulder, around the kitchen, then back. "I'm sure she's around somewhere. She was here a while ago, chewing someone out. Things got messy for a while."

"Well, it may have been messy in here, but everything seemed flawless from a guest's perspective," Nell said.

"Well, that's good. Rachel Wooten came in looking for the chef, too. She walked in at the same time things got crazy. I felt bad that she had to hear all that—the chef laying into a guy big-time out in the hall. I didn't hear much, but am sure none of what she said would have stuck with the guy, anyway."

"Rachel came back here?"

"Just briefly. I think she was embarrassed, because she didn't stick around to see the chef. But back to your message." Shannon glanced down at a *ping* on her phone, clicked it silent, then looked up at Nell again. "Anyway, I'll see that she gets your message, though I'm not sure it'll make a difference to her."

Shannon's reply was a curious one, but Nell thanked her and headed back toward the foyer, where Ben and Ollie were waiting.

Why was Rachel Wooten looking for the chef? Nell wondered, then excused the thought. The food had been delicious and beautifully presented. Rachel would appreciate both those things.

She'd seen her friend only briefly that evening, and had wanted to ask her about Don—to make sure he was okay after what she'd seen in his restaurant the night she and Ollie were there. She made a mental note to get in touch with her soon. But tonight her main thought was getting home to a warm house and even warmer bed.

She'd almost reached Ben and Ollie when she was stopped by the staccato rhythm of stiletto heels on the hardwood floor.

"Nell, I need you." It was Beatrice, hurrying down the wide main staircase.

Nell turned in surprise. "Beatrice, I'm so glad to have the chance to thank you for the wonderful evening—"

Ben joined in with his thanks.

Distracted, Beatrice looked over at Oliver, who nodded, and offered a lopsided smile.

"We're giving Ollie a ride back to Mary Pisano's B&B," Ben said. "Lidia can join him later—"

"That's good. Because the chef isn't finished here." Her eyes were still on Ollie, as if this was somehow his fault.

"Don't worry," Ollie said with a crooked smile. "Lidia will be here 'til the bitter end. She's a pe . . . ectionist."

Nell noticed his words lacked a few letters and was grateful he'd agreed to be taken home.

Beatrice frowned and looked to Ben. "May I ask a favor, Ben? I need Nell for a short while. Very short. Could you take Mr. Bishop into the library and I'll send someone in with aperitifs and coffee. It won't take long."

Nell frowned. "Beatrice, it's late, and I don't think—" But Ben was nodding okay, with Ollie leaning slightly toward him.

After saying good-bye to several other guests, Beatrice ushered Nell into the small, den-like room, where the mayor had earlier chastised Luna Risso. A futile chastise, Nell noticed, having seen Luna enjoying herself all evening. She was even showing guests about the house herself.

"What do you need, Beatrice? I think the evening went really well. The food was wonderful, and your new home is beautiful."

"Yes, for the most part, it was fine. Thank you." The mayor moved slightly away from the door as others walked by on their way out.

"What can I do?"

"Perhaps I just need a friend with a level head. I need the chef to have a photo taken. A reporter from the *Boston Globe* is here, and it's important to me—it looks good to see a small-town mayor showing off her town with influential people around. Who knows what awaits me after being mayor? One must be prepared." She smiled in a conspiratorial way to Nell. An 'it's our secret' kind of smile. And then she continued.

"Anyway, Lidia—who is charging me a pretty penny, mind you—seems to be avoiding me. Earlier, she was fine. She even asked me to point out a couple of people she had requested I invite. I did, and she was happy, or so it seemed. But staff people are coming to me for payment, which Lidia should be taking care of. Famous or not, people make commitments when they're hired for something and she should be agreeable to things I ask of her.'"

"You don't think she is?"

For a moment, Beatrice didn't answer. Then she said, "The truth is, I think Chef Carson considers this job beneath her. My only hope is that my guests don't notice her attitude."

"Oh, Beatrice, I don't think that's true. She agreed to it, after all. She didn't have to do it. Ollie said she was interested in coming here."

"Well, he's wrong. She's interested in something, but it's not me."

"You're tired, Beatrice. And for good reason. Lidia must be, too. She's probably trying to finish up so she can get some sleep. Just like you need to do."

Beatrice sighed. "Maybe you're right. But you're a friend of theirs—Chef Carson and her husband. I need to say good-bye to my guests, so if you could just ask her to cooperate—"

"We're not really friends, Beatrice. I've only just met Lidia. But yes, her husband is an old friend. So sure, I'll help. I'll see what I can do. But I just tried to find her myself and didn't have much luck."

"You'll find her. And have her to come to the foyer." Looking relieved, Beatrice moved toward the front door to bid a few more guests good night. To smile. To be the perfect hostess, the perfect mayor.

Nell stood for a minute near the shining tree, looking around. With so many of the guests gone, she could see the true beauty of the old house. Beatrice had done a fine job of maintaining its old seacoast artistry, its English Arts and Crafts look. The heavy beams on the larger room ceiling looked like they could withstand even the fiercest nor'easter. The mayor had a right to show it off.

She wandered past the dining room again, but suspected that Lidia would leave the cleanup job to her servers. Yet she was a perfectionist, Ollie had said. She'd want to check out rooms the guests had wandered in and out of, which was the entire house, as far as Nell could tell. Touring Mayor Scaglia's home had been encouraged. Maybe Lidia had gone up to the second floor to check the bedrooms for stray dishes or wine glasses left behind, or traces of food on the Oriental rugs covering the wide-planked hardwood floors. It wouldn't be a stretch of imagination to think Lidia might have found a quiet spot and comfortable chair and rested briefly. Nell headed for the staircase.

Although the house seemed large, it took Nell little time to determine Lidia had already checked the bedrooms. Everything was spotless. And she was nowhere to be found

Coming down the back staircase into a shadowy hallway, Nell realized she was in the hall just off the kitchen. She spotted Shannon, pulling on a parka.

Hearing the footsteps, Shannon turned around quickly. "Oh, it's you, Nell. I'm sorry, I never had a chance to give the chef your message." She glanced at the back door, looking anxious to leave and talking quickly.

"You're leaving?" Nell asked, glancing out the storm door into a wintry night.

"Some of the kitchen crew have called it a day and I'm headed out myself. My old Jeep jalopy doesn't love snowstorms. I left a note for the chef, though. And, well . . . I really have to leave—" She paused for a minute, then said, "That's great about Cass's dog coming back, right? Cass said she showed up at the back door. That's great. Right?"

Surprised at the change of subject and the nervousness in Shannon's voice, Nell simply agreed that it was good news. "Dogs have an innate sense of knowing where their home is, where they're loved."

"Yeah, I guess they do." Shannon smiled. Then pulled on a knit hat. "And people do, too."

Her voice held a curious note in it, and made Nell smile.

"It's strange Lidia hasn't come around to check on all of you. Any idea where she might be?"

"Nope. She said something about extra trash bags or something like that. The van or garage maybe? But that was quite a while ago. Someone joked that maybe she just took off. She's kind of finished here—the amazing appetizers and sauces and presentations, all of that. She was supposed to pay us, but I guess the check will be in the mail. I sure hope so. It's the only reason I'm here."

"I imagine these catering jobs can be difficult."

Shannon managed a quick laugh. "Sometimes, I guess."

"Well, the food was outstanding. And the chef must be exhausted. I'd understand if she found a warm spot somewhere and dozed off."

"Sure. Makes sense." Shannon's voice was tight.

"She probably had people interrupting her work tonight, wanting autographs," Nell said. "That can be exhausting, too."

"Folks did come back to the kitchen looking for her, wanting to meet the famous chef they'd seen guesting on cooking shows or somewhere. Someone cornered her in the pantry for an autograph or something. In fact, I think that was the last time I saw her. It's been a really busy night. I don't know about out there"—Shannon nodded toward the rooms beyond the kitchen—"but we had more than enough activity back here. And maybe the chef was trying to get away from extra stresses."

"A top chef is probably like any artist needing time to concentrate, to let her artistic creativity have room."

"Who knows?" Shannon paused for a minute, fiddling with a ski glove, looking again at the door. Then she looked back at Nell. "I don't think the chef liked doing this gig much. It sure didn't seem to be her thing. But then, I don't know her, nor do I especially want to. Not firsthand, anyway."

Nell thought about Shannon's assessment. The mayor's opinion might not be as off base as Nell had thought at first. And it was true that Ollie had expressed surprise when Lidia decided to take the Sea Harbor catering job. It wasn't her usual thing, he had said. She also got the distinct impression that Shannon wasn't crazy about the chef.

Nell looked over as Shannon put her hand on the doorknob. "You don't like her, do you?"

Shannon paused for a moment, thinking through the question, or maybe her answer.

"Like her? She's my boss. And this job pays well. I truly want to finish my degree and jobs like this help. I've learned that it never pays to bad-mouth the one who pays you. No matter how you feel about the person." She looked down, biting her bottom lip, as if to hold other words back.

Nell looked at Shannon's hand as it grasped the door handle. She could see how anxious she was to leave.

Nell touched her arm lightly and thanked her for all her hard work. Then she urged her to drive carefully. "I think the wind is picking up—watch out for drifts. Get home safely, Shannon."

"You too, Nell." And with that, Shannon managed a smile, then pulled open the heavy back door, nearly falling backward as a heavy blast of snowy air blew in. It turned the floor white. "Geesh!" Shannon yelled, stepping out and bracing for another gust as she pushed the door shut behind her.

Nell watched Shannon stop for a minute beyond the door, looking across the drifts in the backyard, the ghostly statues. Then she turned and walked quickly out of sight.

Nell looked back at the empty hallway, then glanced into the kitchen. There was little activity, a few people filling trash bags. But still no chef. She was beginning to feel as if the mayor had sent her on a scavenger hunt that wasn't winnable.

She stood for another minute in the empty hallway, collecting herself. Suddenly she realized that scavenger hunt or not, she wanted to find Lidia. It was no longer to fulfill a favor to the mayor or relay a message about Ollie. Finding the chef had become purely selfish. Finding Lidia was the only way to relieve the irrational knot of fear growing inside her.

She spotted a heavy jacket hanging on a hook. Without careful thought, she slipped it on and stepped outside.

The catering van had been mentioned. And the garage? Maybe that was Lidia's retreat.

Bracing herself against the wind, she walked down the portico to the corner of the house. Some kind soul had already shoveled the driveway, making the walk to the van from the portico an easy one for the workers. But when she reached the door, the van was locked, and there were no visible tracks leading to the detached garage a few feet away.

Nell started walking toward the back portico, stopping at the edge of the house to look out over the yard. To think. To try to imagine why Lidia was trying to make herself invisible. It wasn't the image of the accomplished chef that her husband had presented. Perhaps she truly had left when her job was done.

As Nell's thoughts wandered, she watched the evening wind continue to blow, shaping and reshaping snowdrifts into ever-changing works of art. A curving line of gaslights cast hazy beams of light across the waves of white. It was a mesmerizing view.

The wind shifted then, picking up and creating new drifts, new sculptures across the yard and garage. Nell thought about the Tibetan monks' beautiful sand mandalas, painstakingly created, and then destroyed. Beautiful, but ephemeral. Moving, but temporary.

Her eyes shifted to a new sculpture near the garage, the whiteness of it marred by a colorful object now protruding from the shifting drift.

It was smooth and red, striking against the snow. A snow sculpture, she thought, staring at it. As if pushed by some unknown force, she stepped off the portico into a deep drift, feeling the sting of snow collecting around her calves. A few labored steps took her to the object. Carefully, her eyes teary from the wind, she leaned down and pulled up a wine bottle, its label bright and colorful.

But it wasn't the bottle that froze her in place. It was the hollow in the snow that it left behind.

And the red-stained edge of a chef's toque lying in it.

Chapter 18

It was what Nell Endicott did in a crisis. She swallowed her fear, pushed other emotions to a distant corner of her soul to be dealt with later—and offered whatever she could provide: Healing. Solace. Comfort. Or simply a warm presence. A friend.

On that Saturday evening, as the police sirens filled the frozen air and yellow tape wrapped the snowy backyard of the mayor's home, Nell sat with her old college friend in the well-appointed library of the mayor's home. The room where she had met Ollie Bishop's wife a few short hours before. And where she now tried to be a comforting friend to a man who had just lost his second wife. Not to cancer or some other awful disease.

But to a very expensive bottle of wine.

The early hours of Sunday morning filled the Endicotts' kitchen with doubts and worry and concerns. And deep sadness for an old friend.

"How can you possibly comfort someone whose wife has been murdered just yards from where you were enjoying a Scotch and soda?"

"How did you?" Ben asked.

The couple sat in the kitchen, a bright early sun reflecting off the snowbanks and casting slim white beams across the butcher-block island.

Trying to make sense of the evening that now seemed like a terrible nightmare. A festive, lovely party that was now a crime scene.

Nell poured more cream in the mug of coffee Ben had handed to her, as if she might find answers there in the deep roast with its creamy streaks.

After Nell's terrible discovery, Ben had wrapped a snow-covered Nell in a blanket and immediately called the police, reaching his friend, Chief Jerry Thompson. The squad arrived in minutes, lighting up the neighborhood with spinning lights.

Mayor Scaglia, distraught, begged them to turn off the lights and sirens, be discreet. Be quiet. Do not let her evening end this way.

After talking with Chief Thompson, Nell had taken a moment to find Beatrice, to say something to her, to comfort her, if that was possible, but Beatrice had disappeared. On her way back to the foyer, she noticed movement in the small parlor off to the side. She glanced in, then stopped and looked again.

Mayor Beatrice Scaglia was sitting on one of the matching upholstered chairs, sobbing quietly. She clenched a wad of tissues in her hand. Leaning over her, with a box of Kleenex in one hand, a mug of liquid in the other, and her plump face drawn and sad, Luna Risso awkwardly attempted comfort.

Luna grumbled loudly, "What you really need, Beady, is a straight Scotch." She glanced at a dusty old bottle sitting on the round end table. "It's what our old aunt Gert would have said. In fact, this was probably hers, crazy old witch that she was. I found it in one of the old cupboards in the basement. You need new cleaners, by the way. It was a mess down there. Drink it." She thrust the mug into the mayor's hand, then watched as Beatrice took a drink; the mayor behaved as if Luna might do something bad to her if she didn't.

Finally Beatrice whispered, "Thanks, cuz."

Luna stood, surprised, then stared at Nell in the doorway. "I got this," she said, and Nell hurried away.

It was hours later that Ben and Nell were able to drive a nearly sober Oliver back to Mary Pisano's Ravenswood B and B. And at Ollie's insistence, they left him there and took themselves home, where they sank into troubled sleep.

"Does Oliver have siblings?" Ben asked. "I remember his parents visiting him in Cambridge once. Ollie cooking up an impressive meal for all of us."

"Which didn't impress his father, I remember. Mr. Bishop accusing Ollie of wasting his time cooking for friends when his hardworking dad was paying a fortune for his son to get a Harvard education," Nell said. "But they passed away a while ago, while Maddie was still alive. There were no siblings that I remember. No one to come and be with him now."

"He'll have to stick around until the police figure this out," Ben said.

Unspoken was what they both knew: in murder cases, the spouse was nearly always at the top of the suspect list.

And what Ben and Nell also were acutely aware of: they were Ollie's only friends in Sea Harbor.

His caretakers, Nell thought. For that's what friends do. Friends take care of their friends. And most certainly Ollie—who had been so dependent on Maddie when they were together—would need friends to get through this sudden tragedy in his life.

Nell looked off in the distance. Today the storm had given up its hold on the town, and the day outside her window was truly a winter wonderland. A perfect day for snowmen and snow angels, for sledding and laughter.

Not a day to contemplate a dead body in a snowdrift.

"There's nothing in the paper," Ben said, looking up from the small, soggy newspaper.

"But it'll be online soon." She wondered about Ollie. Had he slept? How early could they call him?

"I called Mary Pisano before making coffee," Ben said, reading her thoughts. "She said Oliver was up early. In fact, while we talked, he was sitting on the B and B's heated porch. He seemed to be enjoying the cook's special spinach-and-cheese omelet and admiring the snow covered trees in the backyard, Mary said."

Nell thought about that. Her own appetite had completely disappeared, as it usually did in times of stress or anxiety or sadness. Even Ben was just picking at his oatmeal, moving the raisins around with his spoon. But Oliver was different, and she wondered if he found some solace in food.

"Ollie seemed in shock when we left him last night," Nell said. "I hope he's okay. But of course he's not okay . . ." She tried to imagine it. She'd been a part of his life when Maddie was dying. It was an unbelievably sad time. But the way Lidia Carson lost her life carried a whole other layer, one that made it impossible to imagine what her spouse was going through.

"Mary said a couple of the catering staff are staying at the B and B. Maybe they'll check on Ollie," Ben said.

Nell nodded. She thought back to the servers she'd seen the night before. Some were familiar, like Shannon, experienced servers from the yacht club restaurant and Don Wooten's Ocean's Edge, notable restaurants with fine, responsible, and friendly staff. "I wonder why Lidia brought her own kitchen help," she said.

"Good question. A vendor or two stayed, too. Apparently, they aren't happy about being detained. All they want are their paychecks and a way to get out of our 'boring burb.'"

Nell was half listening now, her mind replaying the evening. The people she'd seen and talked to. The amazing display of food. Ollie . . . and the awful moment she'd discovered his wife's body. She squeezed her eyes shut, trying to block it out.

She opened them quickly when both her phone and Ben's pinged at the same time.

The chief of police was on Ben's, requesting some time with him.

And Oliver Bishop was calling on Nell's, telling her how sorry he was.

Chapter 19

Cass and Danny slept in late Sunday morning.

Old Dog had been waiting for them the night before, with Mary Halloran beaming at the return of Joey's faithful companion. He had shown up at the back door with a small stuffed polar bear from Joey's collection in his mouth.

"Yes, and it was just as clean and healthy as the pup," Mary said. "Old Dog had simply wandered off and lost his way, not unusual as one ages," she explained again. Cass was skeptical of the story, but hugged her mother tightly, and urged her to be cautious on the ride home.

Sleeping in was an unusual happening for the Brandleys. Since Joey's arrival, six o'clock, no matter the day, seemed more comfortable for the youngest member of the family, and consequently, even on weekends, his parents and Old Dog got up early, too.

Today even the baby had slept in.

A sound from below jolted Cass out of her slumber, sending her upright in the bed.

And then there was silence.

She tried to shake off the lingering sleep, listening to the monitor beside the bed. Joey's baby snore was sweet and soothing. On the monitor screen, she saw his eyes closed, his small body curling around a stuffed polar bear.

Beside her, Danny, too, slept soundly, worn out from the multiple appetizers he'd devoured the night before, not to mention the socializing, which usually exhausted him. Writers were meant to write, not talk, he'd tell Cass. The same held true for lobsterwomen, she'd say, though she could never quite complete the comparison.

She looked down to the foot of the bed, where Old Dog had settled, looking jubilant to be home, if jubilation is possible for dogs. If Old Dog were not so old, and if Joey's crib didn't have a tall side, Cass knew that's where he'd be, stretched out next to the baby and not on their low platform bed.

The shepherd was wide awake now, sitting up, his ears perked, his tail alert, and his eyes moving back and forth from Cass to the bedroom door.

Cass looked over at the clock and her eyes widened. Nine o'clock on a Sunday morning.

Her first thought went to the prowler who had frightened Luna a few nights before, and for one minute, her heart lurched. But that was silly. It was daylight, time for people to be going to church or to Sweet Petunia's for an enormous Sunday breakfast or to Coffee's for a special brew. No sensible prowler would be doing his thing at this hour.

And then the sound came again, a light clicking, a knocking sound. This time, as Cass wiped the sleep away, it was more distinct. It was coming from near the garage. Or the side door.

Old Dog's ears moved forward.

Cass slipped out of bed and grabbed an old sweatshirt from a chair. With Old Dog beside her, she moved quietly down the stairs to the kitchen. The loud creak on the third-to-last step caused both Old Dog and her to freeze, take a deep breath, and finally continue down to the kitchen.

Cass paused for a minute near the table, then bravely followed Old Dog toward the door.

No one used the kitchen door except family and a few friends—and Luna.

But Luna never knocked.

Old Dog whimpered and his paw scratched at the door, as if telling Cass it'd be okay to open it. And if she didn't, he would.

Cass turned the knob slowly.

In the next second, Old Dog was on his hind legs, his paws up and resting on narrow shoulders, and his tongue licking as if someone were holding a giant bone right in front of him.

But it wasn't a bone at all.

Molly Flanigan, with tears in her eyes, stood in the doorway, wrapping her arms around Old Dog, then finally getting free and hugging Cass so tightly that Cass coughed and had to pull away.

"Come in," Cass said, her voice thick. She walked through the kitchen and sat down on the family room couch with Molly and Old Dog following close behind. She patted the cushion beside her, then wiped her eyes and looked at Molly to see if it was really her, or the Molly in the dream she'd been pulled from so abruptly.

"I should be madder than *h* at you," she finally managed to say. But her heart was about to do a dance. Marvelous Molly was back. The world was back on its axis.

Molly wiped away a tear. "Yeah. You should be mad. I'm so sorry for just leaving you like that, Cass. So dumb, so thoughtless."

"Yeah, it was all that. And leaving me with *Luna*? Geesh. What were you thinking?"

Molly managed a small smile.

"So . . ." Cass said.

As if Cass's pause as an invitation, Old Dog climbed onto the couch, too, dropping his head into Molly's lap and warming the couch with his love for the two women sitting on it.

"I'd have gotten it if you had needed a couple days off, Mol. You know I would have. But no note? No call?" But her words weren't angry. Instead, they were filled with concern and complete confusion.

Molly's head was down, her voice raspy. "Like I said, it was dumb. A bad decision. I should have said something to you. But I was upset, worried, then angry, and then it all ended in my thinking it'd be better for you three if I was just gone. Clean and simple. Explaining would only make it worse, because I know you'd step in. Get involved. And you don't need that, Cass. I didn't want to bring my mess into your life.

"But then, after I left, I realized that I had done it all wrong and I was messing up your life, anyway. You can't just run away from things, right? You'd never do that, Cass. Never ever. You're like my mom. An honest person. Brave. You face things. And then after everything that happened, well, how awful . . ."

"Molly, I don't know what you're saying to me. You lost me sentences ago. Speak English, please."

"I thought . . . and then Shannon told me . . . the mess about Dirk . . . but how awful for everyone. No matter what anyone thought of her. How horrible for this whole town—"

"What did Shannon tell you?" Cass scratched her head. "And who is Dirk? And the whole town? I was upset when you were gone for less than two days and didn't tell me where you were going. And now the town, the whole world is ending? Can we back up, start over?"

Molly took a deep breath and released it slowly. And when she spoke again, her voice quavered, as if the world truly were caving in on her.

"Don't you know, Cass? You were there, right? You were at the mayor's party. That's why I went to Shannon's last night and not here. You were there for the amazing food, the famous chef. The . . ."

Cass leaned in closer, listening intently now. Old Dog lifted his head.

"About the chef, Cass. Lidia Carson."

"What about her?"

"She's dead."

Chapter 20

Nell parked in the plowed circle drive and walked up the Ravenswood B and B sidewalk. Piles of shoveled snow banked the walkway, separating it from the sweeping lawn that stretched all the way back to the road, breathtaking in its untouched beauty.

The house itself was stately, an inheritance Mary received from the Pisano paterfamilias, the newspaper baron who liked Mary far better than any of her cousins. He also knew she would care for his home and not deal it out to the highest bidder.

And Enzo Pisano was right. Mary had painstakingly turned it into a first-class B and B, one that welcomed weary travelers with its warm, luxurious embrace. High, comfortable beds with crisp white sheets and fluffy down comforters, throws hand-knit by her Seaside Knitter friends, farm-style breakfasts. It was a place all Sea Harbor residents were proud of.

Mary met Nell at the door and ushered her in. She glanced beyond her, looking out at the day. "It's so beautiful out there, isn't it? Mother Nature fooling us again."

Nell turned and looked back at the swaths of sunlight turning the wide, untouched lawn into a monochromatic painting. "It's a stark contrast to reality, isn't it?" She stepped inside.

"And maybe a reminder that life goes on."

"How's my friend Ollie doing?"

"Well, he's busy. After breakfast, I gave him a pair of snow-shoes and sent him out on the trails behind the B and B while I fielded calls. Apparently, his wife had mentioned on some TV show that she was staying here. Nice marketing for us at the time. Not so much now. Lots of calls from the press, and some from New York restaurants. Oliver wanted none of it right now."

"That's understandable," Nell said.

"An hour later, Tommy Porter came by to talk with him. From a distance, you'd have thought they were discussing some sports game or art exhibit or something. They sat out there on the heated porch, drinking coffee, talking. But the poor man must be in shock. Sad. The whole thing. Not the golden evening I planned to write about in my column."

"You have some others staying here who worked at the party, right? How are they doing?" Nell asked.

Mary nodded. "Tommy talked to them, too. The vendor checked out afterward. Oh, then there was the one fellow and his girlfriend—good-looking, both of them. The man used a few words I usually only hear down on the dock when he was told to stick around because the police would want to talk to him again. Or them, I guess. She seems a little glued to him, if you know what I mean."

"Who are they?"

"I have a roster at the desk that would have names, but the rooms were all booked under the corporate name. A hodge-podge of initials. These two came in early with a van filled with catering supplies. Helping with details, I guess. But clearly here to enjoy themselves, too."

Before Mary could expand, a familiar voice came down the staircase. "Hi, Nellie. I'm glad you're here."

Nell walked over and hugged Ollie tightly, then pulled back and scanned her friend's face.

"I'm okay, Nell. This place puts on a breakfast that even I couldn't match." He offered a small smile to Mary.

But Ollie wasn't okay. Of course he wasn't. She saw it in his eyes. But it wasn't the shock that she expected would be there. Or denial. Or anger. The things that set in before death becomes real. It was something else, and she wasn't sure what. "Ben has a pot of soup simmering for lunch. It seemed good for a wintry day. So may we kidnap you for an hour or so?"

"Which this sure as hell is," Ollie said with a short laugh. "A frozen day. Thawing out with you and Ben sounds like a good thing."

Mary had already grabbed Oliver's coat and held it out. "You go now," she said in a motherly way, though their ages were probably less than a few years apart, Mary being the younger of the two. "The Endicotts are what you need."

Ollie smiled at the innkeeper and walked into the bright day, following Nell to her car.

Once inside, with the car heater warming their feet, Nell looked over at Ollie and said softly, "I don't know how to begin to tell you how sorry I am."

Ollie put his head back against the car seat and turned it slightly toward her. He sighed, a slow release of breath. "I've wanted to see you over these years, but not like this."

She looked at her old friend's face, trying to read his thoughts. "Who could have done this, Ollie?"

Ollie took another deep breath. "I suppose it could be anyone. I think we all have it in us to kill, the circumstances being right. Don't you? It's that survivor instinct."

Nell was taken aback by the answer. She started the car and drove slowly down the long driveway, her thoughts tangled.

"I'm sorry not to have more of an answer, Nell. But I don't know who killed Lidia. I knew a part of her. It was enough for me. But I never knew all of her. She was a very private person in many ways. Secretive. And even the part I knew had sharp, uncomfortable edges. The kind that could cut. Lidia is—was—complicated."

The description made Nell shiver. There was sadness in Ollie's voice, Nell thought. Some fear? But there was something else there, too.

What she saw in Ollie's deep blue eyes, in his long, attractive face—and mixed in with the deep sadness and pain—was a strange feeling of peace.

Chapter 21

The joyful news of Molly Flanigan's return was texted to Cass's close friends immediately, and then she and Joey shared it with Danny, who was waking up to Joey's happy squealing as he crawled over him on the bed.

But although Sunday morning in the Brandley household held happy relief, Molly's return was overshadowed by news of "the murder of the mayor's chef," as a local online reporter referred to the Saturday night tragedy.

Cass and Izzy stood in the yarn shop door later that Sunday while Izzy fiddled with a sign.

"Sam and I didn't know about it until Ben called early this morning," Izzy said, flipping the sign to CLOSED. She stepped outside, locking the door behind her.

"It's so awful," Cass said. "I haven't quite pulled it together. The fact that we were all there, that something like that could happen right beneath our noses. I mean . . . Izzy, we were out there in that backyard."

"It's mind-boggling for sure. And you also have Molly's return to process. You said she was the one who told you about the murder—how did she even know about it? Was that what brought her back today? But why?"

"She actually came back last night. She spent the night at Shannon's."

"But Shannon was working at the party," Izzy said, frowning.

Cass nodded. "I'm not sure how it all happened. But she and Molly are like sisters, and Molly knew Danny and I were out last night. She probably thought it would freak out my mother if she showed up at the door. Which it might have done. But anyway, she's back."

"Of course she's back. We all told you she'd be back."

"I knew she'd be back, too. I did. Deep down. But when you see her, please refrain from an exaggerated account of my falling apart when she left. Which, of course, I didn't."

Izzy laughed, and they turned their attention from disappearing nannies to the sparkling red and green, silver and gold, decorations all up and down along Harbor Road.

"Ah, fresh air," Cass said, tossing her head back and breathing in the cold until it made her cough.

They walked briskly, their thick knit hats pulled tight around their ears, weaving their way among the shoppers, smiling at the tiny gnomes and angels sitting on tools in McGlucken's Hardware Store window and admiring the swags of greenery wound about the old-fashioned lampposts. Harbor Road at holiday time. Magical. Even the colorful Elvis decorations around the door of Jake's Gull Tavern somehow fit in. It was Sea Harbor, filled with expectations of a joyful season.

Cass looked up and down the Harbor Road at the lights and shoppers and kids with Santa Claus in their eyes. She looped an arm through Izzy's as they walked.

"So remind me why we can't just be together at Birdie's all evening?" Izzy asked.

"You mean the Gull thing," Cass said, putting a name to the

reason their meal at Birdie's would be shorter than usual tonight. "It's a benefit for the schools. Jake Risso will donate a percentage of tonight's take to an education fund. Danny's on the board and thought we needed to go, just for a short while to show support. Besides, it's all for Joey's and Abby's education, Iz. The younger generation will save us all. Get with it."

Izzy managed a smile. "Okay. Got it. We'll leave Birdie's right after supper." Izzy looked up at the sky. "And we'll think of Nell and Birdie in the warmth of that cozy den, drinking hot toddies, while we listen to Jake's Elvis Presley Christmas medley in a crowded, smelly bar."

"Right."

Walking the mile or two up from the yarn shop gave the two friends a chance to clear their heads and watch the sunset. The unusual and amazing late day light that always bathed their town. That's what they needed as the news of a murder slowly snaked its way through town.

They knew from both Danny's books and way too many episodes of TV mysteries that the hours after a brutal crime were a dangerous time, the time when news dribbles out in a disorganized fashion and is often "embroidered" as it passes from one person to another. Murder of a well-known chef—and on Sea Harbor soil—was fodder for talk and ripe for exaggeration. And beneath it all was worry and anxiety that where there's a murder, there's a murderer.

Sea Harbor had suffered through tragedy in the past, the loss of friends and neighbors—and sometimes strangers—to untimely death. Townspeople had been forced to face the dark side of humanity. But as they waded through difficult times, the best of humanity would emerge, along with forgiveness and a way of coming together. *This will be no different,* Izzy thought. Sea Harbor had a unique ability to bring itself back to life after death.

"So, how were things in the shop today?" Cass asked. She

waved at Jake Risso as they walked by his Gull Tavern and shouted across the street that they'd be back later. Strains of Elvis Presley's soulful "Blue Christmas" flowed from a speaker near Jake's tavern door, an annual tradition that some towns-folk loved—and the rest had slowly, reluctantly, come to accept.

"The shop?" Izzy said. "Well, busy. Scary. Noisy. Gossipy. Some were already coming up with their own scenarios of what happened last night. But many hadn't heard the news."

"They didn't have much to go on. We were there—and we know nothing."

"That never stops people from imagining. The unknown is too scary."

"I guess." Cass walked a step faster to keep up with Izzy. "Luna told Danny she's working for you now, that you really need it. Your shop's a mess. Did she come in today?"

"Sort of. She came in to tell me she *wasn't* coming in, and that I shouldn't be open on Sunday, anyway, even during holiday season and even if we open late. 'Because of church?' I asked her. But she said no, that no one had a monopoly on Sundays, not even God. It was her day, too. God rested and so did she."

"Luna usually sleeps in on Sunday," Cass said. "And spends the rest of the day reading newspapers and watching political shows on TV. That's probably why."

"Mae told her she could have picked up a phone to tell us that she wasn't coming in, but Luna ignored her. She looked kind of pale and sad, like she hadn't slept much. She was fidgety and stuck around the store for a while, even though, as she told us several times, she wasn't coming in. I felt kind of bad for her, although I wasn't sure why. Maybe she just wanted to be with people."

"She was shaken by everything that happened last night," Cass said. "She nabbed Danny when he went out for the Sunday paper this morning, asking . . . no, telling him to come in and have a donut with her. Danny said she was *clingy*, not a word I'd use for Luna. She just wanted to talk. To repeat what little any of us know. She was leaving as the police came, and then went back in to see what was going on."

"Sometimes I actually feel sorry for Luna. Not often, but sometimes," Cass said.

They huffed a little as they left Harbor Road and made their way up Ravenswood Road toward Birdie's estate on the hill, where Ella would have prepared an "easy" Sunday supper that she'd been working on all afternoon.

Reaching the low granite wall that bordered Birdie's estate, they stopped and looked across the street at Mary Pisano's B and B. RAVENSWOOD-BY-THE-SEA, the new gold-and-white sign Mary had recently put up, now banked with snow, read. It had taken on a different hue because of its present guests. The New Yorkers who had come to town to cater the mayor's event, making it a grand festive party with amazing food that would be talked about for weeks. And instead, the evening had ended up with one of their own murdered.

"I hope Oliver is all right," Izzy said as they walked on, turning into Birdie's drive.

The light tap of a horn behind them moved them over to the side of the drive.

Nell waved, then drove on in, parking in the circle near Birdie's front door. She stepped out of the car and looked around the wooded property, covered in silent snow. The long drive was bordered with pine trees, their boughs leaning in beneath their new winter coat.

"It's so beautiful," Nell said as Cass and Izzy walked up. "Even in the midst of all this, there's beauty."

"Yes," Izzy said, and then the three women leaned in for a circle hug, arms wrapped around each other, a hug made extra thick by heavy down coats and parkas.

"Come on in, you'll freeze out there. And I need a hug of my own." Birdie stood at the front door, wrapping her arms around herself.

A fire was already burning in the grate in Birdie's second-floor den, with holiday music playing softly in the background. The four women settled into their favorite chairs—with Sonny's well-worn leather chair reserved for Birdie. Her long-deceased husband was always there in the room with her, his spirit alive, the scent of his pipe's cherry tobacco in the creases of the old leather.

At first, they had considered canceling tonight's supper altogether. It was a 'sometimes' thing they did when Ben, Danny, and Sam went off with friends to watch a game—or sometimes for no reason at all, just because it was a time to be together. A no-agenda evening to relax and have someone else cook dinner for them, which Ella took great pleasure in doing.

But Saturday's murder clouded everything. In the end, canceling didn't make sense. Being together was more pressing than usual, and besides, Birdie told them, Ella had already baked the lemon bars.

Out of habit, Nell reached into her knitting bag and pulled out the sweater she was knitting for Ben. The annual cable-knit sweater that always drew great surprise from her husband when he pulled it from its wrapped box. She fiddled with the needles for a minute, then put it all back and looked around the circle of women, knowing what each of them was thinking about. Finding a dead body was beyond terrible. It brought a level of grief, of unrest, of images that were difficult to erase. "I know you three well. I feel your concern, but please—don't worry about me. I'll be fine."

"I wish we'd been there with you," Cass said, regretting her push to leave the mayor's party as soon as they could.

"Ben was there. And at my side in an instant. I'm grateful it wasn't Shannon or another kitchen helper—or a random guest—who found her."

"Or Beatrice herself," Birdie said. "Our mayor can handle many things, but I don't think finding Lidia Carson in her backyard would have been one of them."

Hearing the chef's name said aloud and imagining the mayor in such a predicament was sobering. It was no longer a matter of "finding a dead body"; it was finding the wife of Nell's friend, and someone they had all met that evening, dead.

"On the other hand," Birdie said, reviewing her own comment, "who could possibly predict what they would do finding a body, a *person* who had been killed?"

The thought was followed by a light knocking. Ella appeared in the open doorframe. "May I interrupt? I have your supper ready. A light repast." She smiled, carrying in a tray with four bowls of corn chowder, a platter of sandwiches, and freshly baked lemon bars. "Warm pita bread sandwiches," she said, glancing at Cass's skeptical look as she set the tray on the low table near the fire.

"It's very green inside," Cass said.

"And good for you. Lemony broccoli and chickpea salad with olives and avocado. Eat it, Cass. It won't bite." She half smiled, then met each of their eyes, as if she were a mom, wanting her kids to feel better, and turned and left the room.

"Looks healthy," Cass said. She looked around the tray to see if there was ketchup or sour cream she could slather into the pita bread. Maybe some sharp Cheddar cheese.

The others busied themselves while Cass further inspected the food. Izzy walked over to the built-in bookcase, where many years before, Sonny Favazza had put in a small bar, refrigerator, and wine cooler, back in the days before most people knew what wine coolers were. She took out a bottle and opened it.

Then she stared at her grip on the neck of the bottle, as if trying to imagine it being used for more than drinking.

Nell glanced over, then turned away, trying to put to rest the image of the bright red bottle in the snow. At least for now. She walked over to the leaded windows that framed the sky and the harbor, the fishing pier, the Ocean's Edge Restaurant, and Harbor Road. It was Birdie's gull's-eye view of the town, of the ocean, and the lives of people they all cared deeply about.

A sudden breeze from nowhere wrapped around Nell and she stepped away from the thick glass, shivering. Then she turned and walked back to the fireplace, to a glass of wine, a healthy supper. And the warming blanket of friends.

The chowder and Ella's sandwiches were passed around, tasted, then applauded.

"Ella is becoming a master of almost-healthy recipes," Birdie said. She wiped a dollop of cream from the corner of her mouth and put the napkin down. "But first things first. The elephant in the room. How is Oliver doing? This is an unimaginable horror for him."

"I don't know," Nell said. "He's hard to read. He seems calm, remarkably so, but he has to be in shock. Chief Thompson said it'd be best if he stayed around for a few days until things were settled. Over lunch today we invited him to stay in our guesthouse. But he hasn't said he would."

"Why?" Cass asked. She took another sandwich off the platter.

"I think it's because he knows this might be a circus for a while, and he doesn't want us in the ring."

"That's gracious of him, then," Birdie said.

"Well, Ben disagrees with me. He doesn't think Ollie is quite that selfless. But for whatever reason, he's staying at the Ravenswood for now."

"You've been friends for so long," Izzy said. "Geesh, wouldn't you think he'd want to be around friends right now?"

"He may change his mind. But Ollie's always been private. And we'll be here for him, no matter where he's staying. Jerry Thompson had suggested to Ollie that he talk to Ben if he needed any unofficial legal advice, help settling affairs. Things that need to be done. Ollie agreed that it'd be a good idea and he and Ben decided to meet tomorrow. Ben will take another stab at suggesting that he stay with us, too. Mary's had to fight off a few reporters who learned where he was staying—we might be able to save them both from that irritation."

"Talking to Ben about anything can be affirming," Birdie said.

"I think Ben would have reached out to Ollie, anyway, but hearing the chief suggest it was helpful. I don't know what Ben can do, but he's a good listener. It might help Ollie to have someone to talk to." Nell finished the last spoonful of chowder and sat back in the chair. She'd been relieved when Ben told her he and Ollie were going to get together. Their lunch that day had been brief and somewhat stilted. Although both Ben and Ollie were part of their college foursome, it was because of Maddie and her. She sometimes wondered if Ben and Ollie would ever have spoken to one another if left on their own.

Cass interrupted her thoughts. "Does Oliver say anything at all about who might have done this? It's such a freaking awful thing. His wife puts on this amazing, eye-catching spread—and then . . ." Cass shook her head and refreshed the wineglasses, then helped herself to a lemon bar. "Do you think she ticked someone off at the party? Is she that kind of person?"

An empty question, since none of them knew what kind of person Lidia had been.

But the lines in Birdie's forehead deepened as she seemed to be pondering the rhetorical question. Finally she looked up and said, "Was Lidia that kind of person? The kind who 'ticked off' people, to use your vernacular, Cass? Well, she ticked me off. So yes, I think she was."

"What do you mean?" Nell asked.

"Lidia Carson wanted to build a restaurant here in Sea Harbor," Birdie said.

"Hmm," Izzy said. "That's interesting."

"A new restaurant is always welcome around here," Cass said.

"And she's certainly a marvelous cook," Nell said. "But it's strange Ollie didn't mention it—"

"Those things are all true," Birdie said. "But there's more to it. Lidia had her eye on a particular site. She wanted Don Wooten's restaurant so that she could tear it down and build one of her own. Apparently, she had a sentimental attachment to this area, vacationing near here when she was a child. And she thought the Ocean's Edge was the ideal spot. Which, of course, it is. The idea spot for the Ocean's Edge."

Birdie briefly filled them in on the few details she knew— that somehow Lidia thought Birdie could help her wrest the restaurant away from Don Wooten so Lidia could build her glass castle there.

"*Glass castle* were my words, not hers," Birdie said.

"Why you?" Cass asked. Then added quickly, "No offense, Birdie. We all know you can move mountains in a heartbeat, but how did Lidia know that?"

Birdie shushed her. "I'm one of Don's investors—something I don't care to broadcast. I don't know how Lidia knew that. But it doesn't matter. She had the mistaken belief that I could convince the people who needed to be convinced that Don would sell the restaurant, and she could realize her plans."

"Which was to tear it down?"

"It seems so. I can't quite imagine the Ocean's Edge being renovated into a glass castle."

"So, Birdie, you own part of Ocean's Edge?" Cass asked in amazement.

"No," Birdie quieted her. "I'm just an investor. There are a few of us, all wanting the Ocean's Edge to succeed."

"But it's already successful," Izzy said.

"Of course," Birdie said. And then she explained: "It's hard for restaurants to make a profit when they start out. And during rough times, like what they've all gone through these last few years with tight regulations to keep people safe, it can be doubly difficult. So it's a good thing Don has investors. End of subject."

Izzy looked over at Nell. "Kind of like and Uncle Ben did for me when I opened the yarn shop?"

"Not exactly," Nell said. "You paid that back." She looked over at Birdie.

"Yes, this is a little different," Birdie said. "But no matter, Lidia came to me, and probably the other investors, too."

"So Lidia felt that you would have influence?" Nell said. Although Birdie didn't talk about financial affairs with her, nor she with Birdie, it didn't surprise her at all that Birdie would have helped Don Wooten out. She suspected there were many others in Sea Harbor who had been beneficiaries of Birdie's generosity.

"Apparently."

"What did you say to her?" Izzy asked. "If Lidia had offered Don tons of money, would the investors benefit?"

"We never got that far. But I imagine so."

They were all quiet for a moment.

Don was a close friend of Birdie and Nell's. All of them knew him and liked him. And his wife, Rachel, too.

It was crazy for anyone to think Birdie would turn a friend's life upside down for money. Clearly, Lidia didn't know much about the people of Sea Harbor. Or at least some of them.

Cass finally broke the silence. "So, what did you say to Lidia?"

"I showed her the door."

Nell took a drink of her wine and sat back in the chair. Don Wooten, her good friend. She put down the last of her sandwich and thought about the evening in Don's lounge.

"Ollie and I went to the Ocean's Edge on Wednesday night when he came into town," she said. "He never said a word about his wife having any interest in Don's restaurant. In fact, he commented on how nice it was. I wanted to introduce him to Don, knowing they'd have things in common." And then she remembered the way the evening ended, and replayed it now to the others.

"Anger doesn't come easily to Don," Birdie said, when Nell had finished. "Even during times when he had a right to be. Running a restaurant is difficult. He has a lot on his mind—" She let the rest of her thought drop.

"But Don's outburst makes sense now," Nell said. "It happened at the same moment Ollie's wife appeared on the bar TV, talking about plans for a new restaurant. Most people were blaming the bartender for messing up. But I think it might have been the image on the television that upset Don."

"I'm sure Don knew about Lidia's plans last week," Birdie said. "It was clear when we talked at the mayor's party—it was as if we were speaking our own language without saying much. But both of us knew that Lidia wanted the Ocean's Edge. He was visibly upset, but Rachel calmed him down. Clearly, she knew, too, that Lidia wanted to buy the restaurant."

"So Don knew, but Lidia's own husband didn't?" Cass asked. "Could Ollie be in on this?" She glanced at Nell.

Ordinarily, Nell would have said "absolutely not." Instead, she said, "Honestly, I don't know. I knew my friend Ollie, who sat through classes and walked through Harvard Square with me all those years ago. And later, the one who married my best friend. But *this* Ollie? The one who married Lidia Carson, chef and entrepreneur? I simply don't know."

"I wonder if Lidia had other businesses in mind, here in Sea Harbor," Cass said.

They all knew what Cass was thinking. Thanks to an inheritance from an old fisherman friend, Cass's lobster company was situated on another choice piece of Sea Harbor real estate.

"You wouldn't have considered it for a second," Izzy said to her.

"But it's an interesting thought. There could have been other people whose lives might have been sidetracked if offered a significant amount of money," Nell said.

"That could be," Birdie said. "And Lidia was a smart woman. And ambitious."

Nell nodded, realizing that Ollie had said as much. And yet somehow, in the light of Birdie's story, Lidia's ambition seemed tainted in a way it hadn't before.

"Ambitious people aren't always loved," Izzy commented.

"So she may have had enemies right here in Sea Harbor," Nell said.

"We're all talking like her death was premeditated, that someone meant to kill her," Cass said. "Maybe the whole awful thing was an accident. There was some heavy drinking going on last night. Great wines. Imported beer. Maybe an argument got out of hand, fueled by liquor."

"Maybe. But why would they be arguing out in that snowy backyard?" Birdie said, bringing the suggestion down to an improbable level. "If someone had a gripe with Lidia, the pantry might have been a better place to settle it. Or that big van."

"And who would have had a gripe with her? That food was amazing," Cass said. "Just ask Danny. He's swearing off eating for the next week."

"It may not have had anything to do with Lidia's profession," Izzy said.

"That's true," Birdie said quietly. "It was a festive group last night. Decent people. Friends and neighbors. No dark, threatening villains lurking in shadows. At least I didn't see any. But among those decent people was someone who took another human being's life. What was inside them, inside their heart, inside their head?"

The thought was sobering. Nell looked out the window at the darkening night. What would it take? Hate? Revenge? Fear? But if someone hated Ollie's wife enough to kill her, why do it at a party with so many people around? She thought about

Ollie. About this woman he had married. Who was she? And was he grieving? Or in shock? This man she knew so well. Once.

"It doesn't sound planned," Cass was saying beside her, drawing Nell out of her thoughts.

"I mean, do you think it could have been? Killing someone with a bottle of wine?" Cass looked at the bottle on the table, picked it up, then put it down again, as if the bottle were somehow guilty by association.

Ella appeared silently and cleared away the dishes, leaving the extra lemon bars on the table, along with a pot of coffee and mugs.

Birdie leaned over and pushed the plate of bars across the table toward Cass, then poured herself a cup of coffee and sat back in Sonny's large chair. "We may be stressing about all of this for no reason. By now, Jerry Thompson and his men may be ready to arrest someone. These first twenty-four hours are often when things come to light and crimes are solved."

"That's not my take on it," Cass said. "It takes CI Barnaby at least a week, sometimes more, on *Midsomer Murders*."

"You're right," Birdie said. "I'm surprised the man keeps his job."

They all laughed.

"But speaking of unsolved mysteries," Nell said, "our Molly has been overshadowed by everything else going on. Is she doing all right? What's her story, Cass? Why did she leave so suddenly?"

"I'm not really sure. It's kind of complicated, I think. But seeing her this morning was pretty wonderful. She was so upset over causing us worry that I didn't press her on the wheres or whys. And the three of us were so ecstatic to have her back that nothing else mattered much. And then, when she blurted out the news about the murder at the Scaglia house, I was so stunned I nearly forgot she was ever gone."

Of course you were," Birdie said. "She's become a part of your family. Molly is smart and kind, and wouldn't do anything to hurt the people she loves. Where she went or why is not very important in the scheme of things."

"And Old Dog?" Izzy asked.

"Apparently, he'd crawled into the backseat of Molly's car when she was getting ready to leave, and she shut the door without seeing him. She didn't see him until late that night, after she'd already decided that running away wasn't a good thing. So she brought him back as soon as she could."

They laughed, imagining the sweet old mutt enjoying the ride. And greeting Cass's mother and Joey the next night, tail wagging.

Cass agreed. "Danny did ask her if the Peeping Tom at Luna's had anything to do with her leaving—we knew it had spooked her that night—and then he reassured her that we only have Peeping Toms once every seven years, or something like that."

"But the Peeping Tom was at Luna's, not your house," Izzy said.

Cass shrugged.

Nell watched her friend dodge further questions. Cass wanted her nanny's uncomfortable disappearance out of their thoughts, out of their conversations, with no complications coloring it. Her coming back was all that mattered.

But Nell knew that deep down Cass was aware, like they all were, that there was something slightly mysterious about her leaving the way she did. The fact that she might have fled their household because of a random trespasser in the neighborhood didn't sit quite right. But for now, the friends would let the vague explanation rest uneasily on the table.

"Speaking of Luna," Nell said, her voice lighter as she shifted the topic.

Cass looked relieved at the change of subject.

"I know she's a complicated human being, we all know that." And then Nell shared the scene she'd witnesses in the small parlor off Beatrice's foyer shortly after Lidia Carson had been murdered. Luna comforting Beatrice. And forcing a coffee mug of Scotch on her. And Beatrice calling her "cuz."

Birdie shook her head. "Cousins. Of course. I think I heard that a long, long time ago. Jake Risso told me. Luna married a cousin of his and reunions always revealed interesting facts like that. But apparently neither woman seemed to acknowledge their relationship and it became lost in the passage of years."

"Geesh," Cass said. "Well, that partially explains the way the mayor yelled at Luna last night when we walked in. Being related carries its own liberties, I guess."

"And secrets," Izzy said.

"And also the ability to care when it's needed. Goodness in people comes out at unusual times. Luna's just needed the right time and place," Nell said.

"I think that's the same room where Beatrice had chastised Luna a couple hours earlier," Cass said. "So, who's Aunt Gert?"

"I don't know. But I get the feeling the cousins knew her well."

Ella's appearance in the doorway brought them back to the moment.

"Okay, Ella, I admit it," Cass said. "This rabbit food you put together was okay."

Ella smiled, her long face lifting. "I shall convert you yet, Catherine Halloran. But I didn't come up to bask in your effusive compliments. It's to remind you and Izzy that Harold is ready to drive you over to that noisy tavern of Jake's. Don't keep him waiting." Implicit in her tone was the fact that they were slightly daft to leave the comfort of Sonny Favazza's den—and her own lemon bars—for Jake Risso and Elvis Presley.

Ella stacked plates and empty glasses and mugs on a tray. She paused at the door and turned back toward Izzy and Cass.

"Don't forget, you two," she said, balancing the tray with one arm and her skinny hip, and wagging a finger in their direction. "Be sure you use the ladies' room here before you go over to that place of Jake's." With that, she was gone again, down to the kitchen, to let him know the girls were on their way.

Nell sat back in her chair, watching Izzy and Cass finding their phones and bags, getting ready to leave. Her head was suddenly weary, filled with loose thoughts, dangling like misplaced pieces of yarn. Like a cable sweater gone awry. She pulled out Ben's sweater, looked at it briefly, but thought of Ollie, who'd come to Sea Harbor to support his wife. And to see an old friend. Her college friend whose own life was now as misplaced, and as frayed, as her thoughts.

It would all come together in some fashion, she thought. Like the ragged threads knit back into a beautiful sweater. A meaningful life found again. A joyous holiday.

That was the way these things worked out. . . .

Chapter 22

Danny and Sam were seated near the bar, at a four-top, with a half-eaten basket of calamari between them and several bottles of pale ale.

Taller than Cass, Izzy spotted the men first and pulled Cass along with her, winding their way through the crowd.

"It's a good crowd," Izzy said, looking around at the bar, then waving at friends across the sea of people. "That'll be good for the education fund."

A group of regulars were huddled around the bar, while others crowded around tables, laughing, shopping bags with store logos shoved beneath their chairs. Happy people relaxing after a day of holiday shopping. Or hanging out to argue fishing or football, as most of Jake's regulars did.

Cass stopped briefly at the table next to Danny and Sam's to greet several of her lobster crew, joking with them about being out late when tomorrow was a crazy workday at the Halloran docks and they better be on time. They teased Cass back, the kind of easy rapport with an employer that a few beers encouraged.

"It seems kind of festive, not the mood I expected," Izzy said to Danny and Sam as she reached the table. "Maybe the news hasn't hit this end of Harbor Road?"

Sam pulled out two tall chairs, then helped Izzy out of her jacket. "We haven't been here long. But the Patriots game is getting folks revved up. They're about to murder the Colts. That might be the bigger murder topic right now."

"Maybe," Danny said. "But even Jake opens his doors to rumors like someone being killed at the mayor's house. I'd guess people are trading a few comments beneath all this bar racket."

Jake waved at the foursome from behind the bar, and then, a few minutes later, made his way to their table. "So, how are you guys? What can I get you ladies? It's a benefit, you know. For educating the young'uns. Baby Joey, right, Danny? Order big."

They laughed, then ordered wine and avocado dip. "Ella Sampson forced us to eat at Birdie's," Izzy explained to Jake.

"Oh, poor you," he joked back. "Birdie and Nell shoulda all come down here. We have real grease here. Not that healthy stuff Ella's into." Then he shouted the order over to the bar and turned back, his hands on the slightly sticky table, his leathery face serious. "Okay, tell me how are you guys doing? You're looking tired there, all a' you. Sam's about to fall asleep on the table. It musta been a late night?"

"Sam had a rough day, Jake. Three snowmen and more snow angels than the yard could hold," Izzy explained, ignoring the obvious intent of Jake's question. "He and Abby finally went over to a neighbor's and started a new family there."

"Good, good. My snow angels look more like Godzilla." Jake guffawed. Then he pulled back his grave tone, not letting Izzy off the hook. "You all know what I mean, what I'm getting at here. You were all there last night. I keep track of my friends."

"Sure, Jake," Sam conceded. "It's tough, what happened at

the mayor's event. The news is getting out, I guess. You hear people talking about it?"

Jake shifted his stance, checking out his customers again, then said, "Here's the truth. The guys who come in all the time? They couldn't care less about the mayor's big gig, and even less about some cook they never heard of. I mean, half of 'em wonder if the mayor spent their tax money on that poor woman who got killed, so you can kinda understand their attitude."

"Hey, you know she didn't do that," Sam said.

"Yeah, yeah. Well, okay," Jake said, quietly, leaning in on his palms again. "But some of the customers were at the big party, so sure, there's talk. Most of my regulars are in that uninvited group—thrilled not to have to get gussied up and go to a fancy party after a day out on the water catching who knows what. But with their noses out of joint anyway. I won't say I heard a few jokes about how the mayor musta really hated the food that chef cooked, but I won't say I didn't hear it, either. But hey, they don't mean it."

He looked over his shoulder at nearby tables and some of the men and women at the bar, knowing those who could hear above the rising tide of voices were listening in.

"Our mayor has survived a whole lot of difficult things," Izzy reminded them. "She'll make it through this okay." The others around the table nodded their agreement. "She has a good heart. She usually ends up on the right side."

"The right side. Good, good. Good side to be on," Jake said, looking up at Gus McGlucken, who was elbowing his way into the group.

"It was a bad scene over there last night," the hardware store owner said, nodding at the rest of them for confirmation. "Nasty business. I was there for a bit, so I saw the chef for just a few seconds, and I couldn't even believe it when I heard what happened to her. Just awful. I saw her husband, too. Good-looking fellow. Kind of standoffish, but I don't like what I'm hearing about him."

Sam asked, "What are you hearing, Gus?"

"People are saying, 'It's usually the husband when a wife gets killed. And this is his second wife to die, too.' I say, 'Listen, the man is a friend of Nell and Ben Endicott's, and there's no way.' "

"His first wife died of cancer, you tell them that, Gus," Izzy said.

"I will, Iz. What a tough thing for him."

Gus understood grief. He knew the pain of loss. He wasn't being casual. He was thinking of Nell. Of her friend. That empathy was one reason people stayed loyal to his hardware store, even when there was a big chain store up 128 at the mall. Nobody at the big store greeted them by name and asked them how their pop was doing with his arthritis.

"Wow," Jake chimed in. "One wife dies of cancer, the next one gets murdered. That man's been through some stuff."

Izzy said, simply, "Yes."

"Nellie is a good friend to have at times like this," Gus was saying. "She's been good to me during hard times. And you folks have been, too. Things work out. Most of the people in this town care."

At that moment, a cheer shook the tavern as another touchdown prompted more orders for beer and burgers and Jake shuffled off, pumping a gleeful fist in the air as his Patriots team stirred up the crowd and his profits. He turned back to the table long enough to say loudly, over the noise, "Well, we've got a good force working on this. Best chief of police anywhere. Took no time at all to catch that fellow harassing Luna."

He waved and disappeared into the crowd.

"*What* did he just say?" Cass asked, looking startled. "Catch who?"

One of the guys from Cass's lobster crew, sitting at the next table, shoved his chair closer to them. "They caught the Peeping Tom guy. You know, Cass, it was next door to you. We guys thought it was you being peeped on when we first heard about it."

Cass punched his arm. "Watch your mouth, Marco." Then she frowned. "They got him? Who caught who?"

"*Whom,*" Danny said, moving his chair to hear better.

Cass punched his arm, too.

"Ask this genius here," Marco said, pointing to a hulking-looking fellow sitting at the bar, his legs straddling the barstool sideways. "Lou here has friends in high places."

Cass shoved her stool back and looked over at the stranger. "Hi, Lou. So, what's all this about catching someone?"

Sam, Danny, and Izzy leaned in to hear.

Lou laughed, enjoying the attention, his speech slightly slurred. "My best buddy's a SHPD."

"A what?" Cass asked, prepared for some profanity to spill out.

"Sea Haba Poolice, man."

"Got it."

"My buddy was the cop who caught him!"

"Today?" Izzy asked, her eyebrows lifting into her bangs.

"Yep. He told me the whole story." Lou ordered another beer. Then leaned back against the bar as if that's all he had to say.

"So your friend caught someone?" Danny prompted.

"Big-time." Lou grinned. "The guy who snooped on Luna. Crazy, man—"

"It's the God's truth," Jake interrupted from across the bar, pressing hard on the draft tower faucet for the next beer. Foam sloshed up over his hand.

"Good news, right?" Lou interrupted, not willing to let someone take over his story. "My buddy caught the guy red-handed."

"*Red-handed?*" Cass said, looking skeptical. "You mean they caught him peeping on somebody else?"

"No, no, they caught him in another crime, can you believe the luck? Here's what I know." He shifted himself on the barstool, as if settling in to tell a long tale. "You know Mary Pisano's B and B over up the hill?"

They all nodded, including some people at nearby tables.

"Well, this peeper guy, he was staying there. I guess Mary's got stuff all over the place and he snitched some of it, like a picture or painting or something. And some cash, too, which Mary shouldn't have left lying around, and then he tried to sell the painting. Right here in town over at Canary Cove. But the gallery owner knows Mary and recognized the painting and secretly called the cops."

"But how did they know the thief was the peeper?" Cass asked.

Lou raised an eyebrow and, for a moment, looked not only wide, but wise. "Ha. That's the crazy part. When my buddy saw the guy—the thief—up close, he recognized him, because my buddy was one of the cops at the scene of the Peeping Tom crime. My buddy works day and night. He's a great guy."

"But the Peeping Tom was gone by the time the cops got to Luna's," Cass reminded him. "Luna's the only one who saw him, and all she saw was some kind of cap he had on. 'Ugly,' she said. The cap, not the guy. So, how did your cop friend recognize him?"

Lou scratched his head for a minute, then remembered. "It was because of the ugly hat. That was it. Luna's story about the Peeping Tom's ugly cap. The one with the weird colors and stripes and horseshoes around it."

Lou's voice began to fade. As he was oiling his throat with a new beer, Jake picked up the story. "Like one of those ugly hats the Colts fans wear, only even worse colors."

Lou picked back up. "Yeah. When my buddy showed up at the gallery to arrest the guy, he saw the ugly ski cap and remembered Luna's description. He muttered something about the hat and a Peeping Tom. So, get this, you'll never believe this—the guy thinks he's being stopped for peeping in the old lady's window. Get it?

"He was so relieved it wasn't for stealing that he started apologizing, saying he'd made a mistake that night. He'd had a couple too many. He didn't even know the lady who lived there. Said he looked away as soon as he could—"

Marco broke in. "I heard the same story. Seems like old Lou's story holds water."

Lou had had enough then, having his story taken away from him again. He slapped some bills on the bar and seemed to fade into the crowd, weaving his way toward the tavern door.

"That's one weird story," Marco said, and ordered more pitchers, including one for his boss's table in order to cover any remarks he might have regretted making.

"So, who is this guy, this peeper thief?" Sam asked Marco.

"I dunno," Marco said. "You'd have to ask Lou, and he's gone."

"I hope he's in jail," Izzy said, almost a whisper, but they all heard her.

Cass nodded in silent agreement.

Their husbands glanced at each other, and they weren't smiling, either.

"I think I've had enough for one night," Cass told them, and she didn't mean beer.

Danny, the designated driver, suggested they head on home. They had all shown up, done their duty, supported the cause. It was time to go.

The other three were standing almost before Danny had the words out. The weekend had seemed months long. And Lou's story had left them all uneasy.

Danny waved Jake over for the check.

When Jake finally managed to get around the bar and to their table, his brow was pulled into deep furrows. He slapped the bill on the table. "There's one other thing—I just realized I know the guy Lou's talking about. Or maybe I should say I know his hat. He's been in here a couple of times in the last week."

"A local guy?"

"No, no, not from around here, and I don't know his name, although one of the guys around here might. He was here to work the mayor's party. The guy was great-looking, the kind that stands out. Cocky."

"So he worked for Lidia Carson?"

"If that's the cook who was killed, yeah. He was one of the imports. Like I said, good-looking guy, except for the cap. Brown and neon-green and orange or something else. With Colt horseshoes. Can you believe it? In my bar? Mayor B had better count her silver, is all I can say. I sure wouldn't trust them."

"Them?" Izzy asked.

"Yeah. He was always with his lady friend. She was younger. She never said much except to him, just kinda clung to him and whispered in his ear. Crazy about her boyfriend, I guess. *Cray-cray*, as my granddaughter would say. She was working the party, too."

Izzy frowned. "So this guy tried to sell stolen goods *today*, a day after his boss was murdered . . ."

The noise in the bar seemed to get louder as the small group tried to get their thoughts together.

"Yeah." Jake drummed his fingers on the table, then leaned in. "There's something else. That night at Luna's—what night was that?"

Cass told him.

"Lou probably didn't know about this because he only comes in here on weekends."

"What's that?" Cass asked.

"Is there a young woman living on your street, maybe?"

"What's 'young' to you, Jake?"

Jake shrugged. "Twenties?"

Cass thought about it. "A woman moved in down the block a month or so ago. She lives alone, I think. Luna says she's a schoolteacher."

Jake nodded as if something now made sense. "Well, here's what I know. The guy we're talking about was in here earlier that night with his girl. It was our Wednesday oyster special and we were packed. And the new girl on your block was in here, too. I'd seen her around town, but she was new to my place. She came in with her girlfriend. The cocky guy must have seen this gal leaving and tried to catch up with her, but couldn't. He came back to the bar and asked around if anyone knew where she lived."

"That's creepy," Cass said.

"Right. But he explained right away that she was an old friend. It wasn't a pickup. He wondered where she lived, and someone yelled out a street near Canary Cove. He just wanted to look her up to say hello, he said. There aren't that many residential streets over there, so someone filled in that it must be Coastal Road. Your street, right, Cass?"

"Right, Jake."

"And then, here's the capper, he up and leaves without his girlfriend. Just abandons her while he runs out the door, seeming like he's going to try to catch up with his friend, the one you say lives on your block, Cass.

"So this all went down while his girl was in the ladies' room freshening her face or whatever they do in there. She missed the whole show. She comes back in, looks around, and doesn't see the guy.

"She asks me if I know where her boyfriend went. Now, I been in this business a long time, and I'm not about to tell one girlfriend that her man went chasing another woman. But wouldn't you know, one of the guys pipes up and says something like, 'Oh, he saw a woman he knows, and he left to catch up with her.' Let me tell you, that girl was not a happy camper. She gathered her stuff and stomps out on these fancy boots. I mean, you can't really blame her. He shouldn't have just left her like that, alone in a strange bar and town. And I'm watching all this, and as she flies out the door, I'm left thinking, 'Good thing for me that he paid up before he ran out.'"

"I remember that whole scene," Marco chimed in. "It was great. She was madder than Cass when our quota is off. And just like that"—he snapped his fingers—"she was outta here."

The group was still, a small bubble of silence in the middle of a raucous bar. Waiting for something to drop.

And then one of Jake's regulars, listening in from his seat at the end of the bar, took the toothpick out of his mouth and yelled over. "Yeah, I was here that night. The guy yelled as he was heading out that he was looking for someone named Molly Flanigan."

Chapter 23

Danny and Cass both whipped out their cell phones to call home as they hurried out of the bar. Danny put his phone back in his pocket when he saw that Cass was already hearing Molly's phone ring.

They piled in the car as Molly picked up.

"Molly," they all heard Cass say in a calm tone, though they could sense the urgency underneath it. "Just checking in to let you know we'll be home soon. How's Joey? Is he asleep? . . . Good. Everything okay with you?"

Then she said calmly, "Hey, Molly, would you make sure all our doors are locked? I'm sure Danny got them all before we left, but it's never too late to check, right? Like, right now? . . . No, no, everything's fine, I'm being super careful because of Luna's peeper and what happened at the party last night. Thanks, Mol. We're dropping Izzy and Sam off, and then we'll be right home."

"Sounds like things are okay?" Danny asked her when she clicked off. He had already started the car and headed down Harbor Road and the small beach side neighborhood where the Perrys lived.

"Yes. But we never should have left them alone."

"We didn't know, Cass," Danny reminded her. "And things are okay now."

"No, they're not okay. Here're all the things that aren't okay. The guy was looking for Molly. He got close to finding her." Cass tried to keep her voice steady.

"He was looking for Molly. And then she vanished without a word the next afternoon. We don't know if maybe she was forced to meet him somewhere, or ran to get away from him, or her leaving had nothing to do with him at all."

Cass paused for breath. "Does that sound right to you guys?"

Danny, Izzy, and Sam all murmured versions of "yes."

Izzy spoke up, feeling an urgency build. "He told people at Jake's that the woman he saw was a friend. What kind of friend peeks in a woman's window at night? Look how he scared Luna."

"And now we know he was at the mayor's house on the kitchen staff, and then today he stole from Mary Pisano and got arrested for it," Cass said.

Danny pulled the car up in front of the Perrys' house and look relieved. "So he's in jail."

Sam had already dialed a friend at the police department. When he got off, he opened the door for Izzy, then told the others, "The guy's not in jail. Somebody came for him, but they wouldn't say who."

When Cass and Danny got home, they found Molly asleep on top of the single bed in Joey's room. Cass covered her with a down quilt, and then she and Danny went to their own bedroom.

"No point waking her just to give her nightmares," he whispered to Cass.

"We'll talk to her in the morning," she whispered back, crawling in beside him.

Finally, after replaying the evening until it was ragged and jagged at every edge, Cass fell into a restless sleep. Waking only once, when she heard Molly tiptoeing downstairs and out to her own bed. She got up and looked out the window to the garage, seeing the lights go on, and forcing herself to know Molly would have locked the door behind her.

And she knew that, because Molly was Molly. She was careful. She handled things.

And she would never have run off with a thief. She would have tried to handle whatever she thought was happening with Luna's Peeping Tom the way she handled their entire household. With much thought and caring and love. Old Dog included.

Chapter 24

Cass was up too early the next morning. She sat at the kitchen table, drinking a strong cup of coffee left over from the day before, trying to put her thoughts in order.

Even the sweet *da-da* sounds of her baby boy coming from upstairs, the cheerful sounds of Danny playing with his son, couldn't dim the ragged images that had stayed with her during the night, things that hadn't happened, but maybe could have.

A good-looking man she'd never met, climbing up a ladder beneath Molly's window. Knocking on it? Or peering in, waiting. For what? To frighten . . . to steal . . . to harm . . .

He had claimed Molly was a friend.

But Molly ran away. One didn't run away from friends.

One embraced them.

Cass checked the clock above the sink and threw out the rest of her coffee. Izzy'd be there in minutes to drag her out for a cold, wintry run along the shore. Izzy had suggested it when she and Danny drove them home the night before. When Cass hadn't responded to Izzy's suggestion, it was followed an hour later with a late-night text. And then, an early-morning text.

It's what we need, Cass, the text had said. And she promised that the cold, freezing air would clear their heads of all ill will and misinformation, and wash away the weekend's badness in one mighty wave.

"That's Izzy being Pollyanna," she told Danny after reading him the text, which she'd found earlier that morning.

"It's fine with me. Make sure you talk to Molly. I know she'll clear all this up. She was okay yesterday and sure didn't look like she was running away from anyone. Oh, and remember I have a meeting today. You'll need to take over with Joey after his big doctor's appointment"

"Izzy stressed *short* run. I'll be back in plenty of time."

Danny went back upstairs as footsteps at the back door pulled Cass out of her thoughts. She peeled herself from the chair as if she'd been sitting so long her body had melted into it, and grabbed her water bottle.

. "Hi, Iz," she said as the door opened. Then stopped in surprise. "Molly?"

"Hi, Cass," Molly said, slightly embarrassed.

Cass looked confused. She had given Molly the day off. Danny was taking Joey in for his checkup; then she'd take over. She figured Molly could sleep in, something she rarely got to do since becoming a part of the Brandleys' crazy life.

So Cass had planned her day around that fact. She'd run with Iz, because she was given no choice, and then she'd be there when Molly got up.

And then they'd talk, and Molly would explain away Dirk whoever-he-was and together they'd figure out how to cast him out of their lives forever.

Mostly, she would assure Molly that she was safe. And she would be happy. She and Danny would be at her side and help her in any way that she needed. Whatever the problem was, they would find the answers.

But Molly clearly wasn't sleeping in. She was wide awake,

with a water bottle in hand, cold-weather running gear on her body, and a thick merino wool beanie Izzy had made for her pulled down over her ears. Thick blond curls peeked out beneath it.

Izzy came in right behind her. "Molly's going to run with us," Izzy told Cass in a voice that emphasized *don't argue with me.*

"Good idea," Cass approved, "although it's supposed to be your day off, Molly."

"I've had my days off, Cass. I'm grateful you even want my company."

Cass reached out and pulled her into a tight hug. "Of course I want your company, Mol. You and Izzy? Makes my day."

"I was kind of told to come along," Molly said, shivering from the short walk between her garage apartment and the kitchen door. "Who can say *no* to Izzy?"

"Obviously, not me. And it's great you're coming with us. You took all those first-aid classes I read about on your resume and I may need your help when I get frostbite and hypothermia."

Cass glanced at Izzy. Her best friend was doing a masterful job of jumbling up her carefully planned day. But she'd go along with it. Sometimes the best-laid plans of mice and men weren't so great, anyhow. Maybe an Izzy-messed-up day would prove better than her own.

Cass walked to the stairs and yelled up to Danny that they were off for their run, and she'd be back shortly. Molly was going with them. And would he please videotape Joey's exam and get a few photos on his cell phone of Joey sitting on the examining table? Maybe one with the nurse and doc?"

"How about one of Joey reading *Gray's Anatomy*?" Danny yelled back.

Cass ignored her husband and hurried to catch up with her friends.

* * *

The beach was empty, save for a pair of visiting harlequin ducks swimming just off the shore, their sleek blue bodies diving for mussels and crabs.

Had there been others on the beach, they would have noticed the runners—a trio of fit women in colorful running attire, running side by side along the packed sand floor, arms swinging in sync. Their graceful strides were long and even. Their faces held high to the sun above the horizon, lighting up the day in brilliant crimson and blinding golden stripes.

On one side of the runners, waves lapped rhythmically against the shore, and on the other, the town's steeples and old New England cottages and captains' mansions were silhouetted against the morning light.

The three women ran along the beach silently, then looped up through a neighborhood, and down to another stretch of beach. Finally they rounded a bend in the shoreline and slowed to a comfortable pace as they approached the well-groomed beach of the Sea Harbor Yacht Club. The sprawling clubhouse was awake, with lights on inside and shadows of early-morning staff and members moving around inside.

"Coffee," Cass breathed, her body stopping at the wide curve of steps leading up to the patio and the clubhouse. Her single word hung in the cold salt air. She leaned low, hands touching the ground, breathing deeply. When she peeked up, she saw that the others were looking at the clubhouse, too. Warm and cozy and clean. And smelling, at least in their heads, of coffee and freshly risen yeast.

"Frankly, I will die right now if I don't have coffee or a cinnamon roll." Cass straightened her body to full height. "Who's with me?"

Izzy finished a stretch. "Yes, it's a good time. Let's go." She looked at Cass, her brows lifted, then smiled at Molly.

They jogged up the steps and across the patio to the glass

doors, then into a spacious dining area with small poinsettias on each table. A Christmas tree, with tiny ornaments and silver bells, stood tall and stately at one end of the room, and ropes of greenery hung from the wood beams on the ceiling.

With Izzy in the lead, they walked through the more formal dining room to a comfortable bar and lounge, silent in the early-morning hour. Izzy led them to a half-moon of chairs facing the sea, with a low, round table in front of them. In minutes, they'd taken off one layer of running clothes and settled into the soft, comfortable chairs. "I hope we don't smell," Izzy said, lowering her head and lifting one arm slightly.

"No smell that I detect," a familiar voice said. "I saw, not smelled, you guys sneaking in the patio door." Liz Santos walked over to them, her elegant heels clicking on the polished floor and a swirly dress moving with her walk. "You're up early."

The club manager, a longtime family friend, welcomed Izzy and Cass with hugs, then reached out a hand to Molly and shook it warmly. "I'm guessing that I'm finally meeting Marvelous Molly, as you're known around these parts. I'm jealous the Brandleys found you before I did." She whipped out a photo of her two beautiful, tanned-skin babies and showed it to Molly. "Just in case you get sick of the Brandleys' wild household."

They all laughed and oohed and aahed over Liz and Alphonso Santos's gorgeous children, clearly a wonderful amalgam of their mother and their Brazilian father's genes.

Liz motioned to a waitress to bring waters and coffee for her friends. "Showing those photos was shameful of me," she said to Molly. "But Cass, Izzy, and I compete for the cutest shots of our kids. Izzy has a slight edge, since her husband's a photographer." She slipped the photo into her pocket and spoke to the group. "Anyway, I'm happy you all interrupted your run to stop in. You're bringing sunshine into my day. Things have been glum around here, with poor Beatrice's holiday party ending the way it did."

"I thought I saw you and Alphonso from a distance," Izzy said.

Liz nodded. "We weren't anxious to go, leaving the kids on a snowy night, and then there was the whole thing about Beatrice having a guest list, instead of the free-for-all open house it usually is. But Alphonso thought we should go—just a short in and out, you know how that can be. It was worth it, I suppose. The food was grand. I wish we could afford a chef like that here at the club. Everything presented with such amazing artistry. It took a talented, skilled chef to do all that. But then, such a horrible ending. I hope Beatrice is doing all right."

Molly sat in silence, her head moving back and forth as she followed the conversation.

"Have any of you heard anything, any news?" Liz asked.

"Not a word," Izzy said.

"It's certainly affecting the town," Liz said. "Even if people are pretending otherwise. Last night's Sunday seafood buffet had a lot of lobsters left at the end of the evening. We never have lobsters left. Even though we don't know the people involved in this horror movie, even when it's a stranger whose life was ended, it's simply horrific. It just is. I hope it's behind us soon and that people can get back to their lives."

A waitress appeared with a tray of water glasses with lemon slices, coffee mugs, several small plates, and a basket of warm cinnamon rolls, their sweet aroma circling them.

"Compliments of the house," Liz said. She waved, then hurried off toward her office near the lobby. No matter the season, the yacht club was always busy, even when members' sailboats and yachts were shrink-wrapped in plastic or in boathouses, safe from winter storms. And Liz made sure the club's winter life was always fun and went smoothly.

Cass had peeled off a second layer of running gear, and was

reaching for a cinnamon roll. "Why do I feel guilty eating these thousands of calories while in my running duds? It's like magnets. I can't resist."

"You shouldn't feel guilty," Molly said. "That was a good run. You earned it."

"I agree," Izzy said. "By your blood, sweat, and tears."

"Yeah, you're right. I did earn it." Cass licked one of her fingers. And then she wiped off her hand with a napkin and took a long drink of water.

She looked from Izzy to Molly, and then out the window. High tide. The waves gaining momentum.

And the thought: her best-laid plans.

The images were still with her, even after a vigorous run and a cinnamon roll. A man, a thief? A Peeping Tom. And Molly Flanigan, without whom the Brandley family would be circling a huge empty hole in its middle.

"Molly," Cass said.

Molly looked up. She hadn't touched her cinnamon roll, as if she knew the hiatus in their run was for something other than coffee and water and cinnamon rolls.

Izzy did, too. She'd been waiting for the moment. Cass's voice had a curious sound to it.

"It's the elephant in the room, Molly. The Peeping Tom," Cass finally said.

Chapter 25

Molly's face dropped. She put down her coffee mug and stared into it, then swirled the dark liquid slightly.

Cass's voice was uncharacteristically soft. "Mol, I'm not being nosey. Honest. I'm just concerned. We all are. I was so afraid something terrible had happened to you. You were hurt or injured—or who knows what? We love you. And something's going on in your life that's not quite right. I don't know what. But it seems clear now that the creep who was over at Luna's last week was looking for you. Can we help with whatever's going on here? Who is this guy?"

Molly looked up. Her face was still sad, but her voice was clear. "You're right. I owe you that. I'm so sorry for not talking to you, for not explaining everything . . ." She took a deep breath, and then went on.

"His name is Dirk Evans. He's someone I knew before I came here. I met him when I lived in New York for a while. We were in a class together."

Cass realized at that moment that Danny had been right. She really didn't know much about Molly. She'd called references, sure, and talked to people who mattered—teachers in her hometown, neighbors, people she had worked for. Everyone loved Molly Flanigan. How could they not? But boyfriends? Other places she had lived? If she had gone to college? Somehow, once she and Danny and Joey met her, little of that seemed to matter.

"You went to college in New York?" Izzy asked.

Molly shook her head. "No. Shannon and I decided we didn't have a clue what we wanted to study after high school, so we worked for a while in our small Delaware hometown, then finally took off to see the world and find ourselves. We backpacked through Europe on our meager earnings and a little help from generous parents."

She stopped and smiled slightly, dimples appearing in her cheeks, as she replaced Cass's initial question by digging instead into an easy memory. A happy one.

"Did it work?" Izzy asked. "Did you find yourselves?"

"We found the world, I guess, or part of it, anyway. But I did find something during our year of hostel hopping. I found *food*. And I discovered how much I loved everything about the culinary world—food preparation, cooking, sauces, the presentation and the chemistry of it all. Crazy, huh? I lived in hostels and found this extraordinary world I knew nothing about. Well, except for my A's in high school chemistry and the fact that my dad said I was a better cook than my mom. Shannon and I picked up dishwashing jobs in great restaurants all over France and Italy and Spain. I washed dishes for Anne-Sophie, can you believe that? I thought I'd gone to heaven."

Izzy and Cass smiled in amazement, pretending they knew who Molly was talking about.

"I loved all of it. I didn't want to come home. But eventually we ran out of money, so we came back and settled in New York, crashing with friends, finding work so we could go back to school or whatever. Shannon didn't like the city much, though, and finally moved up here to Sea Harbor, a place where she vacationed as a kid. I wasn't that crazy about living in New York, either, though it was exciting.

"But by then, I had set my sights on a school, a place where I could learn about the culinary world. I discovered the Institute of Culinary Education—ICE, it's called—and researched some scholarship opportunities, all that sort of thing. And that was it. I'd go to culinary school."

Cass sat up straighter. She started to say something, then swallowed her words with a swallow of coffee. The brochure from Molly's room now fit into a whole chapter in the young woman's life.

Molly went on. "And in the meantime, I discovered there were lots of cooking classes you could take in New York, which I did whenever I could. I thought it might help me prepare for school, and maybe even help me get some financial aid. It was a good way to meet influential people in the restaurant business who might help me get in. There was one noncredit class, a semester long, that even offered financial aid, depending on how you did."

Cass and Izzy could feel the passion in Molly's voice as she talked about what was clearly a special time in her life. And learning more about Molly was so fascinating that they almost forgot that the conversation had begun on a more serious note. And one that had little to do with backpacking or applying to a college.

As if realizing it herself, Molly paused and took a long drink of water. The smile had disappeared as the story wound down. She put her water glass down and took a breath, letting it out slowly. And then she began again, her voice softer and without the life that had carried it before.

"It was a good plan," she said, running a hand through her damp curls. "Except then it wasn't. It was in that semester class where I met him."

The word *him* landed with a thud.

"You met this guy, this *Dirk*, in New York?" Izzy asked. She expressed the name in a way that sounded more like *dirt*.

Molly nodded.

"In a class," Izzy repeated, keeping the direction of the story going. "He wanted to be a chef, too?"

"No. He never seemed interested in the class, but he was always there," Molly said.

"Were you . . . friends?" Cass asked. A single line from Jake's tavern echoing in her head: *"But he explained right away that she was an old friend."*

"Friends? Oh, no. We were the opposite of *friends*. Well, not at first, but later. Dirk was *GQ* handsome and flirty, a couple years older than I, and for some reason, he focused on me. I was flattered at first. I sure wasn't looking for a relationship—but I went out with him a couple times. Just for fun. But it wasn't long before I saw his mean streak, the dark side. He was the kind of guy who thought running over squirrels or gulls was a sport. His respect for women didn't seem to be much higher than that. I broke it off with him quickly."

"I'm guessing he didn't take it lightly," Cass said quietly. She wanted to ask more about his mean streak. Did this guy hurt Molly? Threaten her? Her hands turned into tight fists? With effort, she held back the words.

Molly nodded, then sighed. "Those were hard days. He followed me, tried to get me back. Not because he wanted me, just because I had left him. He thought it was sort of a failure, I guess. He left lewd notes. Warnings, threats. Then he started spreading rumors about me. And in class, it was awful. Dirk was sneaky in his meanness, in getting back."

"And he was still allowed to stay in that class? Did you report him?" Izzy asked. "Harassment's a crime, Molly—"

Molly was quiet, her eyes shifting to the view beyond the window, the wild, crashing waves. Finally she focused back on the two women sitting across from her, avoiding the question. "Well, anyway, like I said, it wasn't a great time for me. Things, dreams, well, my plans and my life, all fell apart. And then during one of my many late-night phone calls with Shannon, she convinced me to leave the city and come here, and the rest is history." She pushed a smile in place. "That's when you changed my life, Cass. You did. It's the truth. Sharing Joey with me, your family, your life, the way you and Danny have done, is an incredible gift."

No, Cass thought. *Molly has changed our lives.* But Molly was also changing the subject. Pieces of her story were out there somewhere, but definitely not here in the yacht club lounge. She tried to sort it all through in her head, something niggling there that was getting lost in the shuffle.

"Did you ever see Dirk again after you left New York?" Izzy asked.

Molly shook her head. "No. Dirk Evans and the damage he did was put out of my mind and my life forever."

"Until he came back into it," Cass said.

"At first, I refused to believe it could be him at Luna's. He had done that once to an apartment I was staying in, after I broke it off. He scared my roommate to death. Remembering that, I began to think it might be Dirk. It fit. I hadn't paid any attention to the mayor's thing, that party. And that day, the day I left, Shannon suggested I walk Joey over to the mayor's house. She'd been called last minute to work the party and was going over to meet the crew and see the place. And . . ." Molly stopped and composed herself. Then she went on.

"So I went, and as Joey and I were leaving, there he was, driving up the driveway on a bike, speeding, careless and cocky. Self-absorbed. And it all fell into place."

"But why did you—" Cass began, but Molly stopped her.

"What I told you yesterday is the truth. You and Danny would have wanted to solve it. To confront him. To make it all go away. It might have been a mess."

"You're right about one thing," Izzy said, looking at Cass, then Molly. "All of us would have wanted to solve it. We still do. I also understand wanting to solve it yourself."

Molly smiled a thanks. "I needed to figure it out. I knew I couldn't let this guy upset my life again, but I wasn't sure how to do it. And the one thing that I knew was that I needed to be somewhere other than your house, Cass, so he wouldn't be a danger to Joey. Or to you and Danny. So that's why I left. And I actually did scribble a note, but found it later scrunched in my pocket."

Now Cass had gone pale. "Joey might be in danger?"

"No, Cass. No. But I couldn't take a chance. Dirk was unpredictable. I didn't know what he might do.

"Somewhere along the way," she said, as if the thought had suddenly clarified something for her, "life didn't treat Dirk Evans right, and he seemed to spend a lot of time getting back at it any way he could."

The waitress came over and refilled coffee and water glasses, then walked away.

Cass looked at Molly, as if to say something she didn't want the answer to, but couldn't hold back any longer. Finally she asked, her voice quiet, "Molly, did this guy ever hurt you?"

"No, Cass. Not like that. Not physically. But yes, he hurt me. Dirk Evans played with people's heads. There are all kinds of ways of hurting people."

"Do you think he came to Sea Harbor to find you?" Izzy asked.

"No. I don't think he had any idea I was here. Is there an opposite word for *serendipity*? I think that's what happened." Molly tried to put a laugh on top of her words, but it was a hollow and sad sound. "I don't know why life lines up the way it does sometimes. And then to have Shannon end up in the middle of everything."

"Shannon?" Izzy looked confused.

Then Cass spoke up, suddenly remembering something

from the party that had been so unimportant at the time. "Izzy, remember? We saw Shannon talking to a guy that night," she said suddenly. "It was this guy, it must have been—"

Izzy sat up straight. "Of course the guy who was threatening her—"

"It was Dirk," Molly said. "Shannon called me from the party that night. But she's so strong. Dirk was foolish to try to get anything out of her. She'd heard so much about him from me that when she finally realized who he was, she was ready to fight him to the death if she had to."

"She's a good friend."

"The best. She said he has a girlfriend, who was also working at the party."

Izzy and Cass looked at one another. "I think we saw her, too," Cass said. "She came outside and comforted him. A warm and fuzzy one."

Molly winced. "How can anyone touch him? Her name is Darci something. Shannon said she's crazy about him. In an unhealthy way, in her opinion."

"Sounds like they're a match made in heaven," Cass said.

"Well, thankfully, with all the police questionings and the rumors and the terrible tragedy of the chef's death, Dirk is probably long gone. Underneath that handsome façade is a coward. And a weasel who always seems to end up on top. He also has an innate way of avoiding blame."

"Gone from Sea Harbor?" Cass asked. "No, he's definitely still here."

Molly looked confused. "I guess it makes sense that the police are wanting to talk to the staff, too, but—"

Izzy looked at Molly. "It's more than that with this guy, Molly. Maybe you haven't heard—"

"Hear what?"

"About Dirk—"

Molly stiffened.

"He was arrested yesterday," Cass said.

"Arrested?" The single word fell from Molly's lips like a brick. "Dirk was arrested?"

Izzy and Cass stared at her, stopped short by the strength and horror in her voice.

Molly clasped the arms of the lounge chair, looking off at something only she could see. Then she looked back at Cass and Izzy, her eyes wide, her voice strained. She breathed in a bellyful of air, then slowly released it.

"He did it," she said. "He said he would."

"Did what, Molly?" Cass asked quietly, not sure she wanted an answer.

"He killed her. Dirk killed Lidia Carson, our teacher."

Chapter 26

Molly Flanigan's words were still hanging in the air, not fully registered or acknowledged, when Liz Santos came hurrying toward their table, waving a cell phone in her hand and her focus on Cass.

"It's Danny. He says you weren't answering your phone and he needs you home. He has to leave for a meeting with his publisher this morning."

Cass pulled out her muted phone, then checked her watch. And then she slapped the side of her head. "Oh, shoot, I totally forgot. I completely lost track of time."

"That's what he guessed. And he knew it wouldn't be because you were enjoying a marathon run, so he figured you had stopped here for food, knowing I might be the only one who would let smelly runners in."

Cass looked at Izzy, whose eyes were still wide, still trying to process Molly's words.

Molly jumped up. "I'll go. I'll run back. I should be there with Joey, anyway."

Liz shook her head. "No need, you're all in luck. I'm headed to a meeting in town and will give you all a ride. My chariot's waiting."

"Not me," Izzy said quickly. "Two smelly runners in your car is enough. Besides, I need a *real* run, not just a sprint like these guys."

She headed back through the dining room and out the patio doors before Liz could insist. She was into a full run almost before she hit the sand.

To a bystander, Izzy might have been running for her life. Or practicing for a marathon. In truth, she was running to a quiet home, not far away, where there'd be coffee on and a welcoming hug. And a chance to sort through her thoughts.

Nell had gotten up early that morning, restless and wondering what the week would bring. A murderer behind bars was at the top of her wish list.

She rinsed out the coffee cup Ben had left on the counter. In spite of the early hour, he'd gone to meet Sam to fix something on the sailboat while it was in storage, then off to Mary Pisano's B and B to see Ollie.

"I'm looking forward to talking with Ollie," he'd told her before leaving the house. "Not so much because I think I can help him, but just to give him a chance to say whatever he wants to, without anyone passing judgment."

Nell was happy to hear it. Ben was far more circumspect with Ollie than she could be, their friendship histories different.

Ben also promised to put in another invite for Ollie to move into to their guesthouse for a few days. Mary Pisano had had to fight off a couple reporters, and it would be good if they could relieve her of that by spiriting Ollie away.

Nell wiped off the counter for the third time, put on a fresh pot of coffee, and sat at the island with her laptop, scrolling through emails and the news.

*   *   *

In ten minutes, Izzy had arrived at her aunt's door and rushed in, moving through the hallway to the family room, the distance too short to bring her breathing down and her body composed.

Stretching the length of the house, the Endicott family room had been Izzy's refuge through college and law school and practice in Boston, a short drive away, and it still held that spot for her. She loved the wall of windows that looked out onto the backyard, where she and Sam were married; the wooded area at the back edge, with the secret path that twisted through the trees and down to the beach. And she especially loved the small guesthouse tucked in the back corner of the yard, where Uncle Ben and Aunt Nell had let her stay when she had left her law practice and needed a place to figure out her life. Everything about her aunt and uncle's home embraced her and welcomed her and made her feel safe, even if no one was there.

But Aunt Nell was there at the other end of Izzy's favorite room, sitting in front of her computer at the kitchen island, a stack of bills at the side.

"Izzy," Nell said with happiness in her voice. "You're the perfect way to start this day."

Izzy hurried over and hugged her aunt tightly. "Don't let Uncle Ben hear you say that."

Nell chuckled as she finally pulled free. "You are freezing, Izzy. Here." She grabbed a soft alpaca knitted throw from an island stool and wrapped it around her niece. "Are you sick?"

Izzy shook her head. "No. The run was too short to warm me up. Coming here was all I needed. I'm feeling toasty already."

"A short run doesn't sound like you."

"I ran from the yacht club."

"Oh?"

Izzy explained about the run she'd planned with Cass and

Molly, the run that would clear their heads, flush away any uncomfortable feelings about the way Molly had disappeared without a word. Bring things back to normal. And then she took her aunt through Molly Flanigan's journey, on her way from a Delaware small-town upbringing to Europe to New York to Sea Harbor.

And things that were far from normal.

Nell stayed quiet, listening intently. Izzy was a great explainer, lining things up in order, relating events so they followed one after another, logically and consistently and packed with details, but without emotional embellishment. Traits Nell knew had served her niece well as a lawyer.

"So that's where her cooking interest came from," Nell said. "It explains that five-star meal she made for all of us on Cass's birthday. And she learned it all from Lidia Carson."

"Some at least. But she abandoned that dream, all because of this guy named Dirk." Izzy stopped talking and slapped one hand hard on the island, scattering Nell's bills. Her head shot up. "That's it, Aunt Nell. That's where there's a hole. I needed to say it out loud so I'd find it. That's it. Her life fell apart because of this guy."

Nell started to say something, but Izzy wasn't finished, talking partly to herself, with her aunt as an attentive listener. Her voice speaking to a courtroom.

"But why didn't she just report him?" Izzy asked rhetorically. "Get rid of him? Move on and go to that school, follow the profession that she was dreaming about? Instead, she said he had destroyed her life."

Izzy paused. Then said again, "Why didn't she report him? Why? The Molly we know would have."

"Harassment can be a traumatizing thing, Izzy. The newspapers tell us that every single day."

Izzy listened, thought about it, and then said, "You're right, Aunt Nell. Of course you are. We both know that. Maybe I wasn't factoring in the emotional side of it to the degree I should have. Harassment is a horrible thing. Some women never recover."

But Molly had left out words somewhere, Izzy felt sure of it. The knitting group had always characterized Molly as a survivor. Marvelous Molly. Smart, capable Molly, who could do anything.

"I understand now how frightening it must have been for Molly to find out the guy might be here, working at the mayor's party," Nell said. "It's all a bit surreal. But, Izzy, so is her assumption that Dirk killed Lidia Carson—"

"Liz interrupted us with a call from Danny before we even had time to respond to that. By now, Cass has probably explained to Molly that he wasn't arrested for murder, but written up for minor theft. And Luna isn't going to press charges on the trespassing charge. It would bring attention to her that she doesn't want, especially after what happened at the mayor's party.

"But you're right. Molly's response came out of her mouth like a bullet. As if she didn't have to think about it."

"Ben said the police called Ollie after Dirk was arrested, since Dirk was a part of the catering entourage. Ollie said he'd take care of it. He must have been the one who went to the police station for Dirk."

Izzy was distracted, thinking back to Molly's story of Dirk Evans. And then that shocking declaration that Dirk Evans had killed the mayor's famous chef. It seemed a giant leap to her lawyer-trained mind. A giant leap to a conclusion with a lot of possible holes in it. She wondered why an intelligent woman like Molly would have made such a leap.

And then she remembered Molly's exact words: *"He did it. He said he would."*

Chapter 27

It was Ollie who suggested where he and Ben might meet.

"The B and B is a comfortable place. It's quiet in the late morning, Mary Pisano says. It's the lull before the storm, before the true holiday season."

Ben liked the idea fine. Ravenswood-by-the-Sea B and B had been the scene of many happy Endicott occasions—his and Nell's anniversary party, Izzy and Sam deciding to tie the knot, celebrations of friends' special times. There was good energy in the place—something, he suspected, of which Ollie Bishop needed plenty.

Mary had offered to serve them brunch in the comfortable living room. The breakfast room was a little chilly, even with the bright sun coming in. And this way, she knew they'd have privacy. Besides, it was her favorite room, perfect for favorite people.

Mary described the decorating in the room as elegant whimsy, and although Ben wasn't sure what that meant, it seemed to fit the room perfectly. It felt like home to him. The wide-planked floors were covered with elegant old rugs, the walls adorned with New England scenes, and couches and chairs placed around the room in groupings that offered privacy and comfort. On either side of the fireplace, floor-to-ceiling bookcases were filled with books, magazines, games, and some long-ago framed pictures of Pisano gatherings, many of which were left in the house Mary Pisano's grandfather Enzo left her, and which he still watched over from a nearly life-sized portrait of himself above the fireplace.

A sidebar near the bookcases had a built-in warmer, which today held eggs and sausages, and fresh fruit filled a crystal bowl nearby.

Ben stood at the wide-arched entry to the warm room and spotted Ollie over near the fireplace, already comfortable in a large wing chair, with another one angled near him. A basket of warm pastries sat on the table between them. He looked lost in thought, the crackling flames in the fireplace casting shadows across his drawn face.

In that instant, Ben was struck with an unexpected wave of melancholy. He and Ollie had started their adult lives together, similar in so many ways. Then, as naturally happens when graduates go off into the world, their paths had diverged, their experiences taking different forms, different highs and lows.

And now here they both were, in Sea Harbor, Massachusetts, with Ollie sitting alone, far from his home, having lost two wives. And with a murder investigation hanging too close to him for comfort.

Ben had sat with many friends over the years, sometimes just to be company in times of tragedy or loss or misfortune. Or sometimes to help someone think through to solutions for problems that had seemed unsolvable to them. To find wills. To help understand complicated legalese. In Ollie's case, he wasn't sure what he could help with. But in times of grief, things would sometimes come out in conversation, things not thought of ahead of time, or not on any list, or even buried out of shame or purpose or sadness, and then unexpectedly released.

But grieving took a different path in cases of murder.

In any case, he could listen. They had never been confidants in college. But they were different people now.

"Hey there, Ollie," Ben called over, not wanting to startle him.

Ollie looked over, then around the room, looking surprised at where he was. Then he seemed to collect himself and smiled, standing, and lifted a hand in greeting.

Ben strode across the room and shook his old college friend's hand. "Nice place you have here," he joked.

Ollie chuckled and motioned to the empty chair. "It's nice. Mary Pisano has made life mighty comfortable for me the last couple days. Even peaceful. She keeps hounds at the door as best she can, and gives me a snowy woods out back to walk in. What more does a man need?"

A Nell, Ben thought. That's what Ben would need in any kind of difficulty. He couldn't imagine losing her. How empty his life would be.

And then to lose a second wife one loved?

Ben decided in that moment that Ollie must be made of sterner stuff than he had ever given him credit for, but then what choice had he except to endure? Life had thrown disasters at him. When they'd met in college, Ben had judged the future restaurateur as possessing in extroverted charm that made up for what he lacked in inner substance. Now he wondered if he had misjudged him. It was Nell—and Maddie—who had sensed the depth of character beneath the charisma.

Ben took off his coat, looping it over the back of the chair, and sat down just as Mary walked in, greeting him warmly. She filled two plates and placed them on the table between them, then discreetly left the room.

Ollie had Bloody Marys ready in a chilled silver pitcher. He poured two glasses and handed one to Ben, then held his up. "To old times," he said, and clinked his glass against Ben's.

"To old times." Ben nodded. He took a small swallow and put his glass on the table, then settled back in the chair.

Ollie did the same, resting his head back against the cushion. "When Lidia told me she was interested in taking the catering gig and coming up here, I said I'd come along, not something I often did when she was off pursuing business matters. I'd lost all interest in that sort of thing. But I knew you and Nell were here. It'd been a while since we'd been in touch. And now here you are, helping me through this mess. Handling death isn't easy, is it?"

Handling death by murder, even less so, Ben thought.

Ollie looked down at a folder Ben had brought with him and had tucked into the side of the chair.

Ben followed his look. "Nell jokes that I dream in layers of spreadsheets. Not really. I just grabbed some papers that might be helpful in going through logistical things. Details. But you've been through much of this before, Ollie. It may all be super-fluous."

"No, not really," Ollie said. "I was a muddled mess when Maddie died. My lawyer, business manager, accountant—they all took care of those things, the will, directives, filings. So it's nice of you to help ground me. And, as we are both aware, this is different . . ."

There was more to Ollie's thought, Ben suspected, but he let it rest. "You know Nell and I are here for you," he said instead. "Whatever you need. A lot of the bureaucratic things, filings, bank accounts, certificates, don't have to be addressed right now. But I promised Nell I'd put in another bid for housing this morning. She'd really like you to take us up on the guest-house offer. I would, too. Mary tells us there have been hounds at the door, and I think that might escalate. So think about it, anyway. Might be good for both of you. And you'd have all the privacy you need at our place."

Ollie nodded, clearly pleased at the repeated offer. "Thanks, Ben. And as for those other things, there's probably some attorney on our payroll who will have some of those things we need."

It wasn't a surprising statement to Ben. He thought back to the old Ollie. He had never seemed to be the type of person who would know or care about such things. That, at least, still seemed true of him.

"So that attorney has copies of your wills, I suspect—"

"Wills," Ollie repeated, nodding slightly. He looked uncomfortable at the thought, then took another drink and kept his fingers wrapped around the glass. "Wills are strange things, aren't they? You have them written up, sign them, then you stash them in a lockbox and forget about them. Sometimes for years and years. They're like a housekeeping task you do and are done with it."

"Sometimes. Wills can be changed, of course, at any time. You and Lidia probably had a trust, too—"

"I didn't pay much attention to all that. Not after Lidia came and rescued me from it. We had, well, maybe an unusual arrangement in that department. In lots of departments, when you come right down to it." He finished his drink and set the glass down.

Ben was surprised at Ollie's seeming distance from personal matters. He handled most of his and Nell's legal things, but Nell was always on top of it, and she never signed anything without putting him through his paces in explaining it. Nor did he ever make decisions without her input. But each to his own, he thought now. Some people were simply allergic to numbers and forms and figuring out the language of the law, and put that in the hands of their partner or a trusted friend or an attorney.

Ben nodded, not sure of where Ollie was taking the conversation. When Ollie spoke again, it wasn't in the direction Ben was expecting.

"Here's the thing, Ben. I wasn't quite up front with Nell when we met last week, before all this happened. I was looking forward to seeing her, a little like seeing my Maddie again, I guess. Those two were such great friends. Maybe I wanted to impress Nell, let her know Maddie would be proud of me. Marriage to a successful lady. The restaurant Maddie and I started together flourishing. So that's what I told her. But it hasn't been quite like that."

Ben leaned forward, listening, nodding when it seemed to fit into the conversation.

"It's true about Lidia—successful, talented, attractive. We were attracted to each other, but for different reasons. I liked that she was efficient and took care of things. Of me, even. But mostly my restaurant. And then everything else. Another restaurant. More enterprises. And she also loved me, I think. But my feelings were more of need than love."

He winced after his own words came back to him. "How awful that sounds. How selfish. I was always empty inside, knowing I didn't love Lidia, certainly not in the way I had loved Maddie. Maddie was always there, between us. After a while, I found it hard to be around her. It's clichéd to say she deserved more than that, but it's true. Little did I know, though, that she actually *had* more than that."

Ben wasn't particularly surprised by Ollie's confession. Nell had described a man still grieving for the wife who'd been gone for years. Anyone would feel short-changed in a marriage like that. What Ben didn't understand were Ollie's last few words.

"I'm not following, Ollie."

Ollie finished off his Bloody Mary. "I finally told her shortly before coming here that the best thing for us both was to get a divorce. We'd gone out to dinner to try a new restaurant in town, something Lidia always insisted on doing. She was quiet when I told her. And then she smiled and said, quite pleasantly, but firmly, that no, she 'liked the arrangement we had.' It 'suited' her, she said."

Ben sat back, a bit startled.

Ollie's smile held no humor. "I was surprised at her reaction, too," he said. I thought she'd want to separate as much as I did. I was unhappy, so I assumed she was, too. I told her that her instinct was absolutely right on about all the business decisions, but that she was wrong about this one, our marriage, and I hoped she would come to see that. But no matter if she did or did not, I needed to be on my own.

"And that's when she laughed. Not a mean laugh. It was soft, and even caring, like a mother's amusement when her toddler wants to drive the car. And then she explained why we weren't getting a divorce."

Ollie paused for a minute, as if collecting his thoughts, trying to put them in the right order.

Ben sat patiently, seeing the strain on Ollie's face.

Then Ollie continued. "It seems that all our investments, our restaurant deals, everything, are in Lidia's name. All tied up in a prenup that was written at a time when I still wasn't functioning well."

"At what point after Maddie died, did this all happen?" Ben asked.

"I went back to work in body, but it took me a long time to come back fully after Maddie died. Even when Lidia and I began a relationship, I was still with Maddie."

And probably still are, Ben thought.

"The thing is, what she put in place wasn't intended to cheat me. It was because she probably thought early on that I'd have messed up our finances, our business, carelessly. I was in some trouble financially. She built the fortune, not me."

Ben's mind was going in multiple directions. For starters, the whole arrangement didn't sound legal, and any divorce lawyer would be able to come up with an equal settlement. Messy, maybe. But divorces were often messy. Especially with tangled finances.

Ollie was looking at him now, his face suddenly sad again.

Ben had a feeling the sadness was about Maddie dying, however, and not at all about the questionable prenuptial agreement.

"But, Ollie, you must have had to sign things. And what about your accountant and your lawyer and your business manager, what did they have to say about it?"

"They didn't have much to say, or if they did, I wasn't listening. I was fine with Lidia taking charge. And that's what she did. I was grateful. If I ever loved her for anything, I loved her for that. That was the freedom she gave me, Ben, along with freedom to continue loving Maddie."

"But as time went on, you must have talked about financial things."

"There wasn't any reason to. We had plenty of money. She was better at all of it than I ever was. I joke that I'm still the better cook, but the truth is, I'm not even that. I was great, don't get me wrong, but she's better. For one thing, she's up on all that molecular gastronomy—things the culinary schools teach. That nonsense bores the pants off me. She was a respected guru with all those places.

"And as far as running the business goes, well, there is no comparison between us. She is"—he caught himself—"*was* the best, and she managed to meet all needs. Even supporting Dirk the way she did."

"Dirk?"

"Evans. He's a relative of hers. He came here as part of Lidia's kitchen staff. The man has had problems, including financial ones. Lidia takes care of most of it. Apparently, his mother died when he was sixteen and Lidia became his guardian. That ended, of course, when he turned eighteen. But he's had problems and they didn't end at eighteen. Lidia felt responsible for him, even though he was an adult. In fact, he's caused some problems right here in Sea Harbor. But I'm not going to bother you with that right now."

Ben let it go. "You must have had enormous trust in Lidia," he said.

"I do. She was always up front and honest. She never hid anything from me."

Ben wasn't at all sure Ollie, as inattentive as he was, would have any way of knowing that. But he held back his comment, and Ollie continued.

"It probably sounds suspicious to you, but ledgers, papers, bank statements, were always available for me to look at. I just didn't want to. I was fine with whatever she decided. And eventually she stopped trying to involve me. We were making money, pot over pot holder, you might say, by doing things her way, so why should I care?"

"I understand, and I'm in no position to pass judgment, Ollie. But it may take a while to sort through all this."

"It will work out. Things do."

Ben hoped so. He was struck suddenly by the power of grief. And how Ollie had allowed his own to create what could become mighty messes in his life.

Ollie settled back in the wing chair, looking calm. As if he'd somehow unburdened himself. Finally. Gone to confession. Nell had said earlier that she had glimpsed a fleeting peace in him. Ben was beginning to understand it.

As if reading Ben's mind, Ollie said, "But now Lidia's gone, and I finally have the one thing I wanted—freedom from our marriage. There's a certain peace in that. But also a terrible sadness. There's an irony for you, isn't it?"

"'An irony'?" Ben said. "I'm not sure. You lost a wife in a true tragedy. There is sadness when life is taken away. And when it's not a natural thing, like Lidia's, the sadness is mixed with all sorts of other emotions, I would think."

Ollie seemed to have stopped listening. "You know what Lidia said to me when we discussed all this?" he asked.

Ben shook his head, amazed by the whole story.

He was saved from responding by the noise of loud voices on the second floor, where the bedrooms were, and then by the muffled banging of suitcases being pushed down the carpeted stairs on their sides.

After that, the house went almost shockingly silent, so that every other sound—the ticking of the grandfather clock in the hallway, cars crunching along the snowy streets, a beeping from something in the kitchen—seemed heightened.

Ollie, ignoring the interruptions, called Ben's attention back to him.

"She said if I wanted it all, everything, I could have it the next day, because most of it was mine in her will. She had everything, and she took care of it and made it better, and then she planned to give it back to me in her will.

"She said she was pretty sure she'd die first because she'd work herself to death, and she'd chuckled at that, encouraging me to lighten up. But until then, she said, we'd have a decent life. She loved me and didn't want me to leave. She wanted to continue our marriage. It was good for business and good for her personally. And then she repeated that she loved me. It was hard to hear, since I deserved none of it.

"And then she added, trying again in her own inimitable way to get the serious look off my face, that she absolutely wasn't going to voluntarily give anything up in some silly divorce. If I wanted it all back, I'd have to kill her first."

The room fell silent. And then a noise drew Ben's attention to the hallway, where three people stood: a young woman, with long black hair; the owner of the bed and breakfast, Mary Pisano; and the handsome man who had stolen from the inn-keeper.

All three of them were staring in at Oliver Bishop.

Chapter 28

"Good to know, Ollie," the man in the hallway said with a satisfied smirk. His voice was deep.

The young woman next to him reached down to grab the handle of one of the suitcases, but her companion stopped her. "We don't need to bother with those."

Then he pointed toward Mary without looking at her. "Her guy can bring those out for us."

"I'm sorry, Mr. Evans, but we don't have a 'guy' here," Mary said, stepping away from the couple. "You'll have to be your own guy."

Ben watched the look Mary gave the man, sharper than daggers. Had the guy been smarter, he would have stayed quiet. Instead, he stared back at her.

"It's your place," he said.

"Yes," Mary answered pleasantly. "And my belongings."

Her message was pointed, and Dirk looked away, frowning briefly at the young woman hovering beside him.

Then he looked directly over at Ollie. "So. The bill. Have you handled ours?"

Ollie pulled himself out of the chair and walked across the

room. His voice was calm, but color was creeping up his neck, and Ben could see he was on the verge of anything but calm. He got up and followed Ollie across the room.

"It's not your bill, Dirk," Ollie said. "You were a company expense, albeit an unfortunate one. Your expenses will be covered, as well as payment for working in the kitchen Saturday night. The same holds true for you," he said, looking at the woman next to him. "I apologize, I know Chef Carson hired you, I know you work at the New York restaurant—I've seen you there, working hard. But at this moment, I don't remember your name."

The woman was silent, her face unreadable. She started to smile, then stopped it when she noticed the man beside her looking at her.

It was Mary Pisano who answered. "Her name is Darci Fox."

"She's part of the catering crew," Dirk said to Ollie. "If you knew or cared anything about your wife's business, you'd know that."

Ollie looked back at him as if he hadn't spoken. "You may pick up your luggage now and leave."

"May I? Maybe I should let the cops know what we just heard you say. Something about killing your wife?"

Again, Ollie ignored his comment. "Just carry your luggage, Dirk," he said, exasperation now coloring his tone. "I'm assuming you've apologized to Ms. Pisano? She could have made life very difficult for you."

Mary held up her hand to hush him. "It's all right, Ollie."

"You're a gracious person, Mary," he said, and then turned his attention back to Dirk. "You have the address of the place where I've reserved a room for you. They're expecting you. I don't want you anywhere near this place. The police will pick you up if you step on the property. Stealing things from here? What were you thinking? You're lucky you're not sleeping on the dock."

Ben noticed the look on the man's face, his unreadable glance at the young adoring woman beside him. Then the man looked back at Ollie.

"And you, Oliver, are lucky I don't . . ."

Dirk didn't complete his sentence and Ollie went on as if no one else had spoken. "The place you're staying is a boarding-house run by a woman who is expecting you. She has curfews for her guests and instructions to call me—or the police—if there's trouble. Follow her rules or sleep on the sidewalk. Or maybe the police department will accommodate you."

Ben watched the exchange, seeing the tightness in Ollie's posture and the anger coloring his face.

"As soon as the police are finished with this part of the in-vestigation, you can leave town," Ollie said. "We will be in touch."

"In touch," Dirk responded. "And what does that mean?"

"What it means for the immediate future is that you and I have an appointment tomorrow at the courthouse."

Dirk was silent.

Ben wondered what was going through the young man's head. He offered few hints, his strikingly handsome face seem-ingly incapable of it. The chef he had worked closely with, who had somehow supported him financially, if he read Ollie right, had just been murdered, and the man showed no emotion other than resentment. No, it was anger. Piercing anger. But toward what? That she had died? That he was here in Sea Harbor? That he didn't like Oliver Bishop?

The woman beside Dirk shifted her stance, lowering to the floor a large purse that had been hanging from her shoulder.

Ben looked at her for the first time. She was pretty, but with an alertness about her, as if on the lookout for the enemy. A street-wise look. She was listening carefully to the exchange be-tween Ollie and Dirk, her look passing from one to the other, taking in every word of it. She was clearly younger than Dirk. And clearly in love or besotted or enamored with the man standing next to her.

Ollie looked over at her. "You don't have to go with him, Ms. Fox. I'd be glad to arrange a way for you to go home."

"Hey, go for it," Dirk said to the woman. His voice was cold.

She ignored his words and Ollie's too, as if neither had spoken. Instead she took a step closer to Dirk and looped one arm through his, looking up at his face. She placed her other hand lightly on her belly, the beginning of an enigmatic smile curling her lips.

Dirk seemed not to notice, but Ben had. He nodded slightly at her, as if acknowledging it, and Darci's smile grew, as if there now existed an unspoken understanding between them.

Dirk was looking at Ollie. A long, measured, angry look, as if he wanted to say more, but was calculating what it might bring. Or if this was the place.

Then, without a word or a glance at the people sharing the space, he shook free of Darci, grabbed the luggage off the floor and headed toward the door.

Darci picked up her purse and followed him.

Everyone watched as the two of them exited, first the man without a backward glance, and then the young woman.

The front door closed with a slam, holiday bells jingling wildly on the wreath that hung on it.

With relief on her face, Mary looked at the two men. "Thank you, Oliver. I've had some wonderful people stay here, but those two were not among them. I'm sorry to say that—I know they were part of the catering crew. But I'm happy they are gone. I hope you understand."

"Of course I do. I'm ashamed at what Dirk's done. He's a grown man, but acts like the world owes him something. Lidia would have been chagrined. Maybe it was a reaction to her death, stealing those things from here. I don't know. It wasn't even that he needs the money. But I hope he realizes what he's done."

"I just hope they performed their job at the mayor's party better than they have here," Mary said.

190 *Sally Goldenbaum*

Oliver nodded, but his thoughts seemed to be elsewhere. His eyes were still on the door, and the man who was no longer standing in the hallway.

"Did the young woman stay here the whole time, too?" Ben asked Mary.

"Yes, she was here. They were together all the time," Mary said. "Although one night last week, the middle of the week, I think, they went out together, but she came back alone. I was doing some work in my office and heard her pounding on the door. She was clearly upset. I lock up after ten and the guests use their own keys after that. She didn't have hers, or theirs—so I let her in. I don't know where he was, but wherever it was, she wasn't happy about it. And later that night, after he finally came in, there was a lot of foot stomping coming from their room."

"Sounds like a couple's spat," Ben said.

Oliver shrugged. "I don't know if they were a couple. I don't keep track of things like that. The crews, the hires, the chefs, all that was Lidia."

"I can tell you one thing about her," Mary said. "She adores that man, and I don't use that word loosely. But there was so much anger in him that I'm not sure there was room for her."

Ollie was half listening; then he said, "I remember her now, Darci. I even remember when she started working for Lidia, though I'd almost forgotten it. Lidia told me about a young woman who had come in the back-alley door of the restaurant kitchen, much the same way she herself had done. This person had walked in, then spotted Lidia and told her she wasn't a chef, but she could be helpful and wanted to work in that kitchen. She could fix things, help out, wash dishes.

"It was uncanny, in a way. So similar to what Lidia had done, except, clearly, on a different level. She wasn't a culinary person. I guess Lidia had a sense of déjà vu, though, and hired her. Anyway, that's where she must have met Dirk. But I don't know much more about her."

Mary listened to the story thoughtfully, then said, "It's interesting what some people go through to achieve their goals. I wonder if there was something Darci wanted from that job?" She glanced toward the door. "I suspect she may have gotten it."

Ollie was silent for a minute, thinking about that, then looked up. "Well, no matter, they won't be bothering you again, Mary. And if you find any more things missing, or damage to anything, please let me know."

A sound outside took their attention to the front of the inn. Mary opened the door and they looked out.

A small rental car was pulling out of the drive, with Darci at the wheel. But vrooming past her was a black Harley, taking the turn onto Ravenswood Road at high speed.

Mary shuddered at the noise, then looked back at the two men standing behind her. "Seeing that bike reminds me that I was mistaken a minute ago when I said there was one night they didn't come back here together. There were two nights. The night of the murder was the other."

Ben and Ollie gave her their complete attention.

"Dirk Evans never came back that night at all. At least if a frantic girlfriend banging the front door to get in and the absence of that bike in the driveway are any indication.

"The bike and its rider didn't show up until dawn."

Chapter 29

Oliver had agreed with Ben that a move to their guesthouse would be a good thing to do. It would save Mary from dealing with the media, and give Ollie some privacy. Even Mary, who considered Oliver Bishop a new friend, had thought it was a good idea.

"I don't have much to pack," Oliver assured Ben, and he meant it. In a short while, his suitcases were stashed in Ben's car.

But there were still Lidia's things to deal with. Everything had been searched by the police, some things recorded and taken to the station, but the rest needed to be packed up to be shipped back to the apartment in New York.

"I can help with that, Oliver," Mary said. And with her efficient assistance, the three of them emptied drawers and cleared the closet, and the whole of Lidia Carson's week in Sea Harbor was packed in cardboard boxes, double taped, and piled at the door.

Ben looked at the boxes as they got ready to leave the suite. Ollie stood beside him.

"It doesn't get much worse, does it?" Ben said.

"Nope," Ollie said, his voice slightly husky. Then he turned away quickly and picked up one last bag to take with him. "Lidia's personal things," he said. "I'd better take it with me. A couple pieces of special jewelry, wallet, photos. Things she liked to have with her on trips."

Ben looked at the bag. He suspected it was probably the only thing of Lidia's Ollie would ever look at again. The cardboard boxes would never be opened. With no relatives to give them to, they'd end up in a donation center somewhere.

"I'm ready," Ollie said, turning away from the door and heading down the steps, where Mary waited with their coats.

Soon they were back at the Endicott's home on Sandswept Lane, the heat turned on in the backyard guesthouse, and its new occupant comfortable and grateful.

"I'm glad Ollie's here," Nell said late that afternoon. "And I think it's good he didn't want to join us this evening. He needs his time. And we need ours, too." They stood together on the deck, bundled in warm jackets, looking down the sloping yard to the small guest cottage on the edge of the wooded yard, soft light coming from the windows.

They'd each carried out a glass of wine, a toast to the end of the day. To Ollie finding some temporary peace in their cottage. To a quiet moment in a day filled with drama.

The light at dusk in Sea Harbor had always seemed ethereal to Nell, mesmerizing her. It wasn't like the sunsets of her childhood in the Midwest. Or even nearby Boston, where she and Ben had lived for years. There was something otherworldly about the radiant light of Cape Ann sunsets, even on gray days. It was magical. Something they needed that day.

Ben had filled Nell in on his talk with Ollie at the Ravenswood B and B, including the encounter with Dirk Evans and his girlfriend.

"Lidia was supporting Dirk," Nell repeated several times,

trying to get her arms around that one fact, and trying to relate it to everything else that had gone on in her day. Her thoughts were crisscrossing uncomfortably.

Then the conversation shifted, and she told Ben about her day, about Izzy and Cass's day. And Izzy's detailed telling of Molly Flanigan's connection to a murder.

Ben listened carefully, not saying a word.

All the way to Molly's declaration that Dirk had killed Lidia Carson.

When she was finished, Ben said simply, "Molly needs to talk to the police."

Nell took a sip of her wine, then set it down on the deck railing and looked out into the darkening sky, meeting the sea so effortlessly you couldn't tell where one ended and the other began.

"I talked with Izzy and Cass about that later today," Nell said. "We thought that, too. But when Molly realized that Dirk had been caught stealing and hadn't been arrested for murder, she was embarrassed at blurting out the terrible accusation. Suddenly it became her opinion, not a fact."

"Did she retract it?"

"Cass had said yes and no. Molly had heard Dirk say those words, but it was a couple years ago. And lots of people, in a fit of anger or even as a joke, say they'd like to kill someone. Molly couldn't come up with a reason why Dirk would want to kill Lidia. Apparently, Lidia excused disruptive things he did, got him out of jams, and seemed to protect him from his many inappropriate actions in the class. He also seemed to get money from her. It puzzled students in the class, Molly said."

"Nell, the fact that Molly was even connected to the woman who was murdered would be of interest to the police."

"Why? Many people were connected to her."

"And the police are talking to many of them."

Nell thought about it, and realized what she was doing. Trying to protect a young woman who had, very recently, explained that she didn't want people protecting her.

"Do we know where Molly was on Saturday night?" Ben asked.

Nell was still. She tried to remember snippets of conversations, Cass's text on Sunday telling them that Molly was home safely. However, they'd learned later she'd actually come back the night before. . . .

"She came back Saturday night, but stayed overnight at Shannon's," Nell said.

"Do you know what time she got back in town?"

"Don't go there, Ben. Molly's connection to the chef was some time ago. What possible reason would she have for harming her now? This is Molly Flanigan we're talking about."

They stood in silence for a while. Their hands and faces now stinging from the wind that had picked up off the ocean. They watched the light sink into the curve of the ocean waters as they finished their wine.

Finally, when the ocean was nearly black, the lobster boats moored, and the town's evening lights casting a warm glow along the distant Harbor Road, they headed inside, each of them silently sorting through the challenges the new day would bring.

Chapter 30

Wednesday was crisp, the sky sunny, and for the last few days, at least, the snow was on the ground and not coming down from the sky. Sidewalks in the Endicotts' neighborhood were clear of ice, and Nell took the opportunity to bundle up and walk the mile or so to Harry's deli to meet Birdie.

The two friends had agreed to an informal meeting with the library building committee to give them some ideas on a capital fund drive. Having the meeting at Harry Garozzo's deli was extra incentive to attend. "But don't volunteer for anything, Nell," Birdie had instructed, knowing how easily both of them got pulled into things. "I want this to be our winter of rest. We're not off to the best start, so let's not make it worse."

But an hour before the meeting was to begin, they each received word that the gathering had been canceled.

"Canceled," Birdie said to Nell. "Thank heavens. You're the only one I want to see today. I am feeling the weight of all this messiness around us."

Birdie suggested they go to the deli, as planned. It was easy and her taste buds had been whetted by the thought of Harry's *ribollita* soup, his midweek special. That, and being with her dear friend, could help the day along significantly.

Nell felt the same.

The crunch of Nell's boots as she walked across the snow packed street and down Harbor Road was pleasing to her ears. Clean and uncomplicated. The sound and feel of winter. She slowed as she got to Izzy's store, then stopped completely to admire the fairyland of small knit snowmen and Santas, reindeer and bells and tiny sleds, decorating a tree in the window. She thought about going in, just to say hi, but realized Birdie would be waiting at Harry's deli.

Instead, she took out her phone and texted Izzy: **Ribollita soup day at Harry's. Join us if you can get away.** Then she quickened her step and hurried down the block to the aromatic warmth of the deli.

The front area of the delicatessen was crowded as it always was at that time of day, filled with people crowding the glass-fronted cases, waiting for their orders. Nell breathed in the fragrance of basil and oregano, pungent cheeses and steamy wine-laced soups, as she walked through, waving to friends who were waiting in another line for take-out muffuletta and meatball slider sandwiches or Harry's special soups.

The dining room was off to the left, through a wide, curved opening. A bustling area that today looked filled to capacity, the sounds of voices and laughter and Frank Sinatra filling the air.

"Nell, back here." Birdie waved as Nell made her way around tables toward the back of the dining area.

But the wave was pure formality. Harry Garozzo always sat "his girls," as he called them, at the same table. Even the waitresses were known to change customers' seating at the last minute if one of the knitting group came in. It was the most private, Harry claimed—a table for four against the waterside windows, with the best view of the harbor. On a wide ledge beyond the window, a herring gull named Stracciatella, in honor of a special Garozzo dish, spent a good part of each day checking out the pastas and soups just beyond her yellow beak.

"It's packed today," Nell said, unwinding her scarf as she reached their table. "I'm surprised Harry had room for us."

"Holiday shoppers," Birdie said. "And, of course, Harry had room for us."

Nell smiled, then pointed to the front of the restaurant. "There's a whole table of women sitting on the other side of the room, singing along with 'Old Blue Eyes.'"

Birdie chuckled at the image. And they both knew that Sinatra's light baritone would be floating holiday songs through the outdoor speakers until the holidays were over. It was a beloved contrast to Elvis's "Blue Christmas" being sung across the street at Jake's. "Only in Sea Harbor," residents would say to their out-of-town guests, a reluctant note of pride in their voices.

Nell shrugged out of her coat and sat down, her elbows on the table. "I'm going to have to lean in close or you won't hear a word I say."

Birdie chuckled at the truth of it, tapping her ear as if to give it more life.

"Ah, finally. My girls are here." Harry Garozzo's booming voice reached them before he did, his ample body making its way around the tables to the window spot. A smile took over his entire face, jowls moving. Reaching the table, he pressed his fingers to his lips and stretched his hands toward each of them, sending a welcome their way. He straightened up, sliding one palm over his bald head and sighed. "These holiday seasons— lottsa people, long days, and so many steps. *Ack.* They're taking a toll on me, Bernadette. This growing old is for the birds. You never heard me say that, but it's happening."

"You've been saying that for the last ten years, Harry. And you don't look a year older. But you could start taking some time off, now and then. Your Margaret might even like the company."

Birdie and the deli owner had been friends for more years than either of them could count—friends from when they were young and Birdie's Sonny Favazza was alive and well and the center of Birdie's life and that of their group of friends. It was only Harry and a couple of that old group, like Gus McGlucken, who ever called Birdie her given name, *Bernadette*. Sonny loved the name Bernadette, and it's what he always called his young bride. Birdie knew that Harry probably imagined Sonny saying it, hearing his friend's voice, when he used it, too.

Nell loved to watch the back and forth between them, the lifetime memories that wrapped their friendship tight. The warm insight she got of Birdie's early life from these longtime friends had become an ongoing gift. She wasn't a part of their history, but as Birdie's closest friend, she was a beloved, trusted "almost insider."

"So tell me, ladies, what is new?" Harry asked. He wiped his forehead with his giant paw, then grabbed the back of a chair, giving his back some relief.

"You're usually the one who tells us that, Harry. Your little deli oasis here buzzes with news," Nell said.

"Sure, sure. And I listen to the buzz, every bit of it. It hasn't found a murderer yet." He stood and looked around the room as if he might have missed something, but what he saw, instead, was Izzy Perry, hurrying toward him, her loose, streaked waves falling around her flushed face, an unzipped parka flapping against her jeans.

"There's news?" Izzy asked. Her brows lifted into a scattering of bangs. She squeezed Harry's arm and quickly slipped into the chair next to Nell.

"News is that my *ribollita* soup today is perfection." His lips pursed as his fingers squeezed together in the air, saluting the day's special.

"Hey, Harry, before you run, do you know anything about New York cooking schools?"

"Are you asking how I learned to make the best Italian dishes on the North Shore? It was my mama, the finest cook in Italy, God rest her soul."

Izzy laughed. "I know that, Harry. I was just wondering if you'd heard of the Institute of Culinary Education. ICE, for short. But not the government one."

Birdie and Nell were looking at her now, interested.

"Have I heard of Christmas? Sure. My mama could have taught their students some things about how to make *stracciatella*. Nobody did it like her." He gave a nod to the gull, perched outside the window, who was watching the chef curiously. "Margaret and I went to some food conventions early on in the city. Heard some talks by their people. It's a good place, I hear. You think Sam needs you to cook fancy, Izzy? Just bring him here."

"I have a friend interested in studying culinary arts."

"My cousin Tony's wife, Antonietta, works there, but she's no cook. Works in admissions, I think. If your friend wants the scoop, she could call her. She loves to talk. I'll give you her info. But where's your waitress, anyhow? I know you guys don't have all day." He turned around, spotted Shannon Platt in the distance, and waved her over.

Shannon looked up, then came quickly, shoving another table's check into her apron pocket.

"Best waitress in town," Harry said as she walked up. "But she needs to settle on one place—mine. Look how tired she looks."

"Hey, Harry, lay off," Shannon said, forcing a smile. "Now scoot out of here so I can get my friends here some food." She waved him off with her hand.

Harry guffawed at being bossed around and moved on,

greeting another table, then back to the kitchen, where an aproned worker was calling his name.

"Not enough sleep, Shannon?" Nell asked. "I can see why. What a week you've had. But a good one in one respect, Molly's back."

"Absolutely," Shannon said. "That's the best news in the world."

"But you look bothered," Izzy said. "Anything we can help with?"

Shannon glanced around the crowded room, her eyes settling on a table near the opposite side of the restaurant. It was almost hidden behind a wait station.

The three women followed her look. The table was empty.

"*Good,*" Shannon said, seemingly to herself, but the word was audible.

"No problem, I'm fine now. It's just a customer I had. But it looks like he's gone now. That can happen in this business. You meet all kinds. Even no tippers who have lots of money."

"Did he give you a hard time?"

"He gives me a hard time by breathing," she said, her voice hard.

And then she quickly changed the subject, pulling out her order pad, and replacing her grimace with a smile. "Sorry about that. Having you three here is brightening my day."

"Is it true? Mae says you and Molly are taking one of our knitting classes?"

"Absolutely, it's true, Iz. Cass is insisting Molly take time off—spooked by her being gone, I guess. So we signed up. Beware of two neophytes wielding knitting needles." She laughed, and the old Shannon was back, her bright smile in place.

Izzy, Birdie, and Nell laughed with her, feeling her uplifted mood.

"So, what'll it be?" Shannon asked. "Harry's *ribollita* soup?

He's probably already scooping it up for you, so you don't have much choice. But it's terrific, anyway."

They agreed it was terrific, and Shannon was gone, moving between the crowded tables in a practiced way.

"Well, what was that about?" Nell asked. "I've seen her handle rude, profane, impossible diners. She never shows any negative feelings about it."

"You're right, Aunt Nell," Izzy said. "It seems more than a rude customer. Something's on her mind. Did you see who had been sitting there? Her stare was pretty intense."

Neither of them had, but the soup arrived almost immediately, and troubling thoughts were dropped as they devoured the savory Tuscan bread soup. They wondered, as always, what Harry had done to make it taste different from the time before. Each time it was tastier, even more delicious, with different vegetables added, a new spice here or there. And always with Harry's leftover homemade bread floating on top. Kale was holding center stage today.

"I'll have to ask Harry if he massaged it first," Birdie said with a chuckle. Then she dipped her spoon into the thick soup and sighed with pleasure—massaged or not ceased to matter.

Nell paused long enough to look over at Izzy and asked, "Why were you asking Harry about that culinary school?"

"When we found out Molly was interested in it, Cass and I wondered if maybe they had any remote classes, maybe something we could give her for her birthday. Or a 'just because' gift. And maybe, when the time is right, she'd go back in person. Reactivate her application."

"Has she said she wants to do that?"

"No. I think that whole experience with Dirk scared her away from the school, from New York, from everything she had going for her. But it was a while ago. Things would be different this time."

None of them knew how or why things would be different,

but Izzy went on, "Anyway, I told Cass I'd see if I could get some info."

Izzy then went back to her soup, nearly inhaling it. "So good," she murmured, coming up for air. "But I need to get back to the shop."

"Are you AWOL?" Nell asked.

Izzy laughed. "No. Just a busy time, and we have a couple back-to-back classes today. But it's not as urgent as it has been. Mae has Luna doing the young moms' class, and she seems to be crushing it. I saw her holding one woman's new baby for her while she was teaching her to knit a stitch—it was crazy funny to watch. Luna was jiggling the baby on her hip while she chanted that old knitting tune."

Izzy began miming Luna's jiggle while and singing: "'In through the front door, go around back, out through the window . . .'"

". . . and out jumps Jack,'" Birdie finished.

"Right," Izzy grinned. "And with her other hand, she's showing the woman how to move her yarn and needles to the tune. And it all worked. Baby was happy and the mom was on her way to being a knitter."

Nell and Birdie laughed at the image.

"Those young moms love her," Izzy went on. "She's blunt with them, but they talk right back to her. And then hug her on their way out. Who would have thought?"

Birdie was shaking her head, wiping laugh tears from her eyes. "That's just perfect."

"Has she admitted openly that Beatrice is her cousin?" Nell asked.

"Only when pressed. Apparently, the two of them never got along, even when they were kids. Luna's mom made her babysit for 'pretty, perfect Beatrice' all the time, she said, and Beatrice made fun of Luna in front of the other kids, getting them to call her 'lunatic.' They never liked each other."

"So their moms were sisters?" Birdie asked.

"Yes. There was a third sister too, but she didn't have kids."

"That must be the Aunt Gert Luna mentioned," Nell said. "The one who liked Scotch."

Izzy laughed. "Could be. Apparently the aunt favored Beatrice. But there's something else going on there, something about that third sister, and we haven't gotten it out of Luna yet. But we will, now that she has moments of niceness, every now and then." Izzy grabbed her bag and cautioned, "But keep your guard up. She can still be old ornery Luna when she wants to be."

"Ornery or not," Nell said, "she somehow managed to move beyond bad feelings to help Beatrice in those awful moments Saturday night. I don't think I could have done it. Beatrice is hard to approach for things like that. But Luna seemed to know the right things to say. Or maybe to just be there for comfort."

"Even more amazing to me is the fact that Beatrice let her do it," Birdie said.

"It's a season of miracles," Izzy laughed. She gave her aunt and Birdie each a quick hug and disappeared into the throng of diners.

"Luna comforting our mayor. Imagine," Birdie said, shaking her head.

A short while later, she and Nell dropped their napkins beside now-empty bowls and left bills beneath the check, readying to leave.

"This has been not only a delicious meal, but a therapeutic one," Birdie said.

"A little bit of normalcy can go a long way. I needed it, too." Nell pushed out her chair and started to stand.

She was stopped by a familiar voice coming from a short distance away.

Both women looked up.

"Ollie, hello," Nell said, smiling broadly, as he walked over to their table. "It's good to see you. Here you are, staying in my own backyard, and I need to go to Harry's deli to run into you."

"That is one amazing guesthouse you and Ben have. I am so comfortable there, Nell. You thought of everything, even Peet's Coffee and muffins. Thanks."

"We like having it used by special people."

"I'm glad I could oblige. The bookcase in there rivals a library's. You and Ben must have unloaded all your college classics for your guests' reading pleasure."

"We try to keep our friends educated, Ollie."

"Well, I'm deep into *Moby Dick*. Though I have to say," he paused, his brows lifted, a slight smile forming, "the spine on old Melville's work is pretty tight, like it hadn't been cracked. I'm just wondering . . ."

Nell laughed out loud. Having sat through an English lit class with Ollie many years ago, he knew very well she probably hadn't finished it. And more likely hadn't even started it. The famous classic had been a source of frustration for Nell. She was surprised that Ollie even remembered such a small detail of her life.

"You're looking dapper today, Oliver," Birdie said.

Nell checked out his attire—a tailored blazer, dress pants, and a tie—and agreed. "That's almost formal wear here in Sea Harbor. Do you have a meeting?" she asked.

"I suppose you could call it that. We had an engagement at your courthouse today, just around the corner. In fact, it seems everything in Sea Harbor is just around the corner, or down the road a short way. I'm liking that. But as for the meeting, one of our . . . well, one of Lidia's workers got in a bit of trouble."

"I understand," Nell said. "Dirk Evans, I believe."

Ollie nodded. "That's small town for you. Ben met him, as you may have heard."

"As did the nanny of a dear friend of ours," Birdie added.

"Oh?"

"Her name is Molly Flanigan."

Ollie's forehead wrinkled. He repeated the name. "The name is slightly familiar, but I'm not sure why. I don't think I know her. Did something happen here in Sea Harbor?"

"No. This happened in New York. It happened in a class Lidia taught."

"Lidia taught classes sometimes for a culinary institute, but I was removed from that whole business. I know she brought Dirk on staff to help out, but only because he can't hold jobs anywhere else. It somehow satisfied the money she was giving him. Dirk doesn't like to work. I reminded her often that Dirk was an adult. Not a kid. But somehow it didn't seem to matter."

The conversation had turned away from Molly, and Nell was happy to let go of it. For now. "So Dirk wasn't in the class to learn cooking techniques?"

"No. The guy thinks his looks can get him out of anything, but that hasn't always happened."

"So he's an employee with problems, but Lidia kept him around?" Birdie asked.

"Yes, and no. The connection is deeper."

Both women sat up, interested.

"Dirk's mother was Lidia's only relative. She died some years ago and Lidia was appointed Dirk's guardian. He was still a kid, about fourteen or fifteen when he came to New York. We weren't officially married yet, although Lidia was already managing things for me. And we'd been essentially together for a few years."

"That's a huge responsibility," Birdie said. "I have a granddaughter whom I love dearly—every minute with her makes me more alive. But I understand completely how encompassing a responsibility it is."

"Lidia's situation wasn't quite like yours, Birdie. The arrangement was never a good one. Dirk didn't make it easy.

He didn't want to be in New York, and Lidia wasn't the mothering type—and here she had this teenager thrust on her."

"'Thrust on her'? That's not a good way to look at it," Nell said.

"No. But that's how she felt. They may have been related but they didn't know each other. In fact they'd never met until he came to live with her."

"Then why did she accept being the guardian?" Birdie asked.

"I asked the same thing. The lawyer who arranged it said it had been worked out years before, whatever that meant. Lidia had agreed, and she didn't protest the legal agreement after Dirk's mother died. I think she thought it wouldn't be for long. It was never that clear to me, even after we were married, and Dirk remained in our lives, for better or for worse."

"How difficult for the boy. That's a tough age," Birdie said. "It couldn't have been easy for either of them."

"Indeed. Lidia put him into a boarding school for a couple years. But he was around, even after the custodial relationship ended when he turned eighteen. Mostly, he came around for money."

"I know many young people in their twenties, even older, have trouble these days, finding jobs, moving their lives forward. Families help out," Birdie said. "It happens."

"Yes, it does. Lidia tried in her own way with him, I guess. So I'm trying, too. At least until we get through all this."

"He's an adult, Ollie," Nell said, more sharply than she intended.

Ollie didn't answer. He glanced over his shoulder, then looked back. "It's complicated. But Lidia was his guardian, and she was just murdered. Maybe that's reason to give him a little slack, even if he doesn't deserve it. Which he doesn't. But he'll be coming out of the men's room in a minute. I should go."

"Don't forget about coming up to the house, Ollie," Nell

said again. This time, it sounded more like a demand than a social request.

Ollie nodded, a half smile saying he recognized the tone. "Will do," he said.

But Nell wasn't at all sure he would. The Ollie she was meeting all over again had turned into a complicated man.

She and Birdie watched as the older man nodded to the young man coming out of the men's room. A familiar face that now had a name. And a history. They walked toward the front door together, not speaking.

"I guess Ollie's not going to introduce him to us," Nell said.

"That's fine," Birdie said. "What would we say to him? Sometimes it's best to meet people fresh, not knowing anything about them. I'm afraid it's too late for that to happen with Mr. Evans."

Nell and Birdie got up a few minutes later, heading toward the exit themselves.

"I have to make one stop," Birdie said, remembering. "Ella ordered some bread for me to bring home."

Nell moved out of the crowd's way to wait for her. She found an empty space, standing in a small niche near the front door, behind a short divider wall of hooks accommodating coats and boots. And out of everyone's way. She glanced through the front window and watched Ollie walking down the street, alone now. She wondered briefly where he was going, what he was thinking, and made a mental note to repeat her invitation to come up to the house. She wondered, as she did often these last few days, if Maddie was somehow with him as he walked, helping him, guiding him.

She hoped so.

Moving slightly, she craned her neck to look beyond a hanging jacket to see where Birdie was in the line.

But instead of finding Birdie, she spotted Dirk Evans standing near the hostess stand, not far away from her. At first, she thought maybe he was paying the bill, although that was usually done at the table. Then she saw him lift a hand, tapping a waitress on the shoulder.

"Did you like the tip you got?" he said to the woman's back, loud enough for Nell to hear, but only because she was looking and watching his mouth form the words.

Shannon spun around, a look of surprise on her face, followed immediately by one of disgust. Nell watched as she stared down at the handful of bills he held out in his hand.

Nell could almost see the scenario in her head. Ollie had always left generous tips, even when he had little money. Dirk must have scooped it up as they walked away from the table and pocketed Shannon's tip.

But the words that spilled out of Shannon's mouth in a torrent covered more than a tip.

"How do you live with yourself?" she said, her tone cutting and sharp. Several people waiting in line glanced at the couple, then turned back to their own conversations.

Shannon turned away from the hostess stand, her voice low. "You made my friend's life miserable," she said.

Although her words were muffled, Nell could make out most of what she was saying. She moved a step closer, hoping Shannon would just walk away. But she continued.

"You ruined all her plans, you made her feel worthless—even in that class that I wished she'd never ever taken. You manage to destroy everything you touch."

Dirk lifted one hand to stop her words. Nell saw his brows pull together, his face dark. "Hold it right there," he said. "I didn't destroy her 'dreams,' like you call it. What do you know, anyway? Lidia Carson had your friend's application to that school rejected. That's who smashed her dreams. So, what do you make of that?"

Nell could see that Shannon was calm, undeterred. And determined. Her hands were gripping the edge of the hostess stand. Nell though for a minute she was going to try to pick it up and throw it at him.

Instead, she glared at him, then said, her voice steely, "You are ultimately the cause of everything that happened to Molly, Dirk Evans. You're a thief, a misogynist, an all-around awful person. Only time will tell what more we can add to your résumé. What might it be? *Murderer?*"

Nell could no longer see Dirk's expression, but his body language appeared calm, relaxed. Untouched by Shannon's words. When he turned slightly, Nell thought she saw the beginning of a smile.

His voice was modulated, almost easygoing. "Is that what you think, little waitress?" His mirthless smile grew. "Maybe you should do a fact check? And while we're slinging mud about people, why don't you try this on and see how it fits . . .

"Maybe it was your precious friend who killed our favorite chef."

Chapter 31

On Thursday, Shannon and Molly walked up the steps of the yarn shop's knitting room in triumph. They'd finished their first knitting class and felt like pros.

"I can make a stocking stitch," Shannon told Mae proudly. She handed her the pile of yarn she was about to buy.

"*Stockinette,*" Mae corrected, amused. "And what are you going to make with your stockinette stitch, Miss Platt?"

"I'm thinking a cable sweater for my father for Christmas."

Mae tossed her head back, laughing.

"Christmas of 2037," Shannon said, grinning. "Gotcha, Mae." She stashed her purchases in her backpack and headed over to Molly, who was checking out a display of brightly colored knit animals. She gave her friend a brief hug, along with a whispered "call me," before leaving for a work shift at Coffee's.

Mae glanced over at Molly. "And what amazing knitting feat do you have planned, Molly?"

Molly gave a hint of a smile. "Maybe a hot pad? A short scarf?"

"Wise woman. An excellent place to start," Mae said. "But if you're as good at knitting as everything else, it may be a long scarf before you know it."

"Don't count on that, Mae. But I like it a lot. The feeling of that soft yarn between my fingers is so soothing. And I love the rhythm of the needles. A kind of yoga for fingers. It's almost like I'm playing an instrument."

She paused, looking around the room and the two smaller rooms off to each side. Then back to Mae, now helping another customer. "Mae, have you seen Cass around? She left the house this morning before I had a chance to talk to her today and she forgot some keys she's duplicating for me. Ruthie at her office thought she might be here. She had some knitting project she needed Izzy to fix for her."

Mae looked over, chuckling. "That happens fairly often, Izzy fixing knitting messes for her. But yes, I saw her scoot by a few minutes ago. The boss and Birdie are in that supply room Izzy also uses for an office. It's just off that room with the rocking chairs. I imagine Cass found them."

Molly followed the point of Mae's index finger and walked into the fiber room, then spotted the open door to another, smaller room. She knocked lightly on the frame, spotted Izzy and Birdie half-hidden behind a stack of cardboard boxes, and walked on in.

The room was small and stuffy, with the only window pried open an inch.

Izzy looked up. "Hi, Molly. I'm glad you stopped in. How'd the class go?"

Birdie waved a hello from the stool she was resting on.

"I'm guessing she's already better than I am," Cass said from a small desk and chair off to the side. "And that's after, what? How many years?"

"There you are, Cass." Molly looked her way and smiled. She held up the keys, then tossed the ring to Cass. "A better knitter than you? Not a chance. But class was great. Luna was even nice to me, sort of. Except she instructed me not to knit Joey sweaters. They wouldn't be good enough for him, she said. And then she said it wasn't a concern, though, because it might be years before I could knit anything wearable. My stitches were too tight."

"That's our Luna," Cass said. "You can also ask Danny for help. He's a decent knitter."

"Danny is a wonderful knitter," Nell said, coming through the door. "He actually made me a pair of mittens one Christmas."

Izzy laughed, stood up, and walked over to hug her aunt. "How wonderful is all this? My favorite people in one space— one *tiny* space. But why are you all here? What have I done?"

"I was picking up a skein of yarn and some needles," Nell said. "Mae thought I must be here for some meeting and sent me in. Being a curious sort, I came."

"No meeting, no nothing, except supply deliveries, plenty of toilet paper and paper towels"—she motioned to a shelf filled with supplies—"and a new box of alpaca yarn, which my one and only shop volunteer is helping me with." She nodded at Birdie. "But I love to have my best friends stop in like this. It beats unpacking boxes."

"Let's hope no one else pops in," Cass said. "There's not enough air in here."

"Well, I'll give you mine, Cass. I can't stay long, I'm on my way to the market to figure out something for knitting night tonight. I just thought I'd say hi."

Molly spoke up. "Nell, do you have a minute to talk before you leave?" she asked. "It won't take long. I was hoping I'd see you today—this storeroom meeting was meant to be."

Nell chuckled. "Sure, Molly. What's up?"

"Would you like privacy?" Izzy asked, starting to get up from her spot on the floor.

"Oh, no," Molly said quickly. "This isn't private. Well, it is, but certainly not from any of you. In fact, you should hear it, too." She smiled.

A not-quite-relaxed smile, Nell noticed. She took a stack of flyers off a chair and sat down. She could see that the others were perplexed and curious at once. She was, too, probing her mind to figure out what Molly might have needed to tell her.

Except for Ben, she hadn't shared anything about the argument she'd overheard yesterday between Dirk and Shannon. She'd told him about Shannon accusing Dirk of destroying Molly's dreams, making her feel worthless.

Nell looked at the beautiful young woman standing in front of them—like an anxious student feeling stage fright about making a report. A pang of sorrow and anger went through her at the idea that anyone could treat another as Dirk had treated Molly. But, she and Ben had also agreed, although Nell admitted it reluctantly, it was truly a case of "he said, she said."

Nell's instinct was to believe Shannon, or practically anybody, over this man.

Dirk Evans seemed hell bent on hurting people, Molly in particular, and she did wonder if the police might need to know what he'd said. Could someone else end up being hurt by this man?

When she'd talked it over with Ben, he had assured her that Dirk was on the police department's radar, and he wasn't going to be hurting anyone in Sea Harbor, which was comforting. Ben had agreed, however, with her concern about Dirk spreading rumors about a dead woman he disliked.

Especially when it pulled Molly Flanigan into the fray.

Sitting there among her closest friends, Nell suddenly felt overwhelmed by the week, by the party, by finding Lidia's body in the snow.

Molly brought her back to the nearly airless storeroom with her next words.

"Nell, Shannon and I had a long, overdue talk last night.

About all sorts of things. And one of the biggies was that she saw you in the deli when she was talking to Dirk. And she was pretty sure you overheard their argument, and Dirk's accusations—"

Birdie, Cass, and Izzy turned toward her.

"Argument?" Cass said.

"When?" Izzy asked.

"Shannon was right," Nell admitted, then explained to the others. "It was when we were leaving Harry's deli. I did overhear Dirk and Shannon arguing."

She turned back to Molly. "I think I heard most of it. I wasn't trying to eavesdrop. Frankly, I was worried about Shannon. Dirk was behaving so obnoxiously to her, and she was so angry at him."

"Dirk's presence within hundreds of miles causes worry, that's for sure," Molly agreed, with a whole-body flinch that they all noticed. "He can make people furious faster than anybody else I've ever known."

"I'm guessing Shannon told you what he said," Nell continued, keeping her own tone as calm as possible. She remembered how she hadn't felt calm at all as she witnessed the angry exchange between Shannon and Dirk, and how Shannon had leaned toward him as if her anger was pushing her at him. Dirk had tried to look so nonchalant, as if nothing she said could possibly bother him, but she'd also seen how his body seemed to tighten, and how much bigger he was than the young woman confronting him so bravely.

"He's a very angry man," she said out loud. "Imagine, drawing Shannon into something like that, in the middle of Harry's deli. What was he thinking?"

But the argument had dissolved on its own when Harry had walked over and asked Shannon to help him with something, leaving Dirk standing at the hostess desk all alone. A minute later, he had pushed open the front door and disappeared down Harbor Road.

Nell took a deep breath now, to rid herself of those feelings. She looked around at the women looking attentively back at her.

"It sounded to me that he was spreading lies about Lidia Carson," she told them. "And drawing you into it, Molly. But Shannon probably told you all that. She's your best defender, I might add."

Cass and Izzy exchanged glances, still unsure of what was going on. They knew firsthand that Shannon was fully capable of taking care of Dirk Evans.

Molly was quiet for a moment when Nell stopped talking, as if choosing her words carefully. She took a deep breath, released it, and then she said, her voice a little shaky, "They weren't lies, Nell. For once in his damnable life, Dirk wasn't lying."

Chapter 32

Nell was stunned.

Cass, Birdie, and Izzy remained, not yet knowing enough to make sense of the conversation and trying hard to piece things together in their own minds.

"I'm not sure what you mean, Molly," Nell said. "What did Shannon tell you?"

"She told me what Dirk said about Lidia. That she got my application to the culinary school rejected, which meant I lost my scholarship, too."

"Lidia Carson did what?" Cass said.

"That's what happened," Molly told them. Tears came to her eyes. "Lidia arranged for my application to the culinary institute to be thrown out. I'd been unofficially accepted, a scholarship was being considered, but Lidia had a lot of power, and she convinced them to rescind everything. I'm not sure how Dirk knew about it—it was a private thing—but it happened. He clearly thought he'd be shocking Shannon, but he wasn't. She already knew."

Cass was still trying to digest the news about Lidia. "But why would she do that?"

Nell looked at a puzzled Birdie and Izzy and saw they also shared Cass's reaction.

"I'm with Cass. Why on earth would she do that? It doesn't make sense," Izzy said.

"I agree," Molly said, some of the old hurt showing on her face. "But it made sense to her."

"What kind of sense?" Cass asked, looking as if no such sense could exist.

Molly thought for a minute before answering. Her answer, when it came, was simple.

"I think Lidia did it to get rid of me," she said, looking at each of them, "so I wouldn't make life difficult for Dirk. And consequently, I suppose, for her."

"But Dirk was making *your* life hell," Cass said angrily, sounding as though he stood there and she could shake a fist at him. Or throw a punch.

Molly nodded. "Yes. And that was the problem. You asked me the other day why I didn't report his behavior. Well, I did. Not to the police, but I reported it to her. To Lidia. I finally got up the courage to tell her everything he'd done to me. All the harassment, the lies, following me, spying on me. Threats, destroying my things. I told her *everything*, including the things he'd done in class to sabotage me. I told her I thought we should contact the police, maybe even the school, because I couldn't get him to stop, and I was afraid of him.

"I trusted and respected Lidia," she said, her eyes filling with moisture. "She was my cooking idol, my teacher, and my mentor. She had praised me and bragged on me and made me feel as if I could be successful in the culinary world, which I already loved. So I trusted her. I thought she liked me. I thought she wanted good things for me and for all of her students. She had always acted as if she did. I begged her to help me, because I didn't know where else to go for help. She had taught me so much. I guess I thought she would teach me how to handle this terrible problem." Molly managed a smile. "She even praised my soufflé as the best in the class."

"What happened when you told her?" Nell asked. "Surely, she believed you."

Molly was older now, but Nell's thoughts were of that younger Molly, and of the fear and of the strength it must have taken to approach her mentor.

"She listened to everything I said, winced at some of the details, and then she told me she needed time to think about it. I think she *did* believe me, which made the whole mess so much more difficult to handle. And when I left her office that day, I naively expected Dirk to be gone by the next class."

"And maybe arrested, too," Cass muttered.

The others were quiet, and Molly went on.

"But I was wrong. And a few days later, Lidia informed me that the institute was no longer considering my scholarship or admission to the program, and that it would be best for everyone if I no longer participated in her class, either. I was creating too many problems, conjuring up troublesome things that she was having a difficult time believing. It could be bad for the school. It didn't speak well for me, either, she said."

For a minute, the tiny storeroom was deadly quiet.

Finally Cass asked, her voice tight with anger, "Did people know what she did? About your application and your scholarship?"

"No. I never told anyone, except Shannon, and I only told her after I decided to come here. I guess my pride kicked in and I didn't want her to think the school rejected me because I wasn't capable.

"But those years ago—it truly feels like a lifetime ago—I didn't talk about it. I was torn up inside. I felt humiliated. My dream had been touchable, right in front of me, and then *poof*. It was gone. And I was left with nothing but the fear of Dirk."

"But someone, I don't know who, someone needed to know," Cass insisted.

"It was over, Cass. I had to put it behind me and go on with my life. What happened to me, it wasn't fixable. I had to"—she smiled wryly, sadly—"adjust. Find a new dream. I figured I'd be blackballed at any other school, and I was also afraid I couldn't get any jobs in restaurants in the area, not if I had to use her as a reference. I knew I couldn't leave that time blank on a résumé. I didn't know what else to do, and I didn't want it to poison my life.

"So I put it behind me and went back home for a while. I didn't even tell my parents. I was afraid they'd want to sue Lidia or the school, and that wouldn't help me get anywhere in the restaurant world, either. I wouldn't be bringing it up today except I owed you an explanation, Nell, of what you heard." She looked around the room at the others. "And that's really all there is to that. It's a blip in my life."

"More like a black hole," Cass said. "It's not fair, it's not right."

"Could you have gone over her head, Molly?" Izzy asked. "Most schools have committees or departments that handle things like that. Grievances, unprofessional behavior?"

Molly shook her head. "Lidia was powerful in that world. She did favors for people and they returned them. I was no one to them. I didn't really blame the school."

"There must have been some way to let people know what an unethical person she was." Cass's face was flushed.

"Hey, Cass. It's okay. Really, it is." She looked around the small room, surrounded by expressions of caring and frustration. "You are all such amazing women. I love you guys. Maybe if I had had you in my camp back then, we could have put on armor, grabbed swords, and taken up the fight. But the thing is, I didn't think that telling people, even people in the class or in Lidia's own business, would have been good for anyone. Not really."

None of the other women had the heart to say to her at that moment: *It might have helped other women in Dirk's future.* But then Molly answered even that unspoken objection.

"You know who I have worried the most about? Other women who might go into Lidia's classes, and whom Dirk might harass and threaten the way he did me. I feel guilty over that. I wish there was something I could have done, maybe should have done, but there didn't seem to be anybody to help me. I would have handled it differently now, maybe."

"No wonder you left town when Lidia was coming," Birdie said, her voice mixed with sympathy and indignation. "You probably couldn't stand even to be in the same town with her."

"Birdie, really, no. I left because I was afraid Dirk was stalking me after that episode at Luna's. And he was. Lidia was not on my mind at all."

Nell persisted, feeling absolutely baffled by the story of the chef's abrupt change of mind and heart about Molly. "But why would Lidia do that to you?" "Surely, she must have had some idea of what Dirk was like?"

"I think she did," Molly said. "But I had to forgive her and move on."

"How could you forgive her for that?" Cass asked Molly. "I don't think I could."

Molly looked thoughtful, but also tired, as if she had said all that she cared to say, and had the energy to say.

"I guess we all have that part in us that wants to hurt somebody who hurt us," she said softly. "Especially when it seems unfair. I did for a while. I wanted to tell everyone what she'd done. Let the culinary magazines know. I wanted people to think poorly of her. But then I thought, 'why?' To make me feel better?' It wouldn't get me a job or into that school. I realized that I might feel good for ten minutes. And maybe she'd even lose some customers at her restaurant if it got out. But in the end it would only hurt other people, like the cooks and dishwashers who worked for her. And I might not have liked myself much for doing something like that. In the end, that wasn't something I wanted to live with."

Even Cass was silent. Her emotion was visibly softening as she watched Molly, knowing she had escaped a bad situation. And remained whole. But she still said, "But *him*. What he did to you."

"If he hadn't treated you like that," Izzy pointed out, "you would never have had a reason to tell Lidia about him, and you wouldn't have lost your chance at your next training and your scholarship."

"Yes," Birdie said, "we don't know why Lidia treated you as she did, and we don't know what made him abuse you, but we do know they both mistreated you terribly."

Nell caught her eye, and she and Birdie looked at each other with a new, shared worry.

Cass asked, "Why did Lidia take Dirk's word over yours?"

Molly shrugged. "It was a pattern with her. And I don't know why."

"I can guess why," Nell said. "Apparently Lidia had some kind of guardianship relationship with him."

"What?" Molly asked, and stepped back in surprise. "Is that true, Nell?"

"Yes. Ollie explained it to Birdie and me. Dirk's mother was a relative of Luna's. She'd made a promise to step in when the mother died."

"But he was an adult when he was in Molly's class," Birdie pointed out, "so Lidia was no longer his guardian."

"She still might have felt like one," Nell said. "Apparently he had trouble holding jobs and she thought she had some responsibility toward him."

"That might explain why she overlooked so many things he did," Molly said, thinking aloud. "Also, I think she meant it when she said she didn't want trouble. Messes. Anything that might look bad for her, or for the class, or even for the school. Things she didn't want to deal with, like someone she was once responsible for harassing a student big-time. Apparently, it was easier to get rid of me than Dirk."

"An old story," Birdie said with a sigh.

"But honestly," Molly said, "it doesn't even matter anymore. It happened. It's done."

"Molly," Cass said. "It matters. You matter. To us."

They sat in silence, thinking about it. It happened. Life happened.

"And now she's dead," Molly said. "So, especially now, why would I bring it up again? Who am I to sully her memory with an old hurt, an old story? She accomplished a lot, did many things for women in the culinary profession. Let her be known for that. I'm bummed I had to reveal it at all, even to all of you."

Nell listened carefully, watching this put-together young woman. She seemed so very wise.

But in spite of that, Molly was missing one vital part of her story that explained why it would have been good for her to confide in them earlier—in friends who cared for her and might be able to help. Even old stories were sometimes important in a murder investigation.

And from the tone in her voice and the sincerity in her words, she truly hadn't considered the part she had missed.

But Nell could see that Cass, Birdie, and Izzy had felt its weight immediately.

And Dirk Evans, for better or worse, had also considered what Molly had missed.

Lidia Carson, with all her successes and all her misdeeds, had been murdered.

And Molly Flanigan, Cass's marvelous nanny, had a perfect motive for that murder.

Chapter 33

They all were silent for a few minutes, until Molly cleared her throat and suggested she'd better get going. She'd taken up enough of their time.

"No, wait, Molly," Izzy said, grabbing some bottles of water from a small refrigerator near her desk and passing them around. "Can we talk for a few more minutes? There are some things about all this that you may not have thought about."

Nell agreed. "There are parts of your story we might be able to help you with,"

Molly frowned. "I don't understand," she said. "This is all ancient history. It's all behind me, and certainly not as awful as what happened right here in Sea Harbor a few days ago. There's nothing more to think about."

"You didn't think of it, Molly, because you haven't done anything wrong," Izzy said. "Clearly, you've dealt with what happened in New York—and in a really admirable way—and put it behind you. It's understandable that you haven't thought of it in the context of a murder."

"Murder," Molly repeated.

"Lidia's murder. But as difficult as it is, your story is something the police would want to know," Nell said gently.

"And from you," Izzy said. "Not Dirk Evans or anyone else."

Suddenly Nell thought about Ollie. Had he known about this? But certainly he'd have said something. Especially after their brief conversation at Harry's deli. He said he didn't know Molly, only that her name sounded vaguely familiar. But now she wondered if he was telling the truth.

"The police are already on Dirk's case," Izzy explained to Molly. "And I don't think he'd hesitate a second to pull you into this, just like he tried to do with Shannon."

They watched Molly's face as she grappled with the truth of what they were saying. And the anguish of dredging up a difficult time in her life for others to look at. To inspect.

"I understand what you're saying," she said. "Of course I do. It's just that—"

"It's just that it seems like another unfair thing Lidia Carson seems to be throwing at you," Cass said. "This one from the grave." Cass's voice was both angry and sad.

Molly reached over and patted Cass's knee, as if telling her employer that things would be okay.

Then she took a deep breath. "Okay, friends, what you're saying is, I should tell the police that I knew Lidia in an earlier life, and she did some things that hurt me, sort of ruined my life for a while. Do I have it right?" She tried to smile, but they could all see the toll it was taking on her. And though it wasn't mentioned, the topic of Dirk Evans would come up all over again.

Izzy nodded. "The lawyer in me encourages you to do this soon, Mol, before Dirk Evans does."

"They'll ask me lots of questions."

"Which we have already subjected you to. So you're prepared," Izzy said.

"But this time you have us," Birdie reminded her. "With or without armor, we're here, my dear. And we're amazing warriors when we put our minds to it."

Molly gave a small smile.

"One more thing, Molly," Nell said. "Since we're not setting boundaries on intruding on your life, I'll add another suggestion. I have a husband who makes amazing blueberry scones most winter mornings. It's his one talent, he says. But, in fact, he has another one. He has a law degree, just like Izzy, and is excellent at listening and giving advice when it's wanted—also like his niece. But he has one thing over her. His best friend is the nicest police chief you've ever met."

Molly's smile was uncertain, not sure what was coming next.

"Why don't you come for a blueberry scone and see if they're as good as Ben thinks they are. You can talk with him, and when you say the word, he'll introduce you to his friend Jerry. Or respect your right to tell him 'no thank you'."

Molly was reluctant to accept the offer at first. It was clear that she wanted to handle this by herself. The whole discussion, digging up something that she had long ago buried, wasn't settling comfortably with her, and she wasn't sure adding one more person into the mix would help. They could read it on her face.

Then Nell remembered that Molly had once told her that Ben reminded her of her own dad. Wise, patient, and funny. And always honest, she'd said.

So Molly finally agreed.

After everyone had cleared out of Izzy's storeroom office space to breathe clean air and get on with their day, Izzy pulled up a chair and sat at her small desk. She fished in her bag for the number she had gotten from Harry before leaving the diner:

Antonietta Garozzo's extension at the New York school. Izzy pulled out her phone, checked the time, then dialed.

Antonietta answered on the first ring. The students were long gone for winter break, she said, but she still had to show up. And any friend of her husband's old cousin Harry was a friend of hers. She had all the time in the world to talk.

Chapter 34

Birdie hurried into Elliott Danvers's bank, a minute before closing. She had left Harold happily waiting in the town car, the heat on, and his new headphones bringing him an episode of a true-crime podcast, a recent obsession.

She waved to several friends, then hurried across the marble lobby, glancing up at the rotunda second floor offices, then dropped off her papers with one of the bank officers. Turning around quickly, she nearly collided with a well-dressed man in a three-piece suit.

"Elliott Danvers," Birdie said. "Just the person I was hoping to run into. And I almost got my wish, literally."

"I saw you from my office and came down to say hello. It's been a while, Birdie. I've been hoping to see you, too."

"I had a glimpse of you recently, but across 'a crowded room,' as the song goes."

"The mayor's party."

She nodded.

Elliott's smile faded into a solemn expression, as one did when there was a subtle—or overt—reference to tragedy. He shook his head. "Nasty business. Very sad. I hope Chief Thompson brings this to a close soon."

"When I saw you Saturday night, you were talking with Lidia—" Birdie said, letting her comment hang in the air.

"That may have been. Chef Carson called my office the day before, asking for a meeting, but the time wasn't right. She introduced herself to me that night at Beatrice's. Did you meet her?"

"I did. That night. And also two days before."

Elliott nodded knowingly. "So she approached you."

"Yes. She had done her homework to find my connection to the Ocean's Edge, apparently, but she hadn't gone far enough. For some ridiculous reason, she wanted me to convince you and the other investors to get Don to sell. It was foolish of her."

"Don's a friend, yes. But it wasn't a foolish offer, Birdie. I talked to the other investors the night of the party. She'd approached them, too. Don happened to see us, and walked in while we were talking."

"It's Don's restaurant," Birdie said, imagining what Don might have heard. Business associates, but friends, too, toying with his life.

"Yes, it is Don's restaurant. And we all love that place. But investors usually invest to make money."

For a minute, Birdie was taken aback. She looked around Elliott's well-appointed bank, with its gold balcony railing circling a suite of investment offices. Elliott was a generous, community-minded man; his wife, Laura, one of Izzy's good friends. And he did many things that benefited residents of Sea Harbor, usually behind the scenes and without attention. And he owned an investment bank. Elliott was right, of course. And her own financial advisors certainly did that kind of investing for her. It was all about the gain.

But she had never for one minute invested in Don Wooten's restaurant to make money. She had done it to help Don with his dream.

"So the others . . . ?" she asked.

"They were clearly interested. She was offering far more money than could ever be gained from the Ocean's Edge profits."

"And what about Don?"

"Don is a very smart man. He would have been set for life. He caught the gist of the conversation when he came in that night. He listened for a minute and realized then that Lidia Carson's offer had legs."

Birdie imagined the scenario, Don listening to a group of decent men, all friends of his at some level. She thought back to her own conversation with Don that night. And she knew something for sure: Don Wooten was not going to give up his dream, any more than a parent would give away a child. Not without a fight.

Elliott continued. "Don is one of the most levelheaded men I know. But this got to him."

"Of course it did, Elliott. We both know what that restaurant means to him."

"Sure we do. And if we hadn't known, it was vividly clear by the expression on his face that night. He turned and walked out on us, kind of disappeared. I went looking for him later to try and smooth things over, but couldn't find him. I ran into his wife, Rachel, doing the same. He had disappeared. We talked for a minute, and I could tell she was worried. I get it. He loves that place."

"It was unfortunate," Birdie said, turning to go. She was not sure there was more to talk about.

Elliott walked with her to the front doors, holding one open for her.

"But it's all a moot point now," anyway," he said. "And maybe that's for the best. Those uncomfortable moments have passed. In fact, Don was in today talking about updating the place, realizing that it might need some renovations. It seemed he was seeing the place differently. Maybe seeing it through someone else's eyes does that. He's back to the old Don, as far as I can see, and I'm sorry this ever happened."

Birdie had noticed the same thing when she'd had lunch at the Ocean's Edge on Tuesday.

Don Wooten was happy again.

And Lidia Carson was dead.

Chapter 35

Birdie had taken the cork out of the wine before everyone was settled, claiming a dire need for a sip. It was unusual for her. Although she always brought the wine from Sonny's cellar, she measured her drinks carefully. She poured herself a glass and settled down into the fireside chair.

"Interesting day, Birdie?" Nell asked, looking across the room to where Birdie was now fanning the fireplace flames with Izzy's old bellows.

"It will be a fine day, once I get my blood moving again," she said. "What's that I smell?"

"Your dinner."

Nell was standing at her usual place at the library table, stirring a spot of honey and a splash of sherry into a pot of chicken chili. It was her own version, invigorated with green chilies and several spices she was wondering if even Cass could identify. She knew her friend would identify the paprika, oregano, and cilantro, but was wondering if she'd fool her with the cumin and coriander.

"Sorry for two soup-style dinners in a row," Nell said. "Next week I'll go for the exotic."

But her thoughts were far removed from the smells of soup and the exotic. It was the cloud of murder that was hovering over all of them, thick enough that even the thought of Thursday night knitting felt heavy, somehow.

She had wondered aloud to Ben, before she left the house, if he thought having Ollie living in their backyard made it all so present, so close to them? Had that been a bad idea? Maybe for Ollie, too. She had watched him that morning walking down the wooded path toward the beach, restless, as if he needed to get back to his life.

They all did.

"What's up with you, Birdie?" Izzy asked, scattering Nell's thoughts.

Izzy maneuvered her way around the table, placing napkins and flatware on the low table near the fire that she'd started earlier. She gave Birdie a look on her way, placing a hand on her shoulder. "Are you okay?"

Birdie nodded, smiled, and gave Izzy's hand a pat.

Cass interrupted further conversations, coming down the steps slowly, carrying a large foiled wrapped pan.

"Cass, you shouldn't have," Izzy said, walking over to take a peek at the delicacy that could only have come from Molly—no doubt whipped up while baby Joey was sleeping. "What is it?"

"Boozy chocolate fridge cake," Cass said. "That's what it's called. Not fudge, *fridge*. Molly found it in her new favorite cookbook and thought it sounded perfect for the four of us. I'm not sure if there was a hidden meaning in that, but I did see her pour a significant amount of brandy into the batter."

Izzy laughed and took it from her, placing it on the bookcase. She looked back at Cass, who was already sitting down next to Birdie, warming her hands near the fire. She stood back for a minute, looking at Nell, then Cass and Birdie. "Geez, we all look like Abby's old birthday balloons that she still has hanging over her bed—flat. Deflated."

It was the weight of a murder that was too close to them.

And instead of it fading away, safe in the hands of the police or a jail or a courtroom somewhere, each day seemed to bring Lidia Carson's death closer to them.

"Danny was shooting baskets with Tommy Porter last night," Cass said. "Danny's pretty good at asking the right questions and weaseling things out of people. Tommy admitted things aren't moving very fast in Lidia Carson's case. He says they've had lots of calls on the hotline, and lots of dead ends. The fact that Lidia was out of her usual environment makes it hard. She didn't belong here. And neither did her death."

They all agreed with that. Nell, especially, thought back to a week ago, when she looked forward to seeing her old friend. And meeting the woman he'd married. Now it seemed eons ago. And she thought back to it with deep regret.

"I am sure they are finding people who wouldn't have minded if Lidia Carson had never stepped foot on Sea Harbor's granite soil. I am sorry to say, I am one of them," Birdie said. "And I'm sure that's where the police are focusing their attention now."

Cass nodded. "Tommy said that, too, in his own way. They just need something to point the arrow definitively at one of them."

Nell walked over, carrying a tray of steaming bowls of chili and a basket of warm bread. She passed them around and sat in the remaining chair.

"How's Molly doing?" Birdie asked Cass.

"They can't possibly think she had anything to do with the chef's death," her tone daring the police to even consider Moly for two seconds.

And all the while knowing that the police would consider exactly that.

Once wine- and water glasses were filled, and spoons dipped into the chicken chili, conversation stopped, giving way to a crackling fire and creamy chili to lull the discomfort hovering in the room.

Birdie was the first to break the palate-pleasing silence. "I spoke to Elliott Danvers today," she said.

"Elliott?" Nell asked. She took a warm roll and passed the basket to Cass, wondering how the respected banker and community leader fit into the conversation about a murder.

"I'd wanted to catch up with him, to talk about Don Wooten. He knows Don, and I wanted his opinion of how he was doing."

In fact, she'd been spending a lot of time thinking about Don, replaying her conversation with him the night of the murder, then going back over their years of friendship. She remembered the opening of his restaurant years before. A wedding present for Rachel, he'd called it, and they'd all celebrated, toasting Rachel and the wonderful addition Ocean's Edge was to the Sea Harbor coastline. Before sleep finally came and released her from her memories, one thought came to her that she took with her into sleep. A wondering, more than a thought, actually. Wondering about friends—and how many layers deep people are allowed to go to know even their longtime and cherished friends.

"Don's been on my mind, too," Nell said. "He'd been under a tremendous strain. But when I ran into him in the bookstore the other day, he seemed better. More relaxed."

"That's what Elliott said, too. I'm sure much of it is relief. Restaurants can take a toll."

Especially restaurants whose investors, but not its owner, want it sold, Nell thought. But Birdie knew that, too. Wanted it sold to a woman now dead.

"So, what did Elliott say about Don?" Izzy asked.

"Well, we talked mostly about Lidia's proposition for buying the Ocean's Edge. But yes, that's talking about Don. He and the restaurant are one. Lidia had contacted Elliott and the other two investors. That was after I had talked with her and showed her the door, apparently. She was persistent. Two investors were very interested in her proposal to buy Ocean's Edge. The offer was generous and there was a lot of money involved. I'm not absolutely sure where Elliott stood on it. He was noncommittal. Diplomatic. I am thinking Elliott will be our next mayor. But anyway, I want to think that if it had come down to an actual decision, he would have been on my side, or Don's, I should say. The others were considering the sale from a completely financial point of view. Something that they would all benefit from, and Don would have benefitted, too. There were no bad guys involved in any of this."

"But it's a moot point now," Izzy said.

"Yes."

The implications of that hung in the air, and then were set aside.

"Business is business, I guess," Cass said, but her emotions were clearly with Birdie. Cass knew better than any of them what it meant to love and nurture your own company, to treat it almost like your own child. Cass wondered how far she and Pete would go if the Halloran Lobster Company had been threatened somehow.

"This is all too much," Izzy said. "Each day brings this murder closer and closer to us. The murder of a woman none of us know. Yet it's driving these horrible wedges into our lives, our friends' lives." She took a long drink of wine, then set her glass down on the table, a little too hard. She wiped up the sloshed wine with her napkin, then looked over at Cass. "How is Molly handling our advice?"

"Molly's Molly. I'm sure she's not looking forward to walking into a police station and sitting in one of those rooms. If they're anything like the ones on *Rizzoli and Isles*, they're cold and awful. But she's concentrating on finding new games and songs for Joey, and on her knitting. Good distractions, I think."

"She and Ben talked briefly," Nell said. "He's set something up for tomorrow with the chief. But Ben reminded me that it's not going to be a tea party, no matter what. Murder is serious stuff. And Molly, whether she intended to be or not, is in the middle of it."

"She's a strong young woman," Birdie said. "Yet I wonder how strong any of us would be while being questioned about a murder."

"*Suspected* of a murder," Izzy added.

It was a sobering, disconcerting thought, and no one said anything, concentrating instead on scraping up the bottom bits of creamy chili with a piece of roll. For a minute or two, the only sound in the room was the crackling of the fire and a mellow jazz station Cass had found.

Finally Izzy said, "Well, I'm glad Uncle Ben has the time to go over to the police station with Molly. No matter what, he's a wonderful equalizer, and if anything, he'll make Molly a little more comfortable."

Cass nodded. "That's what I told Molly. Having Ben at your side is like walking into the principal's office with your favorite stuffed animal."

That brought chuckles and the mood lightened. A little.

"But like you said, Aunt Nell, it's still serious stuff," Izzy said. "Molly has put the incident behind her, but what Lidia did was pretty awful. And Molly had reason to want to get back at her. We don't think she's that kind of person. But the police don't have that to look at. They don't know her. They look at facts on a paper, in front of them. And honestly? We haven't known her that long, either."

Cass was ready to object to Molly being considered in any kind of bad light. The implications were getting to her. But she held her words back, got up, and headed for Molly's dessert. She cut it into small pieces, grabbed some small paper plates, and passed them around the table.

Izzy took a bite of the boozy cake, swooned slightly, then said, "Okay, I have some news I need to pass on regarding that whole messy incident with the culinary institute."

"Her story's not true?" Nell didn't know if that would be good or bad at this point. Some of Molly's explanations had seemed a little threadbare. Surely, she hadn't misled them about this.

"Yes, and no. Remember when Harry told me about his relative who works at that culinary institute in New York?"

"I remember clearly," Nell said. "It made me wonder if there was any city on the Eastern Seaboard that does not have a relative of Harry Garozzo living in it."

Izzy laughed. "Well, Harry described his cousin-in-law correctly—Antonietta likes to talk. She's worked there forever and remembered the Molly incident—mostly, she said, because it'd never happened before. There was talk about it in the faculty lounge. It upset some of the teachers that a board member could pull rank to 'screw a student'—her words, not mine."

"So she confirmed Molly's story?" Nell asked.

Izzy nodded. "Well, yes. But with some extra information. She also remembered the incident because they'd been having trouble shortly after that with a fellow who was on the payroll in Chef Carson's classes. A guy who was hired to 'help out,' like an assistant. His job was to make sure everything was ready for the classes. Getting kitchen machinery out, all those things. But the word *help* was defined differently by several women in a recent class.

"And even though Molly left New York without having told people she hadn't been accepted in the institute—and why—they'd all heard the story. But unlike Molly, they had nothing to lose, because the women who came forward had decided they weren't as passionate about being a cook as they had thought, and they had canceled plans to apply to the culinary school. In fact, they were happily quitting the class, too. They said it'd become dysfunctional. But first, they went directly to the school and reported the kind of 'inappropriate help' Dirk was providing. 'Bad stuff,' Antonietta said, not enough to call the cops, but plenty to bring the hatchet down on him, she said. Lidia seemed to rise above it all, somehow, but poor Dirk is no longer employed by any class sponsored by the institute. And due to some faculty member's insistence, the part of Molly's file that Lidia had fabricated and sullied was reviewed, and it no longer exists."

"That's an interesting update," Cass said.

"And good news for Molly, should she decide someday to go to school there," Nell said. "The police will check out Molly's story and end up with more information about Dirk. But I don't think there'll be anything there that gives him a motive to kill Lidia. But his actions that night are suspect, for sure."

"He seems so guilty already, I don't know what more they need," Cass declared.

Nell looked at her. Cass was one of the most practical women she knew. Dirk was despicable. But nothing they had learned so far pointed to him being a murderer. Cass knew that, too. And the worry on her face revealed that she also knew, as they all did, that it was now Molly who had the motive. Nell got up and collected their dessert plates, feeling Cass's frustration.

Birdie wiped her hands clean and took a drink of water, glancing now and then into the fire as the others talked, listening carefully. Eventually she slipped on her glasses and leaned down, rummaging in her knitting bag for her needles, the beginning of the second sleeve of Harold's Aran jumper attached to them. She pulled it out and smoothed out several inches of garter stiches with the tips of her fingers, the Irish merino wool soft against her fingers, soothing.

Nell looked over and smiled. "I know you well, Birdie. Your quiet lapses are often filled with some kind of ruminating."

Creases deepened in the corners of Birdie's clear gray-blue eyes. "I'm thinking that my mind is fuzzy and my stitches on Harold's jumper are too tight. And it's because we are all frustrated and talking in circles. It's what we have been doing since

Sunday, trying to pull at stray threads without a pattern. But we won't figure it out that way. We need a better plan."

She took off her reading glasses and offered a small smile. "And now I would like another half glass of Pinot, please."

Birdie had lightened the frustration and brought them back to clear thinking, all at once.

"I think you are like that wine you like," Izzy said, leaning over and refilling her glass. "You get better with age."

Birdie smiled and picked up her knitting, frowning at the tight stitches.

"It's true what you say, Birdie. We care so much for the people tangled up in this tragedy that our emotions are blocking our thinking and we just keep rehashing things. That's not like any of us," Nell said.

"No, it's not. And if we don't slow down and figure out for ourselves who killed Lidia Carson," Izzy said, looking around the group, and then at the half-finished argyle sock on her lap, "we'll never have these projects finished by Christmas."

"Perhaps we should begin with a heartfelt wish or prayer that it won't be one of our friends," Birdie said. She was concentrating on her stitches and not looking at the group.

And then she added, looking up and speaking slowly, "It could be, you know."

Chapter 36

It was the kind of sentence that in a TV mystery would have called for a commercial break. But tight stitches required immediate action, and Birdie, who had proposed the exercise, began, all the while her small fingers working on the precise stitches of Harold's jumper.

"Who seems to have a reason for killing Lidia?" she asked. And then she followed it with a frown, her own recent words coming back to her.

Izzy sighed. "You're right. That's what's awful, Birdie. Some are people we like or love or want to stay exactly where they are in our lives. And in our hearts, we know they didn't do it. But, okay, the only way to remove the awful cloud over those people is to think with our heads first. Prove they didn't. Or better yet, find the person who did."

"So. Our suspects. Including our friends," Birdie said gently, glancing over at Nell, then back to her knitting. "We start with Oliver Bishop. He had motive."

Nell nodded, unflinching. Finding out from Ben that Ollie had misled her about his marriage status had at first surprised her, but not entirely. But the financial agreement certainly put Ollie in a terrible spot.

When Ollie had finally agreed to move into the Endicotts' guesthouse, they had given one another an understanding hug. And Ollie's assurance that he wasn't trying to cover anything up. "I'm heading over to the police station today," he had said. "Chief Thompson and I are becoming buddies."

But Nell also knew that the years between college and the present were filled with experiences and growth, highs and lows, which changed one. Everyone. What she hadn't had time to figure out was how those years had changed her old friend.

Cass was tapping on the table with a knitting needle, bringing their thoughts back to business.

"Birdie's right. Ollie's the prime suspect," Cass said. "Although in Danny's mysteries, it's almost never the husband. I think that's because he is one and he's protecting his breed."

They laughed, and Birdie went on, adding to Ollie's profile. "The night of the party, he had a bit too much to drink. He also seemed to disappear a couple of times. But then, we all wandered around a bit. But it's something to consider."

"And talk about textbook motives," Izzy said. "A husband who will become rich once his wife dies. It's almost too perfect, too obvious."

"But we can't overlook the obvious," Birdie said. "Nor the ordinary. It's where we might find answers. What is right in front of us. The normal . . ." She looked at an imaginary list above the old corner fireplace.

"*Oliver Bishop,*" she said, as if writing it with her voice.

"That sounds a little like *The Hunger Games,*" Cass said, looking up, as if she could see the name scrolled across the air.

Izzy chuckled, then grew serious. She knew Cass couldn't say Molly's name. It was even difficult for her to do it, but it had to be put out there. "Molly clearly had motive," she said.

"We know she was in town that night, though I don't know if anyone saw her at Beatrice's."

"*Molly Flanigan,*" Birdie said. Another name added. "For obvious reasons. What a terrible thing that woman did to her."

"And then there's Dirk Evans. He disliked Lidia," Cass said. "He was there that night—"

"But he would have had plenty of chances to kill her, other than at a party in Sea Harbor," Nell said.

"True. Ollie did, too. But if the murder wasn't planned, and somehow at that moment Ollie or Dirk snapped, that could explain the timing," Izzy said. "I've seen cases like that."

"Definitely," Nell said. "The police are assuming it was not a preplanned killing."

"But not random, either," Izzy said. "It wasn't some crazy person just wanting to kill someone."

"No, it was someone who had something against Lidia," Birdie said. "And what led to the murder could have been festering for a long time. Or not. We humans can be an unpredictable species."

"But as much as we don't like Dirk, he really doesn't have a motive, as far as I can see," Izzy said. "He doesn't like her. But I would imagine there are others who don't like her." She smiled. "I'm one of them. And I don't even know her."

"We know Lidia was Dirk's guardian," Cass said. "That may be a motive all by itself. There are lots of bad guardianship stories out there."

Nell agreed. "Ollie mentioned that Lidia wasn't happy to be named his guardian. If Dirk knew that, it could have left scars with him. With any child that age. It makes me sad just to think of it."

"I think we need more information about the guardianship," Izzy said, making a note on a piece of paper. "Why did she accept being his guardian?"

"And I wonder what kind of life Dirk had before he came to live with Lidia," Birdie said. "It might not mean anything. Or maybe something."

"Let me look into those things," Cass said. "Maybe we should all do some googling for starters, and see what we can find about some of these people."

"All right then, we're adding *Dirk*," Birdie said, looking up at the phantom list.

"Dirk has a girlfriend," Nell said. "She's one of the catering crew. She was working in the kitchen that night."

Izzy perked up. "Yes, the mystery woman," she said, then shared with the others the hug that she and Cass had witnessed the night of the mayor's party. "I presume that was the girlfriend. It was that kind of a hug."

"Ben met her," Nell said. "Her name is Darci Fox. She's staying here until Dirk leaves."

"What's she like?"

"Ben said she's attractive and doesn't talk much. He got the feeling she was slightly frightened with everything going on, but hid it well behind a defensive stance."

"It must be the woman the guys at Jake's bar talked about," Izzy said. "The one who ran out after Dirk the night he went to Luna's."

"Wait," Cass said suddenly. "She followed him. That's what one of the guys said. Dark hair, nicely dressed. Attractive. I think I saw her that night. But not at Jakes. I saw her standing on the sidewalk outside our house, staring at Molly standing in the doorway. So that's the girlfriend. Darci Fox. She must have followed her boyfriend. Interesting."

"Maybe we can find out more about her," Izzy said. "I'll have to ask Mae if she's been in the shop. Usually, when women are detained here because of bad weather or something, they end up in the yarn shop, whether they can knit or not."

"I wonder if Darci knew Lidia?" Birdie asked.

"They must have known each other. At least slightly, since Lidia had hired her to be on the catering crew," Izzy said.

"Yes, they knew each other," Nell said, looking up from a scratch pad she was doodling names on as they talked. "Darci worked in Lidia's restaurant kitchen in New York. I'm not sure what she did, but that may have been how she met Dirk."

"Shannon might know something about her," Cass said. "She was working with her the night of the party."

Nell looked over at Birdie, sensing she was deciding whether to say something or not. "What is it, Birdie?"

Birdie leaned her head to one side, as if still exploring her own thoughts. Then she said, "I was thinking about Shannon."

"Why? Do you think she might have been involved in all this?" Nell asked.

"She told us it was a good job. Good pay," Cass said. "She was happy to get that work."

Birdie's voice was quiet, thoughtful. "I'm not sure. But she was there that night . . ." She looked around the table at each of the women, as if she had more to say, but perhaps wanted the others to follow her thoughts through to their own conclusions.

Izzy sat back in her chair. "You have a point, Birdie. She was Molly's best friend. And she knew about what Lidia had done to mess up Molly's life."

The train of thought was clear. And credible. Shannon didn't want to speak against her boss, but it'd been clear to several of the women at the table that she didn't like her. Quite possibly hated her for what she'd done to her closest friend.

"What if that was the real reason she took the job, not the money, but to be there that night. . . ." Izzy let the thought hang over them.

Cass was frowning. "But it was Dirk, not Lidia, that she was so angry with."

"That's true. Dirk had also harmed Molly. Maybe Shannon thought Lidia should have stopped him, controlled him," Birdie said.

"Maybe not when the ward is no longer a ward, but a grown man," Izzy said, playing another card. "Once Dirk turned eighteen, Lidia had no responsibility over him. In fact, it's puzzling that she continued to hand out money to him."

"I still think it would have made more sense for Shannon to kill Dirk."

"Maybe," Izzy said.

And more "maybe" and more "what if" speculation followed.

Then Birdie said she wouldn't add Shannon to the list. "Not yet," she said.

"We've gone over Don Wooten's stressful week," Cass said.

They all nodded. A person they all liked and respected. Who had a sound motive, and who would have benefited greatly from Lidia's death. And, in fact, he had.

The Ocean's Edge was no longer on the chopping block.

Don Wooten was added to the mental list.

Nell checked the time. It was late, and the discussion had been exhausting. "Before we leave, we need to think about something Birdie has brought up numerous times."

Birdie smiled, suspecting what was to come.

"It's what we need to do when we're trying to know someone better, especially if that person is no longer living. A challenge, no matter what. And in this case, someone we're expecting not to like."

"Getting to know Lidia," Birdie said. She smiled, getting up from the chair and collecting her things. "Yes, perhaps one of the most important things for us to do is to walk in Lidia's shoes as best we can—to find out what she did, who she was, what she liked and didn't like, all those things that might possibly have made a friend or foe or family member—or even a stranger—kill her."

She wrapped herself in her coat and gave each of them a squeeze as she headed to the door. Then she smiled and, with a small wave, said in a very Birdie-like manner:

"Something tells me that Lidia's shoes, as the song goes, 'were made for walkin'"—and so we shall."

Chapter 37

"This murder investigation isn't keeping people inside their houses, no matter what anyone thinks," Mae said. "Look at our shop, Izzy. It's like a Macy's Christmas sale." She spread her arms wide for emphasis. A group of women were heading down to the back room, where a class on knitting Norwegian Selbu mittens was beginning. And their departure didn't begin to clear the main shop area. It was still filled with customers, the thrum of knitting talk mixing in with the giggles of kids in the children's room, and strains of "Frosty the Snowman" coming out the door, while their moms searched for the best yarns for sweaters and hats and warm Santa socks.

"Maybe it's crowded because we're warm and cozy and have free coffee, cider, and Santa cookies," Izzy said. "Oh, and childcare helpers in the children's room."

"Well, sure, that helps a little, I guess," Mae said with a chuckle. "Maybe it's not completely my charm bringing them in. And it's sure not Luna's—"

"You may have to eat those words, Mae. I overheard a customer ask for her specifically today."

Mae harrumphed. Then softened it. "I must admit the cookies she brought in were quite tasty. But anyway, it's great that we're helping people think about things other than murder. I think we should give me a raise for Christmas."

"Who knows, Maybelline? Check that stocking carefully."

Mae chuckled. "And you know I'm half kidding about Luna. She's doing okay. I mean, I wouldn't give her a *raise*, but . . ." Spotting some customers moving her way to pay for their purchases, Mae stopped talking, straightened her narrow shoulders, put on her best smile, and headed for the checkout counter.

Izzy hurried off, hoping to escape to her office to check on incoming orders and deliveries—and a raise for Mae. Hurrying proved impossible, however, as she had to stop every few steps to answer a question, greet a customer, straighten displays. As she made her way, she caught snippets of conversation, convincing her that as safe and secure as the yarn shop felt, her customers didn't feel so safe outside:

"We're not going out at night at all, not until they arrest whoever killed that poor woman."

"I told the kids, they're not going caroling, not this year, not until things are settled."

"It's a small town, for heaven's sake. Why haven't they caught anybody?"

Mae hadn't been entirely accurate, it seemed. People hadn't forgotten that a murder had occurred in their safe town—and even more, that no one had been arrested for the crime.

True, people were out in daylight in safe places, doing festive holiday activities, but even in the comfort of her shop, customers mixed talk about yarn with rumors and conjectures of a mayor's party that ended in a murder.

She spotted Luna on the other side of the room, where her newest employee was straightening yarn in cubicles and talking with customers. Izzy wondered if Luna was being deluged with questions about the murder. Her little secret that she was Beatrice's cousin was now a known fact around town.

It was understandably a point of interest to a lot of people that the slightly eccentric protester and vocal dissenter of many of Mayor Beatrice Scaglia's policies was, in fact, a relative. A curious tidbit for the gossip mill. It also made Luna appear to be a good source of information about a murder at her cousin's home, a festive event that Luna had claimed would be a total failure. A festive event that ended in a murder . . .

Izzy started to work her way over to Luna, to check how things were going, when someone needing help stopped her from behind.

"I've been waiting for twenty minutes," the voice complained.

"Oops, sorry," Izzy responded, turning around. She looked into the face of an attractive young woman and smiled at her with genuine sympathy. When her shop was like this, it truly wasn't easy to squeeze one's way around in it. And while Mae was checking people out as fast as she could, she treated each one as her best friend, asking about sick husbands, new babies, holiday plans. And almost always with a good-natured smile.

Yes, a raise was definitely in order for Mae.

"I need something to knit while I am stuck in this town. Would you show me what you have?"

Izzy's first impulse was to tell this unhappy customer to look around. They had plenty of everything, and it was all out in the open for everyone to see. But she collected herself and regarded the customer kindlier. Then paused, wondering if she should know this person's name. There was something familiar about her. She was tall, almost Izzy's own height, but dressed better, in Izzy's humble opinion.

She glanced down at her blue apron, with SEA HARBOR KNITS scrolled across it in knitting stitches, and a pair of well-worn blue jeans beneath it. Definitely not glamorous, but at least they were clean, she thought, damning herself with faint praise.

Over tight jeans and a black cowl-neck sweater, a gold-linked necklace showing against the wool, the customer wore a blue coat, belted, and a matching knit hat pulled snugly over long, dark hair. There was something familiar about—of all things, Izzy thought—the frown. She was young, but had a semisophisticated look, in the way that Izzy had noticed many teenage girls did these days. Her customer wasn't entirely at ease in it, not born to it, but trying her darndest to be. A Tik-Tok imitation was Izzy's assumption.

"Why are you staring at me?" the woman asked with an increasing edge to her voice. "All I need is help, which is in short supply, it seems."

The woman's age, nineteen or twenty, Izzy guessed, combined with her bad manners, made her manner doubly offensive. But Izzy swallowed her reactions. "Of course. I apologize. I was trying to figure out where we may have met."

The woman shook her head. "Not a chance. I don't live here."

"Somewhere else then?

"Like I said, I don't live here. Of course I live somewhere else."

"No, I meant, maybe we met somewhere outside of Sea Harbor?"

She ignored Izzy this time. Something about this customer was putting her off her stride. But before Izzy could try another approach, Luna Risso showed up beside her and elbowed her way into the conversation.

Or lack of conversation, Izzy thought. Why was this young woman throwing her off balance? She could have been the girl's babysitter just a few years back.

"Who are you?" Luna said to the woman. And then without

waiting for an answer, she said, "It's clear you need help. I will help you." She nodded to Izzy, and Izzy smiled back, relieved.

"Well, thank goodness somebody can help me."

With that for good-bye, the woman followed Luna across the room.

Izzy had the grateful feeling that Luna had come over, not so much to save the customer, but to save Izzy. Another surprising move from her unexpected holiday employee.

She walked back over to Mae and whispered, "Do you know who that young woman is?"

Mae looked over the top of her glasses, following Izzy's finger point. Luna was leading the woman across the store, pointing out yarn and needles, plucking them off the racks as she went. The woman seemed to follow her obediently, letting Luna take charge. Not at all with the defensive tactic she tried on Izzy.

"I don't think I've seen her before. That is, until she walked in five minutes ago."

"Really? She told me she'd been here twenty minutes. And no one was helping her."

"One of those," Mae said with a nod of her head. "Well, it's good you passed her on to Luna. She has a knack for putting difficult people in their place. Being one herself, she knows the right techniques, I guess."

Izzy offered a small smile. Then she asked, "So she hasn't been in here before? You never forget a face, Mae."

Mae squinted, then said, "That's true. And there is something familiar about her. But I think it's actually her coat, not her face." Mae thought about it as she processed a credit card and handed it back to a customer, along with a bag of yarn, a thank-you and a smile. "Okay, I think I remember where. My gentleman friend Henry and I were at Jake's tavern after work last week. Not our usual place to go, but Henry loves their oyster night spread. I think the coat was there. I didn't notice the person in it."

"I didn't know you were so into fashion."

"My twin granddaughters nieces in college," Mae said with a laugh. "Thanks to Rose and Jillian I'm—how would you say it—'with it' these days. That's a coat they'd like. Those cinched-in-the-middle kind. You need to get 'with it,' Izzy."

Izzy watched Luna as she and the young woman made their way into the fiber room, a comfortable space toward the back of the store, with rocking chairs and a couch, and shelves of books about fibers. Framed photos of sheep and goats, alpacas and camels and yaks, lined the walls. One of the customers had cross-stitched a sign that read, OUR SPECTACULAR BENEFAC-TORS and hung it next to a picture of a Hexi Cashmere goat.

"Darci," Mae said suddenly, loud enough for Izzy to turn her head. "That's her name." Mae left her post and walked over to Izzy. "I don't remember seeing the face, but I remember that someone called out to her. Her man friend, maybe. She was with a very handsome fellow. The movie star kind who stuck out in the crowd. I remember the name because Henry sug-gested Darci was short for Darcinda, and people around us laughed. Then he looked it up on his cell. Do you know what Darci means?"

Izzy shook her head, wondering how far Mae would take her story.

"'Descendant of the dark.'" Mae glanced over at a college coed filling in while on vacation who now had a long line of customers waiting to check out. She left Izzy's side and hurried back to help.

There weren't that many women named Darci around Sea Harbor, Izzy thought. Nor ones dating a very handsome man. She bit down on her bottom lip, and narrowed her eyes, and suddenly recalled where she had seen that frown, those eyes, that coat, that long, dark hair, and that attitude before. She hadn't noticed the guy steering the motorcycle that had almost struck her, so she couldn't be sure it was the same handsome fellow that Mae saw, but she was positive the woman with both arms around his waist was the same one whom Luna was currently taming in Luna's inimitable way.

All right, Darcinda, she thought, *let's find out who you really are.*

Chapter 38

Izzy managed to walk through the fiber room without getting stopped again on her way to her office.

She saw a cozy scene, the kind that made her grateful she had left her law firm and turned to yarn with its own long history, its own art, its own professionals and amateurs, and its soft way of soothing hearts, and even sometimes setting crooked lives straight again.

Luna and Darci were sitting on the small couch near the bookcase. Esther Gibson, the police dispatcher, was asleep in one of the rocking chairs on the opposite side of the room, with Purl, the shop cat, curled up on her lap. "I'll Be Home for Christmas" played softly from an ancient CD player in the corner.

The noise and festivity in the other rooms hadn't reached this sanctum yet.

Izzy walked into her office, and closed the door halfway, giving herself a view of the couch while not being noticed herself. The acoustics were such that some of what was said on the couch could be heard in the small back room, even with the door closed. It had interrupted her concentration often enough in the past for her to know. Sometimes the bits of conversation were simply news of schools and kids, and sometimes they were ones that she'd rather she had not heard.

It was Luna's voice that traveled back her way first.

"I can plainly see you've never held a needle in your hand before," she heard her say to the young woman. Luna shook her head and Izzy could have sworn she heard a "tsk-tsk" slip from her mouth. "Shameful neglect is what I call that."

"What's shameful or neglectful about it?" Darci asked.

"Somebody should have taught you. Didn't you have a mother?"

"Not after I was three. She'd have hated knitting, anyway."

"Oh. Well, I'm sorry. How do you know she would have hated it? And what is your name?"

Izzy didn't hear Darci's answer, and apparently Luna didn't, either.

"Speak up, young lady," she said. "I can't hear you. Now tell me your name."

"Darci Lou Fox. And I don't know why my mother would have hated it. She just would. She wouldn't have time for it. She was probably glamorous, not old or bored or poor. Rich and beautiful, that would be my mother. I'll be that way, too. My boyfriend has big plans for us."

"I see. Well, all right, Darci Lou Fox, I am Luna Risso. You may call me Luna, if you want. Or, Matilda, I don't care. Now let's see if you have brains in that head of yours, enough to wrap a piece of yarn around a needle."

"I certainly have brains. You'd be amazed at them. But it doesn't take brains to knit."

"It's time now for you to be quiet and for me to talk," Luna said.

Izzy's eyebrows lifted, expecting to hear the stomp of boots on the hardwood floor as the woman stormed out on her teacher.

But instead, what she heard was Luna's low voice reciting

the "In through the front door, run around back" instructive verse, then the occasional click of needles, and a bossy step-by-step lesson in casting on a row of stitches.

"Not bad for a beginner," she finally heard Luna say. "Definitely not genius, but not bad."

"It's not easy," Darci mumbled.

"That's part of the reason you may find knitted works of art hanging in museums and art galleries," Luna instructed her. "But those are created by geniuses, of course."

Izzy sat quietly at her desk, entertained and reassured by what she was hearing as she thumbed through bills and orders. Soon the only words filtering back to her small room were a litany of knitting terms. Darci was clearly not much of a talker, not that she needed to be with Luna beside her.

Surprisingly, a quiet, clicking, comfortable feeling settled into the fiber room.

Finally Luna said, "All right, missy, you might actually have a knack for this. That's a surprise. I figured you for a dumbbell."

"You're a strange person," Darci said to Luna. "But at least you're real. People in this town are way too nice. Nice can be hard to handle."

"Hmph," Luna said. "Thank heavens I escaped that plague." Her eyes were focused on the most recent knit stitch Darci had dropped.

Darci shrugged. "Who was the woman I was talking to? She's an example of 'too nice'."

"She owns the store."

"And that means . . . ?"

"Izzy is real. She was a lawyer. She's seen stuff. She knows stuff. But she chooses to be kind, which is pretty amazing in this world sometimes."

In the office, Izzy's brows shot up, her eyes wide with surprise. Then she looked back down to her order sheet, smiling.

The couple on the couch was quiet for the next few minutes,

and Izzy shifted in her chair until she had a clear image of the two women.

"Turn that work around, switch hands. You're about to start a new row. And don't drop stitches. Don't mess this up."

"Maybe this'll keep me from smoking."

"Only idiots smoke," Luna said, her eyes on the woman's fingers, the yarn, the stitch. "Don't ever, ever smoke around yarn. It's disrespectful to the beautiful animal who gave it to us."

Izzy watched from her office, half expecting Luna to take a whiff of the woman's wool coat.

"My boyfriend smokes."

"Then he's an imbecile," Luna said. She looked over at Darci's knitting. "That stitch is too tight. Loosen up, missy."

"No, he's very smart. He's going to be someone someday."

"Who is he now?"

"What?"

"You said he'll be somebody someday. So, who is he now?"

"He's incredible, movie star handsome. You can't imagine. He's a few years older than me, so we didn't exactly grow up together, but we knew each other. He lived down the block. I always knew that someday we'd be together, and now we are. She fingered an expensive gold necklace around her neck.

"That's a pretty do-dad," Luna said.

"Tivoli. Nothing but the best from my beautiful guy." She winced as the yarn tangled beneath her fingers.

Luna tsk-tsked again and then helped her untangle it.

"Anyways," Luna went on, "my dad always said I'd be okay in life because I know what I want. It's too bad Dirk didn't have a dad like that."

Luna held Darci's knitting up to the light, nodded, then handed it back.

"My dad's like Dirk. He spoils me. Helps me out. Does nice things for me, no matter what."

"Where are you from originally?"

"From. New Jersey. A nothing town. So nothing it's not even on maps. I hated it there. Dirk left when he was still a kid. Fifteen or something. His mother died and, *whoosh*, he was gone. My dad said he went to New York to live with a relative. My dad's good at keeping up on things. He still lives in that little place and works in a church. He knew Dirk. Knew the family. Everything."

"Sounds like you like your dad," Luna said.

"I'm his only kid. He's there for me."

"But anyway, New York is amazing, nothing like that little Podunk place. And that's where I went the instant I got out of high school. New York City. My dream come true. At least some of it. We'll stay there forever, probably. Dirk and I have big plans. He's crazy about me."

"Aren't we all," Luna said. And in the office, Izzy used her hand to smother a laugh.

She glanced through the door. Darci looked proud, as if she heard it as a compliment, and Izzy suddenly felt sorry for her. Clearly, she was head over heels for a man who had already made his mark in this town by stealing and by stalking, by getting both of them kicked out of a nice place to stay, and by leaning on Nell's friend Ollie to get him out of those jams.

The stalking suggested he would be unfaithful to this child/woman. Izzy looked at her and saw future heartache written all over her. When she'd practiced law, she'd met women like Darci, and men, too, attached to a bad relationship by the pull of good looks, or greed, or loneliness, or a hundred other frailties.

It never ended well—unless by some miracle, it ended early.

"What is superman's family like?" Luna asked her.

Darci shrugged. "Kind of the opposite of mine. I had a dad, but no mom. Dirk had a, well, a mom, but no dad. His mom was old. Very uptight and proper. It seemed to us neighbors that she spent more time in church than she did with Dirk.

Praying for him, I guess. I remember seeing her, walking into the Fairwood Church of Prayer with a little veil on her head. Every single morning, there'd go Miss Patricia, off to light candles."

"She probably wasn't really that old," Luna said, sounding irritated. "Young people think forty or fifty is old."

"Well, it is. Old is old. And you're wrong. Miss Patricia was old. Older than she should have been. She wasn't . . ."

Darci paused and Izzy looked out. Darci had stopped knitting and was looking at Luna, as if wanting to talk, not knit. Then she saw Luna wince as several stitches dropped off Darci's needle, and the moment passed. Luna took the needles away and showed her how to put them back on, her voice turning softer when she talked about knitting.

"Now tell me this," Luna said, handing the needles back and looking at Darci's face. "Why did you abandon your New York City to come here to our little humble town?"

"I'm here for work." Darci's voice lifted.

Izzy heard pride in the young voice.

"My boyfriend and I are—were—part of the catering team for a big party."

Izzy shifted to get a glimpse of Luna's face to see her reaction. There wasn't any.

"So you were helping with the mayor's party, I'd guess?"

"Yeah. I work with Chef Carson in a restaurant in New York City. It's elegant, fancy. She picked me to come help with it. She's very well-known in the culinary world."

"Did you?"

"Did I what?"

"Did you know her?"

"Everyone knew her. In New York, everywhere. Of course I knew her. I worked in her amazing restaurant. Her kitchen. Dirk worked there, too, even before I landed in the big city. My dad found out where he worked. He helped Chef Carson other places, too—teaching classes for famous cooking schools."

Luna pulled out Darci's cast-on tail from being tangled in a row. "Did you know her as a person? I was there at that party. I watched your chef, and I am wondering what she was like."

Darci thought for a moment, as if picking out the right answer. Then she said with a self-satisfied smile: "Well, yes, I did know her, in fact. I knew her real well. She was kind of my mentor, I'd say."

"It must have been an awful night for you when she died like that."

Izzy shifted again, the office chair squeaking slightly. Luna was beginning to sound like an investigator. She wondered what she was up to.

Darci seemed taken aback by Luna's comment. Then her face softened, her voice hushed. "It was awful, horrible. It was terrible for all of us, as you can imagine. Everyone loved her."

"So, why are you staying around now?" She examined Darci's stitches and nodded her approval.

"My boyfriend was working the party, too, and he had to stay on a few days. I thought I should get back to New York, to the restaurant where I work. To help them through all this, but he asked me to stay with him, so I did."

"Why did he have to stay?"

"His mother was related to the chef," Darci said in an odd, formal, stilted way, as if repeating a phrase she'd heard on a TV show.

"This must be a difficult time for him, too, then," Luna said, taking the needles back from Darci and turning the row over.

Izzy could see Darci's face, the frown, then her eyes looking up, a long pause. Finding the right answer somewhere above her head.

"Yes," she finally said. "Yes. But I hope I've been able to make him feel better. Sharing things with him. In some ways, I've known more about him that he did. But now we're on the same track. We're both anxious to get back to New York." She paused for a minute, then said, her voice lowering, "I'm going to move into his apartment soon. It'll be easier . . ."

Izzy could see Darci leaning in toward Luna, the needles idle. As if what she was going to say was confidential. Between student and teacher. And it must have been. Izzy couldn't hear a word she said.

When Luna sat back, she was examining Darci's knitting and pointing out things she'd need to redo.

Darci was complying. And smiling.

"Of course I knew who she was," Luna said to Izzy as she walked into her small office. "I wasn't born yesterday."

She'd just sent Darci Fox off with a bag of expensive yarn and stern directions to come back with twenty rows of perfect stockinette stitches.

"How did you know?" Izzy asked.

Luna put her hands on her hips and stared at Izzy. "I take you for an intelligent person, Izzy Perry. Don't prove me wrong. I know because I saw the woman standing on the sidewalk outside Cass's house the night her delinquent boyfriend tried to peek in my bedroom window."

Izzy held back her smile. Of course. Cass had seen the same thing. She was following her boyfriend.

Luna went on. "I also know you eavesdropped on our whole conversation, and that should prove to you that I knew who I was talking with."

"You sounded a little like one of Cass's television detectives."

"No, they're not that bright. But here's something you need to know about that young woman. That Darci *Fox*. First, she's sharp as a tack and a chameleon. And second, she lies. Not a pathological liar, probably. She probably means well with her lies, protecting her guy and all that. But no matter. She's a liar. A needy liar. Maybe they're the worst kind."

"Why do you say that?"

"Many reasons, but for one, Beatrice and I had an aunt named Gertrude who was a full-fledged pathological liar. She's dead now, buried with her lies, thanks be to God. Beatrice got a house out of it all. But that's another story. Darci Lou Fox isn't nearly as accomplished as our aunt. So I know a liar when I see one.

"But here's what you need to remember, Ms. Perry," Luna continued, her face dead serious now and her eyes narrowed. She pointed one finger at Izzy's face.

"In between those lies, you will find some truth. The trick is finding it."

Chapter 39

Nell had made the mistake of suggesting once that they'd skip Friday night dinners in December. People were so busy, she said, and it was just one more thing to add to already-packed calendars.

She said that the response felt like she'd been attacked by killer bees. She didn't suggest it again.

"It's about time you and Rachel showed your faces around here," Nell said, welcoming the Wootens into the family room.

"Friday nights get a little crazy in Don's business," Rachel said. She handed Nell a holly plant and a bottle of wine. "We're playing hooky tonight, or rather Don is. I finally convinced him that a dose of friends and something from Ben's grill would be the best medicine after a long week."

Nell looked over at Don. "Yes, your wife is wise, Don Wooten. I'm so glad you're here. Both of you." She took their coats and hung them on the coatrack near the back door, then said to Rachel as they walked across the family room, "I've been hoping to run into you all week. But I can only imagine what things are like in city hall, especially in the city attorney's office."

Rachel nodded. "Crazy, yes. And whatever you're imagining, it is probably worse. It's a hard time, with media attention, a couple of attempted lawsuits. People don't always think clearly during emotional times like this."

"And you, Don, how are things with you?" Nell asked.

Don tried to laugh off the question, but Nell held his eyes, seeking an answer.

"All right, Nell, you asked. There were days this week that I felt like I was walking around with a scarlet *G* for *guilty* on my shirt. It's not a feeling I'm used to."

"That's in your head, Don," Rachel said, unsmiling.

But Nell knew it wasn't in his head. Although the police were silent about whom they were investigating, Sea Harbor was too small to protect their secrets. The fact that Lidia Carson wanted to buy—and worse, tear down—Don's beloved restaurant had circulated up and down Harbor Road.

"And then there was the commotion at the restaurant the other night," Don said, ignoring Rachel's glance not to dwell on things. "Do any of you know this fellow named Dirk?" Don asked.

Sam and Izzy had arrived early with their daughter Abby and the family dog that Abby refused to leave behind. While Sam settled Abby to bed in the guest room upstairs, Izzy arranged a tray of cheeses at the large kitchen island. The mention of the name 'Dirk' brought her over to the group. "Dirk Evans?" she asked.

"I don't know the last name," Don said.

"There aren't many Dirks around here," Ben said, walking over to greet Rachel and Don. "You probably mean the guy who was working at Beatrice's party. I met him a few days ago at Mary's B and B. Not under pleasant circumstances, I might add. But this whole mess has affected people who worked with Chef Carson at the party that night. And Dirk was one of them."

"I can add my meeting him to yours, Ben," Don said. "It was

unpleasant as well. He came in for dinner last night with his girlfriend. She was all dressed up—more than usual for a middle of the week date, at least here in Sea Harbor. A knock-off designer dress, or so my hostess informed me. Fancy jewelry, the whole bit. One of the waitresses complimented her on something she had on, a gold necklace, I think—and the guy, Dirk, became irate. Apparently he hadn't noticed it until she took her coat off and the waitress admired it. He started yelling, creating a scene. I wasn't sure who he was mad at, but I got over there in a hurry to protect my server. By the time I got there, the man had grabbed his coat and left. I'd say he has an anger problem. Poor lady was left stranded with the drink tab. I excused it, and she left soon after. The server wasn't sure what happened, except that he had insisted she give him the necklace, which he shoved into his pocket."

"How strange," Izzy said, imagining the scene. She wondered if it was the same necklace Darci had worn in her shop. Clearly expensive, she thought, and then she remembered Darci's comments about Dirk's generosity.

"I agree about the anger issue, Don," Ben said. "The man has trouble controlling it."

Nell stood slightly behind the others, listening and watching people's faces. She noticed the unpleasant expression on the faces of those who had met Dirk, either in person or second-hand, the way she and Birdie had. She wondered briefly if Dirk was aware of Lidia's attempt to buy the restaurant where he was creating such a scene.

She also noticed another curious thing. People still awkwardly referred to the Saturday night event as "the mayor's holiday party," or "Beatrice's event," or "the holiday open house," and other similar versions. It was never called "the party where the chef was murdered." But no matter what it was called now, it would be remembered for a long time, Nell suspected, and not for the festive beauty of Beatrice Scaglia's new home or the amazing food. Nor even that it was a holiday party.

But for a murdered chef.

A rap on a large French door leading to the deck interrupted the conversation and Nell looked over to see Ollie Bishop standing there, holding a couple of Mason jars. Ben got to the door first and welcomed him in. "Hey, old buddy, glad you're joining us. Get in out of that cold." He opened the door wider and Ollie walked in.

"I hear good things about your grilling skills, Ben," Ollie said. "I brought some sauces to throw into whatever. Or feed it to the dog. Ours liked these two especially."

Ben took the sauces and Ollie's coat, thanking him and leading him over to the group.

"I'm feeling a little intimidated here," Ben said. "Here's an acclaimed chef and a restaurant owner who'll be watching me throw flank steaks on the grill. There's something wrong with that picture."

Thank heavens for Ben's ability to make people feel at home, Nell thought. She was hoping it wasn't too awkward for either Don or Ollie. If she'd known the Wootens were coming, she might not have insisted Ollie join them. Yet, she was equally glad to see all three of them.

She moved to Ollie's side. "Speaking of experts, I don't think you culinary-world geniuses have even met one another, though it's not for my lack of trying."

Quick introductions were made, and the awkward moment passed.

Ollie seemed fine with meeting Don. He praised the Ocean's Edge, and mentioned its warmth. "I haven't had a meal there yet, but it's definitely the kind of place you want to come back to. I'll definitely be in again before I leave."

Don, in turn, told Ollie about a long-ago visit he and Rachel had made to Ollie's very first restaurant in New York.

"It was a great place. Clean and warm and welcoming. Unpretentious, but unique—terrific pastas and seafood—a first-class menu and amazing wine list. It was exactly the kind of place I wanted to create here in Sea Harbor," Don said, then smiled. "But maybe mine would have a slightly different view."

Nell knew Don was talking about the restaurant Ollie and his first wife, Maddie, had built together, and Nell could see Ollie warming to this man who was praising it. Imitation, she thought, was indeed the sincerest form of flattery.

And an irony, certainly, since Ollie's current wife had wanted to tear down what Don had built, the restaurant that had been modeled after Ollie and Maddie's dream.

She watched them both, eyes moving from one man's face to the other. Two men who were a part of her life. Dear friends.

And two men who each had a reason to kill the murdered chef.

A chill ran through Nell, and she wrapped her arms around her body, warding it off. She looked at them, thinking about Lidia Carson. Thinking about the fact that murderers could look like neighbors, like best friends, good friends, even long-ago friends. And then she pushed the painful thoughts as far into a corner of her head as she could.

A door slammed and voices floated in from the front of the house, a welcome distraction. Birdie appeared first, followed by Danny and Cass, their arms loaded with loaves of Harry Garozzo's Italian breads and a pan of apple crisp. Birdie carried several bottles of wine from Sonny's wine cellar.

Birdie stopped for a moment at the entrance to the family room, enjoying the view. The living room. The everything room.

At the far end, a fire blazed, complete with the fragrance of sweet and nutty chestnuts roasting in the grate, and there, in front of it, was Sam, his lanky body leaning over to stoke the flames. A giant Fraser fir, lit with bulbs and decorated with handmade and keepsake ornaments, filled the corner near the fireplace. Red, the Perrys' golden retriever, was snoozing in an oversized chair near the fire. And Birdie suspected little Abby Perry was doing the same thing upstairs,

Birdie walked over to the fireplace and gave both the dog and his owner affectionate pats, then walked toward the familiar voices, her smile widening as she looked into the faces of friends milling around the room.

"What a perfect, warm gathering on such a cold and wintry night," she said, breathing in the aroma of a cheesy potato casserole baking in the oven. But mostly, she was delighted at seeing the Wootens and Ollie Bishop tonight. She handed her wine off to Ben and singled out Don Wooten for a hug. She greeted the others, welcomed Ollie warmly, and then headed for the butcher-block island in the kitchen area, where Nell was now tossing a salad.

Rachel Wooten followed her over and helped her out of her heavy coat. "Birdie, your hug for Don was well-timed," she said softly. "You have an instinct for that sort of thing. It's exactly what he needed. Thank you."

Birdie smiled. "Well, I needed it, too. It's been a long week. Don is a good man. And you, Rachel, a fine lawyer, know better than many that a perceived motive doesn't make a murderer. Not in any way. Don is loved in this town. Gossip holds little weight."

Nell noticed that Rachel's eyes misted over at Birdie's words. And also that she looked like she hadn't slept in days.

Cass stood over at the kitchen counter, wrapping loaves of bread in foil to warm in the oven, listening. She set them aside and walked over, welcoming Rachel, then teased her about being too lenient toward one of her lobstermen for a recent complaint that had reached Rachel's office. He'd been speeding in harbor waters. "You're too nice, Rachel. The guy needs a lesson."

Rachel laughed and gave Cass a hug.

Izzy set a plate of cheese and crackers on the island and pulled up a stool. "So, how are things at city hall, Rachel? You're right there in the middle of all this mess."

"Between you and Ben, we should be getting an inside scoop," Cass added.

Rachel's smile faded. "You'd be amazed at how quickly one is eliminated from the inner circle when one is in any way connected to the crime."

That silenced the women for a minute. Then Nell said, "Rachel, that doesn't make sense."

"Well, unfortunately, it does, Nell. Until this investigation is more focused, or better yet, complete—and I sincerely hope that will be soon—I'm not privy to some of the discussions. But it's fine. I've been very busy with a vendor or two who somehow think there might be a way to sue the city for something related to the party that night. Nonsense suits, but they keep me busy and are almost a welcome relief right now."

Ben walked over, interrupting briefly as he set down a tray of martinis and a couple bottles of wine. He handed a martini to Birdie, then told the others to pick their poison. "And if any of you want to join me on the deck to fire up the coals and take a look at a spectacular winter moon, you're welcome." He chuckled at his own invitation, knowing the women comfortably settled around the kitchen island were perfectly warm and content where they were, and he'd have to look elsewhere for help.

As Ben gathered volunteers, and voices drifted off onto the moonlit deck, Nell got out dressing for the salad, then sat down at the island near Rachel.

"Rachel, tell me if I am overstepping here, but there's something I've been wanting to talk to you about all week. It's been playing games with my head. Something that happened that night," Nell said.

Birdie and Izzy perked up, and Cass walked back from rummaging around in the refrigerator, with a Stella in her hand.

"That night" needed no further elucidation.

Rachel went still, her smile dissolving into a look of surprise. Then she took a sip of her wine and pulled herself up on a tall island stool, waiting, clearly unsure of what Nell was about to ask.

The city attorney was older than Cass and Izzy, but a few years younger than Nell. A nice-looking, intelligent woman, Rachel fit in with all kinds of people—native Sea Harbor families, like the Favazzas, Garozzos and Rissos, the Hallorans and McGluckens, and also those considered "newcomers," like Izzy and Sam and the Endicotts, and Rachel and Don themselves. Nearly everyone in Sea Harbor knew Rachel and liked her, because she made it clear she liked all of them. She considered herself "their" attorney, the whole town's, and was especially considerate with teens feeling their oats and ending up needing some court "understanding" and gentle counseling. Rachel was proficient at both.

At that moment, Rachel looked like she'd much rather be with the teens.

Cass took a long drink of her beer, Birdie sipped her martini, and they all looked at Nell.

"Aunt Nell?" Izzy finally said.

"I'm sorry," Nell said. "I don't mean to be mysterious or dramatic. It just occurred to me that maybe I have no right to ask this—"

"It's okay, Nell. I have few secrets from friends," Rachel said. Then she added with a smile, "Well, not any I think you'd ask about." She took a drink of her wine, then set it down. "And I especially don't have any secrets about that night. After several sessions with Tommy Porter, I can probably repeat verbatim most of what that night was like for me. In a few words, it was uncomfortable. Not entirely enjoyable. It was just something we did, then went home and had a decent night's sleep."

"We were with you, Rachel. None us were looking forward to it," Cass said. "And Don couldn't have been looking forward to the possibility of seeing the woman who was trying to kill his restaurant. I sure get that."

"I can always count on you to hit the nail on the head." Rachel smiled at Cass.

"Actually, my question has nothing to do with Don or restaurants or the fact that we all wished we stayed home that snowy night," Nell said. "It's about a conversation I had at the party." She paused, took a drink of water, and then continued.

"At some point later that evening, Beatrice asked me to look for her celebrity chef. She was annoyed with her for some reason, but that's not important. I ran into Shannon Platt, one of the servers, while I was looking for the chef and asked if she knew where her boss was."

"I know Shannon," Rachel said. "A wonderful waitress. She works at the Ocean's Edge sometimes."

"Of course she does," Birdie said, laughing. "Shannon works everywhere."

"And she's observant," Nell said. "In addition to letting me know she had no idea where the chef was, she filled me in on an argument that had transpired earlier, between the chef and one of the catering-team members."

Nell looked at Rachel. "She mentioned that you had come in the kitchen in the middle of it, and she—Shannon—felt bad that you had to hear it all. I think she was embarrassed that you saw the downside of life in the kitchen."

Rachel nodded, then laughed. "Shannon must have forgotten that with a husband in the restaurant business, I've been in on many kitchen dramas. But she's right. I came in through the butler's pantry looking for Chef Carson. She wasn't in the kitchen, but someone pointed toward the back hall. And then I heard the voices. She was out in the back hallway with one of the servers, scolding him about something. Actually, that's a nice word for it. She was *furious* with him."

"Was his name Dirk?" Cass asked.

Rachel nodded. "I think so. Shannon mentioned that name, although I had no idea who Dirk was at that time."

"Shannon apologized that I had to experience their 'kitchen warfare,' as she called it. But added that the man deserved whatever the chef was hurling at him, and plenty more."

"What had he done to make the chef so angry?" Izzy asked. She glanced over at Cass, Dirk's behavior on the portico fresh in their minds. And then she explained to the others the scene they'd witnessed that night, but from a very cold portico and through frosty windows.

"We couldn't hear anything, but unless more than one server was reamed out in the back hall by the chef, I think we were seeing the same thing."

"Talk about coincidences," Rachel said, surprised. "At first, I couldn't hear everything they were saying, either, partly because I was trying not to hear. But that was hard to do, because I'd come in through the butler's pantry, which is near the door that goes out into that back hall." She looked at Izzy. "I guess we learn that as lawyers, right? The less you know can sometimes be better."

Izzy laughed, but in this case, she didn't agree. In retrospect, she was wishing they'd heard more.

"Mostly, I wanted to get out of there," Rachel said. "It was clearly a bad time to talk to the chef. The bits I did hear didn't make too much sense to me. Disrespect of people, maybe. Vague kinds of threats were thrown out, the kind a boss would say to an underling who wasn't doing his job, I suppose. Threatening to change his salary . . . no, not salary, but she was threatening to cut him off or out or something. Perhaps a bonus? At one point, I heard him yell back—loudly—that she had no right to do that to him. And she yelled back that, of course, she could, that she was the only one who could. Or something like that. But at that point, I was more interested in finding the best way out of the kitchen, and as far away as I could get from their angry voices."

"What were the other people in the kitchen doing?" Izzy asked. She glanced at Cass, then back to Rachel.

"Those near the back windows were packing up things and had some music on. I don't think they heard much. Or maybe they were used to that sort of thing, I don't know. Others were cleaning things. One server was hovering near the kitchen door to the hallway, where the two were arguing, maybe listening, and might have heard the whole thing. Gathering some fuel for gossip, I suppose. And Shannon was around, too. I turned and hurried out. I was so relieved to be out of there, I looked for Don to tell him it was time to leave. But when I couldn't find him right away, I found my coat and stepped outside the front door, just to get some air. By then, the crowd was thinning out."

She paused for a moment, as if thinking back to that night. Then frowned.

"And this is strange. I'd almost forgotten it. But I heard a loud noise coming from the garage area. It startled me. I looked over just as a motorcycle tore down the driveway. Then disappeared in the dark. The street was plowed, but the guy was driving crazy. I wondered if it was the fellow Lidia had lit into. Escaping her wrath."

"That's awful. And crazy," Izzy said. "If it was Dirk, Lidia must have said something awful to him."

Rachel nodded. "I'd say so. The whole incident made me relieved that I hadn't met her, as I'd planned. I began to wonder why I'd ever attempted to talk to her in the first place."

Nell leaned in, her elbows on the island. "Actually, that's the question I wasn't sure I had any right to ask," Nell said. "It may be too personal and none of my business. But why did you want to talk with her?"

"Of course you can ask, Nell. You're my friend. All of you are. And it's not a secret, anyway. I also told Tommy Porter about it when he questioned me about that night. I hadn't planned to talk to her, not when Don and I decided to go to the party. I was hoping *not* to see her at all, in fact. I disliked this woman whom I'd never met, not something I ever do, and I didn't want to see her. But once we were there and I saw all that gorgeous food, and then the distress on my husband's face—such a contrast—my emotions took over. Mostly anger.

"The reason I sought her out that night was to try to talk some sense into her. I was so angry at her, so hurt at what she was trying to do to Don. He was going through hell because of her, and it was eating us both up.

"I went to find her to do what I could to stop her from destroying my husband's dream."

Chapter 40

Later that night, Sam woke up in a hazy state, one arm reaching out automatically toward the other side of the bed. He opened his eyes, peering into the dark bedroom, then pulled himself out of bed.

"Hey, Iz," he said, walking across the kitchen, rubbing his eyes. He stood behind his wife, massaging her neck. "Are you okay? Couldn't sleep?"

Izzy was sitting at the kitchen table, the only light in the room the blue glare of her computer screen and moonbeams streaming in the window. She looked up into Sam's sleepy face. "I'm sorry if I woke you."

"You didn't. It was that empty, cold spot in the bed that woke me. The one that was supposed to have a gorgeous woman lying in it. She must have run off."

Izzy smiled. "I had weird dreams. Go back to bed. I'll see if I can find the woman and tell her you're waiting."

Sam dropped a kiss on top of the tangled waves on Izzy's head. "Don't be long."

Izzy went back to her computer. She had carried home

thoughts and worries about Don and Rachel Wooten. And Molly. Ollie. And others whose lives had been turned on their heads by having to stand in the shadow of a murder.

And then her own awful guilt as she considered them, too, trying to find the absolute proof of why they hadn't done such a horrible thing.

Finally she had turned to a different approach and found herself clicking on cooking schools, on churches and obituaries, and facts that didn't fit together. But they would, she knew, if they could just find the stray pieces and cut off the fluff. The tails. Weave in the unsightly stray ends. And she felt in the marrow of her very sleepy bones that they were getting close.

Chapter 41

"I had a dream last night that I was doing what Birdie suggested and walking around in Lidia Carson's shoes," Izzy said. She poured almond milk into her coffee and passed the carton to Cass.

"And?" Birdie prompted.

"I fell down the steps."

Cass laughed and took a glazed donut from the plate.

"It's not so funny. The fall woke me up. I think I even have a bruise from it. Dream bruises are the worst." She wrinkled her nose at Cass.

"I haven't been sleeping well, either," Nell said. "My dreams are mixed up. I can't quite catch the plane or the train, or find my ticket. And when I wake up, I'm still tired. But relieved to have escaped it all."

"Where is Carl Jung when we need him," Birdie said. "Anxiety dreams are troubling ones. Maybe they would help us figure out this puzzle."

An urgent, early-morning text from Izzy stating that she was in need of coffee and donuts and friends, not necessarily in that

order, had brought the four women together in the back knitting room of the yarn shop. They were sitting around the old library table, taking advantage of the quiet, the fire, and the shop
being closed until noon that day.

Outside, the sky was a deep winter blue, the harbor waters
calm, and the people of the town moving into their day,
earnestly trying to revive the holiday spirit.

Inside, the Izzy, Nell, Birdie and Cass were trying to do the
same—but in their own way. By trying to find a murderer.

Cass had brought a carafe of coffee, and Birdie the pastries.
Nell had hastily put together a plate of fruit. For once, knitting
bags were closed, although ready nearby, should they be in
need of quiet inspiration.

"I think I know why I fell out of Lidia's shoes," Izzy said,
talking around bites of a chocolate croissant. Her laptop was on
the table in front of her, along with a yellow pad and loose papers. "The shoes haven't taken me anywhere. It's kind of like
Nell's anxiety dream. I've tried and tried to follow Lidia around
in my head and on my computer, but there's not much there. I
even went to Wikipedia. I can list her culinary awards, her
board representations, school affiliations. But I couldn't find
out the simple things, like where she was raised, who her parents are, any friends she might have. I don't even know how *old*
she was. She's a mystery woman."

"Oliver confessed the same to me," Nell said. "Apparently,
she simply showed up in his restaurant and took over one day.
She never officially applied for a job, so there's no résumé, no
letters of recommendation. None of the traditional things. As
far as Ollie knows, there isn't any family."

"But we know there *was* someone," Izzy said. "That's what
got me thinking. A relative. Someone who knew Lidia well
enough to make her Dirk's guardian."

"Maybe it was someone who wanted to punish her," Cass
said.

"Well, yes, there's that," Izzy said, smiling. "But after reading way too many articles on Lidia's rise in the culinary world, I went back to thinking about this person."

"Dirk's mother, you mean?" Nell asked.

"Yes. She wanted Lidia to care for him, so she must have known her well enough to do that. No matter what we think of Dirk, his mother wouldn't have thrown him to the wolves," Izzy said.

"Maybe," Birdie said, tapping into their unspoken thoughts about Lidia's motherly attributes. But they knew nothing about his mother or what she might have done. "Possibly, Dirk's mother was very ill and had no one else to provide for him. Lidia might have been a better choice than a foster home."

"But how did Dirk's mother even know Lidia?" Cass asked.

"Ollie said they were related. But whatever the reason, I agree that learning more about Lidia is important," Nell said.

"I got a step closer last night," Izzy said. "From Darci, who came into my thoughts in the wee hours of my googling. When Darci and Luna were knitting together, she told Luna the name of the town where Dirk grew up. Both Dirk and Darci were raised in the same place. I wrote it down."

"Did she mention Dirk's mother's name?" Nell asked.

"Part of it. Patricia," Izzy said. "I presume her last name was Evans, like Dirk's. At least if Darci was telling the truth. Luna says she lies."

"But the mother died," Birdie reminded them. "She isn't going to be much help."

"Yes and no." Izzy pulled out a printout and pushed it to the center of the table. "So I checked obits online and found one that matched that name. Yes, she died. But this is interesting."

It was a short obituary, with the traditional information: dates, service details, and survivors' names, little else. It was the kind of obituary that newspapers offered free of charge. But this one was even shorter than most of those.

Birdie put her glasses on and picked it up. She scanned it. And then she read it out loud,

"'Patricia Evans, a resident in Hospice House, a facility run by the Fairwood Church of Prayer in Fairwood, New Jersey, died peacefully after an illness. She is survived by a son and a daughter. Patricia was sixty-five years young. Church services will be private.'"

Birdie looked up. "That's all there is."

"Dirk had a sister?" Cass said. Then she laughed at her own surprise. "What's odd is that we are all acting surprised about the sister, but we don't know any of these people. So, why are we surprised?"

"It's strange the children aren't named," Birdie said.

"That's true," Nell said. "But it makes me wonder why Lidia wasn't made guardian of both children." She was trying to imagine what that would have been like for a young girl. Being sent to a guardian who didn't want either child. It was like a tale from Charles Dickens.

"The daughter might have been older," Birdie said, thinking out loud. "But then why wasn't she Dirk's guardian? Whatever the reason, it would be nice if we could reach the daughter. Maybe she'd be able to tell us how Lidia ended up being Dirk's guardian."

"Hey, wait," Cass said. "Patricia was sixty-five when she died? And Dirk was around fourteen, fifteen, right?" She looked at Nell. "That's weird."

For a minute, they were silent, trying to follow Cass's thinking. And then her math kicked in.

"Darci was right when she told Luna that Dirk's mother was old. She must have had Dirk when she was, what? Fifty?" Cass said.

"It's all curious. And adds a layer to who Dirk is, I guess," Nell said. "I'm sure it wasn't easy on him or his mother. But it doesn't really bring us closer to knowing Lidia."

"Or who killed her," Cass added.

"The obituary just says that services were private. No funeral home or any other place is listed," Birdie said. "Just the church."

"But thanks to Luna playing detective," Izzy said, "we know Patricia went to church. Apparently, often, like every day. So I imagine they knew her at the church. And it's probably the one mentioned in the obit. I'll try to reach someone there, and also ask if they knew Dirk's guardian, Lidia Carson. It may be a dead end."

"But it's a start," Nell said. "It's interesting that Darci and Dirk are both from that town."

"I got the impression during my very fruitful eavesdropping session that Darci followed him to New York once she was able to get out of the small town. She got a job in the same restaurant where he worked. Seems like more than a coincidence. And now they seem to be planning a life together."

"I poked around a little, too, corralling Ollie as he went out for a walk early today," Nell said. "He said Lidia talked once about a small town, but mostly to tell him she hated living in one, and never would again. He had the impression her childhood wasn't happy. But we need to find out more. We have motives and opportunities, but there's something missing. People don't kill people randomly, unless they're psychotic or serial killers."

Birdie had been quiet, drinking her coffee slowly. "No, not normally. But murders happen that might not have been planned. If we assume that Lidia's death wasn't planned, then something must have happened that night that triggered a murder. Something that unleashed a feeling that was already there."

"Yes," Nell said. "But unfortunately we know at least three or four people—people we know and care about—who have reason carry bad feelings about Lidia Carson."

They were all quiet for a moment, feeling the truth in Nell's statement. But not wanting to pursue it. At least not now.

Izzy drummed her fingers on the table, thinking. "The argument between Dirk and Lidia may have been enough. She was threatening him. But with what?"

"Rachel saw him leave after," Cass said. "But he could easily have come back."

"Hmm." Nell frowned. "Mary Pisano told Ben that Dirk never came back to the B and B the night of the murder. Apparently, his pregnant girlfriend was frantic."

"Pregnant?" Birdie said.

"That was the impression Ben got when he met her. It was as if she wanted him to know it for some reason. As if it elevated her to a certain status."

"I wonder if the police know about Dirk's disappearance that night—" Cass said.

"They do," Nell said. "When they questioned the kitchen crew, someone said that Dirk had disappeared before everyone else. When the police questioned him the next day, he claimed he had gotten mad at his boss and left, riding around town. He said he didn't even know she was dead, until the next morning," Nell said.

"Convenient," Cass said. "Riding a Harley in the middle of a snowstorm? All night?"

"Yes. Suspicious," Izzy said. "But it doesn't prove or disprove anything, since he could be lying."

"Or—he could be telling the truth." Cass shrugged.

Birdie had been quiet, trying to digest what they'd learned, but frustrated by what they hadn't. "I feel we are inches away from something. Something just beyond our grasp. We have scattered pieces everywhere, but they need order."

"There are definitely holes that need to be filled in," Nell added. "We are still saddled with friends whose motives are stronger than Dirk's, stronger than a random argument with the chef, which is all we have. Are we piling too much onto a man we dislike because he hurt Molly? Don Wooten was there that night, and he wanted desperately to save his restaurant."

"Rachel too, Nell," Izzy added. "She's our friend and we trust her, but what if she was a stranger? How would we see it then? She hated what Lidia was trying to do to Don's restaurant. What if she came back later to see Lidia? That's how we need to look at these people. They argued. Rachel lost control. We'd do most anything for those we love."

The group grew silent, unwilling to accept what Izzy was saying, but knowing it was accurate.

"Molly admitted that Shannon had called her from the mayor's house that night. She told her about her confrontation with Dirk, that she'd finally realized who he was. She could have easily gone over, maybe encountered Lidia, argued—"

Cass held back the million reasons she knew that wouldn't have happened. But she held her silence.

"And then there's Ollie," Nell said. "He benefits significantly. He gets out of a marriage he'd wanted to dissolve, and he inherits nearly everything."

"And he did disappear for a while that evening," Birdie said. "I remember looking for him myself. I found him late in the evening, coming in the den door, covered with snow. Just out for a breath of fresh air, he told me."

Izzy glanced at the clock. "Mae will be here any minute to open up."

"I've been keeping a list of what we know and don't know," Cass said. "I'll email it to everyone, and let's see if we can fill in the gaps." She grabbed another donut and looked around for her bag.

They knew one another well enough that nothing more needed to be said. They'd go their own ways, then come back together, and each would hopefully bring pieces that would fit into the puzzle.

Even if it meant tripping in a dead woman's shoes.

Chapter 42

Nell walked into the house after leaving the yarn shop, her head spinning with names and motives, confusing puzzles with lots of missing pieces.

She spotted Ben and Ollie sitting at the kitchen island and waved a hello, taking off her coat and walking their way. "You both look industrious. And tired. What's going on?" She glanced at the half empty coffee cups and a scattering of legal-looking documents on the island surface.

Ben nodded toward the papers. "Lidia and Ollie's company lawyers sent these to Ollie, and we've been going through them." He pulled out a tall stool. "Please. Join us."

"Things I hadn't paid much attention to, I'm afraid," Ollie said. "They aren't all here. I'll get the rest soon."

Nell poured herself a cup of coffee, then sat down next to Ben. She looked at Ollie. "Are there problems? You and Lidia had created a little empire. It's probably complicated."

"It's actually very organized," Ben said. "Surprising, though."

"The will?"

"No. That's clear. In a word, everything goes to Ollie. It's one of the trusts we were looking at. It's set up for Dirk Evans. And is sizable."

Ollie looked at the papers again. Then he looked over at Nell. "I knew about it—it's what Lidia drew on when Dirk needed money, which was often."

"Were you all right with that?" Nell asked. "You had no responsibility for him, and it was your life, your money, too."

"Lidia was pretty much responsible for our assets being as large as they were. I saw it as her prerogative, and I was okay with it. It was curious to me, though, because he was never really a part of our family. Not in the way you think about extended family, relatives. But for whatever reason, it was meaningful enough that Lidia accepted the guardianship. There was a magnanimous part of her that surprised me sometimes."

"But Dirk didn't like Lidia, that was obvious," Nell said. "At fifteen, kids often don't like anyone, add to that being taken out of the town he was raised in. I don't think that's surprising. But do you think Lidia liked him?"

Ollie shrugged. "There wasn't real feeling there that I could see. Dirk resented life, sometimes. But he stuck around as long as the money was there."

"And she established a trust for him."

"Yes," Ollie said.

Ben ended the silence that followed. "Lidia was the executor of the trust, so Dirk had to come to her for money. But upon her death, Dirk would get outright control of the trust she had set up."

"Did Dirk know that?" Nell asked.

Ollie took a drink of coffee. "He knew about the trust, but not about the particulars, nor the amount. Lidia made it difficult for him when he'd ask for money. Responsibility. Maybe that's what she was going after. I hoped so, anyway."

"What an interesting relationship," Nell said.

"Interesting? I suppose. I never quite figured it out, and it wasn't a topic Lidia talked to me about. But something happened recently between Dirk and Lidia that intensified the tension between them. It was different from other arguments they'd had, though I'm not sure I can explain why." Ollie grew pensive, as if still trying to figure it out.

"It happened a few days before we came here. Dirk had stormed into the house and confronted Lidia, accusing her of something that had clearly upset him. Some news he'd gotten. About his mother, maybe. Her death.

"I had heard the yelling coming from the den, and hurried that way. Dirk was standing in in the middle of the room, literally red with rage, hurling insults at her, calling her a liar, an awful person, all the comments infused with lots of profanity. Lidia was clearly shaken. Frozen in place. Not yelling back. I'd never seen her like that before. She seemed to be in shock. Her face was white.

"Before I had a chance to throw him out the door, he turned around and saw me. He stared at me for a second, his face filled with rage. But here's the strange part—in the middle of that awful anger, I thought I saw tears. Then without another word, he stormed through the room and out of the house.

"Lidia composed herself quickly. She told me she had to leave for a television appearance soon, and said she'd explain it all later. I assumed it was something about the trust, because I heard that word in the jumble of sounds as I was walking in.

"Like I said, it was just a couple days before coming here and things were busy. And somehow we never had that talk. Lidia was expert at avoiding things she didn't want to talk to me about."

Nell looked again at the papers on the island.

Dirk Evans was a wealthy man.

She looked up at Ollie. "May I ask one more question about Dirk?"

"Only one?" Ollie smiled.

"One for now," Nell said. "Some people heard Lidia arguing with Dirk near the kitchen the night she died."

Ollie nodded. "I heard about that."

"Could she have been angry enough to cut him out of her will? Dissolve the trust? Was that something Lidia would do?"

"Yes," Ollie said without having to think about it. "And I know that for a fact. Here's the reason why."

Nell took this "reason why" with her as she moved into the rest of her day, causing her to have to shuffle around some pieces of the puzzle.

Izzy helped Mae open the store after her friends left, and then said that she'd needed a little time in her office.

Mae had assured her that she had things completely under control. Her amazing twin nieces were on their winter break from college and were coming in to help. "Free yarn is always a draw for those two," she said. "And I suspect Luna will show up, too. She has a little entourage of knitters now who wait for her."

Izzy laughed, enjoying the thought of Luna as a rock star. She went into the small room and closed the door, then sat at the desk, looking at the scribbled notes she had made while they were all together in the knitting room. Then she checked the phone numbers she'd found online during the night, took a deep breath, and dialed the number for the Fairwood Church of Prayer.

The office secretary answered promptly and was pleasant and helpful. Of course she knew Patricia Evans. Well, not personally. She'd only been working there a couple years. But everyone in the church knew Patricia. There was even a brass plate on a church pew with her name on it. The congregation still missed her terribly.

But when Izzy started asking questions, she could hear the uncertainty in the young woman's voice. And in the next breath, the secretary suggested Izzy talk to the minister's wife. "Adele Gunther knows everything," she said. "She knew Patricia better than anyone." She put Izzy on hold and soon a new voice came on, this one older, slightly shaky. But equally cordial and willing to chat.

Izzy introduced herself, but the information had to be repeated several times before Adele was able to make sense of it. Izzy understood. She was a stranger, asking about a person who was dead.

But soon Adele became more comfortable and revealed that yes, she knew Patricia Evans very well. And she seemed happy to be talking about her. Patricia was her closest friend and she missed her terribly. Every day.

And yes, Patricia had a son named Dirk, an incredibly handsome boy. But Dirk was a handful. He had an attitude, Adele said.

"Patricia died before her time, and sometimes I think it was, at least in part, because of him," Adele said. "Of course that's just my opinion. The doctor said cancer, but she cared for that boy, watched him grow, fed him, and she prayed for him every single day. And he did nothing but act like the world owed him a favor."

"Was there a father to help out?"

"Oh, no. Patricia never married."

"Was he loved?" Izzy asked. And then she immediately regretted the words. What right had she? But the words came out. Because Dirk, for all his outward beauty, looked unloved.

"In her own way, she did," Adele said softly.

Izzy moved on.

"Even if he was a problem, it must have been difficult for him when his mother died?"

Adele was silent.

Izzy went on. "I understand he was young, but Patricia had chosen a guardian . . ."

But Adele seemed fixed on talking about Dirk Evans's dear mother and her charitable deeds, not her choice of guardian. "She adopted him when he was born, you know. At first, I wasn't supportive of her decision, but that's the kind of person she was. Patricia was a very moral, upstanding person. Taking a baby into her home was the godly thing to do."

Izzy tried to hide her surprise. It explained the age difference. Yet, it created another dilemma. Adopting a baby as a single, older woman could be a challenge. Agencies might object. "It must have been difficult to do that," she said. "I mean, adopting a baby at Patricia's age?"

Adele's voice was slightly less friendly when she answered this time. "We are a small town. We have a small, fine adoption agency here. It was all done right, mind you. New Jersey has its own way of doing things, you know. Open adoption, I think they called it. But I don't know that it was exactly that. It's a very nice place, run by a member of our church. They would be closed today, or you could call them, and they could tell you how they handle all of those things."

Izzy tried again to inquire about plans Patricia had made for her son after she died. "Patricia's obituary mentioned that she had a daughter. What happened to her when Patricia died?"

"There was no daughter," Adele said. "That was an error made by someone here at the church. We apologized to our newspaper. They printed a correction."

Izzy was silent for a minute. Then she realized she wasn't being up front with Adele Gunther. She owed it to this pleasant woman to be direct. "I'm interested in Dirk because a woman we know died tragically. She was Dirk's guardian. Her name was Lidia Carson, and we think she may have been a relative of Patricia's, of Dirk's. She might even have lived—"

Adele interrupted. "I don't believe there are any Carsons in our town. Certainly not in our church. I know all the members very well, old and new. You are mistaken."

Izzy could tell that Adele was tiring of the conversation, or maybe uncomfortable with Izzy's questions. Or maybe it was the mention of Lidia Carson. She couldn't tell, although Adele didn't impress her as someone who would lie.

"So you don't remember Patricia mentioning a guardian for her son, in case anything happened to her?"

Adele's voice grew very sad. "Yes, we did talk about it after she got sick. I wanted to be that person. I wanted to take the boy."

"Oh, Adele . . ." Izzy began, feeling a sudden affection for this woman. The sorrow in Adele's voice silenced Izzy.

Finally Adele went on.

"But Patricia refused. Truthfully, I think she knew I couldn't have handled him. But I wanted to. For her. But it was all worked out," she told me."

"Do you know why she chose Lidia Carson?" Izzy asked.

"It wasn't my business," Adele said, her voice abrupt in a way that told Izzy it was the end of that particular discussion.

Izzy tried to squeeze a couple more things into the conversation, asking if she could leave her number with Adele, in case she thought of something she might want to add to their discussion. Adele agreed, and Izzy had the impression that Adele, in fact, might actually call if she remembered things Izzy had asked about.

Then she asked her one more question, on a whim, really, she thought later. A last-minute thought. She asked Adele if a young woman named Darci Fox, a former resident of the town, might have been a member of her church?

Adele's response was unexpected.

She sighed. A long-suffering kind of sigh, right into the phone.

On her end, Izzy smiled. The sigh matched the Darci they'd come to know.

"Her father, William, works at our church and does odd jobs around town," Adele finally said. "He loves his daughter very much, no matter what."

"'No matter what'?" Izzy asked.

"No matter what," Adele repeated, and followed it with silence.

"So they're close?"

"Yes, I'd say. Darci Lou doesn't often come to town. But she does if she needs something. She was here a couple weeks ago."

"She needed something?"

"Apparently. Some information, William said."

"Did she get it?"

"William said yes, he'd help, so I suppose it worked out. He's never failed to help out Darci Lou. He's a good man, but . . ."

Adele sighed again, and Izzy suspected Adele thought William helped Darci Lou too much.

Then Adele's voice faded slightly, and she told Izzy she was very sorry, but it was time for her to go. She needed to arrange the flowers for services the next day. But perhaps they'd talk again. She had Izzy's number.

And she hung up.

Cass checked the time as she headed home from the yarn shop, feeling frustrated. She liked it when things lined up straight. And the discussion with Izzy, Nell, and Birdie had left her with a head filled with wavy lines.

She thought of the day ahead. Even that seemed wavy, but she couldn't shake the feeling that one strong wind would line everything up.

She pulled into the driveway and saw Danny's truck gone, then remembered he was helping his parents in their bookstore. Shannon Platt's old Subaru was parked in its place. She went in the back door and was met with a smell that made her briefly forget her wavy lines.

Chocolate. "Hey, what are you two up to? And may I have some?"

"Shh," Molly said, wiping her hands on a towel. "Joey's asleep. I'm teaching Shannon how to make brownies."

Shannon laughed. "Can you believe I never made brownies?"

"You're asking *me* that?" Cass said.

She sat down at the table and watched Shannon open the oven door, carefully stick a toothpick into the batter, pull it out, and then close the door. "Not done yet," she said proudly.

"You look like you've been thinking too much, Cass," Molly said, sitting down on a bench opposite her. Shannon joined her.

Cass sighed, then looked at both of the women sitting across from her. "I was thinking about the night of the mayor's party—"

"I get that," Shannon said. "I've been thinking about that night a lot. Nightmares, actually."

Cass looked over at her. "You heard Dirk and the chef arguing that night, right? Rachel Wooten thought maybe the chef was firing Dirk. And then he walked out?"

"Firing him?" Shannon thought about that. "Well, it wouldn't have been from the catering job, because we were nearly finished. But no, I don't think he left because he was fired. He left because he was furious with her, with whatever she said to him. You could almost feel the heat as he raced through the kitchen and stormed out. The guy had a terrible temper when he was on the job."

Molly was listening intently.

"Izzy and I were out on the portico when that happened. Getting fresh air, Izzy said. But actually we were freezing."

Shannon thought for a minute, replaying that part of the night. Then she said, "Ah. So you saw Dirk and me outside, having a . . . disagreement. That was shortly before the explosion with the boss happened."

Cass nodded.

Shannon shook her head. "He had been obnoxious to everyone that night. So angry. But that encounter with me was truly the worst. He hurled awful things at me. Like everything he hated about women he spewed out on me. Still trying to get even somehow with Molly, who dumped him. The guy is a misogynist, he truly is. He even hated Lidia. The looks he gave her that night could have killed a lesser mortal."

"Well, from the part we saw, you handled Dirk easily."

Shannon laughed. "Guys like that are really weak inside."

"Were you aware that Chef Carson was listening to you both when you were outside? We could see her in the back hallway. It was a little like that old movie *Rear Window*. Izzy and I had good seats."

Shannon's eyes widened in surprise. Then she cocked her head to one side and wrinkled her forehead, thinking. "That explains something."

"What?" Molly asked.

"After I came back inside, I saw the chef come into the kitchen, too. I tried not to pay too much attention to her, but she was clearly angry—'mad as a hatter' is more like it. She looked around the kitchen, her whole face tight. When Dirk finally came in from outside, she called him over, then pulled him into the hall. And that's when she read him the riot act."

"I never saw her do that to him during the class I took from her," Molly said. "It would have been Shannon who was called into the hall."

"Yes, and that might explain her words, too," Shannon said, her eyes lighting up. "I heard her yell something about it being 'the last straw.' Maybe she'd finally realized who or what the guy was, the harm he'd done to others, especially women—" She looked at Molly.

"Do you remember anything else she said?" Cass asked. "Were you the shadow in the mirror? Izzy thought she saw someone intentionally listening—"

Shannon laughed. "I've never been called a shadow before." Then she wrinkled her forehead and tried to think back. "I guess it could have sounded like Chef Carson was firing him, like Mrs. Wooten thought. She said something about cutting him off, maybe? There was something else, though. Like he was expecting something from her, like she owed him some-thing. He seemed to be fighting back. Their voices were muf-fled, and I was trying to concentrate on arranging a tray of sweets I had to take out to the guests. An end-of-the-party kind of thing."

Cass rubbed her fingers across a sticky spot on the table, looking at it, thinking.

"Okay. One more thing," she said, looking up. "What did his girlfriend do when he ran off? Did she try to follow him?"

"Oh, her. She was back there, too. Maybe she was your shadow. She sure shadowed him a lot. But that night, she didn't follow him out the back door, much to my surprise. She looked almost stoic. She walked over to the kitchen windows and watched him go, as if she knew where he was headed. Like he was going to get something for her and would be right back."

"Then what?"

"Then nothing. She went back to work. And I did, too."

Cass imagined the scene, then filed the information away. Letting it simmer. She looked over at the oven.

It was time for brownies.

Chapter 43

Monday. The weekend was gone, and Nell felt that time was at a standstill. She felt anxious, as if she were waiting for something. But she didn't know what she was anxious or waiting for. A series of early morning texts confirmed that she wasn't alone. And Cass's suggestion that they meet at Nell's for lunch suited them all just fine.

Nell had laughed. Cass had a way of knowing what was in Nell's refrigerator from miles away. This time it was a pot of steak soup for a wintry day. And they'd even have the house to themselves. Ben was going into Boston with Ollie to meet with a lawyer from his New York law firm who was coming into town and had the last of the papers Ollie was expecting.

She stood at the kitchen sink in warm cords and a heavy sweater, looking out the window at the bright sky.

How backward the weather was, Nell thought. It was December, and the huge snowstorm was almost forgotten, the white piles on street corners now gray and icy, and neighborhood snowmen looking a bit lopsided, missing hats and carrot noses. Sea Harbor hadn't had a snowfall since the night Lidia Carson had been killed.

She was imagining that there was some sort of significance in that. That it would only snow again—blanketing the town in a quiet peace—when the case was solved, once someone was locked up, once the town could breathe more freely and welcome the holidays fully and joyfully.

A tapping on the deck door pulled Nell from her reverie.

She pulled open the French door and welcomed Ollie inside. "Ben will be down in a minute."

"Good timing," he said, following Nell into the kitchen just as Ben appeared from the back stairs. He greeted Ollie, then looked at the bag he was carrying at his side. "What's that?"

"Lidia's traveling case."

"I remember it," Ben said. "We brought it from the B and B."

"Right. I was up early this morning and decided I should figure out what things I needed to get rid of. Be more organized. I hadn't looked at anything of Lidia's since you helped me move over here." He set the small traveling case on the island and unlatched the top of it.

The case was divided into two parts, one lined with velvet, the other plain.

"She kept her makeup on one side, and jewelry on the other side."

A few scattered makeup tools littered the bottom of one side. A hairbrush. The lined side was empty.

"Oh, Ollie," Nell said, looking into the empty case. She immediately looked out the window toward the guesthouse. "Do you think someone broke in—"

Ollie shook his head. "No, not here. Someone must have taken the jewelry while I was staying at the B and B. I thought the bag seemed light when I picked it up, but didn't pay much attention to it. Just put it with the other things in the car."

"I remember seeing a mess of makeup things on the floor next to it," Ben said. "I assumed you had cleaned it out—"

"No. Whoever took the jewelry must have decided against

the makeup. Wrong color lipstick, maybe." He attempted a smile.

"We should let the police know," Ben said. "Do you remember what jewelry Lidia had brought with her?"

Ollie's voice had the tone of defeat. "I remember a couple pieces. It wasn't something I paid a lot of attention to, and it's probably insured. Let's hold off on the police, Ben. At least until . . ." He let the end of the sentence drop off.

Nell looked into the case again and then at Ollie. "Do you know who did it?" And then she answered herself. "Dirk took the jewelry—"

He nodded. "I think so. I figured it was one last slap in Lidia's face, taking something she loved. He's probably looking for buyers right now."

"Do you remember if there was a gold necklace?" Nell asked.

"Yes. That's the one piece I remember, because I gave it to her. She'd always wanted a Tiffany piece."

"Apparently, Dirk got into an argument at the Ocean's Edge recently," Nell said. "It was over a gold necklace, Don Wooten thought."

Ben recalled the story, too. "Apparently, Dirk was upset to see it on his girlfriend.

He grabbed the necklace off the poor girl, shoved it in his pocket, and left the restaurant."

Ollie listened without surprise. "I suppose he didn't want anyone to see it," Ollie said. "It was noticeable. The kind of thing you probably wouldn't steal, then advertise. Lidia wore it often. She had it on during that television appearance the other night."

Ollie looked at the case again, closed it, and pushed it aside, shaking his head. "The thing is, I don't want to deal with this. I'll talk to him. But he can have the jewelry if he wants it. And

I don't want to make it worse. Dirk is already walking on thin ice for stealing from Mary and for that disruption he caused across town."

Ben and Nell exchanged looks. Then Nell looked into Ollie's eyes, his face, to see if she could read more there. Her old friend seemed to be unaware of the seriousness of Dirk's situation. It was far more serious than "walking on thin ice." Dirk Evans may well have murdered Lidia Carson, and Ollie was forgiving him for stealing her jewelry? Surely, Ollie was aware of the other possibility.

The only reason for his apparent blindness—and it was one that Nell wasn't willing to accept—was that Ollie *knew* who killed her. Knew it wasn't Dirk. And he'd only know that if . . ."

But the more Nell became reacquainted with her old friend, the less she could imagine that possibility. Ollie was not a murderer.

No matter how many reasons he might have for doing so.

After the two men left, Nell bundled up and walked out onto the deck, then down to the backyard. The sun had cleaned the flagstone path of snow and she walked down to the guesthouse, tucked at the edge of the thick stand of trees—the fairy forest, her sweet great-niece, Abby, called it. She stood still, looking at cottage for a long time, wondering about the man staying in it. Wondering what Maddie would make of it all.

What could have possessed Dirk Evans to steal such personal items that belonged to his employer, his old guardian, someone who had a habit of bailing him out, practically supporting him? Especially when he didn't need the money.

She turned and walked slowly back up to the house, reliving Lidia's last argument with Dirk at the mayor's party, and that earlier, tumultuous one days before coming to Sea Harbor that

Ollie talked about. Trying to piece together half sentences that didn't make sense, to make a whole one that did.

She walked up the deck steps and looked toward the house and into three smiling faces, watching her from inside the door.

Nell laughed and hurried inside. "I hope you at least have put on a fresh pot of coffee."

"Of course we have," Birdie answered.

"I've put the soup on to heat up, too," Izzy said.

"And I've brought Molly-made brownies." Cass set the plate down on the island, then noticed a cell phone in a leather case. "Whose cell phone is that?"

Birdie picked it up. "It looks like Oliver's. He must have left it behind. Sometimes I do that on purpose. Maybe Ollie is a kindred spirit."

Nell laughed and sent Ben a quick text to tell Ollie his cell phone was safe and sound in the Endicott kitchen.

And then she shrugged off her jacket and realized how seeing these three women—friends of her heart—was exactly what her mind and spirit needed. What all of them needed. Each other.

In a short while, soup bowls and a basket of warm sourdough rolls filled the round breakfast table tucked into the kitchen's bay window. The four women lifted coffee mugs in the air, toasting the meal, each other, and the puzzle that hopefully wasn't missing nearly as many pieces as it had a few days ago.

Once they were each satisfied with several spoonfuls of the spicy soup, Cass jumped in. "So, Iz, you talked to the church lady over the weekend?" she asked.

Izzy nodded, chewing on a bite of roll. "She was very pleasant, and happened to be Dirk's mother's best friend." She repeated the highlights of the conversation. The adoption item caught everyone's attention, along with Adele's description of it. "We know many adoption records are sealed away," Izzy said, "but Adele invited me to call the one agency in their town. Her church supports it somehow, and I think she wanted to impress me with the wonderful work they do. She's very proud of it. She said it was a loving place, efficient place. They even have 'open' adoptions. That intrigued me. I tried to call there this morning to see how 'open' they were, and got a recording that they open the office at one."

" 'Open' might mean that Patricia knew Dirk's birth mother," Nell said.

They all were silent, thinking about that, about Dirk Evans. About his birth, his adoption. Dirk, who felt cheated by life. And they wondered why, hoping a small town in New Jersey might have some answers.

Cass checked the clock again. "We need to call that agency," she said.

Izzy nodded. She began clearing the dishes away, bringing the plate of brownies back, along with pen and paper for scribbles. It helped them all think.

"So this Adele didn't know who Dirk's guardian was?" Birdie asked as she carried the coffeepot to the table. "That seems off. If they were such good friends, I'd think she would have known that."

"I don't know. She was very vague about that. She didn't recognize the Carson name. I did get the feeling she was keeping something from me. Or maybe had been bound to secrecy. But the adoption agency might be more helpful, if they'll talk to me. Seems it's quite a talkative little town. That might possibly be why Darci hated it."

Nell looked over at Izzy's yellow pad. She had listed a dozen names, some crossed out, others in squares, starting to be connected by lines, events, dates, single words. It looked like a knitting chart that shows what the pattern will look like when knit up. She hoped it would be that easy to figure out. It wasn't complete, but a pattern was emerging. Nell thought she could almost see it—clearer now than it had been for days.

Cass brought up the night of the murder, repeating her discussion with Shannon and what she'd heard in the mayor's kitchen that night. "She had a slightly different take on what Lidia and Dirk were arguing about."

"I think Shannon's interpretation is the more likely one," Birdie said. "Dirk wasn't being fired. And if he had been, it probably wouldn't have bothered him, not from what we know of him."

"Lidia had set up a trust for Dirk, one that she managed. And very carefully, Ollie said. I imagine it was insulting for Dirk, an adult, having to ask for money like a kid. And apparently he had become increasingly angry with Lidia after an explosive discussion a few days before they came here. It was as if Dirk had a new reason to be mad at Lidia, at his life. As if she owed him something. It was very emotional, even hateful, Ollie said."

Izzy latched onto the argument Ollie had witnessed. "So, what could that have been about? Suppose something happened before they came here to Sea Harbor. Something that made Dirk hate Lidia even more?" Izzy asked, doodling more on her chart. Lines being drawn as they all watched, nodded.

Cass checked the clock again and looked at Izzy. It was past one o'clock.

Izzy took out her phone and redialed the number of the Fairwood Happy Adoption Agency.

A man named Ed answered, and when Izzy explained that Adele Gunther had suggested she call, his voice warmed. Adele had left a message, he said. She mentioned that Izzy might be calling for information. The man's tone was enthusiastic, even when Izzy asked if she could let her friends listen in on speaker.

"This is a family place," Ed began. "I wasn't sure what information you wanted. Are you looking to adopt? The message didn't say. We have lots of things for you to read, people to talk to. A fine social worker on staff, too. Born and raised in Fairwood, so she knows her people."

"No, we're not interested in adopting, but we are interested in your organization," Izzy answered. "Adele said such positive things about you. She mentioned you're an open agency—"

"Yes we are, you know New Jersey lets you do that."

"Do you keep track of the children who are adopted? Do they mostly stay in your area?"

"Yes and no. The agency works with families who live here, so most everyone knows someone who knows someone, if you know what I mean. Even the farming folks. So we like to hear the good stories about our kids growing up. Sure we check up on them. Even when they're adults. But no, they aren't all raised here in our county. However, we even keep up with families who move, when we can."

"So you know Dirk Evans?" Izzy asked.

"Oh, Dirk Evans? Well, no, not personally. Funny you're asking about Dirk. Second ask this month. One just a couple weeks ago. Hardly ever happens."

"Oh? Someone else asked about Dirk? Who—"

"Like I said, we keep track of people." Ed's tone told Izzy she shouldn't have asked for a name.

Izzy made a stab in the dark. "Could you tell me when the woman came in? We're trying to get some information and maybe she already got it. Maybe we know her."

They could hear the shuffle of papers as Ed seemed to be checking on something. Then he came back, "Not a she. A *he*. He was in about two or three weeks ago. He said he was a friend of Dirk's mother." The man coughed, then said, sounding embarrassed, "You need to be a little patient with me here. I've only recently moved back to town, so I'm not as familiar with folks as some are. I'm just now getting reacquainted."

"Of course," Izzy said. Then she asked, "So he was a friend of Patricia Carson's?"

There was the sound of more papers being shuffled.

"No," Ed finally said. "Not Patricia Carson—but Miz Carson is a legend in our church, let me tell you. My folks loved her. This person was a friend of—" he checked his papers again, then looked up. "Eleanor. That's it. Eleanor. He was a friend of Dirk's birth mother. But he probably knew Patricia. In a town like this, if you know one person, you know the rest—the mother, the father, the brother. You know what I mean? Not too many secrets around here."

There were four frowns around the table, trying to follow Ed's words.

Ed had a call then, and said he'd have to punch a button to get it, but he'd be back. And then the phone went dead.

There was complete silence around the round table. Ed's words hung in the air above the table like a riddle they needed to solve. Or a sentence badly in need of an old-fashioned diagram. A sentence with a phrase or two missing.

Before anyone spoke, Cass got up and brought Nell's laptop to the table. She put the name *Eleanor* into a search engine. And then, in case it meant anything, and in case Adele hadn't been completely honest with her, she added a last name. "There are no secrets, these days, Ed is right about that," she said, tapping away on the keys. In minutes, they had an interesting answer.

All the names that Patricia's own birth daughter, Eleanor, had been known by.

For a while, no one said anything, each of them putting one more puzzle piece into its proper place. Smoothing out the wavy lines, and feeling a certain sadness for an unwanted child who became a wounded teen who became a selfish, mean, angry adult. And who never felt life treated him right. And maybe it hadn't.

The biggest surprise to each of them was that Ed's information wasn't really a surprise. At least not completely.

But it was a surprise that someone else was seeking the same information.

Birdie looked over at Izzy's diagram. She took her pencil and drew one more link.

"Why did it take us this long?" Cass said, her voice soft.

A *ping* on Izzy's cell phone popped up with an unfamiliar phone number on the screen. And then she recognized it.

"Hello, Adele," Izzy said.

"I lied to you, Ms. Perry," the woman said, her voice loud enough that those around the table could also hear. Then Adele Gunther explained that it was simply too difficult for her to talk about Patricia Evans's other child. But then she proceeded to do exactly that, filling her in, in great detail, with the reasons why she found it difficult. All of them.

"When will Ollie and Ben be back?" Birdie asked an hour later.

They'd finally gotten up from the table and stretched their bodies, looking down at Izzy's chart on the table. Stray pieces had been lined up and the resulting design was as clear as the star on Nell's decorated Fraser fir.

Nell checked her phone. Ben had sent a text: **Back shortly. Depending on traffic.**

"Everything is here," Izzy said, staring at her makeshift diagram. "Except . . ."

"Yes," Birdie agreed. "Except." They knew they were right. Even about the stolen jewelry. It all finally fit.

Except for one thing. Proof. An eyewitness. A confession.

The ring of a cell phone sent them all patting pockets and checking bags, then figuring out it wasn't their ring, their vibration.

"It's Ollie's," Nell said, walking toward the island. Without thinking, she picked it up and said hello.

"Get me Oliver Bishop, please," a stern voice said.

Nell explained he wasn't there, but was expected back soon.

And then the woman on the phone identified herself and explained that "soon" better be "very soon." Mr. Bishop wanted to know immediately if the two people he had registered at her boardinghouse caused any problems. And they were doing exactly that.

And one of them, at least, was about to leave town.

Chapter 44

Mrs. Bridge was standing outside her boardinghouse when Cass pulled up at the curb. The four women got out and greeted her. She recognized Nell and Birdie first and offered a worried hello. Then she greeted Izzy and Cass with a nod.

"I'm a knitter," she told Izzy proudly. "I've been in your shop."

"I know, I've seen you there. And I've also seen some of the lovely things you've knit."

Mrs. Bridge's voice softened with the praise. "I called the police," she said. "The two staying in room 3A are making too much racket, enough yelling to wake the dead."

"Are the police coming?" Izzy asked.

"We'll have to see. Disturbance calls aren't a top priority, I've learned. I've had to call many times with boarders who get out of hand. Sometimes the police show up, sometimes not, and sometimes the culprits quiet down before the cops even get here. You just never know."

Nell had left another text for Ben, saying where they were. And vaguely explaining why.

In the car, they had told one another they were going to do

what they could to calm down Mrs. Bridge. And maybe calm the boarders Ollie had put up there. The truth was, they truly weren't sure what they would do after that. Or what they could do.

"Do you know what caused the ruckus?" Birdie asked.

"No, but I have a bad feeling about all this. At the least, maybe you girls can quiet them down. The neighbors will be banging on my door."

Birdie took one look at the old, narrow staircase and said she'd wait downstairs in case the police came. Mrs. Bridge decided instantly to keep her company, and gave directions to a room on the third floor, along with a key, should they need it. "Just keep climbing until you can't anymore," she said.

Nell wondered briefly if Ollie had asked for that room as a punishment for Dirk. It was a hike, and they were all out of breath before they reached the top.

Music was playing loudly behind the closed door, but beneath it was the sound of things being moved. Something kicked. And voices, the words unintelligible. Angry sounds.

Nell knocked lightly, then slightly louder.

Suddenly the noise stopped.

"I have this feeling that something bad is happening in there," Izzy whispered. She took a few steps away and turned her back, tapping a number into her cell.

Nell stared at the door, waiting. Finally she wrapped her fingers around the doorknob, her heart beating too quickly. Her breath caught in her chest.

The door opened silently, unnoticed by the two figures on the other side of the large room.

Darci Fox stood with her back to an open window, a cold breeze feathering her black hair. Her hands were behind her, her fingers gripping the window ledge, but it was her look that Nell noticed.

Her unblinking stare was glued to a small pistol several feet away, aimed directly at her face.

Chapter 45

Nell took a sudden step back, as if the surprise had forcibly moved her. She stood still, then spoke softly as if speaking to a young child.

"Don't, Dirk," she said simply.

And in that single moment, as she looked at Dirk Evans's handsome face, she saw what Ollie had described seeing so recently. A man in deep pain.

Dirk's head never turned toward Nell's voice, no indication that he cared who she was or why she was there. His hand was steady as it held the small pistol. It was a lady's pistol, the kind advertised to women to keep in their purses or glove compartments. The kind Nell swore she would never own. It had a pink grip, a ludicrous detail in the tense setting, and something that Nell would remember days later.

Izzy had come in behind Nell, watching Darci carefully as she tried to read the scene.

The young woman at the window stole a glance at Izzy and her eyes widened. "You," she said. "What are you doing here? You shouldn't be here . . ."

Then she turned back to the gun. To Dirk. "Tell them to leave, Dirk. They think you're going to hurt me. But I'm not afraid. I know you won't. You don't even know how to use that gun. And I know you love me. Everyone else in your life has failed you. But I won't. You'll always have me."

Nell noticed the disarray in the room, scattered clothes, suitcases open, one partially packed. Out of the corner of her eye, she could see the arrival of Tommy Porter and another policeman. They were standing in the hall shadows, hands on their holsters, assessing the situation. And just behind them, Ollie and Ben came into view, their faces solemn and worried.

"Dirk, this won't help," Nell said carefully. "You have a life ahead of you." She spoke with a calmness she didn't feel, one that seemed to come from somewhere else.

"Yes, Dirk, you do," Darci said. "You have a life with me." She glanced at Nell. "He won't hurt me. We'll be fine. You can go now." She glanced at the suitcases, then back to the gun still pointed at her.

Through the open window, they could hear the ordinary sounds of people coming home from work, the courthouse clock signaling the hour. The sound of the bridge opening over the river and lobster boats coming in.

Inside, in the cold room, the tension was suffocating.

Nell watched Darci glance out the open window behind her. She wondered what was going on in her head as she looked at the three-story drop. And why was the window open in the first place? An escape from Mrs. Bridge's eagle eye? Were they planning to run away? Or was Dirk simply escaping from another part of his life that had failed him?

She could hear Dirk breathing. Heavy, deep breaths. His teeth were clenched, his eyes never leaving Darci.

"We'll help you, Dirk. May I please have the gun?" Nell asked gently. She held out her hand.

"These strangers shouldn't be interfering in our problems," Darci said to Dirk. Her voice was pleading now.

"'Our problems'?" Dirk spoke for the first time, ignoring Nell, and hearing only the words coming from Darci's mouth. His voice was steady—and angry. *"Our problems?"* he repeated, staring at the woman standing a short distance away from him. He took one step closer.

Darci sucked in her breath, her eyes never leaving Dirk's face. "I'm sorry Dirk. I thought you would be grateful that I found out the truth. My dad got the information for you. You needed to know about her. You get that, I know you do. This whole inheritance was yours. She owed you that. And she was going to take it away. I heard her say it to you, Dirk. We had to make sure she didn't do that."

Darci paused, as if to catch her breath. She looked at the gun again, at Dirk's still face, his steely eyes focused on her. "Everything I do is for you," she began again. "Your mother gave you away. You deserve to have everything of hers. Everything. We deserve it."

Dirk took in a deep breath and finally released it. His voice was strained. "There is no 'we,'" Dirk said. "There never was. You're nothing but a thief."

"No, Dirk—"

"Those paintings? And then the nerve to steal . . . to steal that necklace . . ."

"Your *mother's* necklace, Dirk," Darci said. "It's yours. Mine—" Darci's voice had weakened as she talked, her last words barely audible.

Nell listened, her heart heavy, knowing what Darci's father had found out for her. Information she needed to lay out for Dirk so he would understand. He'd know that she, Darci, was the only one who loved him. His birth mother didn't want him. But Lidia's devout mother, Dirk's grandmother, felt shamed by her daughter's pregnancy and adopted the baby to do penance for her daughter's sins. Dirk Evans was his grandmother's penance, his birth mother's shame.

Nell saw Dirk's hold on the pistol tighten.

But Darci continued: "Everything I do is for you. Everything . . ."

Nell watched in dismay. "Dirk, we can make this better. Nothing you can do will change what's been done—"

"She's right," Darci said, her eyes now on the doorway. "You're not making anything better." She looked at Nell. "And you aren't, either. Not any of you. Leave our room. We will work out this problem." Her voice had risen.

"No, Darci, you can't work it out," Nell said.

Dirk stared at the pistol in his hand for a long time. As if wondering how it had gotten there. Then he looked at Darci, his voice hoarse. "You . . . you killed my mother."

He opened his fist and let the pistol drop to the floor. "Take it. It's yours."

Then he turned around and walked out the door, past Nell and Cass and Izzy, then stepping aside as Tommy Porter and the other policeman walked in.

Chapter 46

By the time they left the boardinghouse, a cold, wintry night had settled down on Sea Harbor. Without a conscious plan, they all headed back to the Endicotts' house, exhausted. And hungry.

Birdie, Izzy, Nell, and Cass walked into the warm house, greeted by the smell of burrata pizza and a blazing fire.

"I suspect Santa's elves are here somewhere," Birdie said, walking across the family room and giving Sam, Danny, and Ben warm hugs. "You three are quite wonderful."

The men had each received a jumble of texts over the last few hours from their wives, brief updates that didn't give a clear picture of the day, of their thinking, of the seemingly disparate facts that had finally become linked together for them. Part of a whole. But there was enough in the brief communications to know that it had been an emotional, draining, and tumultuous day. And dangerous enough to add a few gray hairs to each of them.

Pizza, calzones, and beer would help.

"What will happen to Dirk?" Birdie asked Ben as they gathered around the table.

"I left Ollie at the police station to deal with things. "The gun incident will be resolved," Ben said. "He was holding it, pointing it. It was definitely a silent threat. But Darci was right when she guessed that Dirk didn't know how to use it. Ollie, Dirk and the police will work something out. But as far as his life long-term? I don't know."

"He's been rejected his whole life. Damaged. It will be a long journey for him," Nell said. "But I suspect Ollie will stay in touch as best he can."

"I can't get Patricia Evans off my mind," Izzy said, settling into a chair next to Nell. "And Lidia—the daughter she completely rejected for having accidentally gotten pregnant. There was hurt all around."

"But then Lidia did the same thing to her own child. Dirk was never made a part of the family when Lidia became his guardian. Not even treated like a real relative. Why didn't Lidia tell him?" Cass asked, her tone upset.

"Or tell Ollie," Nell said. "She even kept it from her husband."

"Maybe Lidia did the best she could do," Birdie said. "She made a decision she thought was best for her when she gave up her baby for adoption. She knew she wasn't mother material. You can't blame her for that. A decision like that takes courage, no matter who you are. And then, without ever wanting it to happen, that child was brought back into her life."

Ben walked around pouring wine and water for the non–beer drinkers. "Ollie got hold of a document when we were in Boston today that explained details of Lidia's guardianship. Apparently it was something her mother made her sign, whereby she agreed to assume responsibility for Dirk if something should happen to Patricia before he was eighteen. Lidia also was bound to never tell anyone, including Dirk, about him being her son, for reasons that were unclear."

"Her mother died relatively young," Birdie said. "I suppose

Lidia never imagined that her mother would die before Dirk came of age. So she signed it."

"Adele, the mother's friend, said that Patricia thought giving up the baby to a stranger compounded her daughter's sin, so she took the baby herself," Izzy said. "Even Patricia's best friend didn't understand Patricia's thinking and the way she cut her daughter out of her life completely. But it certainly took a toll on lives."

"On Dirk's, for sure," Cass said.

"And Lidia's. But she supported him, we have to give her that. And left him a trust. There was some conscience at work in her," Izzy said.

They nodded, agreeing.

"How did Darci know about the money, the trust?" Sam asked.

"Darci was the shadow in the mirror that night at the party," Izzy said. "Cass and I were outside, and we saw someone, but we didn't know who it was. Rachel Wooten was in the kitchen, and she said she saw someone listening also. Shannon finally figured out who it was. Darci must have heard Lidia's whole tirade, and heard that she was cutting him out of the will."

"And thanks to Darci's dad, she found out Dirk was Lidia's son, which was even better for her. A real inheritance—mother to son," Nell said. "She thought it would be gone if Lidia changed her will."

"She seemed to really love the guy," Cass said. "So a double motive. She wanted Dirk and she wanted the money he'd get. The solution to everything was to prevent Lidia from changing her will."

"The threat of being cut out of the will is a textbook motive, for sure," Danny said. "For either of them."

"And that's what Darci thought would happen," Nell said. "But according to Ollie, Lidia had no intention of changing her will to eliminate that trust. And Dirk wouldn't have been affected by her threat, because Dirk knew she wouldn't change it, no matter what Lidia said.

"Apparently, Lidia threatened it often, whenever they got in an argument. It was an 'in the heat of the moment' threat, and never a real one. It had almost become a joke, something Lidia herself admitted to Ollie. A tension reliever, at best, when Dirk had somehow irritated her."

"But Darci Fox wouldn't have known that," Izzy said.

"That's right. So she had the motive. But Dirk didn't. At least not a money motive. He had anger issues and probably hated being chastised in front of his fellow workers, which probably was why he walked out that night. But Lidia was good to him, as far as money goes."

"So Darci knew everything there was to know about Dirk Evans," Danny said. "But not about his mother. Not that Lidia had a habit of making idle threats. She didn't know Dirk's trust was his, no matter what."

The pizza and calzones were passed around once more, along with drink refills, as Danny's comment took a sobering hold on the group of friends.

It was all for nothing.

A senseless, meaningless taking of a life.

Chapter 47

"The lull before the wonderful festive storm," Birdie said, looking around at the mess they had made of the cozy back room in the yarn shop.

The murder of Lidia Carson still lingered over their lives, the sadness of it, and how the power of money—and love—could destroy lives. But it was fading to make room for life.

It was the end of their knitting night, and the flames in the fireplace were nearly gone, a bed of shimmering embers giving off a final glow.

Around the room, chairs and the coffee table and floor were littered with ribbons and wrapping paper, scissors and gift cards, and gifts they'd wrapped to take home and put under their trees.

It was the Thursday before out-of-town relatives arrived, before Santa came, and before last-minute shopping trips were squeezed in between planning menus, delivering food bags, and finishing up final projects.

And it was the one Thursday night of the year that the Seaside Knitters didn't knit. Instead, they sat together in Izzy's shop and celebrated their friendship with toasts and small knit gifts, ones that often resembled the same ones they'd given to one another the year before. Or maybe regifted.

Friendship, Birdie always said, didn't come wrapped.

Izzy held up a sock in wild colors that Cass had made for her. "Cass, you've outdone yourself."

"Yes, I have," Cass said, pointing to the lopsided heel. "It's my first sock, and I thought you should have it. You may get the mate next year."

They laughed and began packing up their things and cleaning the mess they'd made.

In minutes, the shop was almost normal, the fire completely out, and the floor free of debris. Clean enough so Mae wouldn't have Izzy's head the next morning.

They pulled on coats and hats, reluctant to say good-bye, when Izzy frowned, looking around.

"Did any of you hear something?" She looked toward the front of the store.

"I think it's those bells you tied to the door," Cass said. "Or Santa."

"A delivery?" Nell suggested. "The services are working late during the season. Maybe they saw the light."

"Maybe," Izzy said, unconvinced. She headed up the steps and toward the door.

The others followed close behind.

It wasn't Santa, after all, unless he was hiding in the circle of smiling faces that appeared when the door opened. And that, Nell thought with a wide smile, was a distinct possibility.

As the door opened wider, and a pitch pipe sounded, voices rang out, greeting the surprised group.

"'We wish you a merry Christmas . . .'"

There was Luna Risso in the middle, the shortest in the group, her surprising soprano voice mellow and clear. Gus McGlucken was right behind her, and Jake Risso from the bar, along with a couple of waitresses. Mary Pisano stood with Harry Garozzo and Don Wooten, all with floppy Santa hats on their heads. Shannon Platt and Molly Flanigan were in the very front, alternating between directing the group and singing their hearts out.

The group paused long enough for Shannon to introduce them.

"We are the Harbor Road Carolers," she said. And then explained that it was a group newly formed—actually, like the day before—to dispel all ills during the season and fill Harbor Road with goodwill and singing and laughter and love.

"We're open to new members," Molly added, "no tryouts necessary." It was the beginning of a fine tradition, she added. Next year, she was signing up Joey Brandley and his parents.

Several shoppers stopped on the sidewalk to see what was going on. They looked over the eclectic, unusual group, then formed another row, greeting familiar shopkeepers. Ready to sing.

Not to be left out, Izzy, Nell, Birdie, and Cass stood together on the yarn shop steps, arms around one another's shoulders, waiting for the sound of Shannon's pitch pipe. When Molly's hand made the motion to begin, their voices rose up as one into the Sea Harbor sky:

> *"Faithful friends who are dear to us*
> *Gather near to us once more . . .*
> *And have yourself a merry little Christmas now."*

Acknowledgments

My thanks to Kristen Frederickson, who has given permission to publish one of the recipes from her newest cookbook, *Second Helpings: more tonight at 7:30.* The book is a wonderful compilation of photography, personal and geographic information, and recipes that will have you wanting to rush to London to shake her hand—and sneak away with some of her sourdough bread.

Thanks also to designer and yarn shop owner Kate Brennan Dailey, who has given permission to print the pattern for Nell's project in this mystery, the Marblehead Cowl. The cowl is a wearable reminder of the rocky coast of Massachusetts North Shore, which is home to Kate's wonderful yarn shop, Marblehead Knits, and just a few miles north of Sea Harbor and the same rocky coast the Seaside Knitters call home.

A huge thank-you to June Steel and Susan Alvey, who generously offered me writing sanctuaries in which to write this book.

Thanks, as always, to my agents, Christina Hogrebe and Andrea Cirillo, and the whole wonderful Jane Rotrosen crew. Also, my editor, Wendy McCurdy, Elizabeth Trout and the Kensington team that polishes these mysteries to a fine shine. And my "board," Rosemary Flanigan and Mary Bednarowski, who have been there from the birth of the Seaside Knitters and never abandoned them.

And my endless thanks to my good friend Nancy Pickard, who held my hand from 1,003 miles away during the writing of this book. Her encouragement, editing, suggestions, and being at the short end of a cell phone call 24/7, were instrumental in *A Dark and Snowy Night* maturing into its adult life. My grateful, forever thanks.

And lastly, my love and thanks to my always-supportive family who makes all things, including writing books, possible. To Don, my amazing husband, who has weathered a year like no other, and whose spirit and courage inspire his family each day. And to Aria and John, Todd, Danny, and Claud.

Marblehead Cowl

Designed by Kate Dailey

A Broken Rib Cowl that will be about 46" around and 10–12" deep. The gauge is flexible: 3.5-4 sts per inch in broken rib pattern. It should be loose and cozy.

Materials
250–300 yards of Bulky Yarn
#10 32" Needle

Instructions
Cast on 180 Stitches.
Join in the round being careful not to twist.
Place marker at the beginning of the round.

Row 1: (Knit 1 Purl 1) repeat around.
Row 2: Knit.

Repeat rows 1 and 2 until desired width, leaving enough yarn to cast off.
Cast off all stitches and weave in ends.
Enjoy.

Visit Marblehead Knits website www.Marbleheadknits.com for an inside glimpse into this charming and popular yarn shop, and to meet its creative owner, Kate Dailey.

Marblehead Knits
128 Washington Street,
Marblehead, MA 01945

In *A Dark and Snowy Night*, Nell Endicott is knitting the Marblehead Cowl for her Midwestern sister, as encouragement for her to visit the North Shore, Sea Harbor, more often.

CHRISTMAS MORNING SOUFFLÉ

Kristen Frederickson

This extraordinarily rich and simple dish is perfect for Christmas because you can assemble it the night before, then put it in the oven when the festivities begin in the morning. By the time the first present-unwrapping frenzy has abated, it's ready. This version is vegetarian-friendly and completely simple, but you can jazz it up with sliced tomatoes on top, and you can also slip in some slices of cooked sausages if feeding meat-eaters.

(Serves 8)

12 eggs
520 ml/2¼ cups single cream
1 tsp red pepper flakes
350 g/3 cups grated sharp Cheddar
20 slices commercial white bread, crusts removed, cut into
  bite-sized cubes
sea salt and fresh black pepper
6 tbsps. butter, melted

Beat eggs and cream and add pepper flakes.

Butter a 20 x 30 cm/9" x 13" baking dish. Sprinkle ⅓ of the cheese on the bottom. Scatter ⅓ of the bread cubes on top, then repeat until you've run out.
Pour the egg mixture over the cheese and bread cubes, season, then drizzle with the melted butter.
Refrigerate overnight, covered, then bake at 180 C/350 F for 45 minutes to an hour, until it reaches the browning you desire.

Serve with a large fruit salad to balance the richness of this dish.

This recipe for Christmas Morning Soufflé, reprinted here with permission from the author, is from my favorite new cook-book, *Second Helpings: more tonight at 7:30*, written by Kristen Frederickson and Avery Curran. More information about the recipes and the cookbook authors can be found here: https://secondhelpings.net

And more about Kristen and the evolution of her cookbooks, along with her life in London, can be found on her blog: https://www.kristeninlondon.com

The recipe for the Boozy Chocolate Fridge Cake that Molly bakes in *A Dark and Snowy Night* can also be found in the *Second Helpings* cookbook.

Printed in the United States
by Baker & Taylor Publisher Services